*Praise for*
CHRISTOPHER BRAM

"Extraordinary. Brimming with atmosphere, charged with powerful insights, it is as wise as it is witty, as entertaining as it is original. A wonderful book."                                  —Clive Barker

"Christopher Bram draws on such a seemingly unquenchable wellspring of imagination that he never ceases to freshen our own lesser imaginations with astonishment and delight. . . . Using the yardstick of the adage that truth is stranger than fiction, this fiction is so hauntingly strange that it just may be truth."                                          —*Lambda Book Report*

"Swift, penetrating, and intelligent. . . . Bram's best novel yet. . . . It shows how gay and straight are bound together in an unstable embrace full of affection, misunderstanding, violence, and the desire for meaning."                            —David Bergman

"Bram creates a curiously appealing portrait of a director on the verge of extinction and in doing so, revives some of the feel and taste of early Hollywood."                    —*Dallas Morning News*

"Monstrously good. . . . Christopher Bram brings to his creation a wickedly witty intelligence and a vivid sympathy. His James Whale is a clever, complicated, and edgy man exhausted by age and illness but still relentlessly fascinating as he looks back wryly at his life and loves, and sketches a final scene of dark sexual mischief."                            —Patrick McGrath

"An engaging read. . . . Bram's prose has an evanescent quality that evokes his protagonist's fading consciousness."

—*Bay Area Reporter*

"A most moving, sympathetic, bitingly witty portrait. . . . Painfully beautiful imagery and haunting lyricism make this a book for everyone who has ever been afraid of the darkness, inside or out."   —*Los Angeles Daily News*

"An ingeniously imagined novel. . . . Wickedly disconcerting. . . . Bram cleverly mines his material's potential from nostalgia and comedy to the grimmer secrets of carnal and charnel knowledge."   —*Publishers Weekly*

"Bram is, quite simply, the best American gay novelist going."   —*L.A. Gay*

"Bram's blend of fact and fiction creates a morality tale that grabs the reader and compels a page-turning flurry to resolution."   —*Our Own*

"This moody, almost 'film noir' novel has a lot going for it. . . . Bram is a solid storyteller, capable of spanning history and consciousness."   —Gannett News Service

"A glorious read from an intelligent and talented writer, and worthy of a space in your library."   —*Frontiers*

"With finely tuned lyricism and a sure sense of drama, Christopher Bram paints a portrait of two men locked in a startling psychological relationship that is complex, fascinating, and, in the end, deeply moving. . . . Offers the reader a host of keen pleasures, not the least of which is to be in the hands of masterful storyteller."   —Paul Russell

"A touching fictional portrait of old Hollywood and of one of the curious geniuses who made it what it was."

—NPR's *All Things Considered*

"Bram's remarkable imagination explores the mystery of an obscure legend's last days and turns out a rich tale of pseudo-historical suspense."

—*Gay Net*

"Witty, moving, entertaining, and enlightening. . . . One of the most remarkable and satisfying novels to come along in quite some time."

—*Island Lifestyle*

"Bram mixes his tale with bygone glamour and gossip, keen wit, and deft compassion. Juxtaposing the gay and straight worlds within the framework of class boundaries adds weight to the characters. Bram shows himself to be a subtle and seductive stylist."

—*Cover*

"As compassionate as it is phantasmic. . . . Bram constructs a compelling fictional narrative."

—*Independent Weekly*

"A masterful account of one man's 'summing up' and his acting on his convictions about how and when his life should end."

—*Harvard Gay and Lesbian Review*

# GODS AND MONSTERS

# GODS AND MONSTERS

CHRISTOPHER BRAM

HARPER
PERENNIAL

HARPER ● PERENNIAL

A paperback edition of this book was previously published under the title *Father of Frankenstein* in 1996 by Plume, a member of Penguin Putnam Inc.

P.S.™ is a trademark of HarperCollins Publishers.

HarperCollins books may be purchased for educational, business, or sales promotional use. For information please write: Special Markets Department, HarperCollins Publishers, 10 East 53rd Street, New York, NY 10022.

First Harper Perennial edition published 2005.

*Original hardcover designed by Steven N. Stathakis*

Library of Congress Cataloging-in-Publication Data

Bram, Christopher.
 [Father of Frankenstein]
 Gods and monsters / Christopher Bram— 1st Harper Perennial ed.
  p. cm
 Originally published under the title: Father of Frankenstein.
  ISBN-13: 978-0-06-078087-6 (pbk.)  ISBN-10: 0-06-078087-8 (pbk.)
 1. Whale, James, d. 1957—Fiction. 2. Frankenstein films—Production and direction—Fiction. 3. Motion picture producers and directors—Fiction. 4. British—California—Fiction. 5. Los Angeles (Calif.)—Fiction. 6. Gay men—Fiction. I. Title.
  PS3552.R2817F38 2005
  813'.54—dc22                                    2005040221

05 06 07 08 09 ❖/RRD 10 9 8 7 6 5 4 3 2

FOR
DRAPER

*Friend?*
—THE MONSTER

# GODS AND MONSTERS

**1**

NIGHT. RAIN. A WHISTLING SEETHE OF WIND. SPECTERS OF AIR
swirl around a scaly roof and dark Gothic steeples. A bright sol-
itary window stares out like a caged eye.

Lightning splits the sky, a jagged mile-high spark that leaps
to the earth with the boom of an iron door slamming shut. In
the hard white flash, the twisted vines around the window's case-
ment flare into view, as sharply rendered as an engraving in an
old anatomy book.

The landscape of churned darkness stretches all around—
mud and stumps and pools. A single shattered oak stands above
the desolation. Lightning crashes again. There's a glimpse of
movement, a shape like a man stumbling past wiry coils of brier
before he gutters out in darkness. The wind grows louder. The
horizon thuds and flickers with distant lightning, a great short-
circuiting of the world.

Another crashing blink, and the human silhouette reappears, upside down now, reflected in a grainy, rain-pricked

puddle. The top of his head is flat, his arms long and heavy, his boots weighted with mud. Lost again in blackness, he is no longer out by the puddle but continues to move, shifting farther off in the dark, or coming closer, very close.

And suddenly: everything changes back.

The gale fades, as quickly as the dying spin of a backstage wind machine. The lightning abruptly stops, as if someone threw a switch, and birds begin to sing, real birds, martins and nightingales, as light creeps into the scene, and color: the dark green steeples of cypress trees, the soft red and ocher of brick trim, the clamshell white of clapboard. The grass is fogged with no more than a light dew as the sun rises from behind the next ridge.

A two-story Colonial-style house stands above a shaggy, grassy slope bordered with privet and boxwood. It's the rear of the house and there's a swimming pool at the foot of the hill—seen from the air, both sides of the little valley are blue-eyed with swimming pools. The rectangle of still water mirrors a cloudless sky that pales into woolly brightness as the sun dissolves in milky haze. Off in the distance to the right, a triangle of ocean tucked in the valley's mouth loses its horizon and melts into white sky. A water sprinkler suddenly blooms on the lawn next door, a hissing, twirling corkscrew full of rainbows. We're in Los Angeles, in Santa Monica Canyon, on a spring morning in 1957.

One bird sings louder than the others, a catbird who has no song of its own but sings fragments and snatches of other songs, in rapid, scrambled succession.

On the patchily tarred road at the foot of the hill, a pickup truck appears, rusty and in need of paint. It turns and bounces up the bumpy dirt drive behind the swimming pool, springs squeaking like tin flutes. It comes to a halt behind the gray-shingled studio beside the pool. The radio in the cab is turned up loud and the morning is broken by Elvis Presley furiously grumbling "Hound Dog." A young man gets out, tall with broad shoulders and a flattop haircut. He lowers the tailgate and wheels a lawn mower across the truck bed, a red power mower with a spiral of blades up front and large spoked wheels in the rear. The machine is heavy, but he lifts it, back muscles tensing beneath his T-shirt, thighs and buttocks flexing in his fatigue pants; his knees bend and he lowers the machine to the ground.

He doesn't notice the white shadow in the house's bay window fifty yards up the hill. The shadow watches as the young man props a foot against the engine and jerks at the starter cord, once, then again, and the machine catches, its roar drowning out the birds. He braces himself behind the handles and begins to mow. The shadow continues to watch.

The shadow is a man, of course. He stands on the pegged oak floor of his living room, a living man in a white dress shirt and seersucker jacket. A folded handkerchief droops like a lily from the jacket's pocket. There's a cold fireplace behind him with two ceramic spaniels on the mantel, and walls hung with paintings that appear valuable—Velázquez, Rembrandt, and Titian—but are in fact copies the man has painted for his own amusement. He is English, with a lean, rectangular face, blue eyes, and heavy lips. Pale wrists peek from his coat sleeves. His dove white hair is precisely parted on the right and thinning at the temples.

His name is James Whale. He returned home recently after two months in the hospital, where he was treated for a series of strokes. He was once a movie director, under contract at Universal. He is retired now, sixty-seven years old, although the world thinks he's only sixty. It's one of several facts he's reinvented about himself. The eight-line obituary printed next month in *Variety* will be full of errors.

"I'd have more peace of mind if the live-in nurse were still here."

"She was nothing but bother. I not like her, Mr. Jimmy not like her. Stuck-up and bossy. We do better alone."

In the dining room, visible through open double doors, a man sitting at the table speaks softly with the housekeeper, a short, round-faced Mexican woman dressed in black, her hair cinched in a hard bun. The man is slight and bald, with a pinched face and the tiny eyes of a mouse. He wears a pin-striped suit that suggests he's on his way to something important.

"You'll contact me if there's an emergency?"

"Certainly, Mr. David. I call you at this number."

Whale cannot hear them but knows that he is the topic of conversation. He hates how illness has reduced him to a problem whispered about by others, a difficult child, an embarrassment.

"Mr. Jimmy?" the housekeeper calls out. "More coffee?"

"What? Oh yes. Why not?" He returns to the dining room with the delicate smile of a man determined to be friendly despite a hangover. He sits down. "Isn't Maria a peach?" he observes.

She ignores him, refills his cup, and returns to the kitchen.

"So nice of you to drop by for breakfast," he tells David for the third or fourth time. "Such a pleasant surprise."

"Yes, well. I wanted to visit before I went out of town."

There's still a mild vertigo over seeing David's face again, like gazing into a mirror. They look nothing alike—David Lewis is ten years younger, but life as a studio producer has aged him badly. Still, his face is one that, over time, Whale has seen almost as often as his own reflection. Until David moved out four years ago, they were a couple, living together for twenty years, fifteen in this very house.

David has difficulty looking Whale in the eye. "Maria says you haven't been sleeping well."

Whale frowns, then shrugs. "The ridiculous pills they prescribe. If I take them, I spend the next day as stupid as a stone. If I don't, sleep is nothing but fever dreams. Last night, for instance. Foolish, trashy dreams. Hardly sleep at all."

"Then take the pills. You need your sleep."

"I've spent too many weeks asleep. I wanted to be alert today. So that I might try my hand at painting again." He attempts a self-mocking smile. "I am making a slow but steady return from the dead."

David is silent. Never comfortable with the physical, he is disturbed by talk of misery almost as much as talk of sex.

Whale happily changes the subject. "Where again are you flying off to?"

"New York."

"Oh yes, I remember. For how long?"

"A week. Two weeks. I don't know yet. I'm to meet with the new management and find out what's to happen with my picture."

"I thought it was finished." It has to be the same big movie that David was producing when Whale went into the hospital.

"The New York office is running MGM now, and the money people don't seem to know what to do with the damn thing. There's even talk of shelving it."

"You poor boy. It never ends, does it?"

"Yes. This picture." David sighs. "It was to be my golden opportunity. My name above the title as producer." He disappears into his own troubles. "But it's been an endless nightmare. First the script, then the weather. Then Clift's car wreck last year. We were shut down for months. And when Clift returned? Just awful. He was still handsome, but craggy rather than boyish. As if the hospital aged him ten years. The cutter had the damnedest time matching shots. And the change to his personality? Never easy at his best, he was impossible. So morose. I'm certain it was alcohol he had in his thermos when we were in Mississippi, but its effect was worse than any drink I've seen. He was a zombie. When we tried to talk sense to him, Miss Taylor always jumped to his defense, playing the protective big sister. It's a miracle we finished. And now that Dore Schary is out and the studio has no head—"

Whale tries to listen. It's the sort of thing he thought he wanted to hear, news from the Rialto, but he has difficulty even following David. The mention of someone else in a hospital throws him, and when he hears "Clift," he pictures Clifton Webb, whose looks wouldn't be affected one way or another by a car crash. Only when David has moved on to struggles in New York does Whale realize that it's Montgomery Clift, one of those mumbling street-corner cowboys now treated as stars, although so elegantly handsome that even Whale has found him dreamy. Miss Taylor is the English beauty, of course, one of the current crop of would-be Garbos. David's movie is called *Raintree County,* another would-be *Gone with the Wind.* Hollywood now repeats itself like a broken record. Whale hadn't asked to see the rough cut before his illness, but then David hadn't offered to show it to him either.

Whale grows frustrated over his inability to be interested in any of it. Is his mind such a sieve he can't follow gossip? And he grows irritated with David, after the fact, for speaking about that fellow in the hospital without a bit of sympathy or sorrow.

David begins to look at his watch while he talks. A clumsy device, but he's full of such devices picked up from his years on stage. He was a pretty yet mannered juvenile in the theater before he became a studio flunky.

"Miss Taylor is supposed to be in New York this month, visiting Clift, but I can't say I ever want to see either—"

Whale breaks in. "What time is your plane?"

David looks at his watch more blatantly. "Oh yes. Thank you for reminding me. Sorry. I really should be going." He slowly stands up, pretending to be reluctant to go.

Whale rises too. "So nice of you to drop by. So good to see you. Especially since I saw so little of you in the hospital."

The remark hits its target: David is full of remorse. "I'm sorry, Jimmy. Again, I apologize for not visiting more. But with this project and two difficult stars, I could never get away."

A chance for wit suddenly lightens Whale's smile. " 'The fault is not in ourselves but in our stars.' "

But David misses the pun. "You remember how a production eats up one's life."

Whale sighs. It's such a bore when people miss your jokes. But it was a good one, wasn't it? He's pleased by his use of Shakespeare, relieved. His mind isn't a complete wreck after all.

"Oh, David. There's no pleasure in making you feel guilty. I shouldn't have mentioned it. You don't need to feel obligated to me. After all, I threw you out. For the love of another man."

"You didn't throw me out, Jimmy."

"Not literally. But it makes the more dramatic tale."

David takes on a noble, selfless look. "I only wish that Luc had still been here when you got sick."

"I'm glad he wasn't. I was drawn to him for his spirit and spontaneity. I would've hated to see the boy play nursemaid." Whale dislikes thinking about Luc, who grew homesick and returned to Europe almost a year ago, long before Whale's mind shorted out.

"You *should* get back to your painting," David tells him. "You need to keep yourself occupied."

"You better go, my boy. Your flight."

They do not kiss or embrace when they say good-bye, not even as friends. They manfully shake hands. Whale doesn't walk David to the door but lets Maria see him out.

He drifts back toward the living room window, relieved that the visit is over. He sings to himself so he won't listen for the closing of the door or the sigh of the car driving off.

*The bells of hell go ting-a-ling-a-ling*
*For you but not for me.*

It's a ditty from the war, not the last war but the one before. Whale continues to sing even as he watches the young man pushing a lawn mower back and forth on the hillside.

He remains fond of David, especially in his absence. They know each other too well. They cannot spend any time together without trodding on old guilts, tendernesses, and regrets. They are too different, although it took them twenty years, and Whale declaring himself free of his career, to discover that. David is so safe and conventional, you'd think he were the Englishman.

Whale is glad that he didn't give the full reason for neglecting his pills last night. He needs to be alert today, not only to paint, but because another visitor is coming this afternoon, a university student who wants to meet the great horror picture director. Old directors have no fans and the boy probably just wants to hear anecdotes about Karloff. No matter, it will bring a fresh face into the house. He hopes the lad will be half as striking as the manly fellow doing his lawn.

Whale pulls at the window, suddenly wanting to smell the fresh-cut grass. He is weak but only bed weak; the stroke hasn't affected his muscles or coordination. The window sash lifts to the roar of the mower. But instead of grass, he smells smoke. Coal smoke. The bitter fumes of the cheapest grade of coal, a gloomy childhood smell of narrow rooms and narrow streets, a Midlands sky blackened by the smoke of a thousand chimney pots. This has happened before; Dr. Payne warned him it will continue. Damaged tissue presses on the patch of brain where smell and memory mingle, or something like that. He has hallucinations in his nose, luxurious whiffs of things from forty and fifty years ago. It could be amusing if the odors didn't carry the emotions of lives he can remember only abstractly, if at all. He breathes deeper, determined to crowd the past from his nostrils. Finally, there, an American aroma of mown grass, like watermelon rind.

The young man stops, straightens up, and slips his T-shirt over his head, baring a beefy pink torso and shoulders. He resumes mowing. There's a tattoo on his right shoulder, like a faint bruise and too far away to read. Ah, shirtless youth, Whale thinks with a smile. He waits for a familiar flicker of lust but experiences instead a twinge of sadness. The half-dressed body only makes him feel old, detached, and oddly sexless. He sighs and turns away from the window, determined to get on with his day.

"Maria?" he calls out. "I shall finish my coffee in the studio today. High time I did a little work, don't you think?"

"Yes sir, Mr. Jimmy."

He picks up the *Los Angeles Mirror* folded on the telephone table, then chooses a cane from the basket of walking sticks and umbrellas. He doesn't really need a cane, but the path to the studio is steep and he wouldn't want to fall in the presence of a stranger.

"Who's the new man, Maria? I don't recall seeing him."

"Bone? Boom? Something Bee. Mr. David hire him while you were away. He comes every Monday."

Whale nods. He steps out into the sunlight and fragrant air.

It's a beautiful morning, although what day here isn't beautiful? The other side of this valley they call a canyon has a few modern houses poking through the cypress and eucalyptus trees. The jacaranda at the back of his own house is in full bloom, limbs dotted with purple flowers in an orderly pattern a child might use when painting a tree. The unmown grass is sprinkled with poppies, not red like the paper ones worn in buttonholes on Armistice Day, but orange, the innocent orange of California poppies. Whale steps jauntily down the hill, keeping to the path and singing to himself again:

> *The bells of hell go ting-a-ling-a-ling*
> *For you but not for me.*
> *Oh death where is thy sting-a-ling-a-ling?*
> *Grave where thy victory?*

The gradient of the slope makes his footsteps brisk and pleasantly jarring to the bones. It feels good to find he has a body, something more corporeal than the achy joints and hospital gown floating behind him like a wedding train during his long weeks in hospital. But does the body have a mind? His skull is a vacancy edged with ache, like a mild hangover that won't go away.

He looks around for the yardman, but the fellow has moved into the narrow strip between the privet hedges and the side of the house. The mower roars in the distance.

Whale has not been down here since his return home. The studio, not much bigger than a garage, was built when he left the movies. He had rediscovered painting, and David thought he'd work better in his own building. They bought the slope behind their house, had it cleared of scrub and pine, and commissioned a simple shingle box. The swimming pool is newer, installed after Whale returned from a trip to Europe with a young Alsatian in tow, not a dog but an auto mechanic in his early twenties. Luc was to be an employee, a chauffeur or assistant, something official. David moved out. They'd talked about separating before the trip. Whale was a free man, but David was still in the thick of it, and the studios were not so cavalier about men who lived together as they had been before the war. Whale built the pool for Luc before it became clear that a wiry French mechanic was not what he wanted, after all.

The pool has not been used in over a year, yet Whale likes to keep it filled. He never learned how to swim, but loves to see this slab of gemmy color set in his property. The gray-green canoes of eucalyptus leaves speckle its surface this morning.

He opens the door to the studio—there's no need for locks in Santa Monica Canyon. He hopes to feel at home, to come to a place where he can be his old self again. Maria has done her work well. The windows are already open, the tabletops clean. There's a faint aroma of turpentine and oils. The empty easel stands in the corner. Squares of sized canvas lean against the wall, some already sketched with charcoal, one dabbed and smeared with blocks of color. Whale rolls out the easel and lifts the half-painted canvas in both hands, expecting to remember what he intended to paint. A blotch of green in the bottom left corner, a patch of yellow in the center, a few chalk lines connecting them together. It suggests nothing to him. Absolutely nothing. He sets it on the easel and stares, baffled by his failure to see anything resembling a picture.

He hears shoes scuffing down the path. He quickly sits in the wooden armchair, opens the newspaper, and is reading when Maria enters with the coffee service. Eisenhower played golf on Sunday; all is right with the world. Maria sets down the tray, pours a fresh cup, and leaves, neither of them saying a word.

Whale folds up the paper and looks at the canvas again. I

am tired, he tells himself. I didn't sleep well last night. The picture will come back to me. But he fears that much more is wrong, that his stroke erased not only all memory of this picture but his ability even to think in pictures. Up on the wall is a finished painting, nice but not nice enough for the house. A Dutch still life, with a vase and glass of water and handful of wildflowers. Yes, he painted that, but when? And why? He vaguely remembers taking pleasure in getting the play of light in water just right but wonders why he went to such bother. Could the painting give pleasure to anyone besides the painter?

There's a bookcase full of art books by the window. He pulls out a heavy volume of Rembrandt, turns the pages with their harsh perfume of foreign ink, and tries to remember why he painted. Imitation is a form of understanding; he had wanted to understand the Old Masters. He had nothing to say as a painter himself; he only wanted to get deep inside things he found beautiful. There was nothing beautiful in the movies he made, only noise and shadows and some nasty cleverness. But to understand Rembrandt by making a perfect copy? It was like coming into a clearing after stumbling through woods full of maddening branches and briers. That is what he had hoped to find in his studio this morning: a small, still place, like a quiet room in his own head, where he could gather himself and lose himself by being fully engaged with the beautiful.

Outside, the lawn mower shuts off. A few minutes later there's the chop-chop-chop of clippers snapping at hedges.

Begin at the beginning, he tells himself. He carries the art book to the drafting table, sets it down, and opens a drawer. He takes out several sheets of thick vellum and a handful of sharpened pencils, and pulls up a stool. He goes through the book, looking for a painting or a detail he might want to draw. Here. *The Polish Rider.* There is such a look of repose in the Old Masters. Their people know who they are. Their identities fill their bodies to the brim, without uncertainty or vagueness.

He works freehand, beginning immediately with the eyes, the arched brows, hooded lids, and hard pupils, so that the whiteness of the paper seems to gaze back at him. For a moment, there's an echo of the old pleasure, the cool excitement of creating life with fine marks on vellum. But the self-forgetting concentration never takes over. It stands off in the distance, like a word that doesn't come when it's needed. And as his fingers scratch and dig, Whale sees he's getting details right—the twist of hand clutching a riding crop, the droop of mane along the horse's neck: in his movies too Whale always worked in details— but the whole, the constellation of parts, is awry, distorted. The proportions are off, the figure a grotesque cartoon.

He balls up the sketch and starts again, lightly penciling a series of boxes that he can fill with the man and his horse. He is usually such a meticulous draftsman that he doesn't need these temporary lines but holds them in his head as he draws. Made visible on paper today, even they look wrong, a child's geometry, the simplest square or rectangle coming out squat and flabby. He forges on, working in details and shading, but the nose and lips of the young man, the isolated eye of the horse, are as dark as the lines that cage them, like body parts snagged on wire. Nothing connects. Not the man on the horse, not his own hand and eye and mind.

Whale closes his eyes. The stroke, he tells himself. It is not just a lack of sleep or even laziness but something wrong with his brain, a snarling of wires, a blown fuse. The world is no longer round and real but as thin as nerves, as fractured and feverish as the dreams that came to him in lightning flashes last night. He searches the darkness under his skull, hunting for the headache that never goes away, a simple explanation for his failure. He has to see around his pain to the world outside. He needs something intense and strong to distract him from this pain. He had always been able to lose himself in work, whether with an army of artists and technicians in a motion picture production or, more recently, in the soundstage of his own head. No more. Would he be like this for the rest of his days? Would he end his life in one long hangover?

There's a smell like a suggestion of smell, as if caught from the corner of his nose. Like fish or rotting meat. Yes, a stench of meat that's lain out in the sun so long it's as pungent as dead fish on a beach. He sniffs the back of his hand, then the air, but it's from inside his head, another stinking memory of the past. It fades before he can identify it.

He examines his sketch. How modern, he thinks with a sneer. Modern art is the art of civilization after a stroke. He wads up the sketch and tosses it to the floor with the first one. Maria will pick them up. Patience, he tells himself. And rest. Except that this dabbling in art is the only rest he can imagine.

He lifts the Rembrandt book from the table. The back cover falls open and something slithers out and hits the floor. Whale looks down. A magazine is splayed at his feet, black-and-white wings with a young man in blue jeans on the cover: *Physique Pictorial.* Whale puts down Rembrandt and takes up *Physique.*

Oh yes, he tells himself, going to the armchair to flip through the pictures. This I remember. Muscles, bodies, skin. Except for the robust figure on the cover, none of these fellows wear more than a bit of string. Their bodies are shaved and shiny, with an occasional tattoo to suggest lives outside the glossy fantasies. Beefy from the neck down, their faces are as blandly American as highway billboards. This one is too young—Whale does not like children—and this one too silly: who could be aroused by a naked man drying the dishes? Perhaps it's to appease the censors. Whale finds the pictures ridiculous yet touching. No, they don't touch him in the way they were intended, but they touch memories of being touched.

Here is where he will begin. Here is his clearing in the forest. Why waste time with forgeries of Rembrandt when he could be drawing pictures that might move him in a more immediate, primal way? Not today, but tomorrow. It gives him something to look forward to. He flips through the magazine again, searching for a figure who will move him to art.

There's a soft gurgle outside the window. The yardman is skimming the pool.

Luc's pool, Whale's gift to a last fling at love that never took.

He was too old for love, too comfortable with his solitude. Luc didn't seem to care one way or the other. The swimming pool attracted Luc's friends, though, all-American boys he met at the beach or gym and brought home for cookouts and swimming parties. Whale would sit in a deck chair at the door of his studio, a martini in one hand, a cigar in the other, a harmless old uncle watching young men splash and swagger and sun themselves. Late in the evening, when the mix of mood and alcohol was right, bathing trunks were sometimes peeled and the dark pool became a pit full of naked shadows.

Whale has gone to the door while he remembers those evenings from two summers ago. The yardman combs the water with a muslin screen on a pole, fishing out fallen leaves and drowned insects. He has big shoulders, a hairless chest and, in profile, a pouch of youthful gut. His face is older than it looked from the house, older than the boys in the magazine, with a gently flattened nose. He has a handsomely thuggish quality.

"Good morning," Whale calls out.

"Mornin'," the fellow grumbles without looking up.

Whale comes toward him, keeping both hands in his pockets. He will not indulge in the ridiculous practice of shaking hands with the servants. "My name is Whale. This is my house."

"Nice place," the fellow answers, with a sidelong glance as he makes another sweep with the pole. A little whirlpool spins across the fabric of water.

Whale stands close enough to read the blue tattoo beside the bulge of bicep, three words, each above the other: Death Before Dishonor. What a quaint, young sentiment. To think that death could be preferable to anything.

"And your name is—?"

"Boone. Clayton Boone."

"You do nice work, Mr. Boone. Very nice."

Whale pretends to examine the yard, chiefly to see if Boone will steal a look at him. No, Boone continues to give his full attention to the pool.

"Excuse me. I couldn't help but notice your tattoo," says

Whale, determined to get his eye. "That phrase? What does it mean?"

The fellow lifts the pole from the water and irritably stands by, head twisting for an impatient look at Whale. "Don't mean squat, mister. Just means I was in the Marines."

"The Marines? How admirable." Yes, he does have that stony, sullen masculinity that Americans found dangerous in juvenile delinquents but becoming in their soldiery.

"Yeah. *Semper fi*," the fellow mutters.

Whale assumes he served in Korea—he looks to be the right age—but has no desire to fight his silence just to hear more war stories.

"Getting to be a warm day," he observes. "A scorcher, as you Yanks call it." He likes to play up his Englishness. Foreigners can get away with murder.

"Yeah. I better get on with my work," Boone grumbles.

Whale clears his throat behind the back of his hand. It's been so long since he's done this, but he has to give it a try, for old time's sake. "When you're through, Mr. Boone, feel free to make use of the pool. We're quite private here. Quite informal. You don't have to worry about a suit."

Boone glances dumbly at Whale.

"And more healthy, don't you think? Swimming as God made us?"

The glance hardens into a stare, as if seeing Whale for the first time. What does he see? An old faggot, a withered fruit. Yes, he finally understands. His upper lip lifts in disgust. The stare ices over as he turns away, muttering, "No, thanks. I got another job to get to this afternoon."

"Some other time perhaps?" But Whale feels he's touched something dangerous. Most men, whatever their predilection, nervously laugh, but this one looks insulted. "I should let you finish your chores. Keep up the fine work, Mr. Boone. Good day."

He hurries into his studio, smiling to himself, pleased to be naughty again. It doesn't matter that he failed. There will be others. He has that university student coming to visit this afternoon. But when the fellow glared at him, there had been such resentment in his eyes, such animal anger that, for a brief instant, Whale was frightened. Traces of that fear still twitch in his chest when he's alone. He's not been afraid of any living man in so long—except for doctors—that he finds this fear oddly exciting, and interesting, very interesting.

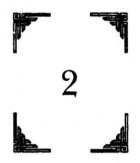

# 2

He feels terribly open to the world and the world pours in. The gangly young man with wavy red hair is nervous, excited, even fearful, but cannot move a muscle.

"Hold still, Jimsy. Turn your head back a mite."

Tozer sits in the grass ten feet away, a bulky sketchbook in his lap, a bowler hat on the back of his patent-leather hair. Their spidery bicycles lean against the stone wall of the ruined granary behind him.

A summer morning in 1910, a Sunday when everyone else is at church. Two men lounge in a clearing behind the ruins, away from the towpath of an abandoned canal outside the factory town of Dudley, in the Midlands region known as the Black Country. The ruins are hardly ancient, dating back only to the time of Napoléon, before the railway and a new canal made this route obsolete. The water is black with runoff slag from the steel mills upstream.

The men sit on squares of rubberized cloth, standard equipment for any Sunday artist. John Tozer is dressed in the white shirt, winged collar, and waistcoat of a respectable workingman. He's removed his coat and tugged the celluloid cuffs up his arms so he won't get charcoal on his sleeves. He has a smudgy new mustache.

In front of him, against the yellow ferns and soot-streaked tree trunks, young James Whale, twenty-one years old, reclines on his elbows in the classical pose of "The Dying Gaul." He is uncomfortably, nervously naked.

There's nothing classical about his nudity. He looks like a skinned rabbit. His long torso is not much thicker than his limbs, and his flesh is the color of rice pudding. His arms are surprisingly muscular, however, the hands dark and leathery from working with metal. Like his father and brothers, Jimmy Whale works six days a week in a factory. He attempts the stuffy expression of a photography studio portrait, but his skittish eyes continue to dart and blink.

"Can't you be quicker?" he mutters.

*"Ars longa, vita brevis,"* says Tozer, who's had more school and Latin. "Or maybe arse *longa?"* he chuckles.

"Just drawr."

Both men have Midlands accents, like head colds that smother their consonants and flatten their speech. Whale fights against his accent with genteel enunciation, but he gets careless when he's preoccupied. There's a girlish lilt to both his diction and gesture whenever he forgets himself. He cultivates an air of gentlemanly reserve not just out of ambition but because it's the one disguise he's found for the effeminacy that gets catcalls and sneers from his workmates. He's ashamed of almost everything about himself.

"Relax, Jimsy. Nobody's gonna come this way."

"I don't care about that," says Whale, although he does. He also hates keeping still, which can't help but feed his fear and excitement. He is afraid of his own nakedness and, odder still, afraid of his clothed friend. "What I don't like is I sit and you draw. Not fair, John. Not democratic."

"You lost the toss, Jimsy."

"But I'm the better artist, John. You say so yourself."

Slightly superior to Whale, not a manual laborer but a hauler's clerk and engaged to be married, Tozer tends to take command in all things with his chum, except art. Among the men improving themselves in evening classes at the Dudley School of Arts and Crafts, Whale stands out in talent and seriousness. He invited Tozer to bicycle with him into the country this morning to sketch trees. It was Tozer who proposed they sketch each other instead, a bit of the life study that the school won't give them. Only full-time students are allowed to work with models. The evening classes are restricted to plaster casts of body parts, for fear that whole bodies, even in plaster, might corrupt less educated minds.

"What are you wanting, then?" asks Tozer.

"I want you to finish so's I can have a go."

"I need the practice more than you." Tozer chews his mustache while he thinks. "What if we model for each other? Two birds with one stone?"

Whale only wants to get dressed, but if Tozer too is naked, then he should feel less humbled, less a servant to his chum's eye. Nevertheless: "A fine pair we'd look if someone comes larking about."

Tozer lets out a laugh. "A couple of Red Indians? A pair of Greek gods by the Old Birmingham Canal! That's what they'd see. But nobody ever comes this way." He is completely taken with the idea. "All right, then. Fair is fair." Chuckling to himself, he gets up and begins to undo his tie. "Why should you be the lucky one, the happy heathen sitting nature-ale in the woods?"

Whale almost protests but doesn't. This is what he wants, isn't it? For Tozer to undress? He tries not to watch but reaches around to get his sketchbook, pencils, and lump of gutta-percha from his satchel. "Whoever saw a Greek statue with a drawing pad?" he worries aloud.

"We don't put our books in the pictures."

There are a dozen buttons for Tozer to undo, even on his

shoes. Soon he is standing there in his bowler hat and one-piece
suit of short-sleeved underclothes. He doffs the hat before his
final unbuttoning. His shoulders emerge and he steps out of the
legs, like a man stepping from his own skin. He has a hairy belly
and whey-faced buttocks. He hangs his empty skin on the bobbing branch of a pin oak.

"Feel better already," he declares, slapping his stomach. He
sits down again and flips to the next page.

Whale is relieved, pleased. They have corrected the balance
of things, made themselves equals. One of the joys of art is that
it introduces a new hierarchy into the world. As an artist, a workingman could sidestep class and origin, even earn a knighthood
as John Millais did.

They lie on their sides and face each other, ten feet apart.
Scratching at unbleached paper with an oval-barreled pencil,
Whale can forget his own body and concentrate on Tozer's. He
sees in isolated details where the instructors prefer general im-
pressions, the smudge of wholeness that can be captured with
charcoal. Whale works quickly, getting the foot, then calf and
raised knee and Tozer's pursy middle. As a clerk Tozer spends
most of his day perched on a stool, so his body is softer than
Whale's, fleshier. Neither body is beautiful. They are like weak
imitations of beauty, awkward cartoons, just as their nudity in this
shabby glade is like a caricature of a scene in Poussin or Claude.
Whale sometimes fears his whole life is a poor cartoon, his love
of beauty a clumsy aping of his betters. "Y'are getting above yar-
sef," his mother tells him. "Who are ya to want to get above yar-
sef?" But he can forget these doubts and anxieties when he
concentrates on capturing the accordian crush of abdomen, the
nonclassical squint of Tozer's belly button.

There is a soft rustle of air in the trees, and the sharp whispers of pencil and charcoal. The little clearing between the
woods and ruins grows more peaceful, more mysterious. Whale
feels a strange oneness with the world, himself, and his friend.

"Now leave off that," says Tozer.

"Leave off what?"

Tozer keeps his eyes lowered to his sketch. "You know what."

Whale does know. His face is suddenly very warm—he's blushing—but he can't stop the warmer, heavier blush nodding at his middle. It stole into him unnoticed while he shaded the hair-filled cup of an armpit. He's horrified Tozer can see him like this, but the horror only deepens the blush, turning it to stone. He is too embarrassed to do more than mumble, "Sorry."

"Spoiling my symmetry," says Tozer, trying to joke away his own embarrassment.

Their faces become more solemn as they look deeper into their books. Whale is too paralyzed with shame to continue drawing. One wants beauty from the human body, not barnyard crudity. He closes his eyes, desperately wishing his body would go away.

Tozer takes a deep breath. He steals a sidelong glance at himself. "Now you have me going," he grumbles.

Because where Whale left only a crosshatch of shadow, Tozer too has stiffened. It's like an attack of giggles during church: once one person starts, the other can't help but join in.

Whale feels a flood of relief. Shame shared is less humiliating. They both stick out like coat hooks.

Tozer begins to giggle.

"Not funny," says Whale, but he bites his lips together to keep from laughing too.

"In the style of the French," Tozer declares, "I should draw it in, don't you think?"

"No!"

But he's already begun. "Jimsy Whale. The stallion of Plessy Lane," he chuckles. "Who'd have guessed."

"Don't, John. Not funny."

But the thought of Tozer drawing it is like having his hand touch him there.

"Warning you, John. Do me and I'll do you. Show it to your Lucy."

"Righto. Give her a gawk at what she won't so much as

poke." Tozer turns his sketchbook around to show Whale. The clumsy charcoal figure has a great prick sticking between its legs.

"Gimme that!" Whale grabs at the book.

Tozer laughs and rolls away, swinging the book out of reach.

And Whale leaps on top of him, laughing as he pins his pal to the ground.

"No better than a donkey!" cries Tozer, laughing too and trying to roll Whale off, but he has only one hand free and it's all he can do to keep his sketchbook out of Whale's grasp. "Where's the great artist? Where's the next Millais?" He tosses the book out on the grass, then grabs Whale around the waist to keep him from going after it.

"You milksop clerk," laughs Whale. "You fat-arsed sod. You know I'm stronger than you."

They are two schoolboys having a friendly wrestle, except these boys are men, and naked, and suddenly there is no fight in Whale's horseplay.

"Yes? Yes?" Tozer continues, still laughing.

The warm depth of skin against skin—not flat like a picture but as round as sculpture—stuns Whale. He stares in alarm at Tozer's face.

Tozer continues to grin and squirm, but the look in his eyes has changed too. His hands relax but remain perched on Whale's hips.

Whale is breathless. "Do you kiss Lucy?" he asks. "How do you kiss her?"

Tozer is too frightened to answer.

"Like this?" And Whale kisses Tozer's cheek. "Like this?" He gives a quicker kiss beneath the bristly threads of mustache.

"Like this," Tozer whispers, and takes his friend's head in both hands to show him.

Nothing in Whale's life, nothing in his previous experience, matches the confusing glory of what follows. Not his first glimpse of a real painting—the Titian in Town Hall—not even the rush of joy he feels when a touring theater company comes to Dudley and the curtain rises on new worlds magically conjured out of painted flats, colored shadows, and carbon arc lamps, their fakery part of the thrill. But John Tozer is real, warm and hairy with a faint taste of aromatic bitters. The redheaded factory worker has always loved nude pictures of men more than those of women. And he has guiltily known what he wanted from certain living men; he has had it in dreams. In the midst of his joy, he imagines spending the rest of the day doing this with Tozer, one time after another, again and again.

The glory builds to frantic clinches, startled gasps and jolts, and a light splash of pinfeathers.

And it's instantly over for Whale, with a completeness that surprises him. His need disappears, and all love for John Tozer. Their mess of limbs feels damp and unseemly. He rolls over on his back to gaze up at a sky heaped with scumbled clouds worthy of Constable—another genius from the lower classes—and a single broken line of black smoke climbing from the power station a mile away, the only furnace burning on a Sunday.

Tozer lies beside him, his arms still around Whale, his breath moist and ticklish. "That was lovely, Jim. Better than what I ever got from a girl."

"I liked it too. Very much." But there's nothing more he wants from his own body, or from Tozer's either—except to resume sketching it. He lifts an arm to make Tozer let go.

Tozer tightens his embrace. "No, let's lay like this for a spell, eh? I feel so good right now."

"Then have a nice lay. I can sketch you while you rest."

"You don't want to sketch. What do you need with sketching?"

"My one free day and if I'm to get anywheres with art—" He pulls free of Tozer and returns to his book in the grass. He sits cross-legged on his square and turns to the unfinished drawing. "Get the way you were," he commands. "Least get your head up so's I can finish your face."

Tozer obeys, with a smirk. "You're a daft one, Jimsy. Don't know how to relax."

"We had our fun. Now I should work." But the pencil

doesn't feel as natural in his fingers as it did before. And Tozer's body, now that he's known it with his own body, is no longer as important to his eye. He makes a few idle marks where the head should go.

Tozer watches him. A squint of concern comes into his face. "You don't feel bad about what we just did?"

"Course not. What makes you say that?"

"The way you hide in your work."

"I want to finish this. Nothing to feel bad about."

Tozer considers that. " 'Tis a sin, I suppose. But so is so much else in the world. Little fellas certainly enjoyed it," he claims, flicking himself with his thumb and index finger.

"Keep still."

Whale's fingers are slippery with Tozer's hair oil. He rubs his hand through the grass before taking up the pencil again, but it doesn't help. The picture will not come.

Tozer grows thoughtful, gnawing at his mustache, staring off in the direction of town. "Lucy," he mournfully declares. "I cannot do this to Lucy."

"No. You cannot," Whale agrees, simply to suggest they shouldn't do this again. He does not feel particularly sinful. The Methodist religion he knows is stern yet spacious enough to include all manner of sin—fornication, drink, blasphemy, even murder—without singling out one as grounds for expulsion. No, Whale's guilt is over his failure to continue working. A man in his situation cannot afford such distractions. Sex is as bad as drink for the way it consumes energy, and look at what drink did to two of his brothers. Until today, sex hasn't been a possibility, so it hasn't been a temptation. He is sorry he enjoyed it so much, because it squanders the passion he needs to climb out of common life into the greater world.

" 'Tis a sin, after all. A sin against my future wife," Tozer mutters, as suggestible in his conscience as he'd been in his privates. "This cannot happen again, Jim. Fun though it be. Not fitting for someone who's to be a family man."

"Good, then. I promise never to do it with you again, John."

"Thankee, Jim. Yes, we must forget we did this thing. But no bad feelings?"

"None."

Tozer instantly feels better. He lifts his head to better enable his chum to draw it.

But Whale can only make marks like exclamation points along the margins. He might be able to close the door on this, but he's unable to lock the door shut. He sniffs at his left hand, still scented with sex and hair oil. When I get where I'm going, he tells himself, when I get up in the world, then I can have this when I please. Anytime and as often as I like. But not before I arrive.

When they are dressed again and wheeling their bicycles along the towpath toward the macadam road into town, Tozer behaves as though nothing extraordinary happened today. He natters away about Lucy and his hopes that an upcoming promotion will give him enough money to finally marry. In the canal beside the granary, the torn pieces of a pencil sketch drift across the black water.

Over the next months, Whale sketches no more men, clothed or otherwise. He limits himself to architecture. He's only a guest at Tozer's wedding the following year. They are seeing less of each other, and Tozer's best man is his supervisor at the hauling firm, a gruff bearded bachelor who bullies employees and regularly attends meetings of the Friends of Walt Whitman in Birmingham. It is this boss who will read aloud from *Leaves of Grass* five years later, spitting out verses through the tears soaking his bushy beard, at the service for Corporal John Tozer's effects. The body itself has been buried in France. Whale only learns of the death from the "Local Heroes" page of the Dudley newspaper, thoughtfully sent to him by his mother.

# 3

AFTER A LIGHT LUNCH FIXED BY MARIA—WATERCRESS SALAD, AN omelet, and a glass of red wine—Whale watches *As the World Turns* on television, then goes to his bedroom for a nap. It is a safe, dreamless sleep. He wakes up clearheaded, his headache diminished.

He occupies the next hour preparing himself for afternoon tea and his visitor. He changes his shirt twice and tries a necktie before deciding on a blue polka-dot bow. He spends a long time studying his face in the mirror over the dresser. He lifts his chin for a manly, military pose, then stretches his long upper lip for a look of aristocratic inscrutability. He can pass for sixty, can't he? Even fifty-nine or fifty-eight? One of the nurses said he reminded her of the Duke of Windsor, but Whale believes he has a younger, more sensuous mouth than the lovelorn abdicator. Twenty-five years ago, David said he looked like that paragon of male sexuality, the Arrow Shirt Man. No more. He needs the tan he lost in the hospital to hide the deep lines etched around his

eyes, the furrows scored down either side of his mouth. He gives
his white hair a few final licks with his monogrammed, silver-
backed brushes.

He knows he has no business going to such fuss, but it's
been so long since he entertained a guest. There had been a
letter among the four or five get-well cards waiting for him when
he returned from the hospital.


Dear Mr. Whale, sir,

I am a student of cinema at the University of South-
ern California. I have always been a great admirer of
the movies you directed, not only the horror ones but
also the original *Show Boat.* Would it be possible for me
to interview you for a paper I hope to write? You must
have a very full and busy schedule, but I will do my best
to work around it. I am trained in shorthand and will
be able to record every precious word you have to share.
                    Sincerely yours, Edmund Kay


This was interesting. He was touched a stranger even knew
who he was. Once you stopped working and were of no use to
people, even friends in the industry forgot your existence. The
last time anybody sought him out was a year ago, when a brash
young television producer from New York came to ask, not that
he direct something for TV—a prospect Whale considered with
both hope and alarm—but that he appear as a contestant on a
game show called *I've Got a Secret.* "Your secret could be something like, 'I created Frankenstein.' " Whale politely yet firmly
said no. He would not give up his privacy for the sake of five
minutes of notoriety, a funny old coot in a sideshow.

But this letter was different, personal and intriguing. A
young man wanted to sit and talk with him at length. On the
morning his doctor let him discharge the day nurse, he had Maria telephone Edmund Kay and set a date for afternoon tea. It
might have seemed a little desperate if Whale made the call him-

self. "Just a boy. Very young," Maria reported with a shrug after her conversation with him.

"There is iced tea, Maria?" Whale asks when he comes from his bedroom. "The cucumber sandwiches?"

"Yes, sir, Mr. Jimmy."

The sandwiches might be excessive, but they are what a young American would expect at a proper English tea. Whale goes to the hutch and selects two weighty Havanas from the shallow mahogany box. Allowed only one cigar a day, he takes an extra in case Mr. Kay partakes. He runs a smoothly foliated, spicy cylinder beneath his nose before slipping both cigars into the inside pocket of his jacket.

The doorbell rings and Whale goes to his club chair, settling in while Maria answers the door. He opens a maroon-bound book left on the end table—the Dickens he put aside last week when he found he couldn't read anything denser than a newspaper. He waits until Maria ushers the fellow into the room before he looks up.

"Mr. Kay, sir," Maria announces.

"Yes?" He feigns surprise that he has a visitor.

A slim boy in a V-necked sweater stands by his fireplace, staring. Short black hair hangs in a Roman fringe on his forehead. He rests his weight on one slouched hip, his boneless arms nervously twined behind him. Whale certainly didn't expect a football player or fraternity rowdy, but he's mildly disappointed that Edmund Kay is so clearly a baby poof.

"Ah. Mr. Kay. I'd almost forgotten. My guest for tea." He stands and holds out his hand.

"Mr. Whale? Mr. Whale," Kay repeats more confidently. He untangles his arms to shake hands. His voice is froggy, like a hoarse child's, his handshake as light as a feather.

He also appears to be Jewish, although that's of no matter to Whale. He has no romantic notions about Jews, negative or otherwise, not in this city. Even David was born David Levy.

"This is such an honor. You're one of my favorite all-time

directors," Kay blurts out with a grin. "I can't believe I'm meeting you."

"No. I expect you can't," Whale says gently, intending to be
both teasing and self-deprecating.

But the boy is too excited to catch the mockery. "And this
is your house. Wow. Double wow. The house of Frankenstein."
He looks around, maintaining his smile. "More housey than I
expected," he admits. "I thought you'd live in a big old mansion
or villa."

"One likes to live simply."

Maria stands solemnly by, wrinkling her implacable face at
Kay, glancing suspiciously at Whale.

"Oh yeah. And I know people's movies aren't their lives."
The boy suddenly leans in and growls, "Love dead. Hate living."
He laughs, a high, girlish giggle.

Whale fights a cringe with a polite smile.

"That's my favorite line in my favorite movie of yours, Mr.
Whale. *Bride of Frankenstein.*"

"Is it, now? I made so many pictures, I can't remember them
all."

"Surely you remember your horror films? They're the
greatest."

"Maria?" says Whale. "I think we'll take our tea down by
the swimming pool. Will that be good for you, Mr. Kay?"

"Sure. And the interview. I can interview you, can't I?"

"If you like. Although I'm afraid you'll find me an old stick
as a raconteur."

He had originally intended to give Kay a tour of the house,
but the boy's gush and fervor will seem less loud outdoors.

"After you, Mr. Kay," says Whale as he opens the back door.
Inspecting the boy from behind, he notices his wide hips and
plump posterior. No, not his physical type, but an amusing character.

The yardman is gone, but the sweet smell of mown grass
lingers on the sloping lawn. Kay chatters away on the path to the

pool. All initial shyness in the presence of "the great director" has vanished. "I love the great horror films. Not like this new junk at the drive-ins. The science-fiction horror junk? Creatures from outer space and black lagoons. And giant insects. Lots of giant insects. I saw one last month about giant snails in the Imperial Valley. But the old ones? The movies made by you and Tod Browning and Robert Florey—"

Whale winces at the company he's been given.

"But yours are the best, Mr. Whale. The Frankenstein movies. *The Old Dark House. The Invisible Man.* They look great and have style. And funny! God, audiences back then must've flipped their wigs at the stuff you were doing. Like that 'love death, hate living' line. When Dr. Pretorius meets the Monster in the crypt and the Monster holds the skull that's going to be his bride? And then Pretorius says"—Kay's deadpan murmur is perfect, even if his English accent isn't—" 'You are wise in your generation.' "

"This," says Whale, pointing ahead, "is the studio where I now paint. A hobby. Mine and Winston Churchill's."

"Nice," says Kay. He refuses to be sidetracked. "And your lighting and camera angles. You got to go back to German silent movies to find anything like it. Did you know any of the great German silent directors, Mr. Whale? Pabst and Lang? Murnau? Was F. W. Murnau an influence on your work?"

Finally the boy has mentioned someone Whale doesn't despise. "No, I met Mr. Murnau very briefly, when I first came here. Shortly before his death. A great director. But no, I can't say he influenced my work in any way."

"You know how he died, don't you?"

Whale frowns. "I've heard tales. Here, please be seated." He gestures at the white cast-iron chairs around the table beside the pool. The umbrella overhead has been cranked open and casts a cool oblong shadow. "Our refreshments will be down shortly."

Kay sits and flips open his steno pad while Whale adjusts his bones against the iron scrollwork. "So. When were you born?"

Whale smiles again, but his smiles are growing less indulgent. "Mr. Kay. We'll talk. You may interview me. But we must take this slowly."

"Yes. Sorry. Right," says Kay, grimacing at himself. "It's just I'm so excited to meet you I can't control myself. I mean, I wasn't even sure you were alive until your secretary called."

There's no malice in that. There appears to be no guile or ulterior motives at all in the boy, and his dancing on Whale's toes is nothing more than the headlong rush of youth. Lucky child, Whale thinks. He could never afford to be so thoughtless and carefree. If only he had been born an American.

"Let's get better acquainted, Mr. Kay." The name has taken on a sinister, alphabetical sound. "You said you were a student at the university?"

"USC, yes, sir."

"And you study . . . motion pictures?"

"Oh yeah. Film history."

"As one might study ancient history or Elizabethan drama? Curious. I had no idea it might be an academic field. At Oxford in my day, people studied only what had been dead and gone for a hundred years at least."

"You're English, right?"

"Ah, you've guessed my little secret."

Maria comes down the path with a tray loaded with finger sandwiches, a pitcher of iced tea, and a plate of sponge cakes.

"Thank you, Maria. Very nice."

She makes a highly audible sigh and starts back up the hill.

"I confess I've acquired the American fondness for iced tea," he tells Kay. "What's lost in flavor is more than compensated for by a refreshing piquancy. Uh, cucumbers," he explains when Kay makes a face after a bite of sandwich. "Sliced very thin."

Kay opens his sandwich to peek inside. "Righto," he laughs.

"I presume you want to make pictures, Mr. Kay?"

"Not me. I just like to watch them. And write about them. The old ones. New movies stink. Jerry Lewis and Doris Day? *The Ten Commandments?*" He rolls his eyes. "I hate color, don't you?

All that bright, flat lighting. They don't make them like they used to, that's for sure."

Whale wants to be flattered—recent movies are as cold and shiny as the newest automobiles—but he can't help feeling like a quaint Victorian sideboard discovered by a chatty little antiques dealer. Kay is only a boy, but he has an old queen's love of the past. The old is good because it's old and has no teeth. One hopes to keep a contemporary bite, as the Old Masters do. Whale has to remind himself that they are only talking about horror pictures.

"Shall we begin?" he asks. "What did you want to know?"

Kay wipes his hand on a napkin. "Everything. Whatever you want to tell me." He picks up his steno pad and ballpoint pen. "When were you born?"

"The twenty-second of July. In 1896."

He waits to see if Kay writes that down.

"The only son of a divine who was a master at Harrow. The family was full of divines. And military officers. Grandfather was a bishop—Church of England, of course." Whale shifts his gaze out toward the ocean, relaxing into the role. "I was a bit of a rascal when young. In and out of scrapes. I attended Eton—it wouldn't do for a master's son to attend where his father taught. I was to go up to Oxford the year war broke out. The Great War, you know. You had a Good War, but we had a great one."

He glances to see if the boy smiles at the quip, but Kay only continues to write.

"I never did make it to university. I enlisted. After serving as a lieutenant, and spending a year in a prisoner-of-war camp, school seemed redundant." When Whale first came to Hollywood he told people he had actually attended Oxford, until one day a smart-ass screenwriter asked which college.

He pauses so Kay can ask about his experience as a prisoner of war—it wouldn't do to draw too much attention to that oneself. The boy only nods and says, "Go on. I'll catch up."

"It was a source of great shame to the family when I went

into the theater after the Armistice. People from good families didn't, you know."

Inventing this life used to give Whale such strange pleasure. As the lies were refined and repeated over the years, he could almost believe that this was his past. But the lies feel different today. Maybe it is the ease with which Kay swallows them, or the fact that Whale has not repeated this fairy tale in such a long time. Perhaps it's an effect of the stroke, unplugging his facility for make-believe. But this pretty story, made from the odds and ends of people he's known and books he's read, doesn't feel as convincing as it once did. It hangs on him like a suit of clothes he's too thin to wear anymore. The truth stands closer to him now, peering over his shoulder.

"You went into the theater," says Kay.

"Yes. I developed a taste for it as a prisoner of war. We had so much time on our hands we engaged in amateur theatricals. The Boche encouraged us, expecting we'd do *Hamlet* or *The Tempest.* The old Germans were very keen on Shakespeare, you know. They were sorely disappointed when our first program was *Charley's Aunt.* Our chaps loved it, but the Huns in the front rows just sat there, Prussian and stone-faced over our silly little farce about an Oxford student in women's clothing."

Again, not so much as a nibble from the boy. Whale skips the war as a lost cause.

"So when I returned"—he loudly clears his throat—"I had been bitten by the theater bug. I wanted to be part of that world. Footlights and make-believe. I began as an actor. I had the looks and made up in eagerness for what I lacked in talent. I joined a small troupe doing the theatrical circuit in the provinces. Leeds, Newcastle, Birmingham, Dudley. A wretched grind of drafty houses, moth-eaten costumes, and equally moth-eaten plays. A slightly desperate, seat-of-your-pants sort of life." He has let the truth into his story, but it doesn't embarrass him as it once did. "It was good for me. A valuable experience. You learn to live with the fickleness of the public, the vicissitudes of fate. You learn to go with the punches. And I met people important to me later in life, including Mr. Ernest Thesiger. He played your Dr. Pretorius in *Bride*, you know. He was Mr. Femm in *The Old Dark House* as well.''

Kay's pen scribbles more excitedly.

"Ernest came from a background very different—I mean, similar to my own. Good family, service in the trenches, a spit-in-the-wind attitude about life. Quite a nasty fellow at times, in a droll, withering sort of way. Much like Dr. Pretorius himself. And utterly unashamed about his, uh, eccentricities.'' No, he won't talk about that, especially since the boy tilts that way himself. "For example, in the theater and later on the movie set, this former company commander would relax by sitting in a corner with needle and thread and quietly embroider.''

"What did he embroider?''

"Oh, I don't know. Scarves and such.''

"When did he die?''

"He hasn't. At least not that I've heard.'' The thought that Thesiger may be dead is oddly disturbing to Whale.

"He seems awfully old in your movies.''

"Thesiger was born old and desiccated, a bit of a fossil. No, Thesiger will never die.''

"Karloff is still alive.''

"Yes. I suspect he is.''

"But Colin Clive is dead.''

"Quite dead.'' This is a distressing line of talk; Whale irritably pushes past it. "But so I returned to London, a wiser, more seasoned trouper. Roughly around, oh, 1925.''

Kay resumes writing, less eagerly than before.

"I continued to perform but understood my limitations. Oh, I was pretty enough. I could play juvenile leads for a few more years, but my days were numbered. Luckily, I had a knack with pencil and paper, an idle hobby in school. I began to design sets, often for the very plays I performed in. It was a gypsy time in London theater, quite slapdash and bohemian. I met Elsa Lanchester then—''

"The Bride!"

"Yes, the Bride. But at that time a cabaret artist. She had danced as a child with—a famous dancer. That American woman. But when I met Elsa, she and a friend ran a little cabaret café called the Cave of Harmony. Just a hole off an alleyway in Soho, but quite charming, quite bohemian. Elsa used to perform there, old comic songs. There was one in particular called"—he smiles as he remembers—" 'I Just Danced with a Man Who Danced with the Girl Who Danced with the Prince of Wales.' " He can almost hear Elsa singing, her schoolgirl mouth curling comically above her gums as she mimes the character's ludicrous delirium; he suddenly smells sickly-sweet perfumes and smoking paraffin—the place had been illuminated by candles stuck in wine bottles. "You can't imagine what life was like back then, for someone who'd been through—so much. So much." The rush of emotion takes him by surprise. He hasn't thought about the Cave of Harmony in years. "The twenties in London were like one long bank holiday, a break from everything dour and re-spectable. The Bright Young Things were out and about. Mit-fords and Sitwells and that novelist fellow, Evelyn Waugh. He once came to the café. But all of us, high and low, were happily splashing about. Your latest batch of bohemians, these poets with their bongos and beards, have nothing on us. We had booze and jazz. I never especially liked jazz, but I loved the attitude that came with it. Do what you will and the devil take fuck all." He laughs at the obscenity he let slip. "And Dora. Dora Zinkiesen."

"Is that a name I should know?"

"No. Just a friend. A lovely Scotswoman with whom I danced the tango. At the Cave of Harmony." He remembers in his shoul-der muscles the stop-and-go energy of the tango, he and tall Dora darting from pose to pose like two wind-up flamingos. He had loved to dance with Dora, so much that he mistook the tango for love and proposed marriage, which Dora was wise enough to refuse. "But we were all so young. Beautiful, careless, and young. Except for Charles. Gloomy old Charles. Charles Laughton, you know, before he and Elsa were married. He took an immediate dislike to me. I thought it was my vulgar past that made him uncomfortable—he was awfully hoity-toity for someone whose people ran a seaside hotel in Yorkshire. But no, years later, when we'd all gone Hollywood, I understood we had something else in common."

"A friend told me a story about Laughton," Kay offers, with a sly wiggle of eyebrows.

"Yes, there are several young men in this city with stories to tell." Whale frowns to signal that he does not need to hear another. "I was his son in a play called *The Man with Red Hair*, whose set I designed. I was the stage manager too. Difficult man to act with. You never knew what he was going to do next. Which can be marvelous for a real actor, keeping you on your toes, but I'd come to the conclusion I was not a real actor. I did less acting after that, more designing, and finally a little directing. I was hired to design the set for a play called *Journey's End*. Nobody expected much of it. The thing had been written by an insurance clerk, Bob Sherriff, a sweet if oblivious fellow. He had the broadest shoulders and smallest derriere of any man I've known. He was a rowing chap, one of those sports who mess about in boats, and lived happily with his mother. Still does, last I heard. But Bob wrote the play for his rowing club to perform to raise funds for new boats. They wouldn't touch it. It was too morbid, too sad. The whole thing took place in a dugout in the trenches. No singing, no dancing, no roles for pretty girls. I thought it a beautiful play. Every experienced director they approached turned it down. Not commercial, too much work for too little reward. I offered myself, bullying and begging that I could do it. And I did. *Journey's End*, to the surprise of everyone, myself included, was a huge success. It made the careers of all who were associated with it."

"I've never heard of it."

"That doesn't surprise me. Although it was also my first motion picture, you know."

"How much longer before we get to *Frankenstein?*"

The bored whine of the question startles Whale. He glances

at the steno pad to see what the boy has written. He cannot read shorthand, but Kay seems to have recorded little since Whale last looked. "Sherriff is spelled double *r*, double *f*."

But even with Whale watching him, Kay doesn't write; he hasn't included Bob at all.

"Am I correct in assuming, Mr. Kay, that it's not me you're interested in, but only my horror pictures?"

The boy becomes flustered. "Oh no, I want to hear everything. I just didn't think most of that important enough to write down."

"I see."

He took such joy in remembering his London days that it hurts to think it was all idle chatter to his interviewer. What had he expected? The interest of posterity in a child with bangs? Someone who'd be as eager to hear about his life as David was when they first met? He has not told anyone his whole true story since he shared it with David.

"You must understand, Mr. Kay. The horror pictures were trifles. Entertainments. Grand guignol for the masses. The film I am proud of is *Show Boat.* With Paul Robeson and Helen Morgan."

Kay looks shocked. "*Show Boat* is great. But . . . you can't really believe that, Mr. Whale. Your horror films are classics. Everybody knows them."

When people praise his horror pictures, Whale fears they are being condescending. When they dismiss them as trash, however, he feels hurt and insulted. "Yes. They certainly have a life of their own. They've gone on without me."

"But you should be remembered too. I remember you. That's why I'm here. I want to hear about the man who made *Frankenstein.*"

"Who did other things with his life as well."

"Sure. But it's the horror movies you'll be remembered for."

Whale's change of mood, the anger and resentment following his joy, is so abrupt it feels insane. "I am not dead, Mr. Kay."

"No. I never said you were. Or will be soon," he adds, without conviction.

Whale feels an inexplicable hatred for the boy. He fights it by concentrating on his youth, his delicate hands, his turned-up nose. Not beautiful, but not unattractive. Years ago in London, meeting such a fellow backstage or at the Cave of Harmony, Whale would overcome his feelings of resentment and challenge by going to bed with him. Sex was a great equalizer, if only for ten to thirty minutes. But sex has remained off in the distance since his return from the hospital. The idea of feeling lust for this boy is like glimpsing something at the bottom of a well.

"But *Journey's End,*" Kay asks. "You were going to tell about making it as your first movie." He leans over the steno pad, determined to be more worthy.

"I have a proposal, Mr. Kay. This mode of question and answer is getting old, don't you think?"

"I don't mind."

"I do. I need to make it more interesting. And it'll enable you to distinguish between what you find necessary and what you find trivial. I will truthfully answer any question you ask. But in return, for each answer, you must remove one article of clothing."

Kay's little mouth pops open. He laughs, not his girlish giggle but a single guffaw that catches on itself like a cough. "That's funny, Mr. Whale."

"It is, isn't it?" Whale agrees. "My life in a game of strip poker. A biographical striptease." He feels better already. "Shall we play?"

"You're serious."

"Quite."

Kay glances around, needing a witness to confirm that the old man really proposed this. He peers at Whale from the corner of his eye. "Then the rumors are true?"

"What rumors might those be, Mr. Kay?"

"That you were forced to retire because, uh—a sex scandal."

"A homosexual scandal, you mean? I think we can call a spade a spade, now that we understand each other. But for me to answer a question of that magnitude, you'll have to remove both your shoes and your socks."

Kay just sits there, squinting and smirking. Whale wonders if he will pass on this question and try another, or simply end the interview. There's a screech as Kay pushes the cast-iron chair across the flagstones. "You're a dirty old man," he declares with a grin, and bends over to remove his argyle socks. He's already kicked off his penny loafers.

"You are kind to indulge your elders in their vices," Whale declares. "As I indulge the young in theirs."

Two pale feet with neatly trimmed nails emerge; the big toe of his right foot fidgets and flicks against the second toe.

Whale has leaned forward to examine them. He leans back again. "No. There was no scandal." And he reaches into his coat for a cigar, letting the boy stew in the possibility that this is all he will say on the matter.

Kay waits, nervously covering one foot with the other.

Whale slices a neat hole at the base of the cigar with his penknife, then lights the cigar with a wooden match, sucking and rotating until the tip is roundly lit. Clouds of blue smoke drift out across the swimming pool.

"Ah. My only other vice," he explains, and smiles at Kay. "I suppose you'd like a fuller answer to your question?"

Kay nods.

"I was bored." He perches an elbow on the back of his chair and holds the cigar at a rakish angle. "That's why I quit. Nothing more. I was bored with my assignments. Which were nothing but tripe. I'd made enemies at the studio, and they punished me by handing down worse and worse assignments. Until finally, in the middle of a loathsome picture titled *They Dare Not Love*—and no, my dear Kay, it had nothing to do with the love that dare not speak its name—I walked. I packed it in. I'd been saving up my berries for quite some time and didn't need to suffer their drear routine another single day."

"Did you make enemies because of your, uh, private life?"

"Because I was a pansy? Not at all. A full answer to that question, Mr. Kay, will cost you your sweater. I do hope you're wearing a vest today. If not, we'll break the bank very soon."

Kay hesitates a moment, then sets his pen aside to pull his sweater up over his head. "Too warm for a sweater," he claims. His sleeveless T-shirt displays a pattern of freckles across his shoulders. He brushes his hair forward before he takes up his pen again.

"You must understand how Hollywood was twenty years ago. Nobody cared a tinker's cuss who slept with whom, so long as you kept it out of the papers. And that was true only for the stars. A character actor? A writer? A director? To care about our behavior would have been like worrying over the morals of a plumber before letting him mend your pipes. Outside of Hollywood, who knows who George Cukor is, much less gives two spits about what he does with those boys his pals bring home from the malt shops along Santa Monica? We directors, we artistic types, were already looked upon as freaks. Nothing we did surprised the people in the front office."

Kay is staring at him in disbelief. "George Cukor? Who made *A Star Is Born?* You mean—"

"As gay as a goose," says Whale, always happy to take another swipe at Cukor. "A close friend of mine was his associate producer on *Camille.* Two of a kind, and nobody batted an eye. And when you toss Garbo into the soup as well . . ."

Kay is still too stunned by the first revelation even to hear the second one. "George Cukor! I never guessed."

"We are new to the life, aren't we, Mr. Kay? You haven't heard about George's notorious Sunday brunches? Gatherings of trade. Eating the leftovers from his oh-so-proper Saturday dinner parties. His pals regularly bring him fresh bodies, since Georgie-Porgie can't seem to keep a boyfriend."

But Kay doesn't laugh or sneer in disgust. He only nods to himself, amazed by his discovery.

"If a goat like that can continue about his business, my more domestic arrangement could've raised very few eyebrows." Whale fears his envy has peeked out; he won't say another word about Cukor. "This same close friend insists things are different now. David was always a puritan, but attitudes do seem changed since the war. Along with McCarthy and the Red Scare a few years back, there was a kind of Lavender Scare. Masculinity is all the rage now, not just in actors but in the people who work with them. You can't have a fellow like Alan Ladd being directed by a fairy. We'll spoil his red-blooded manliness. The fact is, there's nobody like a fairy for distinguishing real masculinity from the wooden variety now in vogue. But in 1941, when I walked, my hint of mint was not an issue."

"Then why did you have enemies at the studio?"

He thinks a moment. "Maybe it wasn't so much the presence of enemies as an absence of friends. I was lucky my first years at Universal. The Laemmles, father and son, Carl and Junior, indulged me. They gave me full approval on scripts, they let me improvise on the set, they stayed out of my hair. In return I gave them pictures that made heaps of money. The fact is, they didn't know the first thing about moviemaking. Laemmle Senior was a short, sweet, chatty German Jew whom everyone called Uncle Carl. Universal *was* a family affair. Uncle Carl filled the lot with relatives from the Old Country, most of whom could barely speak English. Junior could be the dullest fellow on earth, but he understood that I knew more than he did, so we worked well together. All went smoothly, until they lost the studio. Uncle Carl had negotiated a loan with a bank back east. If a certain sum weren't repaid by a certain date, then the bank could buy the Laemmles out. The old fox thought this bank wouldn't be able to raise the money for the purchase, but, for the first time in his life, he was wrong."

He has not thought about the Laemmles in years; he suddenly misses them, and not just because of the turn of his career.

"There was a rumor," he admits, "that they needed the money because I'd gone over budget on *Show Boat*. Utter nonsense. They were hard up because that prima donna of prestige pictures, John Stahl, made a royal balls-up of *Magnificent Obsession*, shooting hours of film with no end in sight. But suddenly, the Laemmles were gone, replaced by people who knew just as little, but who had no inkling how little they knew. They let me have my way for another picture or two, until we made one called *The Road Back*. Do you know it?"

Kay shakes his head.

"Do you know the novel? Sequel to *All Quiet on the Western Front* by Erich Remarque."

Again Kay shakes his head.

Whale is so involved in explaining himself that he's forgotten their game. "Take off your vest and I'll tell a story."

Kay nervously plucks at it, glancing toward the house.

"Don't be shy. There's time to stop before you go too far."

"Oh. I guess." Kay peels the shirt up, from the neck, and tosses it on his shoes and sweater. His pouter pigeon chest is covered in freckles, with two brown nipples and not a trace of hair. "Was *The Road Back* a horror movie?" he asks hopefully.

"Not at all. Horror pictures were a thing of the past by now. I'd done *Show Boat*. Major success. Great box office. But now I was to do something important, an indictment of the Great War and what it did to Germany. A remarkable story with remarkable people involved. I brought Bob Sherriff back over to write the script. It was my masterpiece, better than *Western Front*, better than anything Cukor ever did." Had it been a masterpiece? Whale wants to believe it was but knows he cannot be sure.

"Why haven't I heard of it?" asks Kay.

"Because the studio, or rather, the bank that now called itself a studio, butchered it." His headache, always present, flickers with sparks and splinters brought on by anger. "They cut away the guts and brought in another director to add slapstick, for fear the truth might depress the public. And they were afraid they'd lose their German market. The Boche consul in Los Angeles had been making a fuss ever since work began on the picture. Remarque's novels had been banned by the Nazis, publicly burned in their literary bonfires. They certainly didn't want this story seen by moviegoers around the world. And the bankers, those foolish, petty money people, caved in. They let the Nazis have their way, claiming the changes would improve the box office. And it still laid an egg. A great expensive bomb. For which I was blamed. After that, nothing went right for me at Universal. Nothing."

"You couldn't have gone to another studio?"

"I could. I did. Loaned out for this picture or that. But I'd stopped caring. I'd given them my best and it was rejected. All I wanted was to gather up my berries and spend my time making pictures alone—painted pictures. Like Winston Churchill."

"You stayed here during the war? You didn't go home?"

Whale has always hated this question, whether it came from countrymen or Americans. It is especially infuriating coming from this child. A tightening of muscles behind his eyes increases his headache. "Take off your trousers," he tells Kay.

Kay smiles, lowers his head, and says, "Never mind. I'm saving these for something I really want to know."

"Ah, the stakes have become higher. You have to be more selective in the cards you play." But Whale needs to explain why he stayed. "There was no reason to go home. What could I do? Offer myself to the RAF? Man an antiaircraft gun during the Blitz? No, I'd have been just another potential casualty. I had offered myself as a casualty to Mother England for one war. I felt perfectly justified in sitting out the next."

Kay takes a deep, bored breath. "Can we talk about the horror movies now?"

The slightest irritation tightens the threads and knots of pain in his skull. He desperately needs his guest to distract him from this hurt. "Certainly, Mr. Kay. Is there anything in particular you want to know? So badly that we'll be able to get you out of your britches?"

"You really want to go on with this?"

"Of course. Don't feel shy if your linen isn't clean. Although I understand women in this country tell their daughters they must always wear clean underwear, because you never know if you'll be hit by a car. The same should be true for curious boys who visit lonely old movie directors." He draws a hot mouthful from his cigar for dramatic effect, then opens his jaw and sets the smoke free, watching the small cloud slowly somersault from the shadow of the umbrella into the sunlight, curling and scrolling upon itself in elaborate arabesques—like the pinching convolutions of his own brain. He has to close his eyes so he won't feel sick.

"Will you tell me everything you remember about making *Frankenstein?*" asks Kay. "Can that count as one question?"

"Perhaps," says Whale, opening his eyes and seeing Kay. "Oh, of course. Why not?" He'll still have the *Bride* to get the boy out of his knickers.

"I can't believe I'm doing this. But—" Kay stands to unbuckle his belt, glancing around the yard again. His freckles are mixed with little matte goose bumps. "I do this all the time at the dorm or gym. It's doing it in front of somebody famous that makes it creepy." But he has already unzipped and is stepping out of the sharply creased flannel legs. His thighs are pale and skinny; white BVDs swaddle his hips like a bandage. "Just like I'm going to go swimming, isn't it?" he mutters as he lowers the trousers on top of his other clothes. A whey-colored eye peeks through a hole in his seat as he bends over.

"Maybe you would like a swim when we're through?" Whale gently suggests. He suddenly regrets putting the boy through this, especially since seeing Kay in scanties gives him so little pleasure.

Kay sits down again, scrapes his chair up to the table, and leans forward. His shoulders bunch behind him like vulture wings. "Okay. *Frankenstein.* Tell me everything." Undressing has made him arrogant and demanding.

"Righto. *Frankenstein.* Yes. Let me see." But returning to his thoughts brings Whale back into his headache. It is as though a nail has been driven into the base of his skull, one intense pain echoed by a chorus of smaller pains. "*Dracula,* you know. Universal had a big success with *Dracula*. They wanted another project for La—? Lou? Lay—?''

"Lugosi?"

"Of course. Bela Lugosi." He's angry he couldn't remember something so simple. "They conceived the project for him, and somebody else was to direct. That frog. Florey. Yes, Robert Florey began it. But the studio wanted me for another story, and wanted me so baldly—I mean badly, not baldly. I was given the pick of stories being developed. And I picked that one, snatching it from under that silly frog's nose."

"You stole somebody else's idea?"

He hadn't meant to tell Kay that, but the headache leaves him no room to say anything except the truth. "Happens all the time in the studios. Florey would have made a hash of it. He shot tests. Looked ridiculous. Lugosi with a ton of clay packed around his head. Like that children's doll with a potato for a head."

"Mr. Potato Head?"

"He was supposed to be a golem but looked instead like Mr. Potato Head." Whale finds it more difficult to feel his way to the words he needs. "And then La-la-la-gosi"—he hopes that sounds like a joke and not a speech impediment—"refused to do the part. No more monsters. That's what he said. And he did not want to play a monster who couldn't t-t-talk. So I was free to pick my own monster. And I picked a contract player named Karloff."

Kay is writing quickly, eagerly, paying no attention to the sputters and erratic tones of Whale's speech.

"You may have heard of him." A bit of sarcasm should disguise his condition. "English. Real name—Pratt? I don't know who called him Karloff instead. He was playing mostly gangsters when I cast him."

"Who came up with his makeup and look?"

"My idea. Muchly. My sketches. Big heavy brow. Head flat on top so they could take out the old brain and put in the new, like tinned beef." How he longs to do that with his own. "And the makeup artist. Terrific man, very clever. Jack? Jack Pierce.

He did good stuff. Brilliantly good. The electrodes on the neck? Those were his. We couldn't decide what to do with the eyes. Karloff's eyes were soulful, but intelligent. Too intelligent. Finally we melted wax on the eyelids, for a heavy, imbecilic look. Heavy shoes with foot-high soles. Padding. Heaps of padding. So much, poor Boris couldn't sit between takes. Someone rigged a plank he could lean against. With armrests. We used to prop the Monster there between takes and give him his tea. Which he had to sip very daintily so as not to spoil his scars."

"He's one of the great images of the twentieth century," Kay declares. "As important as the Mona Lisa."

"You think so? That's very kind of you." Stumbling through the briers and barbed wire of the headache, Whale catches up with what the boy just said. "Oh no. Don't be ridiculous. Just makeup and padding and a large actor. Hardly the Mona Lisa."

"But it's as familiar now, as famous."

"So is Adolf Hitler. So is M-m-mickey Mouse." He has to become angry to get the name out. "Definitely not the—"

His hand is suddenly empty. He clutches at the air, twice, and remembers he'd been holding a cigar. He looks down and sees it on the flagstones, flakes of ash crumbled open like petals around the ember.

"Colin Clive as the doctor. Where did you find him?"

Whale bends down to retrieve his cigar—and the change of gravity drives the spike through his skull.

For a split second, as if in a flash of light, everything else disappears. There is only a sensation so intense it can't register as pain until the shock of it passes. He freezes, stunned by the first shock, terrified there will be another, slowly understanding that he's still in great pain and that it feels like peace only in comparison to what preceded it. Is this death? He wants death to save him from the next bolt of lightning, the next artillery shell screaming toward him, until he remembers what death means and thinks: No, not yet, not yet.

"Colin Clive, Mr. Whale. How did you cast him?"

Whale turns his head toward the froggy voice, and sees the

boy sitting at the table in BVDs. "Take them off," he whispers.
"Quickly."

"No! We haven't finished *Frankenstein.*"

"Please. Now." He fears he will lose consciousness, will
black out and never be conscious again. It seems fitting that the
last thing he'll ever see should be a naked man, even one who's
not his type. Which is ridiculous. He cannot die. Not yet.
"Never—," he whispers. "Excuse me. I must go lie—" He forces
himself up with one hand pushing against a cast-iron arm.

Kay bounces his chair back, ready to run if the old man
pounces. But then he sees Whale's face, the colorless lips, the
desperate eyes. "Mr. Whale? You all right?"

"I just need to—lie down. Studio. Daybed in the studio."
He feels his way around the table, breathing deeply, straining to
exhale the pain and save himself from death.

A scrawny angel with a pigeon chest and no wings stands two
yards away, frightened of him. Not until Whale lurches from the
table does Kay jump forward, catching him under an arm.

"Oh my God. What's wrong, Mr. Whale? Is it your heart?"

"Head. Not right. Not right." There is an instant of comfort
when he feels another body against his side, but it's a small body,
a weak one. He's afraid to rest his full weight against it. "In the
studio. Help me there. Please."

The single blast of pain has left him weak and helpless. The
memory of it nauseates him. He is afraid he will vomit on the
boy or forget his bowels and soil himself. "Forgive me," he whispers. "Forgive me."

Kay steers them through the door into the cool darkness of
the studio. He sits Whale on the sticky leather of the daybed and
eases his head against a bolster. He follows Whale's pointed finger to the intercom and presses the buzzer.

"Yes, Mr. Jimmy?" The voice is full of static.

"An emergency! Mr. Whale's had an attack! Call an ambulance! Call the doctor!"

"No bloody doctor!" Whale snarls. "Tell her to bring my
pills. My painkillers." The thought of a doctor and ambulance

sickens him more than the idea of death. He refuses to go back to hospital. He cannot return to that white hell so soon after he escaped it.

The boy rapidly relays the instructions, his cheek pressed against the intercom.

The pain grows more familiar, less terrifying. It continues to sicken him but no longer feels like death.

"Nothing," says Whale when Kay kneels by the daybed. "This is nothing. Sorry to panic you. Only a headache. A terrible megrim." He lies with his head on the bolster, both feet on the floor. Kay moves to raise the feet. "Don't! Blood to my head. Blood makes it worse."

The boy stands back, wrapping his arms around his chest and rubbing them, as if to rub away the touch of sickness.

Gravel scatters outside as Maria comes running down the path. She swings open the screen door—and freezes when she sees Kay. Her little frown tightens. She catches sight of Whale on the daybed and snaps back to life. "Water," she tells Kay. "Glasses at the sink." She goes to Whale, scooping different bottles from the pocket of her apron. "Which one? I bring them all. This one, yes?" She holds the prescription up for Whale to read. He nods and she empties two capsules into her palm. Whale tilts them into his mouth and takes the glass of water Kay passes over her shoulder. The water is cool in his mouth, painful in the throat, nauseating in his stomach. The capsules won't take effect for several minutes, but to know that pain will pass makes pain bearable.

He lies there, catching his breath after the exertion of swallowing. Maria has recovered from her panic and stands above him, stiff and censorious. With her round face, tight hair, and imperious little chins, she looks like Queen Victoria. The guest for afternoon tea peers around her in his underpants.

"Mr. Kay," Whale declares in feigned surprise. "You're not dressed."

"Oh! I was—we were—" Kay frantically crosses arms over

his chest and middle, blushing pinkly from his forehead down to his nipples. "I was going to swim!" he tells Maria.

Maria cuts her eyes at her employer.

"Yes, I suggested a swim," Whale declares. "I'm sorry I spoiled it for you, Mr. Kay. You should probably go home."

"Yes. Right. I'm going." Kay hurries outside to where he left his clothes.

And Whale feels better, as if the boy's presence had created this pain, although he understands that what lifted was merely his shame over Kay witnessing his helplessness.

Maria bends down to undo Whale's bow tie. She makes no attempt to be gentle.

"You must think I'm terrible, Maria."

"I do not think you anything anymore, Mr. Jimmy." Then she adds, "I think you are a crazy. Just back from the hospital and already you are chasing after boys."

"All we did was talk. We were having a little talking game. My attack had nothing to do with him. It might have happened if I were watching television."

"Hmmmph." She has lifted his shoulders to pull his jacket off. "How is your head? We should get you uphill before the pills knock you cold. Maybe your boy can help?"

Whale winces. "No. We should send him home. He's seen enough for one day."

"Don't be ridiculous. I cannot get you up the hill alone. You are not ashamed of your monkey business, but you are too proud to let this boy see you sick?"

"You're right, Maria. Always right," he says with a sigh. "Let me lie here a moment longer. Ask him to give you a hand." There is still pain, seams of ache beneath his scalp growing smudged and indistinct as the barbiturates take effect. In another minute the shame of having the boy see his helplessness will be smoothed away as well.

"Boy! Oh, boy!" he hears Maria call as she steps outside and goes to Kay. They speak softly out there. Whale cannot make out the words.

Portions of consciousness wink out as the pills take effect, his hard emotions first, then the gentler ones. Whale remembers feeling great pleasure at one point this afternoon. Over what? The Cave of Harmony. But more than his nostalgia for that, there was a feeling that he has whole worlds inside him, forgotten worlds that would die with him. He would die, wouldn't he? Death is the only alternative he can imagine to such pain and helplessness. The narcotic stillness stealing over him isn't peace. But he doesn't want death either. Not yet. Not yet. Only what does he need before this "yet" becomes acceptable? Fame and recognition? Late wisdom over the meaning of it all? The chance to see one more naked man? Only the last item is likely, but all seem poor trades for oblivion.

"Ups-a-daisy, Mr. Jimmy. We go now."

"I got him on this side. You okay, Mr. Whale?"

A boy and a woman stand on either side and lead him toward the door. The light ahead is shockingly bright. He closes his eyes and walks in slow motion through a red landscape without trees or grass, only mud that reduces his walk to a drunken stumble over a featherbed.

"When you're better, Mr. Whale, can we finish the interview?"

"Quite," Whale mumbles in answer to a half-heard question about an inner-view. What is an inner-view? Another new invention like tele-vision?

The long, dreamlike walk up the hill is interminable. He grows impatient with the diminutive fellows propping him on either side. He is afraid they won't reach their lines before nightfall. He longs for someone large and strong to do the job quickly, someone who can cradle him in his arms and take him home, an athlete of death who'd carry him as easily as his monster once carried Mae Clarke off into the night.

# 4

FOUR COLUMNS OF POWDERY BLUE LIGHT CLIMB THE NIGHT SKY over Hollywood Boulevard, swinging out and back, crossing and turning, a drunken set of ladders to heaven. The source is visible up ahead: electric cauldrons of arc light and a teeming lake of people outside Grauman's Chinese.

"Oh God," says David Lewis. "There's thousands of them."

"Out for a peek at immortality," says Whale.

"Guess I got time for a smoke," says Miss Crews, fishing in her handbag. "Looks like we have a bit of a wait."

Their limousine joins the queue of mammoth autos along the curb, Cadillacs and Bentleys jeweled with lights reflected around their polished hulls. Through the closed windows can be heard the murmur of spectators and portable generators, and the squawking of the radio personality who announces each arriving star.

A January evening in 1937, a Hollywood premiere. A searchlight beam clips the ornate overbite of pagoda roof, then sweeps across the banner over the forecourt: Tonight *Camille*.

It is David's night, not Whale's. Universal rarely spends money on gala openings, but this is Metro-Goldwyn-Mayer. As associate producer, David inherited and finished the picture when its real author, Irving Thalberg, suddenly died during production. The director, George Cukor, quit MGM to work with David O. Selznick and is out in Atlanta, shooting tests for a Civil War extravaganza. David is left to represent the makers tonight, and to escort Miss Crews, a former Broadway star of a certain age who's found a second career playing plump maiden aunts. She will be Aunt Pittypat in Selznick's new movie. Appearing in both *Camille* and the picture Whale is fighting his studio over, *The Road Back*, she knows the two men without being close to either. Having spent her life in the theater, she accepts their relationship as commonplace.

The car moves forward. The stationary herd of Americans glides past, a shadowy frieze of men and women in hats and sweaters, pressed against the barricades, gawking into each window. Whale amusedly gazes back at them. He sits straight and English but is giddy tonight with the gorgeous absurdity of it all, and the many cocktails they had back at the house.

"Look at them out there," he declares. "What do the sweet dears possibly hope to see?"

"Not us. We're the poor relations," Miss Crews quips. "Garbo's feet, perhaps?"

David broods between them, a handsome man with a boyish face and full head of dark hair. He twists a pair of white gloves in his hands. "She will show, won't she? She's not going to plead a headache at the last minute?"

"If she said she would, she will," Miss Crews assures him. "She's screwy, but she's no liar."

Tonight David is responsible for Garbo, who didn't want to appear but promised she would, on the condition that she could come alone. She said she did not need an escort, "like a prizoner."

Three cars up, a door opens and a man and woman climb into an electrical fire of camera flashes.

"Oh my. They've paired poor Robert Taylor with that awful Joan Crawford," Miss Crews declares.

"We are the poor relations, aren't we?" Whale echoes. "Invited to the Christmas dinner. And what a dinner. The wine is colored water, the goose is papier-mâché."

"Nobody forced you to come," David snaps.

"I'm not complaining. I wouldn't miss this for the world."

"Then will you give the catty remarks a rest?"

"Catty? Was I being catty, Miss Crews?"

"Uh-oh. A spat," she says. "Don't mind me, boys. Just go on like I'm not even here."

"Oh, David," Whale groans. "Don't carry on. I'm only bringing us to earth with the humorous realities."

But David is not mollified. "I'm in no mood to hear you go on and on in this vein. Anyone who didn't know you would think you were bitter."

*"Bitter?"* He almost says, "Of MGM?" but says instead, "Of what, for God's sake?"

"That's what I ask myself. Forget it. We can't talk now."

There is one more car ahead of them. David stuffs his fingers into a glove.

"Don't wear them," Whale scolds. "Clutch them. You look like a waiter if you wear them." He's striking back, but he doesn't want to be nasty to David, not tonight. "Look at me."

David faces him.

"Let me just—" Whale gently straightens David's tie, then brushes his starched shirtfront. "There. Now you look smashing."

The Bentley ahead of them pulls way. Their own car eases into the space beside the red carpet. The door is jerked opened. A red-cheeked usherette in trousers and candy-box hat beams at them like a painted doll.

Whale gets out, then David. They shake their coattails loose and help Miss Crews to her feet.

"Time to pretend I'm the village idiot," she mutters.

"And here comes everybody's favorite aunt," announces the woman at the microphone. "Miss Laura Hope Crews. A featured player in tonight's marvelous motion picture."

They walk arm in arm up the red carpet, Miss Crews rolling her head from side to side, sharing a brainless grin with the mob along the ropes. Whale wears the droll half smile of a visiting foreign dignitary. Only David has no role to hide in.

"With her tonight are Mr. David Lewis, a producer on this picture. And—?" The announcer pretends not to have the name in front of her. "It's the King of Horror himself, Mr. James Whale. Who's come out specially from Universal to see this fine motion picture. I'm only glad he didn't bring Frankenstein along."

Whale holds his head higher, miffed not to be identified as the director of *Show Boat.* But that time will come. If the new movie is released as he made it, the horror films will be forgotten and he'll be recognized once and for all as a gentleman artist, a director of prestige pictures.

A smart aleck in the crowd lets out a spooky, "Oooooh!"

They walk past the wolf pack of executives grouped behind the podium and through the open doors.

"Ahhh." Miss Crews spits out her smile and can breathe again.

Despite its gaudy red-and-gold chinoiserie, the lobby feels civilized after the madness outside. In the theater proper an orchestra plays selections from *La Traviata.* Men in impeccable evening clothes line up to buy bags of popcorn.

"Are we staying?" asks Miss Crews. "I am. I haven't seen the damn thing yet."

Whale saw it a month ago, with David, at a preview out in the dusty sticks of Riverdale. They both intend to stay, however, hoping David will be congratulated afterward.

"I'll join you shortly," David tells them. "I can't go in until she arrives. I promised I'd arrange her escape."

"I'll wait with you," Whale offers.

"That won't be necessary," David says brusquely.

He's still angry, which makes Whale angry. He decides to stay with David so that they might clear up this nonsense.

Miss Crews goes with her ticket to an usherette at the door. Whale follows David around the dribbling fountain in the middle of the lobby. They stop a few feet behind the small throng who loiter just inside the doors, at an angle where the illuminated length of red carpet is visible. David refuses to look at him.

"Would you rather I went home?" Whale says coldly.

David closes his eyes. "I wanted you here. But I have no sense of humor tonight. I cannot enjoy your mocking. I'm sorry I lost my temper out there. I had too much to drink."

Whale recognizes he's tipsy himself or he wouldn't be so impatient to continue this. "I am not bitter," he whispers. "Or envious or any of that. I'm happy for both you *and* MGM."

"Can we talk about this later?"

"You take this folderol much too seriously."

"How else am I to take it?"

"With a grain of salt."

David frowns. "I know you have your own studio troubles right now. But you can afford to be satirical, Jimmy. You got your piece of pie."

"My piece? What are you talking about? As our friend said outside, I'm just a poor relation here."

"You don't really believe that. You go on and on as if everybody else's grapes were sour. Which is very ugly when your mouth is full of grapes too."

Whale thinks about that. "No. They're not sour," he admits. "They're quite sweet, in fact. But it's difficult to believe that they're real. Or that they'll last. Which is why I mock them."

A bald, pink-faced executive rushes inside and wildly looks around. He spots David, puts on a smile, and walks over. He keeps the smile even as he says, "Where is that damn cow?"

"Frank, she's on her way."

"We promised this mob Garbo. If she doesn't show, we're going to have a riot on our hands."

"She'll be here, Frank. Don't worry."

"She better." The cold smile briefly takes in Whale. "All right. It's your fanny, not mine, sweetheart. You don't have Thalberg to protect it anymore. You screw this up, you'll wish you were back in the chorus." He hurries outside again.

"What a glamorous evening, ladies and gentlemen," sings the radio announcer. "Lionel Barrymore and his lovely sister Ethel, the royalty of American theater."

"The happy family of MGM," Whale says sympathetically.

David's face is pale, his eyes burning. "One of L. B. Mayer's lesser toads," he explains. "Still, it hurts that a nobody like that can call you a fairy at your own premiere. And worrisome."

Whale understands what he means. "They won't take away your grapes, David. This picture will do very well."

"I hope you're right. On both counts."

"When the lunacy gets too much for me," Whale offers, "I remind myself that one can always walk away. I've saved up my piece of pie. I could contentedly spend it on a life of leisure."

David smirks at him. "You don't believe that for a minute, Jimmy. You love to work. You'd be miserable doing nothing."

"I wouldn't know. I've never done nothing."

Outside, at the far end of the corridor of eager faces, a maroon Duesenberg pulls into view.

"Thank God," David moans.

The door opens. A slim figure unfolds itself from the depths. The crowd goes, "Ahhhh."

It's her, alone. There seems to be someone else in the back, but the usherette shuts the door on the shadow and the Duesenberg pulls away. Garbo stands perfectly still. Then, staring straight ahead, she starts up the red carpet, in a brisk, cool, floating gait, a walking hieroglyph in an unbuttoned full-length coat. Along the velvet ropes, arms reach out, autograph books and a hundred hands desperate for a touch. She keeps the self-absorbed calm of a woman alone with sad thoughts on a walk in the country.

Even Whale is impressed. A papier-mâché goose, perhaps, but one with far more spirit and panache than the others.

She struts out of view toward the podium. The crowd goes wild; she has stepped up on the dais and is visible to all.

"And here she is," declares the announcer. "The brightest star in MGM's firmament. Miss Greta Garbo."

A hush passes over the crowd—she must be bending over the microphone. Then the throaty, honeyed, piping voice says, "Is such a beautiful night. Thank you."

Applause and screams again. She comes through the doors into the lobby, followed at a distance by a handful of executives. Everyone stares after her, even the bald man who called her a cow, but nobody dares to approach. She coolly glances left and right as she crosses the room, as imperturbable as a cloud.

David goes straight to her. Whale automatically follows, needing a closer look. They catch up with her in the corner, outside a silk screen shielding the door marked Ladies.

"Miss Garbo? Thank you."

She sees David and turns.

"Ah, Mr. Lewis. All right. I came. Now can I go home?"

"You don't want to see the picture? We have a private box for you in the balcony."

She winces, as if he proposed a tour of a slaughterhouse.

Whale has seen her only on film, never in life. He expects her reality to disappoint, but, even without the mediation of a camera, her face has the unreal simplicity of a portrait by Ingres. Her only makeup is the mascara on her long, long lashes. She seems ready for bed, wearing a kind of pajama under her coat that on closer inspection proves to be an elegant gown.

Suddenly, the lashes and eyes are directed at him. "You are Mr. Whale," she says. "Mr. Lewis's friend." She smiles. "I like your work. I would luf to have been your Monster's Bride."

Whale is stunned, amused, skeptical, touched.

A forlorn look comes into her eyes. She laughs. "Maybe one day you could star me in *The Invisible Woman?*"

He laughs with her. "Wouldn't that be interesting?" They seem to understand each other perfectly.

"Very well, then. Let me go," she tells David. "There is a secret passage I can leave by? My car is around the block."

"There's a fire exit down here. Right this way, Miss Garbo. I'll meet you inside, Jimmy."

"Good night, Miss Garbo," Whale says proudly.

You are such a hypocrite, he tells himself as he watches them disappear down a dark hallway. You can be as gaga as any secretary daydreaming over a magazine. And yet, for a moment, the fact that Garbo knows his horror movies, and teased him about being in one, made Whale proud of his monsters. It is all a beautiful joke, and Greta Garbo appreciates the joke with him.

He rejoins Miss Crews in the theater. "Garbo came and went."

"I told you she would."

"We exchanged a few words. She was very cordial."

"She's mad as a loon, you know."

"Aren't we all?"

David joins them a few minutes later, his tension and temper gone. The house lights dim and the movie begins. After the first reel, time enough for the crowd outside to clear, several stars quietly get up to leave. Whale is happy to stay, wanting to see how Garbo might look to him now that he's met her.

The movie is what it was in Riverside, a romantic, creamily photographed, clunky thing, Robert Taylor a stiff, Lionel Barrymore a shameless ham. Miss Crews dithers and prattles so obnoxiously that Whale is embarrassed for the no-nonsense woman sitting beside him. But Garbo is magnificent. Natural, luminous, alive.

"Thalberg couldn't have done better," Whale whispers to David halfway through, squeezing his hand below the seats.

She dies beautifully in the end, gracefully, all pathos disarmed by the witty way she mocks her own suffering.

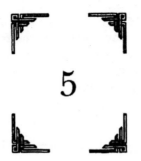

# 5

NIGHT. WIND. THE FIRST HARD SPITS OF ONCOMING RAIN. IT APproaches in the darkness, a steady roar like a waterfall down the highway. The only shelter in sight is the dark house at the top of the hill. He goes up the steep slope, slipping and stumbling in grass as black as hair, until he reaches a tall wooden door. He hammers at the door with his fist. The knocks are barely audible. He pounds harder, with the flat of his fist, then both fists, before he notices the brass door knocker. A curved shaft weighted with a pair of spheres. He swings the knocker against the door. The entire building booms like a drum. It continues booming after he lets go, banging like a clock striking the hour, rattling like a great tin drum.

Suddenly the door is open. In the bright light stands a woman in a one-piece bathing suit, a shapely blonde holding a glass in one hand and open bottle of Coke in the other. There are freckles on her face and cleavage, even in her smile. He slowly realizes that this Technicolor blonde is Doris Day.

The hammering continues, sheet metal banging and buckling under a fist, shaking Clayton Boone from his dream.

"Boone! You awake? Eight o'clock."

"Fuck off!" Boone hollers, desperate to dive back into sleep and get a cold drink from Doris Day.

"You told me to make sure you were up when I left, asshole." The voice belongs to a baseball-capped head visible through the louvered glass in the trailer's door, Dwight Joad, his neighbor.

"Right. Damn. Gotcha." They sat in Harry's Beachcomber drinking beer and talking shit late last night. When they stumbled back across the highway to the trailer park, Clay told Dwight to wake him this morning; his alarm clock was busted.

"You up?"

"I'm up. Thanks."

"*Hasta la vista,* Boone. I'm off to the mines." Dwight's shoes grind away on crushed shells and asphalt. Already there's a baby squalling out there against the low, overlapping roars of traffic and surf.

Clay's head is gummed with sleep, his bed damp with sweat. He kicks off his sheet and discovers he's bare-assed, with an ugly door knocker of a boner. He dislikes waking up naked, dislikes getting naked at all except when it has a purpose—washing or screwing—but he ran out of clean shorts two days ago and there's no point in getting dirty what you don't need. The pinstripes of bare mattress are covered with overlapping salt-line profiles of his body. He sits up and reaches for the crumpled pack of Luckies on the sink opposite his bed, hoping the nicotine will wake him up. He lights a bent cigarette and sits there smoking, a blond man like a half-skinned ox. His face and arms are covered with brown hide, but his chest is brick red, his legs and middle as white as lard. Off by one hip is the serrated smirk of an appendectomy scar. His prick still sticks out like a bridge going nowhere.

Doris fucking Day? What's she doing in his dreams? A woman like that would have you in a three-piece suit before you could get to first base. If you ever did score, she'd probably want to get on top. What had he and Joad been jawing about last night anyway? Sex and marriage and the meaning of life. Dwight has a wife and two kids, but Clay is free. Free to do what is another question. In foul moods like this morning's, he feels like a bum to be his age and have no wife or family, no house, no future. He is twenty-six years old.

He drops the cigarette in the sink, runs the water to put it out, then steps to the back of the trailer for a long piss and a quick shower. His trailer is a single tin room, toilet and shower stall in the rear, a dinette table up front with paperbacks and magazines piled on it, *A Farewell to Arms* and *Mad* magazine among them. Clay comes out of the shower and looks for his calendar, needing to see where he has to go today. Up above the Canyon, 788 Amalfi Drive. He can't remember which house that is, but he better shave anyway. A couple of his customers act like they thought mowing the grass required a coat and tie. When Clay started this line of work last year, he assumed he'd be his own man and wouldn't have to kiss ass anymore. But you still have to placate the bastards, play their little games.

A half hour later Clay steps out of the trailer, clean-shaven and dressed in dungarees, a T-shirt with a fresh pack of Luckies flipped into one sleeve, the little rectangular cap they called a piss-cutter in the marines pulled over his crew cut. Dwight's wife, Jackie, is already hanging up wash on a rotating clothes tree, even though the trailer park will remain in the shadow of the jagged sandstone cliffs until noon. When Clay first came here three years ago, this box canyon off Pacific Coast Highway was little more than a gypsy camp for beach bums. Now the place is full of families. A couple of neighbors hide the tires of their mobile homes behind trellises, ashamed of being mobile. There's even a white picket fence around one yard. The ocean is still across the highway, though, fading off into haze this morning, muscular swells shifting to the right and turning into breakers. In the parking lot of Harry's Beachcomber, the roadhouse opposite the trailer park, a surfer unloads an unwieldy wooden board. A waste of energy, thinks Clay, who's tried it and can't keep his balance, not on those old mahogany canoes or the new fiberglass-and-Styrofoam jobs either. But those guys do attract the girls.

He weight-lifts his secondhand mower onto the bed of the truck, wedges it in with chock blocks and gardening tools, then checks the jerrican to make sure he has enough gas for two lawns before he remembers he has only one today. The Pendergasts canceled last week, telling him they'd found an Oriental who did the job cheaper. So he's down to thirteen lawns a week, which gives Clay enough to live, but not enough to improve his life, or even keep it properly maintained. The ocean air is eating his truck. It gets at the fenders and gunwales through the chipped paint. He has to scrub white fur from his battery every week or the starter won't work. The battery's clean this morning and the engine turns over on the first twist of the ignition. Clay drives down the narrow lane between trailers, carports and wash lines, slowly so as not to run over a kid. The place is getting too crowded and it's time he think about moving on, but where? Oregon? Alaska? Not back to Joplin, Missouri, that's for sure.

The drive down the coast to Pacific Palisades takes twenty minutes. There's no traffic on a weekday and it's a pretty drive, if you enjoy that sort of thing. The radio is on and Clay catches the Patsy Cline song that Betty likes so much. He turns left on Sunset Boulevard, the engine racing in low gear to get up the steep hill. The air grows less salty, more earthy as he climbs Santa Monica Canyon. The boulevard twists and curves after it levels out. Clay swings down a side street into a neighborhood of old-fashioned bungalows and bright new split-levels. Not until he comes to 788 Amalfi and sees the semicircular driveway out front does he remember he has to park in the back. He drives around the corner and down the hill. The next street below has fewer houses, its downhill side full of thorny brush in vacant lots. He pulls into a dirt driveway between a gray-shingled hut and a bright blue swimming pool. When Clay sees the pool he remembers that this is the job where that English fairy propositioned him last week. Well, didn't proposition him exactly but wanted

Clay to swim in the raw. Great. Just what he needs this morning, some old vulture getting friendly while he tries to do his job. But there's nobody around. The umbrella in the patio table is shriveled shut. The house up on the hill still looks like it's fast asleep at ten o'clock.

Clay unloads the heavy mower, fills the tank with gas, and attaches the canvas bag that catches the clippings. A couple of yanks at the cord, and the roar of engine makes him invisible. Tilting the machine back on its oversized rear wheels, he pivots it around and begins with the flat area around the pool. The noise levels the grass and occasional poppy; the furious vibration in Clay's hands smooths out his mind. His thoughts drift in and out of daydream.

Clay's daydreams are usually about sex. When he first began doing lawns, he had swank erotic fantasies that seemed less like daydreams and more like real opportunities. After all, Hollywood is nearby and it wasn't impossible that he'd mow the grass of a beautiful actress, even a movie star. And it wasn't completely implausible that such a woman, alone all day and watching a former marine, former jock march up and down her lawn, might be moved to invite him inside for a beer or a Coke. She'd greet him in a silk kimono. One thing leads to another until there's a trail of clothes from the kitchen to a luxurious bedroom, and a famous face—or one so beautiful it should be famous—tosses deliriously on satin pillows while her yardman bodysurfs in high-price honey.

But there are no movie stars among Clay's clients, just a movie electrician, a car dealer, an aeronautical engineer, several dumpy wives with pesky kids, and this old English fairy whom Clay didn't know existed until last week. He'd been doing the lawn for a month, seeing nobody except the Mex maid who gave him his money and, when he asked for something to drink, tap water. She said something once about the Master—she really called him that—being in the hospital. But suddenly, last week, there'd been that tall, white-haired geezer strolling about, watching Clay. The guy had to be a fairy, only with Englishmen you can't be sure where English leaves off and fairy begins. It's not like Clay is afraid of fairies. He doesn't think he's ever met one. He knows homosexuals only by their reputation, the same way he knows Communists and flying saucers.

He gets to the slope, which is always a bitch. He goes back and forth on the diagonal, beginning in the bottom right corner and working his way uphill and to the left. He has to make one leg shorter than the other on each swatch, gravity coming at the mower from odd angles. His daydreaming turns peevish. His sex life is nothing but daydreams these days. At the bar last night, Dwight complained about being married and said he wished he was Clay—Jackie didn't like her husband spending too much time with their bachelor bum neighbor. If they only knew. Clay enjoyed Dwight's envy too much to set him straight about Scottie Deerfield, the USC coed he saw for three weeks before she got tired of slumming and stopped coming to the Beachcomber. Clay made a point of keeping clean sheets on his bed for her, but he never got to use them. The bitch was a cock-tease, stroking and even kissing Clay inside the bar but wiggling out of his embraces when he got her alone on the beach. And now that it was over, Betty wouldn't put out anymore. Even Betty, who worked at the Beachcomber and was divorced and thirty and used to jump into bed with Clay anytime he asked.

"I know why you're being so damn friendly," she told him last night while Dwight was in the toilet. "Forget it."

"Why? You seeing somebody else now?"

"You wouldn't know, would you? You couldn't give me the time of day while that snotty brat had you wrapped around her pinkie."

"What's eating you?"

"Me? Nothing. I should love being treated like the town pump again, after being invisible for the past month."

"You're not a pump, Betty. You're a pal."

"Hey, thanks. What a guy."

"We're just good pals who have the hots for each other," he reminded her. He didn't think a man and woman could be pals, but it's what Betty once said and he wanted her to think they were playing by her rules.

"Even the hots got feelings," she toughly declared. "You hurt mine real bad. Run after all the unattainable sweethearts you like, Boone, but don't think you can crawl into my bed after they give you the heave-ho. From here on out, you're just another tired old face on the other side of the bar."

Clay can't understand her. She should be grateful he didn't care that she was divorced and on the horsey side. What else did she want from him? He knew what he wanted from her. But even there you have to play a game. You have to kiss ass just to get a piece of it. The world was one stupid, kiss-ass game after another. Betty went on his list of the world's bullshit, along with college and football, women in general, and the whole fucking United States Marines.

You got to make up your own life, alone. Thoreau with a lawn mower, Clay tells himself as he approaches the top of the hill. He reads books, although not as many as he pretends. He wants to think of himself as Thoreau, but he's a bitter, often angry Thoreau. He wants to see all the failures of his life as escapes from bullshit, except he doesn't like what he's escaped into. You're either married with a nine-to-five job or you're nobody. You're either one of them or a bum, a white nigger no better than a criminal. You might as well be a criminal. There are days when, for no reason at all, Clay feels a wild, irrational anger, becoming so angry he wants to slit somebody's windpipe, the way they'd been taught at Pendleton. Only whose throat was worth cutting? It's just another daydream with which he amuses himself now and then, and not as much fun to think about as screwing a starlet.

As the lawn levels out behind the house, Clay feels like he's being watched. He steals a look as he wheels the machine around and sees nobody, not even the maid at the kitchen window. The catcher bag is full. Clay unhooks it and lugs it down to the gray hut. He empties a damp mound of clippings on the mulch pile there, then carries the empty bag back up the hill, checking out windows as he climbs. Is anybody even home? Steering the mower like a plow under the bay window, he looks in and sees a shadowy living room full of empty sofas and chairs, paintings on the walls, and a pair of china dogs on the mantel. He wonders if the old guy went back into the hospital. He hopes the maid is home at least. He hates it when he has to come back another day to get his money. But he continues to mow: the strip along the side, then the front yard where there's more driveway than lawn. The garage door, at a right angle to the long shallow front porch, is closed. Clay finishes the front and cuts the engine. The sudden silence is eerie. He trundles the dead machine down the sidewalk behind the garage's back door and stops to peek inside and see if their car's here. A new model Chrysler crowds the dark garage. You'd think an elderly Brit would drive a fogey car, a Packard or something, but no, it's a wide, chromey '56 Chrysler convertible.

Down by the truck, Clay hoists the mower up on its rear wheels to clean out the thick cud caked underneath. He begins with a stick, then finishes with the garden hose. The muscles in his back and legs ache and twitch. The mindless half of the job done, he now has to think about the more brainy chores of trimming and weeding, whether he gets paid today or not.

*The bells of hell go ting-a-ling-a-ling* . . .

A song comes out of nowhere. The chassis slips from Clay's hand; the mower slams upright with a bang. But when he looks, there's nobody there, just the long slope diagonally cut and combed, the house on top as blank as ever.

"Drop something, Mr. Boone?"

The gray hut is five feet away, a raised window above the spigot of the hose. The Englishman's inside.

"Uh, just cleaning my tools," Clay quickly answers. "Sorry to disturb you." The old coot must have come down while he was doing the front yard. Clay turns off the spigot and crouches by the mower to wipe down the engine housing.

The screen door around the corner squeaks open, clatters shut. A leather slipper and rubber-tipped cane appear. The white-haired geezer strolls into view, smiling.

" 'I am the Mower Damon, known / Through all the meadows I have mown.' " His lips disappear in a wrinkled, close-mouthed smile. "Andrew Marvell," he explains. "You don't, perchance, have a girlfriend named Juliana?"

"Uh, no." Clay gets up, but resists the impulse to stand at attention. He declares his independence by wiping his nose with the back of his hand.

"Perfectly all right. And your name isn't Damon, but Boone. Am I correct? Clayton Boone." He seems pleased to know Clay's name. "We met briefly last week."

"Yeah. I remember. Mister—?"

"Whale. Like the aquatic mammal. Not the lamentation."

The old guy seems more nutty than fruity today, senile, even drunk. He leans on his cane, looking like an old photo in his seersucker jacket. Crinkly striped fabric and wavy white hair are lit up from behind, his rabbit pink ears nearly transparent. The sun seems to shine straight through the man.

"I was just about to ask Maria to bring down some iced tea. I'd like it very much, Mr. Boone, if you'd join me."

"Thank you, but I should finish this."

"Oh, please. You look very hot, very tired. You'll make me feel like less of a villain for making you slave in the sun."

Clay plucks at his soggy T-shirt. "Thanks, but I stink to high heaven right now," he says, before he remembers last week's business about swimming in the pool.

The man does glance poolward but only lifts his chin and observes, "The honest sweat of one's brow. I assure you I won't be offended. Let me tell Maria to bring tea for two. Or would you prefer a beer?"

Clay wonders why he's resisting; he is thirsty and he needs

a break before he continues. What's he afraid of? "No, iced tea's fine. Sure. Why not? Let me wash off my hands, okay?"

"Smashing. I'll speak to Maria." He turns, hesitates, then briskly steps around the corner.

You're such a pushover, Clay grumbles to himself while he hoses the crumbs of grass off his arms. But it's always easier to dislike somebody in his head than when he's talking with them. It'd be ridiculous to turn down a cold drink just because he's afraid the guy's a fruit. Even if he is a fruit, Clay can take care of himself. The worst thing that could happen is he'll ask Clay to swim naked in his damn pool again. Clay's not sure why he can't let go of that idea, but it's the only solid threat he can find to explain his unease around the guy. He dries his hands and arms with his hat, then wads up the hat and stuffs it into his shirt to wipe out his armpits.

"Come in," Whale calls out when Clay stands at the door. "Refreshment is on its way."

Inside, a moment passes before Clay's eyes adjust to the light. The old man lounges on a daybed like a psychiatrist's couch, the newspapers beside him making clear he doesn't expect Clay to sit there. He gestures at a wooden armchair across from him. Clay sits in it and sees a spatter of red on the wooden floor. He nudges the spot with the toe of his boot.

"Yes, my shop, my studio," the man explains. "Hardly somewhere in which a sweaty workman should feel out of place."

There are other spatters on the floorboards, white, yellow, and black. Clay sees unframed canvases on the wall and stacked in the corners, then an elaborate easel with oversized wing bolts and a long screw. A couple of the pictures look familiar, even famous. Clay suddenly wonders if the old coot is somebody important.

The coot is watching with blank blue eyes. He sits forward with his legs crossed at the knees, an elbow on the top knee, one finger tapping his pouting lower lip.

"These are your paintings?" Clay asks.

"What? Oh, yes." He gently smiles. "They are now anyway."

"Excuse me, but—are you famous?"

The smile extends and thins. "What a question, Mr. Boone. A less humble man might take offense. If you have to ask, then the answer must be no."

Clay makes a face and shrugs. "I don't know squat about art. I'm just a hick who cuts lawns." He likes to play dumb; it makes life simpler. "But some of these look familiar. I was just wondering if I should know who you are."

"They were familiar when I painted them. That one's copied from a Dutch still life done almost three hundred years ago. And that one's a Rembrandt. Surely you've heard of Rembrandt?"

"Yeah. I know Rembrandt," Clay says irritably. "They're just copies then. Gotcha." He's embarrassed not to have known that, and disappointed the old guy's nobody. He wishes the iced tea would come so he could drink it and get out of here.

"But before I retired, you might say I had a brief time in the sun. Fame, as it were. I used to make talking pictures. Before I made copies of quiet, already famous ones."

It takes Clay a moment to realize he means movies. "You were an actor?"

"Oh, no. Nothing that grand. Only a director."

"Yeah? What were some of your movies?" Clay knows how important directors are, although this guy looks like he hasn't worked since the Keystone Kops.

"This and that. The only ones you maybe have heard of are the Frankenstein pictures."

"Really?" Clay sits up, surprised, skeptical, and impressed all at once. "*Frankenstein* and *Bride of* and *Son of* and the rest? Jeez, everybody knows Frankenstein."

The old man frowns. "Yes, well. I made only the first two. The others were done by hacks." He pauses for a wistful sigh. "A long time ago. Before you were even born, I wager."

"Still," Clay insists. "You must be rich. Making a couple of famous movies like those."

"Comfortable. Merely comfortable."

Clay can't help looking at the old man more closely. Something about him is changed. His smile looks less senile, more proud, a secret pride. He's no longer a frail old fruit but has weight now, grandeur and importance. The man who made *Frankenstein*. And Clay Boone cuts his grass.

"Whatever happened to what's-his-name?" Clay asks. "The guy who played Frankenstein?"

"Colin Clive? Colin died many years ago."

"No, another name. He did lots of other horror movies."

"Ah, you mean the man who played the Monster. Karloff. People are always confusing the Monster with its maker. Frank- enstein is the doctor, the Monster is simply the Monster."

"You would know," Clay says with a laugh. He wants the man to see he's impressed without making a big deal of it. He tries to remember the movies themselves, but all he can picture is the Monster looking very stern and powerful, and himself as a little kid scared shitless in a third-run movie theater in Joplin, his sister clutching his arm when he wasn't clutching hers. The mov- ies were kid stuff and kind of sweet.

"Ah. Here's Maria with our tea," Mr. Whale announces. "Can you get the door, Mr. Boone?"

Clay jumps up to open the screen door. The Mex maid in her black dress and white apron steps briskly past, refusing to look at him. She sets the tray on a table very hard, ringing the glasses and silverware.

"How are you feeling, Mr. Jimmy?" she demands. "How is your mind today?"

"My mind's lovely. And yours?"

She flares her nostrils at him. "You remember what the doc- tor tells us."

"Yes, yes, yes," the old man chants, wearily closing his eyes. "I merely invited Mr. Boone to take a glass of tea. We'll have a brief chat and he'll finish the yard."

Clay watches the senora, who looks almost as old as her boss, wondering why he lets his maid nag him. She treats him as haughtily as she treats Clay whenever he has to deal with her.

"I am not forgetting your last brief chat."

"Just go," the old man tells her, shooing her with the back of his hand. "We will do the honors without you."

She stares up at Clay. "He looks plenty big. You won't need my help if anything goes flooey."

"Nothing will go flooey. I feel tip-top today."

"Suit yourself. I do not care." She shakes her head and marches out the door.

Clay returns to his chair and timidly sits down again.

"She's a love," says Whale. "Been with me now fifteen years. And very possessive. When they stay in your employ that long, servants begin to think they're married to you." He smiles at Clay, suggesting he doesn't think of Clay as a servant. "Please, Mr. Boone. Help yourself. There's sugar."

Clay takes a glass and spoons sugar into it. Poor guy. The man who once terrified little kids at the movies is now run ragged by his own maid. "What did she mean by something going flooey?"

"Nothing at all. I returned from hospital a couple of weeks ago. Maria, bless her soul, still thinks I need more rest and solitude. The day will come when one can do nothing but rest, I fear."

Is he that old? "What were you in the hospital with?"

Whale shrugs. "A touch of stroke."

Clay nods knowingly, although all he knows about strokes is they affect the brain, like sunstrokes. He can get a little dizzy himself when he works in the heat too long.

The tea is cold and sweet, and Clay chugs half of it at a single tilt. When he lowers the glass, he finds the old man watching him again. His chin is raised, his eyelids slightly lowered.

Clay brushes a corner of his mouth with his thumb.

The old man smiles. "You must excuse me for staring, Mr. Boone. But you have the most marvelous head."

"Huh?" Clay isn't sure he heard right.

"To an artistic eye, you understand. Have you ever modeled?"

"You mean, like posed for pictures?"

"Sat for an artist. Been sketched."

Clay laughs, a deliberate snort that he hopes will make him feel like laughing. But all he feels is ticklish, and oddly shy. "What's to sketch?"

"You have the most—architectural skull. Your haircut. That's a flattop? And your nose. Expressive. Very expressive."

His head flinches, although the man only talks as if he's stroking it; the clasped hands are perched safely on his knee. "Broke is more like it," says Clay.

"But expressively broken. How did you break it?"

"Didn't break it, really. Squashed it a little. Football in college."

"You went to university?" He sounds dubious.

"Just a year. I dropped out to join the Marines."

"Of course. Yes. *You* were a Marine." His gaze deepens, grows more admiring. He lightly laughs. "I apologize for going on like this. It's the Sunday painter in me. I didn't mean to make you uncomfortable."

"Not uncomfortable. Just surprised. Nobody's ever wanted to paint or draw me before."

"Now that surprises *me*. But I understand your refusal. It's a great deal to ask of anyone who's unaccustomed to modeling."

Still puzzled over what the man wants, Clay is alarmed that Mr. Whale thinks he's said no. "This is for real? You want to draw me. Is that what you're saying?"

A feathery white eyebrow rises an inch. The rest of his face remains bland and apologetic. "That wouldn't possibly interest you, would it?" he timidly asks. "Models do get remunerated. I'd pay you for the privilege of drawing your head."

"How much?"

"What do we give you to mow the grass?"

"Five bucks. Plus five for extras. The hedges and pool."

Whale calculates, gazing steadily at Clay. "What if I paid you five an hour for modeling? Two hours each session. It can be tiring to hold a pose. As tiring as pushing around your red machine."

"You mean it'd be more than once?"

"That depends. On how you like it. And how much variety and challenge I find in your physiognomy. Your face, you know."

Part of Clay has been tempted all along. Now he can tell himself he's doing it for the money. Ten bucks for sitting on his can. And yet, he still feels uneasy, afraid of something, either in himself or Whale, he's not sure which. He glances again at the pictures on the wall and sees only faces and flowers. But he has to ask. "And it's just my head you want. Right? Nothing else."

Whale smiles. "What're you suggesting, Mr. Boone? You'll charge extra if I include a hand or bit of broad shoulder?"

Clay takes on a tough look to let the man know he's not kidding. "You don't want to draw pictures of me in my birthday suit, right?"

For a split second, the old man is perfectly still, mouth straight, eyes unblinking. "Not at all," he says. "I have no interest in your body, Mr. Boone. Only your head."

Clay can find no other reason to object. If he says no now, it'll be like confessing he's timid, shy. "All right, then. Sure. I'm game."

The blue eyes blink in surprise. The smile returns. "Smashing. I was hoping you'd prove amenable."

"No skin off my nose. And I could use the dough." Clay immediately needs to make his decision less important, the idea of letting a man draw pictures of him less peculiar. And not just any man but the man who made *Frankenstein.*

While they discuss scheduling, what time and which day, it does feel less peculiar, more like just another job. Whale proves surprisingly flexible when Clay explains that mornings aren't good for him; that's when he likes to cut grass. They settle on late in the afternoon the day after tomorrow, Wednesday.

"I have a doctor's appointment in the morning. Nothing serious. Minor consultation," Whale grumbles. "But I'll be quite rested by the time you arrive. Raring to go." A shadow suddenly passes over his eyes. He quickly glances at Clay, as if with second thoughts, before he blinks a few times and the shadow goes away.

"I should be letting you get back to your other job. Or Maria will accuse me of spoiling you."

Clay stands up when Whale stands.

"Four o'clock sharp Wednesday," Whale announces, and holds out his hand.

Clay takes it: long and narrow, the loose skin around the bundle of bones clammy, as if from the iced tea. The bones grasp back, startlingly strong, like the grip of a bird claw.

"We'll have a most interesting time, Mr. Boone."

The hand lets go and Clay snorts, "Maybe you will. I just got to sit." He drops his own hand to his side, careful not to shake the weirdness from the joints in front of Mr. Whale.

Out in the bright sun again, Clay tries to laugh off the weirdness of the whole business. What the hell is he getting himself into? Why should he feel so pleased to be doing this? Because he is pleased, nuttily tickled. He goes to his truck to fetch the hedge clippers and can't help stopping by the side-view mirror to look at himself. Was his head really so interesting? He sometimes likes his looks, and secretly loves it when women call him craggily handsome. But it feels funny coming from a man, even one who's an artist. Clay no longer suspects the guy might be a fruit. He can think such a thing only about strangers, men he does not want to know any better. This man made *Frankenstein.* And when you get to be his age, you can't help seeming a little weird and creepy.

Clay is sorry he doesn't know where his sister lives this year so he could write and tell her he's working for the man who scared them silly when they were kids. Back before alcohol and sex, getting scared at the movies had been the keenest physical pleasure, the most thrilling confusion the human body could experience.

# 6

Two skulls. One faces forward. The other is in profile, turned toward the first as if gazing at a spouse or lover. The pair of X rays are slapped wet on the doctor's light board. Pearl gray shadow surrounds the white bone like a memory of flesh.

"Here," says Dr. Payne, pointing to a smudge in the side-view X ray. "This is the area of infarction. By which we mean the portion of brain affected by the stroke. It read more clearly in the fluoroscope, but it's faintly visible here."

The venetian blinds of the examining room are closed. James Whale sits in a low chair in the soft light that shines through two grinning skulls. He watches calmly, flanneled legs crossed at the knees, a cuff-linked wrist balanced on his thigh. Fully dressed again after spending most of the morning in a hospital gown, he still has the disquieting sensation his backside's exposed. He pretends to be unafraid, unmoved to see himself bared on the screen.

"Brain tissue can't replace itself," the doctor continues.

"We still don't know exactly what zone does what job, but it's a surprisingly plastic organ. Other zones often take over tasks when one is shut down. But it alters the balance of power."

Whale came to the hospital today full of brave disdain, treating the visit as a noxious chore, a dental appointment that must be patiently suffered. He expected nothing; he will get nothing. He used his hatred of the place to lift himself above fear. They undressed and explored him, flashed lights into his eyes, tested reflexes and injected him with a radioactive isotope. He sat very still with his head behind a fluoroscope screen while Payne and another doctor murmured over things Whale couldn't see—he imagined light trails blossoming on a radar screen like slow-motion fireworks. They took two X rays and returned Whale to the waiting room again. Now he has been called into Payne's office to be told what they found.

He looks and listens, but mostly he looks. There is still the fascination of seeing himself as he's never appeared in any mirror. His teeth are startlingly long. Overlapping washes of light—the dispersed isotope—fill the lopsided cathedral domes. The brief tail of vertebrae seems as delicate and crunchy as sardine spine. But even as mind looks at itself with worldly amusement, the brute fact of the image sinks in. More than a trite symbol for death, that's his own skull up there, his own death. It has no hair, no eyes, no face. There's a flutter of nausea in Whale's throat, as if over a smell of bad meat, but the only odor in the room is the antiseptic sting of alcohol.

"You're a lucky man, Mr. Whale. Whatever damage was done by your stroke, it left your motor abilities relatively unimpaired."

They keep telling him that, over and over. "Yes, yes," Whale mutters. He nods at the X rays. "But from the neck up? What's my story there?"

"That's what I'm trying to explain."

"I don't give a tinker's cuss for the explanation," Whale snaps. "What I want to know is when am I going to come out of this fog? I can't concentrate. I can't close my eyes without thinking a hundred things at once. I could live with the occasional killing headache if I could be myself the rest of the time. But I'm not myself and it's become *very* boring."

Payne says nothing. He turns off the light board and goes to the venetian blinds. The room is instantly full of sun. The X rays on the board become meaningless squares of black celluloid. And here is Payne beside the examining table that's covered with fresh butcher paper, not the omniscient elder his deep voice suggests but a bland young neurologist with horn-rimmed glasses. Without the headbands and silver disks that once made doctors look like high priests, a white coat gives Payne no more authority than a soda jerk. His name is much too obvious for puns or poetry. He appears embarrassed to find a living man in the chair in front of him.

"Yes?" says Whale, more politely. "What can I expect?"

Payne leans against the table for a more casual stance. But he resumes speaking science, the only language he knows.

"There is much we don't understand about the brain. As I said, your balance of power has changed. The central nervous system is important not only for what it takes in but for what it blocks out. It selects items from a constant storm of sensations, things inside as well as outside the brain. Whatever was killed in your stroke appears to have short-circuited this inhibitory mechanism. Your olfactory phantoms are one symptom, but other parts of the brain are also firing at random."

"You mean there's an electrical storm in my head?"

"Yes. That's as good a way as any to describe it."

His dark and stormy nights? His dreams were nothing more than physiological disturbances.

"I've seen far worse cases, Mr. Whale. Elderly patients who are utterly non compos mentis after their strokes. One old woman whose memory is so incontinent she can't tell past from present."

"Incontinent." Whale pinches his mouth in disgust. "Yes, I'm cacking myself with my past."

"Cacking? Oh, I get it." Payne smiles. "An English expression. Yes, we need to keep our sense of humor. A stiff upper lip. And better your memory than your bowels. You might even learn to enjoy these walks down memory lane."

Whale winces. He has spent his life outrunning his past. He can't bear the thought of having it flood over him. "But the rest of it? My constant fog, my inability to concentrate? That's nothing more than bad electricity?"

"In a manner of speaking."

"There's no way you can get in there and make things right?"

"Surgery? No. We don't know how. We're not even sure what to look for. We risk doing so much damage that we avoid neurosurgery except when it's a life-and-death situation. And I know you must hate hearing me say this again, but you're comparatively well off, Mr. Whale."

"But my attack last week? It was like I was hit with a pickax. Surely that's not well off."

"The pain I don't understand at all. The brain is mostly insensate, despite what headaches suggest. Your first stroke was so painless you noticed only the effects. I considered the possibility of a minor aneurysm in the cortex, but we saw no trace of that in the fluoroscope."

"It's not the beginnings of another stroke?"

"No. Definitely not. What I suspect, and Dr. Ransom concurs, is that these are ghost pains, hallucinatory pains, much like your hallucinations of smell."

Whale glares at him. "No! If you'd felt this pain yourself, you wouldn't call it a hallucination."

"I'm not denying you were in pain. But we couldn't find a physiological cause. Which leads me to believe it's another bit of short circuitry, more bad electricity, as you call it."

How could pain not be real? Whale is stunned by the idea, and fascinated. Pain that only seems like pain. As if pain were just an idea, and like all ideas could be either believed or disbelieved. A ridiculous sophistry. What difference does it make when, real or illusory, it's identical in its hurt? Whale almost smiles, amazed by his own unreality.

"I know that doesn't make you feel better, or the pain more bearable, but it does mean it's not a symptom of a new cerebral catastrophe. The mind is a strange place."

"Is there anything that might set off an attack? A change in blood pressure or—something I should avoid?"

"I don't know, Mr. Whale. My guess is that it simply comes and goes, random discharges, like migraines."

"So what can I do?"

"Take the Luminal. The phenobarbital I prescribed. Use it whenever you feel an attack coming on. It should also be used to help you sleep."

"There's nothing else I can do?"

"You should take things slowly. You need to take it easy."

"But you seem to be saying that this isn't just a case of resting until I'm better. This will last to the end of my life."

And Payne, who has hardly looked at Whale during their conversation, opens his eyes a little, producing a confused look of sympathy that's followed by an angry tensing of his mouth.

"Yes. I suppose that is what I'm saying."

Then I should just go ahead and kill myself?

It's the next obvious question, but Whale can't say it aloud. The words are too melodramatic, too desperate. They would sound like a plea for pity, and Whale does not want pity. No other question comes to him, however. The unspoken sentence crowds his mouth.

"Here," Payne offers when the silence has lasted too long. "Let me walk you back to the waiting room."

"That won't be necessary. I know my way out." Whale stands, more casually than he thought possible. "Thank you for being so forthright, Doctor. About my chances as well as your profession's ignorance."

"There are people worse off," Payne repeats yet again. "And one never knows what might happen down the road. The brain is its own place. A remarkably plastic organ."

Whale wants to end with a dry quip, the expected display of stiff upper lip. Nothing comes to him except, "Good day, Payne."

He goes out the door and his first feeling in the bright white corridor is relief. He is finished and can go home. The hospital's artificial chill and light, its vodka smell, depress him. It's not like he's been told anything new. Hadn't he expected this all along? It's not the bad news that throws him but the absence of any kind of hope, not even the whistling-in-the-dark hope of doctors. Payne has paid him a compliment in refusing to paint a make-believe door on the wall of his prison cell. The skull he saw on the light board is his prison, a bone box full of confusion and nightmare. Walking past nurses in starched caps and patients in stained bathrobes, Whale sees himself as a healthy-looking gen-tleman in Savile Row clothing, who secretly carries a prison on his shoulders.

The waiting room for outpatients is full of old men and women today—there *are* people worse off. They sit on green Nau-gahyde sofas, stoop-shouldered and collapsing into themselves, some accompanied by adult children, others with private nurses. Whale has only Maria waiting for him. She is in her Sunday best—white gloves and a dress layered with flounces—as if they'd come to church together. The others sit apart from her, unable to place a Mexican woman who isn't dressed like a maid.

"All done, Mr. Jimmy?"

"Quite." He goes to the hat rack and gets his Panama—yes, a skull needs a hat—then waits for Maria to gather her things and follow.

"He give you a new prescription?" Maria asks as he holds the front door open for her.

"No."

"He tell you how much longer before you feel better?"

"I remain a medical mystery."

"Then why did he need to see you?"

"I have no idea."

"Doctors," she spits. "They are all butchers or thieves."

"Rather."

The noon sun is ferociously bright and he takes his gold-framed sunglasses from his coat pocket. The interior of the Chrysler is a sticky vinyl oven. He sits up front beside Maria, who is so short she can barely see over the futuristic panel of gauges. They have shifted the seat forward so her feet can reach the pedals; Whale sits with his knees pressed against the molded dashboard. He purchased the car last year for the long jaunts he loved to take alone, racing up the coast or across the desert with the top down and the wind whistling around him. Never again. Now he has to be chauffeured everywhere by his own dour little puritan. Looking at the hand on his knees, he seems to see through his skin to a jointed fan of bones. How does one live when all doors to the future are shut?

Maria aggressively hums to herself as her white gloves wrestle hand over hand with the steering wheel. She hates to drive and keeps her spirits up with music. Usually she hums old Spanish songs Whale doesn't know, but today's tune sounds familiar. It takes two bars before he recognizes "Land of Hope and Glory."

"Where did you pick that up?"

"Pick what up, Mr. Jimmy?"

" 'Land of Hope and Glory.' "

"I know no hope and glory."

"You must. You're humming it." And he angrily hums it back at her.

"Ah. A theme song from TV. *Queen for a Day*. They play it at the end of each show, when they crown the contestant. Dooo do-do do doo do."

"Well, don't. It annoys me."

"Yes, sir, Mr. Jimmy." She shrugs but hisses one more bar to herself, trying to find what in the tune might disturb him.

If he can't control his brain, he can at least control his housekeeper. Land of Hope and Glory? Land of smoke and drizzle. England means nothing to him now. He has escaped and forgotten England. This is his home, this open city of automobiles and palm trees and khaki-colored hills.

But as they slowly drive home, Maria keeping well below the speed limit, Whale sees nothing he recognizes. He doesn't know these derelict storefronts and vacant lots. Then they come around a corner and he sees something he remembers, a newsstand stretched along a side street off Hollywood Boulevard, books and magazines exposed to the open air.

"What are we doing over here?" he barks. "We're in Hollywood. You've gone the wrong way!"

"I know, Mr. Jimmy. I take a wrong turn where they are building the freeway. We're going the right direction now."

But even here Whale sees little he recognizes. Has his mind deteriorated so much he's forgotten the city where he lived and worked for twenty-some years? No, it's not his mind but the city that's died. It's terribly changed. Where are the orange groves that used to be visible behind the office buildings? Where are the crowds of people who once trooped along the broad sidewalks in fedoras and cloche hats? Where are the streetcars? Tramlines still hang overhead, webs of bedsprings pulled apart and stretched across a smoggy sky, while down below only red-and-yellow buses belch exhaust. The preposterously blue sky of the thirties is gone. And in the midst of this sunlit squalor stands Grauman's Chinese, a winged island of the past, its wings sadly exposed and in need of paint, its marquee full of *The Ten Commandments.*

This is where he will die? And he will die, won't he? Death is the only door that remains unlocked, the only future he can count on. But when? Next month? Next year? To think that his blighted state of mind could last for years, disintegrating into more fog and helplessness, is sickening.

Then I should just go ahead and kill myself?

He is pleased he didn't say that to Payne. It has such a cheap sound. But why turn it into words? Action is more eloquent. A self-made man deserves a self-made death. Whale has considered it before, but always from afar. Even now, with the X rays of a bone box still clearly remembered by that box, he considers suicide from a great distance off, separated from it by despondency.

The black mood that enables him to think about death is so deep it makes all action impossible, even that one. What is he afraid of? What does he hope to gain by hanging on a little longer? Is this mood real or is it, too, nothing more than bad electricity?

"Will your guest be joining you for dinner?" Maria asks.

"My guest? What guest?"

"The yardman. He is coming this afternoon?"

"To do the yard?"

"No. You are wanting to paint him. Or something."

The note of disapproval in her last phrase finally brings the man to mind. "Oh. Him. The Marine. What's his name?"

"Boone."

"Of course." It was only two days ago when Whale played his little game with the fellow, flattering him into agreeing to sit for a picture. Why? He can't remember. All he remembers is a pleasant bubble of anticipation, both last night and this morning, as if he had something to look forward to after the visit to the hospital. His hours there sever him from everything that preceded it.

"When he arrives, I will tell him you are tired or that you are ill," Maria offers.

"No. If I invited him, I should see him."

"He is only the yardman."

"I want to see him. I'd like to sketch him." She doesn't know he can no longer draw a straight line, much less render a man's face. But the truth is Whale can't remember why he wants to see the Marine, what he expects from him. He conjures up an image of the fellow: broad shoulders and flattened nose, the enormous hands that would form fists like mallets. That blue tattoo like a price stamped on a melon.

"Please, Mr. Jimmy. You have a full day in the hospital. And you remember what happens last time?"

"Bloody hell, Maria, I know what I want. Don't treat me like an infant."

She is silent for a moment. "Whatever you say, Mr. Jimmy. Yes, sir, Mr. Jimmy," her respect turning sarcastic.

Now he wants to see the Marine merely because Maria opposes it. But he seems to want something else from Boone. What? Thirty years ago the answer would be simple enough: he wanted him in bed. Before his stroke, the answer would've been equally simple: he wanted to see him naked. And that desire must be tucked somewhere in his attraction to the fellow, the gentle violence of skinning a man of his clothes. The Marine is more of a challenge than the baby poof whose disrobing was much too easy, but the challenge is part of his appeal.

Whale sees Boone more clearly in his mind's fractured eye: the fists like mallets, the dumb animal squint of his face. He seems irrational, dangerous, your classic American killer. Yes, Boone frightens him, but it's exciting to be frightened by another human, sharper and more real than the debilitating fear of losing one's mind to incontinent memory and hallucinatory pains. He needs to play with fire. He wants to feast with a panther, if only to take him out of himself for a few hours. And if he gets eaten, well, it's more exciting to be eaten alive than to be slowly consumed by your own bad electricity.

"What?" Maria suddenly asks.

"What do you mean, what?"

"You laughed. What did you laugh at?"

Had he laughed? "I told myself a silly joke. Not worth repeating."

"Never mind. I do not get your jokes anyway."

No, it isn't worth repeating, not even to himself. It's an absurd and ridiculous notion, about as real as Santa Claus. A Marine might lose his temper and take a swing at him. Where's the pleasure in that? Why should it feel so appealing, even sexy?

He's tired. His consciousness is as slippery as ice. The faintest breath can blow his mind this way or that, without logic or order. He tries to reconstruct the sequence of thoughts that brought him to the hope his marine would be violent, but can't.

The traffic has swung up the hill to Sunset Boulevard. There are fewer real buildings, only service stations and used car lots and billboards full of smiling faces two and three stories tall.

Whale looks out the window, desperately needing to see something on which he can lock his mind and stop its slide into absurdities.

And he sees a spaceship. A great disk like a slow spinning top reclines against the sky, as big as a house and orbited by tubes that must be neon lights at night. The monstrosity stands over a ring of parked cars where a bare-legged girl on roller skates waltzes out with a tray of paper bags. Whale solemnly watches the spaceship and girl drift past.

This is where he will die?

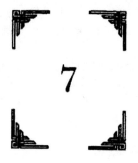

# 7

"Where's the city proper, James?"

"Everywhere and nowhere, my dear. There is no city proper. Only the city improper."

The windows are down, the soft air blows through the car. They happily raise their voices over the roar of the motor.

"It looks like Egypt," says Elsa. "Without Egyptians or pyramids. Don't you think, Charles?"

"Wouldn't know," her husband grumbles from the backseat. "Never been to Egypt."

"But one can imagine. All these palm trees."

Over the low buildings with flat roofs, royal palms parade across a crystalline blue sky. The street below is full of boxy new autos like enameled biscuit tins, an occasional Model-T, and a stately, high-windowed streetcar.

"Give them time," says Whale, "and there'll be pyramids."

Early one evening in 1932, James Whale takes the Laughtons out to dinner. It's their first night in Hollywood. They arrived

that day on the train called the Twentieth Century. Whale picked
them up at their hotel in his new car, a buff-colored Buick sedan.
He's overjoyed to see them again. They are pale and he is
tanned, and *Frankenstein* has been a smash since it opened in
December.

Elsa Lanchester constantly looks left and right, her enormous eyes delighted by everything she sees. She wears a beret on
her frizzy red hair.

Whale's own red hair is neatly pomaded and graying at the
sides or, rather, pinking as white comes into it. His face is smooth
and brown, his body trim in an elegant charcoal gray suit.

"The buildings look like marzipan."

They're on Hollywood Boulevard now, driving past the elaborate pastel facades of office buildings and movie palaces.

"The adobe effect, my dear. Splashed with stage paint."

"Oh look, Charles!"

They pass a hot-dog stand shaped like an enormous green
frog.

Charles Laughton sits in the backseat, an enormous white
infant suspiciously eyeing the city.

"We're dining in a restaurant that looks like a big hat?" Elsa
asks.

"No, that's for tourists. The Brown Derby we're going to is
for picture people. Its oddities are all interior."

Whale hasn't seen them in three years, not since his first
trip to America. He was always closer to Elsa, although he once
had a bit part as Laughton's bullied son in a play. Laughton is
ten years younger than Whale, but he's such an odd, intense,
inward fellow that one can't help but feel intimidated by his si-
lences. Only onstage does he fully express anything.

In the rearview mirror, Whale catches him surreptitiously
stroking the soft leather of the new car.

"You're going to love it here, Charles!" Whale cries over his
shoulder. "The weather. The vegetation. The salaries. Nobody
deserves such salaries. But who'd be so foolish as to turn them
down? I pour the gold through my hair."

Elsa laughs, enjoying his mock vulgarity. Laughton shifts uncomfortably.

"I'm only here for a couple of pictures," he grumbles. "And then it's back to London and the theater. Where I belong."

"That's what I said when I first came out. But once you get a taste of it, there's no returning to bad climate and tepid English pleasures."

"What about me?" Elsa asks plaintively. "Do you think there'll be work for me?"

"Oh, someone is sure to find a role for a woman of your remarkable gifts."

Ever since he heard they were coming, Whale has been thinking through the uncast parts of his current project, *The Old Dark House*, wanting to share his success with old friends. He's already cast Thesiger in the picture. Much as he loves Elsa, however, her comic talent and quirky looks would be all wrong for the tart who's one of the stranded travelers. Laughton, on the other hand, might be good for the Yorkshire businessman. It'd be fun to order his former "father" about, and in a picture so bizarre that this perversely original actor will seem relatively normal. Whale intends to wait until after dinner before he makes his proposal.

"But Paramount is good?" Elsa asks, where Laughton has his two-picture contract.

"Oh, Paramount is . . . paramount." Whale laughs. "Don't you just love the names? Paramount. Universal. Metro-Goldwyn-Mayer. Which sounds like an expensive lady horse. I've become friends with someone over there. Irving Thalberg's assistant. They're the crème de la crème, but the rest of us don't do too badly." He would like to have brought David tonight but was afraid that he couldn't be his new American self with people who knew only the old English one.

They reach Vine and Whale turns. He comes to the Brown Derby and turns again. The silhouette of a hat stands on the peaked roof. Whale loves to drive but hasn't quite mastered the art of parking. The Buick rises up on a curb and rests there, listing to port. He hops out and comes around to open the door for Elsa. She daintily steps down from the running board. Charles follows.

Whale is surprised at how dowdy they look, even Elsa, who always seemed so vivid in London. She takes her husband's arm, frightened by the world they're about to enter.

"Just be yourselves," Whale tells them. "Although you mustn't laugh too much. When I first arrived, I was laughing constantly, which makes them nervous."

They enter a dark front room with a bar, and Whale gives his name to the maître d'.

"Of course, Mr. Whale. Your table is ready."

"They know you, James?" Elsa whispers as they follow the man toward the bright dining room.

"Perhaps. But one can never tell who's important and who isn't here, so it pays to pretend a certain familiarity." Whale is now a favorite son at the studio, but it was Karloff who got the publicity and fame.

The dining room is white and noisy. They're seated at a banquette in the back. Several faces cursorily glance their way.

"The other animals are curious," says Whale. "I wonder if any will come over and sniff us."

"But there's nothing to sniff," says Elsa. "Charles hasn't made a picture yet."

"Which makes him more mysterious. Everyone's wondering who this brilliant young Englishman is that Paramount brought out."

Laughton shyly hides behind the large cardboard menu. Elsa brazenly continues to take everything in with her wide eyes and big-toothed Kewpie doll smile. "Anyone famous here?"

"I think I saw Jean Harlow in the corner. And that's John Barrymore's raucous drunken laugh we hear in the background. Other than that, nothing but a couple of lowly directors."

Whale orders for everyone, so that he might introduce them to the foods of the natives. He reads from the menu, not bothering to look at the waiter until, glancing across the table, he sees Laughton staring at the man. The waiter is young and rather good-looking, like virtually every man and woman in this town. The look on Laughton's face, an odd mix of interest and disdain, means nothing to Whale. Then he sees Elsa frown at her husband and lower her face for a closer study of the menu. The waiter takes her menu and goes, and she contemplates the silverware.

"We can't afford any more sofas," she mumbles.

"What?" says Laughton. "What was that, dearest?"

"Nothing. Sorry. Wool-gathering aloud." She brightly smiles at Whale.

Whatever the private reference means—they're an odd pair, but Whale always assumed they are perfect for each other—her use of it goads Laughton into finally talking. "You're serious, Whale, when you say you don't miss London?"

"What's to miss? The yellow fogs? The dingy little flats? The people on the dole?"

"They have the Depression here too," says Elsa, snatching up a new topic.

"It hardly touches Hollywood. And I'm not depressed. I have success here." They know who he is; he can be shamelessly honest with them. "Over there I was poor. Over here I am rich. I own my own car. I rent an entire house. Can you imagine? They give me more money than I know what to do with. And for what? For having fun with a camera and actors. For telling whatever story happens to catch my fancy and talents."

"Ain't we the 'umble one," teases Elsa, putting on the accent of a Cockney char.

"I am finished with being humble. Knowing one's place? I knew it all too well in London. I could never forget I was an intruder. Here, I can be anyone I choose. If I wish I'd gone to Oxford, abracadabra, I'm an Oxford graduate. If I hate being in my forties, presto change-o, I lop off a few years and tell interviewers I'm in my prime at thirty-six. It's all make-believe, my dears. The whole world is made of plaster of paris."

Elsa looks amused, Laughton appalled. Whale hadn't intended to be so full of himself, but he can't help it, not with friends who knew him when he was nobody. It's good that he didn't ask David along, or the boy would be shocked by his gaucherie.

"We have not yet seen your horror picture," Elsa confesses. "They can't show it in England, you know."

"Oh yes." Whale amusedly shakes his head. "Too violent for the lower classes. Imagine that. They ship us off to war, yet are hot to protect us from a mere motion picture." Even Laughton spent a year in the trenches.

"But we want to see it," says Elsa. "I certainly do."

"I'm eager to see it myself," says Laughton.

Whale smiles. Elsa is being loyal, but anything that upset so many people would have to attract Laughton's interest. "I'd love for you to see it. It's a dark, curious thing. An entertainment. Yet there are moments I am proud of. Strong meat. Perhaps you could come out to the studio for a private screening?"

"Oh yes. That'd be lovely. Wouldn't it, Charles?"

Laughton nods. "Definitely. Uh, can Paramount visit Universal?"

"Charlie, dahling. Welcome to Hollywood."

They turn to look. The rusty female voice does not prepare them for the beautiful, languid young woman who slouches by their table.

"Miss Bankhead," says Elsa. She has to prompt Laughton to stand as well as remind him who this lady is.

"Please. Don't. I'm on my way out. Just wanted to say hi. Elsa, right?" She takes the hands of the husband and wife. "We met in London. I can't tell you how happy I am," she tells Laughton, "that you're in my picture."

"Yes. Quite," Laughton mumbles. "Good to work with you."

"Miss Bankhead," says Elsa. "Mr. James Whale."

"An honor," says Whale. "I saw you onstage in London."

"Betcha don't recognize me with clothes on," she growls.

He laughs—she did have that reputation—and waits for her to acknowledge that she knows who he is. She doesn't, but Whale is not too disappointed. A year ago he wouldn't have dared to hope for such a thing.

"I trust you limes aren't too at sea in our fair city. I can't keep my date waiting. But if you need anything, please feel free to call. Cheers, dahlings." And she slinks off, a few eyes following her, others lingering on the trio she greeted.

"*Her* picture?" says Elsa. "It also has Gary Cooper in it."

"That's the woman I'm to make love to?" worries Laughton.

"You'll do fine, love. Just close your eyes and think of her as a very bad dog that must be punished."

"You see," says Whale. "You already belong here. You know Tallulah Bankhead."

"If she represents Hollywood—" Elsa finishes the remark with a roll of her eyes. "You don't intend to stay forever, do you, James?"

"I don't know yet. Perhaps I will go native. I could be American. Listen to this: Sidewalk. Apartment. Garden hose. Don't I sound like the real thing?"

"What about home? Your native soil and family? You can't just pull up your roots and float in thin air."

He laughs freely. "Come now, Elsa. We know about each other's hearth and home. Yours was larkier than most. But Charles's? Mine? Gloomy Dudley, where me mum and dad spent the evenings staring at a lump of coal glowing in the grate? I'd just as soon have an ocean and continent between me and it, thank you. And those people who smile so politely while they secretly listen for a syllable or phrase that might betray who you really are? No, I enjoy being free of them. Here, I'm limited only by my talent and imagination. I truly believe that this is where I belong."

The waiter returns with the first course. Whatever about him alarmed the Laughtons has passed. Their unease is now directed at their salads, pear halves topped with glossy white mounds.

"Mayo-naise," Whale explains when the waiter goes. "A tasty combination. Believe me."

Laughton tries a small bite. He solemnly swirls it around with his tongue. Then he takes a bigger bite. "Yes. It is good. Quite good. I could learn to like this." He polishes off his salad and greedily helps himself to his wife's plate.

# 8

THE HOUSE OF THE MAN WHO MADE *FRANKENSTEIN* LOOKS STAR-tlingly ordinary today. Clay has never seen it at this hour. He pulls into the semicircular driveway at four o'clock, and the clutter of afternoon shadows and shaggy forsythia out front is identical to the clutter of shadows and shrubs in the neighbors' yards. Clay parks his truck by the garage. A guy who's come to sit for his portrait should enter by the front door, Clay tells himself. He feels good. He mowed two yards this morning and has been back to the trailer park to shower and change. He wears dungarees and a white dress shirt he bought at Robert Hall on the way home when he remembered he had nothing clean to wear. The shirt-front is still crisscrossed with package creases. Clay feels foolish having to think about how he looks, but it isn't every day a famous man draws your picture. His dungarees are turned up in denim buckets at the cuffs. A folded copy of *TV Guide* is wedged in his back pocket.

He rings the doorbell.

The Mex maid answers. Her little mouth horseshoes in a frown as she looks up at him.

"Don't worry, senora. You already paid me," Clay quickly explains. "I'm here because Mr. Whale invited me. He told me to come today so he could—"

"The Master is waiting for you," she says without emotion. She gestures him in, shuts the door, and hurries down the hall, a squat little Sherman tank in a black dress, with a starched petticoat whistling underneath.

Clay follows her. The cool hallway is sweet and musty in a way he thinks must be English. The place doesn't feel rich or famous but like an old lady's house, only bigger. The ceilings are high, the varnished oak floor dotted with dark plugs, the walls full of real paintings. The hard tread of his boots suddenly vanish in a soft Turkish carpet. Other people's houses always feel strange the first time you enter them.

In the black-and-white-tiled kitchen, the maid goes to the wooden counter where there's a TV tray with two glasses, two bottles of beer, a bottle of Coke, and a church key.

"He is in his studio," she says. "Here. Take this with you." She thrusts the tray at him.

He accepts before realizing she's treating him as a servant.

"You know the way," she declares when he sourly stands there.

"It's your job, lady, not mine." He thrusts the tray back at her. "I'm here so he can draw my picture."

She folds her arms across her chest. "I am keeping away. It is none of my business."

Clay refuses to let a Mex maid lord it over him. That's what this is about, isn't it? Who's the servant and who isn't? He slides the tray back on the counter.

"Take it, take it," she insists. "It is for you, you know."

"But you're the one who's paid to carry it."

"I tell you. Today I am keeping out of this. What you are doing is no bloody business of mine."

He twists his squint at her. "What're you talking about?"

The maid grimaces. She wags a little hand in front of her wide face to erase what she's said and start over again. "What kind of man are you?"

Her English sounds good enough that it should make sense, but Clay is more lost than ever.

"Are you a good man?"

"Yeah, I'm a good man. Something make you think I'm not?"

She gives him a stern, indignant look. "You will not hurt him?"

The old senora is nuts. "No. I'm going to sit on my ass while he draws pictures. Is that going to hurt him?"

"No? No," she slowly agrees, closing her eyes. "I am sorry. He is in such a mood, he is so crazy after his stroke, it is making me crazy. But he is weak and you are large. I can't help worrying—"

Clay laughs in disbelief. "You think I'm going to beat him up? Why? So I can rob him? Gimme a break. I cut your grass. I don't go around robbing old people."

"I am sorry. I do not know what I am afraid of. Forget everything I say. Here. I will take the tray."

"You do that," he commands, but he opens the bottom half of the Dutch door for her to show there's no hard feelings.

"Thank you."

He follows her into the bright sunlight. She steps down the path, the glasses and bottles jingling on the tray. She slows down until he is walking beside her.

"Please do not tell him I have talked crazy," she says in a low voice.

"Nothing to tell."

"But if bad happens, there is the intercom. Buzz me. Any attacks, I can handle him."

Clay continues beside her, trying to understand what she's said. "He has attacks?"

"No. Not yet," she admits. "But if he attacks"—her English keeps slipping—"you will not do anything but call me?"

Clay once saw a guy have an epileptic seizure, at Pendleton in sick bay, and it scared the shit out of him. But the maid is fretting about seizures the poor guy doesn't even have. Old people baffle Clay, and an elderly Mexican female is triply foreign. There's nothing for him to say except, "Sure. No sweat."

"He is harmless and old," she whispers. "Do not let him worry you." They have reached the studio and she calls in through the screen door, "He is here, Mr. Jimmy."

"Mr. Boone?" Whale's voice is strong and clear. "Won't you come into my parlor?"

Clay opens the squeaking door and enters behind the maid.

Whale stands at a drafting table with his back to them. He has a knife in his hand; he's sharpening a pencil.

"Almost ready. One can never be too prepared." He glances over his shoulder and sees the maid set the tray on the low table. "Very good, Maria. Now good-bye."

She goes toward the door, wrinkling her forehead at Clay.

"See you," he tells her, not knowing what other promise she expects from him.

She nods and leaves. The screen door bangs shut.

And Whale slowly turns around.

His lips are sealed in a smile, his blue eyes clear and calm. The snow-white hair is neatly brushed and he wears a bow tie. The man looks perfectly okay.

"I'm sure you'd like a beer," he offers, stepping toward the tray. "Something to wet your whistle while I work." He uses the church key to open a bottle. He pours it into a glass, very carefully.

Man to man, without the senora there to make him nervous, Clay feels perfectly comfortable with the old guy.

"You'll be sitting there." Whale nods at a straight-backed chair with a leather seat. "We'll go slow today. Since this is your first time as a model, and my first life session in . . . months. Cheers." He hands Clay a glass with a two-inch head. "Please be seated. We'll be ready in a moment."

Clay sits, and snags the chair with his *TV Guide*. He forgot all about it while struggling to understand the maid. "Oh, did you see this?" He reaches back and pulls out the little magazine, opening it to the dog-eared page. "They're showing one of your movies on TV. Tomorrow night."

"You don't say?" Whale gives his full attention to attaching a large pad of paper to the board on his easel. He shows no interest in what Clay thought would be big news.

"I guess you know already."

"No. Can't say that I did. But I'm not surprised. Television is such a hungry beast, they'll shovel anything into its maw. Which picture?"

"*Bride of Frankenstein.*"

"Oh yes. That was one of mine."

"The late show," Clay adds.

Whale continues to fuss with clamps and screws. "Is there a description?"

Clay reads: " '1935 sequel to Boris Karloff horror classic, with Elsa Lanchester as the monster's mate. Creaky in parts but superior to later sequels. A must for buffs.' "

"Hmm. No mention of Clive or Thesiger."

"They don't mention you either."

"Well, a director is among the peons." Whale grips the easel with both hands and gives it a shake. It seems solid.

"You going to watch?"

"I don't think so. It's an old thing, and much too late past my bedtime."

"I want to catch it. If I can find a television."

"I don't encourage you to go to great bother. Unless you have nothing better to do that evening." He flips the cover sheet of the pad over the top bar. "Shall we begin?"

Clay takes a deep swig of beer and sets the glass on the floor. "Ready when you are."

Whale stares at Clay. He stands ten feet away. He looks more serious now, even glum. Clay can't tell if he's getting artistic or if he's pissed over hearing he's on television. Maybe the late show is the equivalent of the glue factory for old movie directors.

"That shirt, Mr. Boone."

"It's new."

Whale shakes his head. "I'm sorry. It will not do."

Clay tugs at the collar, wondering what's wrong with it.

"Exactly. Your collar. The way it frames your face." Whale holds his hands on either side of his own face. "I can't work with that."

"I can fold it in," Clay suggests.

"No, the shirt's too white, too distracting. Would it be asking too much for you to take it off?"

"I'm not wearing an undershirt today."

"Pish posh, Mr. Boone. I'm not your aunt Tilly. I won't be offended."

"But it's just my face you want to draw."

"Oh, if it's going to make you uncomfortable—" Whale gives in with a sigh. "Perhaps we can find you something else to wear." He looks around. He lifts an old drop cloth off a foot-locker. "We could wrap it like a toga round your shoulders. Would that help you overcome your schoolgirl shyness?" His mouth remains straight, but there's a smile in his eyes, like he's making fun of Clay.

Clay doesn't know which is sillier, Whale's dislike of the shirt or his own desire to keep it on. "All right already. I'll take it off." Scoffing at himself, he unbuttons the top and pulls out the tail. "Kind of warm in here anyway."

Whale watches, the smile passing from his eyes into his mouth. "Yes. Much better." He abruptly steps forward. "Here. I'll hang it for you." Standing over Clay to take the shirt, he calmly examines Clay from above, front and back, then walks away with the shirt draped over his arm.

Clay adjusts his belt buckle over the slack of stomach muscles and makes sure his belly button is clean. He often goes shirtless when he works, but to do it while you sit and someone else works feels funny. Clay suddenly has to think about his navel, his nipples, the blond gig-line of hair on his stomach, little facts of himself he never considers.

Whale has hung the shirt on a wall peg and stands beside the easel again. "I think what we shall do, and what will make you most comfortable, is to have you to sit slightly sideways, so you can rest one arm on back of the chair. Yes. Just so."

Moving helps Clay forget his self-consciousness, although it returns as soon as he settles into position. The arm with the tattoo faces the easel.

"Now, is that a pose you're comfortable in? You'll be holding it for a while."

"No sweat," says Clay, shifting so his skin won't stick to the chair. His head is turned in such a way he can see Whale and the easel only by straining his eyes hard to the left.

"Very good, then." But Whale remains at the far edge of Clay's strained field of vision, just looking.

"Take a picture, it lasts longer," Clay says with a smirk.

"What? Ah." Whale lightly laughs. "That's exactly what I intend to do." He steps behind his pad of paper.

There's a clatter of pencils in the easel's tray. A moment of silence. Finally, a long, low, whistly scratch.

Clay concentrates on keeping still.

More scratches follow, short, long, loud, soft, like people whispering in the next room.

Clay focuses on the open window in the corner, although there's nothing to see except the pie slice of sunlight on the screen and a cracked blister of paint on the sill.

"You seem to have no idea how handsome you are, Mr. Boone. Which makes you even more handsome."

"Yeah?"

"Oh yes. Rembrandt would have adored you." Whale continues to draw while he talks. "Goya and Hogarth too. It has to do with how snugly your face fits your skull."

Being admired is like being tickled, and Clay strains to stop himself from wincing. But he finds he enjoys being admired when it comes from an artist, a professional. He's alarmed that he enjoys it so much. He feels like he's admiring himself in a mirror, which would be wrong except that he's getting paid to do it by a man who made famous movies, and this mirror won't give him his reflection for another half hour or so. He wonders how he's going to look. His waist tickles with beads of sweat. The back of the chair digs against his forearm.

"Would you be more comfortable barefoot?" Whale suggests. "Feel free to remove your boots and socks."

"No. I'm fine."

The pencil continues to sizzle and hiss.

"It's a bit like being at the doctor, isn't it? You have to remain perfectly still. While I examine and scrutinize you."

"No," says Clay. "Not like that at all. Thank God. Those guys give me the creeps."

"Do they, now? I feel much the same, Mr. Boone," Whale softly confesses. "Much the same." He turns sad and thoughtful, or rather his pencil does, concentrating on a series of soft, slow marks. Whale himself is silent.

Clay wishes he'd resume talking, and that he hadn't mentioned doctors. He has Clay thinking about being on an examining table in Joplin. Going in for a checkup every summer before football practice began, he had to lie face up on clammy leather in nothing but his drawers. His heart was in his throat while Dr. Sturgis indifferently thumped and poked his way down. For a teenage boy who was still a virgin, being touched was as frightening as having someone stick his hand right through your skin. No, this ain't like that. It's nothing like that.

Whale loudly sniffs, as if smelling something. He sniffs several times but continues to draw.

"Dripping?" he murmurs to himself.

Clay cuts his eyes hard to the left; Whale is hidden behind his easel.

"Do you ever eat dripping in this country? Beef dripping." He seems as surprised by the subject as Clay is. "The fats from roasts and such. Congealed in jars. Used like butter on bread."

Clay doesn't care what they talk about so long as they can talk. "Never heard of it. Sounds like something you feed a dog."

"It is. Only the poorest families ever ate it. I don't know

what made me think of it. I haven't tasted dripping in years."
He continues to draw as he talks. "We kept ours in a crockery
jar. In the cupboard."

"Your family ate dripping?"

"Buckets of it. Our mother replenished the jar every week
with the juice of the Sunday roast. When we had a roast. You
could follow the family fortune by the level in the jar, like a bank
book."

"But you said only poor people ate it."

The scratching stops. Whale thrusts his head around to look
at Clay. He ducks back in and the scratches resume. "So I did.
Had you thought I was of the gentry, Mr. Boone? A silver spoon
and a country estate? Fox hunts and hey what?"

"Never stopped to think what you were." Clay hadn't even
bothered to think that there must be poor people in England.
Every Englishman you see in the movies is a lord or a butler.

"No. You wouldn't. That's what I love about Americans. So
natural, so democratic. But I come from the slums. Yes, beef
dripping and four to a bed, and a privy out back in the alley.
Our dear old privy. You froze your arse in the winter and were
eaten by flies in the summer. Land of hope and glory? Land of
privies and dripping."

Clay feels he's come in on the middle of a conversation.
Hearing that Whale was once poor only makes him seem older,
like he has a past that goes back to the Stone Age.

"Are you from the slums, Mr. Boone?"

"We weren't rich, but we weren't poor either."

"I know. You were middle class. Like all Americans. Rich or
poor, you need to think of yourselves as middle class." He sounds
disappointed.

"I guess you'd say we lived on the wrong side of the tracks,"
Clay admits. One of the humiliations about lying on the examining table was the ragged state of his underwear.

"Very good. I didn't want to think you were a well-to-do
youth who'd fallen from grace." He clears his nose with a snort.
"In Dudley, there were more sides of the tracks than any Amer-

ican can imagine. Every Englishman knows his place. And if you forget, there's always someone present to remind you. My family knew its place quite well. My father was a laborer. His only ambitions in life were a full jar of dripping, a proper home without fleas, and good standing in our church.''

Whale seems to be saying whatever comes into his head. Clay figures he does it deliberately to help him sit still. He's impressed the man can draw and talk at the same time.

"Good Methodists we were. My father marched us to chapel every Sunday morning. Seven and eight of us. In scratchy hand-me-down suits that were always too small. They pinched you in the crutch. We paraded up the hill and through the snicket by the pub. Rancid puddles of slop and a drunkard or two sleeping off the Saturday night revels. No, our Dad weren't like them, although that was Mum's doing. Strong drink was the devil to her. She allowed him and herself no glass of cheer. But they did not deny all pleasures of the flesh. They loved to spawn. Yes, they clearly loved that, or else they wouldn't have continued long after the house was packed with progeny.

"But they fed what they begot. They worked hard to keep us clothed and fed. They were good people. Proper people. They had no doubts about who they were. Or who their children were either. They never knew who I was. I was an aberration in that household, a freak of nature. I had imagination as a child, cleverness, joy. Where did I get that joy? Certainly not from them. They never even noticed I was different. They took me out of school when I was fourteen and put me in a factory.''

He no longer sounds mocking. Clay wonders if he should say something, hum or grunt just to show he's listening.

"Oh, but I hated and feared them when they did that. I was such a child. I thought they were punishing me for being too clever. A promising lad was ripped one winter morning from the warm bed he shared with a little brother, marched out to the cold privy in the dark, then seated in the kitchen with his father and grown brothers for strong tea and bread with dripping. Nobody apologized, nobody said a word. Out in the street you could already hear the clack of wooden shoes—the most depressing sound in the world. Like a funeral march.''

He hums a mournful, royal-sounding tune.

''And the factory whistles. Our days were measured in factory whistles and church bells. And the foundry itself. The iron shutters over the windows were closed tight in winter. The only light came from the smelting furnaces and the hot melt being poured into molds—like staring at the sun. Machine parts we made, gears and such. With an endless banging of hammers, the clank of chains hanging from the overhead tracks, the screech of wheels up there when the chain was wrapped round a quarter ton of iron. The noise of the shop floor was deafening. Men shouted themselves permanently hoarse in that place. I kept my voice only because I had nothing to say to anyone. Great blackened men with singed beards and massive arms. I was tall for my age but slim, frail. Everyone else was a giant. They had me fetching tools and water at first, then gripping the hot castings with tongs while they hammered away the flaws. They cursed me when a blow fell wrong, whether it was my fault or not. I was in constant fear of having my ears boxed, although nobody laid a hand on me.

''I hated and feared those men my first winter there. Until the weather grew warm enough for them to strip off and wash at the pumps in the yard. And I saw that they were human. Very white and human. I stopped fearing them, but I still hated them. I despised and pitied their existence. I had to rise above these men and escape this life. It was hatred that enabled me to keep a small piece of soul alive in that soul-killing place. And among these hated men, in this very factory, was my own poor, dumb father. Who did nothing to protect me. Who had put me in this hell to begin with.''

The whisper of the pencil stops. A bird sings in the cypresses outside, a little tune that spins once, then twice in the hot sun.

Clay has heard old people talk about hard times before, but always to bully you for not suffering as much as they had. Whale does not sound proud of his suffering but confused, which confuses Clay.

"I haven't thought about my first winter of work since—twenty-some years ago? Only now it feels fresher, worse," Whale murmurs in astonishment. "Because I grew accustomed to that place, that life. I lived it for ten years, most of it in a gentler factory, where I beat lovely patterns into fireplace fenders. And I forgave and forgot my parents long ago. They meant no harm. They thought I was just like them. They were like a family of farmers who've been given a giraffe, and don't know what to do with the creature except harness him to a plow. There's no dignity in hating the dead."

He slowly peers out from the square of paper. His face is paler, his eyes wide and frightened, like he's not sure where he is or what Clay's doing here. He rubs a hand across his eyes and steps into the open. His voice changed while he spoke, becoming more pinched and nasal. He quickly recovers his old accent.

"Excuse the prattle," he says dismissively. "Since my stroke, I am often overcome with nostalgia. It's clinical. Nostalgic diarrhea, they call it. Or some such medical term. I seem to be purging myself in talk."

"I don't mind," says Clay, not knowing what else to say. "Everybody's got stories. I'm not crazy about my old man either."

Whale looks at him. He frowns and goes back to the easel. "Why don't we break for five minutes? I should sit down. You probably want to stretch your legs. More beer?" He pulls the cover sheet over the pad to hide what he's drawn so far.

Clay slowly stands, stiff and awkward after sitting so long and listening to these tales from another planet. He likes Whale for telling these stories, although he's not sure why.

Whale is watching him with a forlorn, rather bitter smile.

"Are we absolutely sure, Mr. Boone, we wouldn't be more comfortable with our boots off?"

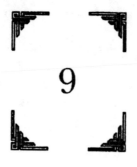

# 9

"So you just sat there and this old limey banged his gums?"

"Yep."

"Would've bored the shit out of me."

"Well, I liked it. English slums and factories and art school at night. You learn stuff listening to old-timers." Clay didn't understand everything Whale talked about, but he's not going to tell Dwight that.

"And you never got to see his picture of you?"

"He didn't want to show it yet. Said he needed to work it up when I wasn't there."

Dwight flips the bill of his Lockheed softball team cap, with the exaggerated care of a fellow who's had too many beers, so he can light a cigarette without setting the cap on fire. He's not impressed to hear a famous man is doing Clay's portrait. Nobody at the Beachcomber is impressed. Clay wishes he hadn't told anyone, except he needed to explain why he wants to watch an old movie on the TV tonight. *Bride of Frankenstein* comes on in ten minutes. The battered Motorola perched on the pinewood wall to the right of the bar remains turned off.

Harry's Beachcomber is dead on a Thursday. There's only Clay and Dwight sitting at the bar, and Harry himself parked with a book in a bright corner by the liquor bottles—Harry always has a book with him. Out in the darkness, in a wooden booth under the seine nets hung with old life buoys, Kid Saylor is sweet-talking the cute girl he brought in with him tonight. Saylor really is a kid, a cocky twenty-year-old who was suspended from college and is spending his semester surfing and tomcatting. He makes Clay feel old. His date is a shy, ponytailed thing who looks like she's still in high school. The silent chrome-trimmed jukebox opposite the bar projects its illuminated guts on the ceiling. Through the screened-in windows out front come the intermittent drone and whine of traffic on Pacific Coast Highway. The long, low snores of ocean can be heard through the screens in the back.

"You ever hear of this Whale fellow?" Dwight asks Harry.

"Can't say that I have. Can't say I've heard of a lot of people, though," Harry drawls without looking up from his book. He has a mumbly drawl, his tongue filling his mouth like a wad of gum. He reads almost anything—poetry, philosophy, science fiction. In his fifties, with a bald head and Uncle Sam tuft of beard, Harry was a beatnik before beatniks existed. He bought this shack and turned it into a bar fifteen years ago, when the beach was in the middle of nowhere, to give himself a place to live and just enough income to sit and read. He lets Betty or whoever else he hires do all the work.

"I wonder if this guy even made movies," says Dwight.

"You think I'm making him up?"

"No, I wonder if he's making himself up."

"You think I'm too dumb to tell if he's bullshitting?"

Clay knows his friends think he's dumb. He got that in college too, where smart friends thought he was a dumb jock and jock friends thought he was an egghead. Dwight isn't so smart himself or he wouldn't be married to a woman who wants a life straight from the *Saturday Evening Post*. Dwight can play the hard-drinking man of the world only when Jackie and the kids aren't around.

"I'm not saying you're dumb. I'm saying he sounds fishy."

"What's fishy?"

"If he really was a famous movie director, why didn't he tell stories about movie stars? Instead of talking about how his family was so poor they ate bacon grease for breakfast."

There's no arguing with a drunk cynic, especially one who has a point. Why *didn't* Whale talk about his movies? "If you don't believe me, let's watch this movie. See if his name's on it. How about it, Harry? Can I watch my damn movie?"

"I told you," says Harry. "I don't turn on the TV except for ball games."

"What, we're going to burn up fifty cents of electricity? I'll give you the fifty cents. Hell, Harry, I'll give you a dollar. Although I spend enough money in here, I'd think you'd let me watch one stinking movie."

"Come on, Harry," Dwight joins in. "Boone's got me curious. Let's watch this *Frankenstein* movie and see if his pal is for real or not."

"It's not the money, it's the principle," Harry declares. "I'm not going to let my place become one of those joints where the idiot box is always blaring."

"One stinking movie, Harry."

"Let me think about it."

"Starts in five minutes."

"Then you better shut up and let me think about it in peace!"

Betty reappears behind the bar, lugging a bucket of ice from the storeroom. She wears a man's checkered shirt with the tail out and the sleeves rolled up—Harry does not stand on ceremony—and bright red lipstick. Betty is big-boned and almost as tall as Clay, a softly muscular farm girl with heavy eyelids and a doughnut of brown hair spiked with bobby pins. She's stuck to her resolve tonight, saying even less to Clay than she'd say to a perfect stranger. But Clay caught her in the mirror earlier, listening when he told Dwight and Harry about Whale.

"A spooky movie," she grumbles. "Just what this place needs tonight."

"Couldn't make it any deader, doll," says Dwight, and wags his empty Pabst bottle at her. "Hit me with another."

"Sure. Your friend want one?"

"Yeah, one for what's-his-name here." Dwight is amused by the silent feud between Clay and Betty.

Clay wishes she'd knock it off. He hates playing games and he's still not sure what he did wrong. "Thanks, doll," he says with a doggy smile when she sets a cold bottle by his elbow.

She ignores him and turns to Harry. "I say let the dopes watch their movie. And be grateful Boone's not cutting Shirley Temple's lawn."

"Gimme a break," Clay groans. "I've gotten to know this guy and I want to see one of his movies. Why is everybody giving me crap?"

Dwight laughs. "Jesus, Boone. You come in here proud as a peacock just because some old coot you think is famous wants to paint your picture. We're just bringing you back to earth."

"Sounds screwy to me," says Betty. "I can't imagine a real artist wanting to spend time looking at that kisser."

Clay is angry. He doesn't know how angry until he grumbles, "This kisser wasn't so bad you couldn't lay under it a few times."

"Ooooh," goes Dwight, and Clay realizes he's gone too far.

Betty glares at him. She sniffs and turns away. "I bet this is just some old fruit pretending to be famous. So he can get in the big guy's pants."

"Oooh," Dwight goes again, with more pain.

And Clay explodes. "You got no fucking right to say that! What makes you say that?"

Betty refuses to be frightened. "Just thinking aloud."

"Keep your dirty thoughts to yourself, damn it."

"All right, then. He's interested in you for your conversation. We know what a great talker you are."

"Screw you."

"Not anymore, you don't. Doll."

Clay is furious. He wants to hit her, but he can't hit a woman. He's angry not just for himself but for Whale, for the stories Whale told and the trust he showed Clay. All a bitch can see is sex and perversion. Clay grips his full bottle and taps the base against the bar. "We're watching the movie, Harry. You got that! We are watching my fucking movie."

"Calm down, Clay. Just calm down." Harry sounds worried, afraid of trouble now that Clay's angry. He has closed his book around a finger. "We'll watch it. If that's going to make you happy, we'll turn it on."

"Good. Fine." Clay pulls out his wallet. "Here, lady. I'm buying this round. Give one to Harry too. You want a beer, Harry? And the lovebirds in the corner. Take them a couple of cold ones." He flips a five across the bar top. If she's going to call him queer bait, he's going to treat her like dog shit.

Betty does not look insulted as she takes the money and works the cash register. She slides Clay's change in front of him and plucks three beers from the cooler. She comes around the bar at Harry's end, hands him his beer, and strolls across the gritty floor toward Saylor and his girl.

"Turn it on," Clay tells Dwight. "Channel four."

Dwight stands up and pushes the button. There's a pause while the cathode tube heats up; the screen blinks twice and opens wide on a commercial for shaving cream.

"This is gonna be good," Clay assures everyone. "Gonna be real good." He feels like a jerk for losing his temper, but there are times you have to get angry to get what you want.

Betty returns from the shadows. "I don't think they appreciated the interruption. Smells like a henhouse back there."

Harry takes on a lecherous grin. "Hey, you kids," he calls out. "Don't forget you're in a public place."

"Mind your own business," answers a croaky, swollen voice.

"Turn up the volume." Clay doesn't want to think about Saylor playing stinky finger while they watch Mr. Whale's movie.

"Reminds me of the old days," Harry sighs. "When I came here after the war, beach was like a grunion run every night, only it was people flopping instead of fish. Not like now. Everybody's so middle class now. Back then, you couldn't walk the beach at night without tripping over fornicators."

"Especially if you were a dirty old man out looking for them," mutters Betty.

"Shhh, shhh, it's starting," says Clay. He leans on an elbow so he can see around Dwight.

There's an old-fashioned clock face on the screen accompanied by the late show's signature tune. A television voice announces: "Tonight, Boris Karloff in *The Bride of Frankenstein.*"

A toy airplane drones noisily around a toy globe.

"Ooh, I'm getting scared," says Betty.

"Shhh!"

Music comes on, buzzy, kazoolike music, and titles: "Karloff in"—white letters against black—"*The Bride of Frankenstein.*" More names follow, actors and writers, the art director and composer. Nasal, sneering horns announce something evil. Then the phrase "Directed by" floats over a white blob. The blob jumps forward to form letters: "James Whale."

"*There!*" Clay shouts. "What did I tell you? It *is* his movie. You believe me now?" Clay had begun to doubt it himself. But there he is, his name given special treatment as if it were an important name.

The sound track hiccups over a break in the film. A building burns on a hilltop at night. The building collapses and the scene dissolves to a howling mob in the flaming wreckage. The fake sky behind them is full of storm clouds. A hatchet-faced woman in a little hat with fluttering ribbons cackles happily over the monster being roasted alive.

"This looks corny," says Betty.

"Go wash glasses if you don't like it."

But she remains where she is, standing beside Harry who sits in his corner. They all face the blue gray postage stamp blinking and buzzing on the wall.

An old man tells his wife he needs to see the bones of the beast who killed their little Maria. He climbs into the smoking ruins. There's a puff of flame and he drops through the floor. But he lands in a flooded cellar down below. He splashes around in waist-deep water, shouting for help. He doesn't see the great white hand rising from the water.

Yes, it's him. The familiar head peeks out angrily from behind a pillar.

"Oooo, somebody's gonna get it," Dwight whispers.

The head looks like a white clay jar, cracked and patched, with a human face. Clay remembers the face being green, but that must've been the posters. The famous steel bolt sticks through the neck. The Monster growls. He splashes out to the screaming man, grabs him, thrusts him underwater, and kills him instantly—they told you over and over in boot camp that killing is harder in life than it is in movies.

The Monster quickly climbs from the cellar. The old man's wife, thinking it's her husband, takes his hand to help him out. The hand is cold and slimy. The woman lets out a scream, and the Monster flips her into the cellar. Her body bounces down the bricks like a rag doll. An old owl watches wearily.

"Not bad," says Dwight. "Two down and it's just started."

The hatchet-faced woman with fluttering ribbons is alone outside. The Monster towers beside her like a wet statue; she slowly looks up. Her eyes go wide, her jaw works up and down. She squeaks and whimpers and, finally, she screams. But it's a funny scream, a comic shriek. She flees in a bowlegged jig up the hill, long skirt dancing around her little boots.

Dwight and Harry and Betty all laugh. A commercial cuts in.

"These old movies are such a hoot," says Betty. "They thought they were being scary, but they're just funny."

"Maybe it's supposed to be funny," Clay says defensively.

"I can't believe that," says Betty. "Comedy is comedy and scary is scary. You don't mix them."

"People weren't as sophisticated back then," Harry drawls

knowingly. "Movies could get away with stuff they can't do anymore."

Clay knows they're probably right, audiences are smarter, but he doesn't like to think Whale didn't know what he was doing. Still, he wants the movie to be scary and strange the way he remembers it as a kid, and it's not. Well, it is a sequel and sequels are never as good as the original.

Things drag after the commercial. The injured Dr. Frankenstein—it is the doctor and not the monster who's called Frankenstein—has been taken to his castle where his pretty fiancée frets and fusses and makes him promise to stop his experiments. But there's a knocking at the front door. A man wants to see Dr. Frankenstein. A scarecrow fellow in a black cape and soft-brimmed hat comes inside and removes his hat. The lean, beaky face looks familiar, but Clay can't remember seeing this actor before or even this character: Dr. Pretorius. His springy white hair curls across his head like smoke. A pair of snaky eyes gleam over a wrinkled, close-lipped smile. His upturned nostrils shrivel shut when he sees the fiancée.

"Guy's a fruit," says Betty.

"You don't know that," says Clay. "They didn't have fruits back then." She's obsessed with fruits tonight.

"I calls 'em as I sees 'em."

"So where's the Monster?" Dwight demands. "I want the Monster. Good time to take a leak." He climbs off his stool and goes to the toilet.

Pretorius takes Frankenstein to his own laboratory, shows him his experiments—glass jars with little people inside—and suggests they collaborate and create a bride for the Monster.

At long last, after Dwight returns, the movie gets back to the Monster. He wanders in a phony indoor pine forest, hungry and hurt, more pathetic than scary. Clay can't remember feeling sorry for the Monster. He doesn't look so frightening when there's nobody around to show how big he is. He moves like a linebacker staggering off the field with a broken arm. His growls sound like the gunning of an engine with a bad muffler.

Suddenly the forest is filled with armed men. They chase the Monster and corner him on a high rock. He groans and swats at the poles surrounding and beating him. Hands grab his legs, ropes are thrown around his arms. His contorted face is both fierce and helpless.

> *You ain't nothing but a hound dog*
> *Crying all the time*

The song suddenly blasts from the jukebox. Kid Saylor has come out of the shadows and bends over the console, wagging his denim butt and tapping a high-top sneaker to the hit that Clay is sick of hearing. His girl must be in the john.

"Hey! Some of us are watching a movie!"

"Go ahead. Free country," Saylor smirks over his shoulder. His face is blotchy, his lips swollen. His eyes have a sleepy, smug look.

The Monster is strapped to a pole and hoisted over a cart, hanging crucified before he's dropped into the hay.

But the song is too loud, and Clay too angry to watch. He jumps from his stool.

Saylor sees him coming. He steps aside; he's smaller than Clay. "Hey, you want me to turn it down?"

Clay stiff-arms him out of the way, slamming the heel of his hand against Saylor's chest. The boy staggers backward, almost falling. Clay bends down and grabs the rear corner of the jukebox. He jerks it from the wall; the needle screeches across the song. Clay yanks out the plug, tosses the cord behind the machine and faces Saylor, daring him to fight.

The kid stands back, keeping his smirk but holding up both hands in a nervous surrender. "Hey, like, I didn't know. It's your favorite movie. Sorry, okay?" The apology sounds insincere, mocking, like he thinks Clay is a crazy old man.

Clay takes a deep breath. He hates the kid for making him feel old. "I don't have time for this shit," he growls. He returns to the bar and uprights the stool that fell over when he jumped off. "I'll plug it back in after my movie," he tells Harry.

Harry only shakes his head. "You're like a dog with a bone over this movie, Clay."

"I just want to watch it, okay?"

But it's hard to get back into the story after losing his temper. The muscles in his gut and shoulders remain alert and jumpy, although no exertion was required to lift the jukebox or knock Saylor aside. Clay waits, even hopes, for Saylor to tap him on the back and suggest they finish this in the parking lot. But when Clay cranes around to look, Saylor's in his booth with the girl again, snickering. He feels like the people at the bar—his friends—are looking at him funny, leaning away even though they remain exactly where they were.

The Monster has escaped the village jail. He's stumbling through the indoor forest again, howling like a wounded animal. He comes to the cottage of a lonely old man, a blind man. The man can't see the Monster's a monster. He invites him inside, feeds him, tends his wound, puts him to bed and prays over him, thanking God for sending a friend. Blackness closes around the picture so there's nothing but the crucifix over the bed.

Clay doesn't need Betty or Dwight to tell him it's a sappy scene. But nobody makes any cracks. Clay wants to think they've gotten into the movie, but he worries they're just afraid he'll blow his lid again. Clay buys another round of beers to remind them he's not such a bad guy.

The Monster meets Dr. Pretorius, in a crypt full of cobwebs and skeletons. Pretorius is having a midnight snack on top of a closed coffin. He doesn't bat an eye when the Monster appears. He gives the Monster a drink, then a cigar. He has a bantering chat with him—the blind man taught the Monster a few words—and announces that he and Dr. Frankenstein intend to make a woman for him. The Monster holds a skull in both hands and happily growls, "Wiiife."

"Ooh, what a creepy scene," says Betty during the next commercial, rubbing at her arms. "Just listening to that creep talk about women gave me the heebie-jeebies."

"Makes sense to me," Dwight proclaims, sounding more drunk now than the last time he spoke. "All that monster needs is a good piece of ass."

"Sick stuff," says Harry. "Necrophilia. I wonder if they knew how sick they were."

"Nothing sick about it," Clay insists. "The Monster's lonely and he wants a friend, a girlfriend, somebody. What's sick about that?"

Saylor escorts his girl toward the door, quickly, so he won't have to prove himself in another encounter with Clay. "You guys still watching that?" he asks. "I got to get my darling home before Daddy starts cleaning his shotgun. Night, all." The girl keeps her head lowered as they hurry out, more likely headed for the beach than home.

The movie continues. More talk: Frankenstein and his wife —they've been married since we last saw them—Frankenstein and Pretorius—Pretorius brings the Monster to bully Frankenstein into helping him make the Bride. Then, finally, they are in Frankenstein's castle laboratory, in white tunics and shiny black rubber gloves. Kites rock and strain in an electrical storm. In the cavernous room below, a tall contraption like a three-story coil of refrigerator tubing crackles and sparks over a neatly bandaged mummy. Coil and mummy rise together, shakily, through the roof of the castle into the storm. Eerie light glows on the lizardy face of Pretorius, on the smooth face of Frankenstein who's sprung a cowlick. The coil sticks up from the top of the castle, popping from top to bottom like a Roman candle.

Then, to the music that sounds like "Bali Hai," the contraption descends into the laboratory again. A drum beats like a heart. The mummy has wide hips and small but definite tits. Pretorius lifts a bandaged hand. Something whimpers beneath the gauze. Frankenstein tears a strip from the face. A pair of eyes stare out, frighteningly alive.

Church bells are ringing and here's the Bride, already un-wrapped and not naked or even in her underwear, but fully dressed, in a wide white surgical gown the doctors hold out by the hems on either side of her, like moth wings that were co-cooned inside the bandages. Her hair is molded in a stump with electrical squiggles on the sides; the black lips catch on a pretty overbite. Her eyes are wide open. She looks up, down, left, right, startled to be alive, uncertain who she is.

The Monster comes down the stairs, and sees her. He stares tenderly, desperately. "Friend?"

She spins around. Her wide eyes snap wider. The Monster approaches, huge hands hovering in front of him. He timidly touches her arm, and she screams.

"All right!" cries Betty. "You don't want *him.*"

But Clay thinks she should. It's unnatural she doesn't. She was made for the Monster.

The Monster tries again. He sits beside her on a couch. The doctors watch as he takes her hand and nervously pets it. She stares at her own little hand in the Monster's paws. He touches her shoulder, and she shrieks again, louder than the first time, jumping up from the couch into Frankenstein's arms. The Mon-ster is heartbroken. Nobody loves him, not even his Bride.

His pain turns to anger. He tears through the laboratory, knocking over tables, chasing the Bride and the doctors. Fran-kenstein's wife is banging at the door outside. The Monster comes to a handle sticking from the pipes.

"Don't touch that lever! You'll blow us to atoms!" cries Pretorius.

The Monster grips the lever with one hand and waves the other at his maker, ordering Frankenstein to escape with his wife. But he wants Pretorius and the Bride to stay. "We belong dead." The bride opens her mouth wide and hisses at him from the back of her throat, like a cat.

The Monster pulls the lever. The castle begins to explode. Bricks and beams crash into the laboratory.

Outside, Frankenstein and his wife scramble up a hill. They watch as explosion after explosion blow the tower apart. They embrace.

Music, and titles. And that's it. The movie is over. Which doesn't seem right. A guy gets snubbed by a girl and he blows up himself and everybody else? He didn't even get a chance to prove his love for his bride. Clay feels tricked, like the whole thing was a shaggy-dog story.

"Weird movie," says Betty. She goes to the television and turns it off. "Weird, weird, weird." She begins turning on lights, so the bar is no longer surrounded by darkness.

Harry stands up and stretches. "They don't make them like that anymore. Can't say I remember they ever made them like that, to tell the truth."

Clay remains seated, still not believing that was the end. "So what did you think?" he asks. "Did you like it?" He needs to ask because he can't tell if he liked it.

Betty answers when nobody else does. "Wasn't boring, I'll say that. Wasn't scary either. Was weird, though. Funny but creepy."

"I loved it," says Dwight. "Love that ending. Yeah, I want a switch like that in my trailer, so I can blow us to kingdom come when things don't go my way." He wobbles when he climbs off his stool. "Damn but it's drunk in here." He tilts toward the door. "Late too. The bride of Dwight is going to bite my head off. You coming, Boone?"

"I think I'll hang around." He wants to talk to Betty, at least about the movie.

Harry lifts the money tray from the cash register. "Go on home, Clay. You got to see your flick. We're closing up."

"I thought I'd give you a hand since I kept you open." He waits to see how Betty reacts.

Betty shrugs. "Sure. So long as you're not expecting anything afterwards."

"Hey, I'm nobody. Remember?" And to prove it, Clay goes to the front to shut the windows.

Dwight staggers outside. Clay sees him out by the highway, looking left and right for a full minute before he races across to the handful of lights in the trailer park. Not a single car passes the whole time. Clay is a bit drunk himself, but he holds his beer better than Dwight. The big fumbliness of his hands feels more like a memory of the movie than an effect of alcohol.

Harry takes his book and cash drawer to the back door. "You think you'll be okay, Betty?"

"I'll be fine," she tells him.

"I'm next door if you need . . ." He lets his thick tongue drown his words. He gives Clay one last look and goes out to the breezeway and his apartment.

Betty swabs the fixtures behind the bar. Clay finishes the front windows and begins on the back. The Beachcomber is large and desolate with its lights on, the knotty-pine walls, fishing nets, and grainy wood floor dingy in the fifty-watt glow. Clay doesn't know how to begin or even what he wants them to say to each other.

"So you hated the movie?" he says.

"I didn't hate the movie. Can't say I loved it." She gives him a skeptical glance while she scrubs something. "Why should it matter what I thought of it?"

"Because I know the guy who made it, that's all."

"Knowing this guy has sure put you on a high horse. God, you're touchy tonight. You looked like you were going to rip Saylor's head off."

"He pissed me off, acting like he owned the place. The punk's got his whole life ahead of him, so he thinks the world is his for the asking. Here, I'll get the garbage." Clay has to explain why he's coming toward the bar. "I'm not the one who's touchy. Everyone else was touchy. What was eating you tonight?"

"Me? I'm fine. What was eating you?"

"Not a damn thing."

Clay takes the garbage pail from under the bar and carries it to the back door. The long desert of beach shelves down into the night, a few ghostly breakers floating like clouds in a darker

darkness. He empties the pail into the rusty steel drum and returns, with a new thought.

"I think you guys are jealous."

"Jealous?" Betty laughs. "What's for us to be jealous of?"

"I've gotten to know somebody who made a famous movie."

"You cut his grass and he's drawing your picture. Big deal.
It's not like he's going to be putting your name in lights."

"I don't expect to get anything out of knowing him."

"Then why should you be so damned pleased?"

"I don't know." He doesn't, which is why he wants to talk
about it, hoping Betty'll respond to Whale the way Clay has and
justify his pleasure. He's pissed that she doesn't think it means
a damn thing. "I like hearing him talk. He treats me like I'm
somebody worth talking to. And hey, he's kind of famous."

"Not so famous any of us have heard of him."

Clay considers that. "If he were that famous, he probably
wouldn't give me the time of day. This way, he's like *my* famous
person." He hears how ridiculous that sounds and laughs at himself, although it has a truth to it. "Yeah, my own personal famous
person. Nobody knows about him except me."

But Betty doesn't laugh along. She's silent while she wrings
out the rag. "You take more interest in this old goober than you
ever showed me."

He's annoyed she's gone back to that. "He's a man, you're
a woman. It's different."

"Uh-huh." She grabs a handful of padlocks from a drawer.

"You had no business calling him a homo."

"It was just an idea. It never crossed your mind?"

"No," Clay lies. To admit he'd considered it might make
him look queer, or if not queer, then meek and stupid that he
could spend time with a man he once suspected was a faggot,
even take off his shirt for him. "He's an artist. A gentleman. And
old. He's too old to think about any kind of sex with anyone."

"The old men I've known seemed to think about nothing
*but* sex." She is snapping padlocks on the cabinets and cooler.

"I haven't met him. But after seeing his movie, I picture him looking like that old fruit in the movie. Dr. Whatcha-torius."

"He doesn't. Not a bit." But he did, didn't he? A little. The lizardy close-lipped smile. His accent. Except he was thinner than Whale, his nose beaky where Whale's is normal, and the movie was made twenty years ago, when Whale would've looked completely different.

Clay can feel himself getting angry again, and he remembers the jukebox, still dead and angled out from the wall. He goes over to fix it, ducking behind and sticking the plug in. Straining his muscles to shift the machine back makes him want to use those muscles for something better. He suddenly wants to make love to Betty, peel back her toughness to the sweetness at her core, and prove how silly she is to think there could be anything queer between him and Mr. Whale.

He pulls a handful of change from his pocket and considers playing the Patsy Cline song she likes, but he has no nickles.

"You almost done?" he asks.

"Just about."

"You want to walk on the beach?"

She looks at him, calmly, curiously. "I got to go home."

"You didn't want to go for a swim?"

She begins to smile. Then she snaps her mouth wide open and goes, "Hghghgh"—the Bride's furious cat hiss.

He laughs, lamely. "What's that mean?"

She laughs with him and shakes her head. "It means it's too cold to go swimming. And I don't mean the water."

"I wasn't going to try anything."

"Yeah, and I'm not going to smoke more cigarettes. Uh-uh, Clay. You vamoose. I'm going home."

But she's talking to him again, which is a good sign. He won't give up. He patiently waits by the front door while Betty turns out the lights. Why did she have to ruin a good thing by changing the rules on him? She's thirty and divorced, but the body beneath her sloppy clothes can still look good when he's in the right mood. They were both in the right mood the first time a few months ago, another night when Clay closed out the place and it was Betty who suggested they go swimming. They were both tipsy and the moonless night was so dark he didn't know her white patches were bare skin until they were in the water and a wave knocked them together. She burst out laughing when she found Clay was still in his shorts. She pulled them right off him and he was all over her, in the water, on the beach, then later back at his trailer. His shorts will have washed up in China by now.

Betty walks briskly through the jack-o'-lantern glow of the jukebox, waving Clay outside with her hand. She pulls the door shut behind them and bends over to lock it. There's a glimpse of skin in the side slit of her shirttail.

"Come on, Betty. Let's go for a walk. Walk and talk. That's all. You complain we never talk."

"Talking about an old man who made a creepy movie isn't the talk I had in mind."

He goes with her out toward her car, a fat late-model Chevy, two-toned like a saddle shoe, parked in the white cone of the streetlight by the highway. The car is all Betty got in her divorce settlement. The ocean softly grinds in the darkness behind them.

"We'll talk about whatever you want to talk about."

"Give it a rest, Clay. Some other time, okay?" She opens the door on the driver's side.

The window is rolled down. Clay grabs the thick sill with both hands to keep her from pulling the door shut. "Look, I'm sorry about that girl."

It works. Betty does not get in but remains beside the car, the opened door between them.

"I didn't mean to hurt your feelings," Clay tells her.

She sharply looks him in the eye. "Yeah, you hurt me," she admits. "My pride more than my feelings. Don't go thinking I was in love with you. But getting sour over seeing you chase after that tease in a turtleneck made me wonder what the hell I was doing to myself. Letting you pull me into bed whenever the spirit moved you."

"You liked it."

"Oh, I loved it. It was fun. The screwing was fun."

"Yeah. So come back to the trailer." He jiggles the door, wanting her to step away so he can close it. "We'll pick up where we left off."

"No, Clay. That's all it was. Screwing. And I've decided it's time I stop screwing around."

"If you enjoy it, you should do it. Come on," he pleads, thrusting his head through the open window, propping his elbows inside the frame. "What else you going to do tonight? Sleep?"

"Clay, I'm telling you. I'm through with screwing around. With you, with myself. Look. I'm thirty years old."

"I still find you hot"—although the halogen glare of the streetlight brings out the bags under her eyes.

"No, Clay. What I mean is—I've got to get my act together. Just because I fucked up one marriage doesn't mean I should fuck up the rest of my life. I got to look at who I am, see what I want, and—get back on the damn horse. Another horse. I still have time to try again and get it right."

"You want to get married?"

"Yeah. Don't you? One day?"

His reflex is to pull back, but he's caught in the window. "You don't mean us?"

She bursts out laughing. "The look on your face! Uh-uh, loverboy. You're not marriage material. You're not even boyfriend material." The laugh relaxes her and she becomes humorously matter-of-fact. "You're fun. A big, fun, irresponsible kid. You treated me like the town pump, but I always wanted to know what it was like to be the bad girl in school. Now I know."

"I'm not a kid."

"No? What are you, then?" She lifts an elbow to park it on the roof of her car while she studies him. "What will you be ten years from now? Still cutting lawns? Still banging horny divorcées in your trailer?''

He withdraws from the window and straightens up, looking at her across the top of the door. ''I like my life. I'm a free man. I want to keep it that way.''

''A free man?'' she says with a sigh. ''Yeah, part of me wants something like that. But a free woman? There's no such thing. You're either a slut or an old maid in this world. No thanks. I've decided I can't live that life. Seeing some of the unattached broads who drift in and out of this joint. Uh-uh. You can live that way when you're young, but when you get to be my age . . .''

''You want a washer and dryer and Lassie.''

''Or something. Something with shape. This living from day to day, hangover to hangover, fuck to fuck''—she smiles pointedly at Clay. ''It's depressing. I don't have the stomach for it.''

''So you're going to husband hunt,'' he sneers.

''I'm not so cold-blooded as that. I've begun to hunt for a nine-to-five job in town, receptionist or secretary, something that'll give me a more conventional life. The chance to meet conventional men.''

''You're buying back into the bullshit.''

She lowers her head and grimaces. Her faces goes dark in the shadow of her forehead. ''You know, Clay, all your talk about bullshit sounds sometimes like sour grapes.''

''What does that mean?''

''The world didn't give you what you want, so it's all bullshit.''

''The world doesn't owe me squat, which is how I like it.''

''Do you? I wonder. You must think somebody owes you something, or you wouldn't go around with a chip on your shoulder the size of a cinder block.''

''Shit. A guy goes his own way, and everybody thinks he's got a chip on his shoulder.''

''I calls 'em as I sees 'em. Maybe I see that because I've got my own chip. I'm pissed at the world because I was a washout at marriage. Maybe you're pissed because you were a washout at everything you tried."

"I didn't wash out in college. I quit college, remember?"

"So you could join the Marines. I know," she says wearily. "But you were a washout there."

"That wasn't me. That was my frigging appendix."

"I'm not saying it's your fault. I'm just saying you didn't get what you wanted. Why you'd want to go to Korea and get your butt shot off is beyond me. But you wanted it and didn't get it."

"I wanted it because I was stupid. I've wised up since."

"You once said it was because you wanted war stories."

He glares at her, his jaw working forward. She makes it sound like kid stuff. He's furious with himself for having told her so much. Tell anyone about yourself and, sooner or later, they use it against you.

"I don't know, Clay. Seems like you mostly want things you can't have. Like being in a war or Scottie the virgin or being pals with an old movie director. You make yourself miserable."

His anger jumps from his jaw into his shoulders and arms. He suddenly wants to hit her.

But Betty keeps talking. "Me? I've decided to go after things I can get. They might not be the best things, but—"

"So you don't want to fuck. That's what you're telling me?"

She screws up her face at him. "Is that all this conversation means to you? Am I going to put out or not?"

"Damn straight. I'm sick of playing games." He grabs the door handle and jerks his head at the front seat. "Just get out of here, you think you got all the answers. Why're you such a bitch tonight?"

Her mouth goes slack and she stares. Clay does not know how he looks when he's mad, only what he feels and how other people react. She quickly gets into the car. Before she can pull the door shut, Clay slams it on her, hard. Her hands leap in front of her face, as if he'd hit her.

He steps back, wanting to hit her, terrified of hitting her.

He opens his hands with the fingers spread apart so he won't make a fist and punch at the windshield.

She frantically turns the key in the ignition. "I'm not being a bitch. I'm just being honest for once. No, I don't have the answers, but you don't either."

"Well, I think you're full of shit." He needs to hit something, not to break it but to break his anger, a force he can stop only with pain. There's nothing in sight except the creosote pole with the streetlight, and the car with Betty inside. He turns on his heel and walks away, before his violence takes over. He charges across the highway.

"What the hell are you afraid of?" she shouts after him. "You can't talk about anything real without blowing your stack!"

But Clay keeps going. He hears the pop of the clutch, then the ricochet of gravel and shells against the chassis as the Chevy peels out. A pair of headlights swing past him, but he's already twenty yards up the lane into the trailer park, too far away for her to shout more taunts and insults.

He didn't want to hurt Betty. He wanted to kiss her and love her and make her love him back. For tonight anyway. Why did she turn it into a contest, setting his life against hers, with one of them the loser? That's what triggered his anger, he thinks, being called a loser. His blow up with Saylor was nothing compared to what he feels now, a rage as blindly solid as a fist. The emotion alone should knock over the garbage cans he passes as he storms up the lane. He hates this blind fury. He was once able to burn it up on the football field, then in boot camp at Pendleton. He wants to think he could have burned it out of himself for good if they sent him to Korea five years ago. But his own body fucked him there and left him stranded.

He walks right past his trailer. He can't shut himself in that fucking tin can. He continues up the lane, slapping his pockets for cigarettes, slapping himself on the head for having told Betty so much. He doesn't want things he can't have. It's just that none of the things he can get are worth wanting.

A dog in a carport starts to bark, as if set off by the silent hum of human anger. The porch light is on and Clay raises his arm to cover the glare so he can see if the dog's tied up. And he glimpses again the damn tattoo that he paid to have needled into his skin one night in San Diego after boot camp.

He had loved the Marines. It was where he belonged, he once thought, a man among men. There was a war in Korea, not a world war but something more real than the idiocy of cooling his heels in classrooms or bumping heads with other dumb jocks on a playing field. He was nobody at Kansas State, a second-string lineman, just another piece of meat on scholarship. But the Marines made Clay feel part of something important, feeding him skills and pride and a selfless love of the Corps. And then, when he was keyed up to such a pitch that nothing short of combat would release him, his body screwed it. He was running an obstacle course with his buddies, scrambling over a wooden wall when the dull ache in his side exploded into a handful of knives. He dropped to the ground and writhed while the drill instructor called him a candy-assed maggot, a no-good pussy who had to pee sitting down. The man continued the name-calling even when he understood what had happened, radioed for an ambulance, and rode with Clay to sick bay. They cut him open that night. The infection was so bad that he had to spend a full month in the hospital. If a gook bullet had done it, they would have patched Clay up and sent him back to the front. Because his own body did it, they dumped him out with a medical discharge.

That was five years ago, just down the coast at Pendleton, but it feels like the day before yesterday. Time has stood still since then. The tattoo now disgusts Clay, but you can't cut off your own arm. Despite himself, he plays it up now and then, even letting strangers believe he served in Korea. He comes away from their assumptions hating himself as a failure and a phony.

The pavement and trailer park give out and he stomps up the chalky dirt road toward the end of the box canyon, his boots pounding out smokelike puffs of dust in the dim starlight.

It's not just war stories he wants. He might have said that to Betty, but it's not what he meant. It's bigger than that. He wants to burn his soul clean by being part of something terrible and real, an intense experience that would prove he'd been somewhere. The world beats it into your skull that you must be a man, a real man, then denies you the opportunity to do anything about it except get drunk or fuck. Clay knows he'll never be famous. He doubts he'll ever be a success, whatever that might mean. But he wants to have something like a war story. He wants to have passed through an extraordinary experience, combat, a love affair, a harrowing adventure, even a crime. Heaven or hell, it didn't matter which, but a great drama that would take him out of his dead-end life and justify his existence. Then he could sit quietly on his laurels, or his thorns, knowing he had lived. Without such an experience, everything is bullshit and he is twisted in a knot, paralyzed.

Meeting the man who made *Frankenstein* doesn't count here, but it's something, isn't it? It's got to mean something.

Clay comes to the dump at the end of the canyon. He climbs into it, kicking at loose cans, looking for a thing he can punch without busting his hand. He learned the hard way not to hit things that can break, like windows or mirrors, or things that can break him, like brick walls. New-model refrigerators are good, the metal hulls flexible enough that they won't shatter your knuckles. But there's no Frigidaires up here, only a hard ancient icebox, rusted bedsprings, a pyramid of empty tins, and the shell of an old Buick squatting on bare hubs.

"Fuck!" He shouts the word at the cliff, for the raw, sudden violence of shouting. "Fuuuuck!"

He turns around. The trailer park is at his feet, dark boxes and streetlights, with no trees, only TV aerials and telephone poles over those canned lives. The distant dog continues to bark.

"Fuck you!" he shouts. "Fuck all of you!"

No light comes on down below. Nobody calls out for him to shut up. The nearest trailer is a hundred yards away.

"You spend your fucking lives asleep!" he cries. "You're fucking dead! Every one of you dumb fucks!"

His obscenities probably sound no worse than the howling

of a coyote down there, but Clay continues to shout, blasting out
his throat and lungs, getting the poison out of his head, proving
to himself that, dumb as he is, he's smarter than the rest of them.
They are all in a world of shit, but nobody knows it better than
Clay knows it.

# 10

It is after midnight in the house on Amalfi Drive. The shadows of the living room furniture tug and snap in a twitchy blue glow. The ceramic spaniels on the mantel keep changing their expressions. A square little ghost twitches in a window, the reflection of the seventeen-inch Magnavox softly roaring in its cherry-wood cabinet.

James Whale sits up late with Maria to watch an old movie. Both are in bathrobes and slippers, and there is a half-empty glass of milk and a plate with cookie crumbs on Whale's TV tray. Maria's hair is down, a loose black hood that spills around her shoulders. She sits in a corner of the sofa, her arms folded tightly across her chest, her chin lifted in disapproval. Then the Monster reappears and her frown pops open to suck air through her frightened little teeth. Whale sits lower than his knees in the leather club chair, unamused by her fear, unafraid of the movie, moved now and then only to pity.

His poor sad movie. He has stopped being angry over what they've done to it. From the start, the thing is a shadow of itself, not just pixeled like a newspaper photo and shriveled to fit inside a piece of furniture, but amputated, butchered. They chopped off his pretty prologue: Elsa as Mary Shelley daintily chatted about monsters with Percy Shelley and Lord Byron while lightning flashed outside their mountain villa. The prologue was intended to let people know this was not just another horror picture but something stylish and different, and to show the studio he could do a costume drama they had not yet assigned. But the prologue is gone, and scattered throughout are scenes he never shot, episodes involving filter-tipped cigarettes and a local automobile dealer and the spasmodic cartoon beaver who wants you to brush-a brush-a brush-a with Ipana. Yes, he knows these are "commercials" and every viewer will understand they're not part of the picture, but it's disconcerting to see Karloff stumbling through the woods on his way to a rendezvous with—a woman in a white owl costume peddling cheap cigars?

Maria unclenches her arms to close the bathrobe over her throat. "Oh, that monster," she says in a chilled voice. "How could you be working with him?"

"Don't be silly, Maria. He's an actor. A very proper actor. And the dullest fellow imaginable."

But Whale can't connect what he watches with memories of being on a soundstage with Karloff and the others. A finished picture is as seamless as a completed jigsaw puzzle. You forget the anxiety and excitement of finding each piece. The puzzle has a life of its own, as if it had been assembled by somebody else. Whale never watched any of his movies after the previews. All he saw back then were a thousand mistakes and missed opportunities. All he notices tonight, at first, are actors, old friends, people he hasn't seen in years. He goes in and out of his movie as if he were idly flipping through a photo album.

Here is Una O'Connor as the hysterical biddy—those ridiculous ribbons were an inspired touch. It's good to hear her gobbling like an old turkey hen again, and her lovely comic screech. He hasn't spoken to Una in months. He should ring her up. Una's the only cast member with whom he's stayed in touch.

Here is Colin Clive as Frankenstein. Alive again, or as alive as anyone can be when preserved in a performance, pickled in aspic. He was quite handsome, in his wooden, shell-shocked way, and not wooden with narcissism as most handsome actors are, but with nerves, stage fright. You could get a good performance out of Clive if you tapped into those nerves with the help of a drink or two. Otherwise you just let him run on in his West End leading man fashion, as he does in his conversation with Mrs. Frankenstein—Whale can't remember the actress's name—and trust the audience to know they're not to take the scene seriously.

They chatter about mysteries of death and secrets of eternal life, and Whale is startled. He doesn't remember this dialogue, pious blather thrown in by the screenwriters to fake a little moral purpose. The phrases play differently tonight, sound more meaningful than intended. The movie had been nothing more than a bit of fun, an elaborate joke at the expense of the studio that insisted he make a sequel. He wasn't saying anything serious here. Was he?

Ah, but here is dear Thesiger. Whale feels his heart lift when the familiar turned-up nose and delicately crow's-footed eyes are thrust into the camera. He has not seen his old friend in years, not since Thesiger returned to England. He had loved the man like an older brother, admiring his originality and aristocratic disdain for what other people thought of him. They managed to get some of his droll perversity into Pretorius, he and Thesiger conspiring to make Pretorius as gay as a goose, a woman-hating auntie. They were subtle about it, an inside joke in a picture full of inside jokes. Junior Laemmle and his father never guessed what was going on. Oh, but you can have fun when you're working for innocents.

There is comedy throughout the picture, macabre yet genuine wit. They laughed constantly while making *Bride*—everyone except Karloff, of course. Has anybody ever noticed the picture is deliberately funny? Whale doubts that the people watching tonight will catch the humor, even with Franz Waxman's music constantly declaring where one should chuckle. People are so earnest nowadays. Will anyone except a few antiquarians like that Kay fellow even be watching? Some children perhaps, and teenage boys who hope to frighten their girlfriends into vulnerable snuggling. Whale wants to be pleased by the thought that, all over greater Los Angeles, young men are using him to get into girls' knickers.

What do women want? A TV announcer answers the question with the phrase "The Tappan Self-Cleaning Oven and Range."

The movie in the cherrywood cabinet is as fragmented and scattered as the mind of the man watching it.

The scene with the blind hermit is more earnest and sanctimonious than Whale remembers. He rotates his hand at the wrist, trying to hurry the players on and get it over with. But then, at the fade-out, he sees something he forgot. He lets out a sharp, "Ha-ha!"

Maria turns, alarmed he laughed at what she probably thinks is sweet: the Monster has a friend.

"He is not going to kill the old man?" she asks worriedly. She knows his humor all too well.

"No, Maria. My heart isn't that black. A private joke. You wouldn't understand."

Because, seen from behind, the hermit praying and shuddering over the prostrate Karloff seems to be rendering him an obscene service. Neither Karloff nor the contract ham with the beard ever knew, only the camera operator who called Whale over and said they might try another angle, this one looked like a blow job. "My boy, you have a very dirty mind," Whale told him, secretly delighted with the chance for mischief. When he saw the rushes, however, he was sure they'd gone too far. During the editing, he had the printer quickly iris in on the crucifix on the wall, which might add insult to injury but should throw the Miss Grundys off his scent. And it worked. Junior fretted over

CHRISTOPHER BRAM

what the Hays Office might make of a moment when the villagers
hoisted Karloff like Christ on a cross over the cart, but he never
noticed the fellatio religioso.

Karloff lurches through the cemetery. The blasted, treeless
landscape is seen from a low angle, as if viewed from the fire
step of a trench. Whale's heart beats faster. But it's only a set on
a Universal soundstage, scaffolding and wire mesh covered with
dirt in front of a painted cyclorama. Karloff lifts the lid of a
sarcophagus and climbs down into the crypt.

Dear old Thesiger again, in the vaulted crypt that, without
the cobwebs and skeletons, had been the vaulted entrance hall
of Frankenstein's castle. Oh, they were clever in their doubling
of stage sets. Then Karloff and Thesiger chat, over the coffin lid
that Thesiger uses as a dinner table. The cigars they smoke are
Whale's own brand of hand-rolled Havanas, selected so that he
might keep any leftovers for himself.

"Love dead. Hate living," Karloff groans.

And Whale is startled once more. Here it is again, more talk
of death. "Wiife," says Karloff, tenderly cupping a plaster-of-paris
skull in his hands, as if it is death he wants to marry.

It's only a joke. The whole scene was intended as a joke,
impudent and funny, but Whale is struck by it, excited.

Love death, hate living. Yes. He definitely hates living the
life now allowed him. But does he love death? No, not yet. The
movie suggests he did, at one time. The whole picture is about
death, a comedy about death, but its jokes do not have the naive
flippancy of a young man who knows nothing of dying. They have
the slippery weight of dream. Whale wants the jokes to mean
something, to show him a truth, the way dreams can show you
things that you're not yet ready to see awake.

This isn't a dream, of course. It's a movie, an old job of
contract storytelling with a few private jokes worked in. But the
darkest jokes can have a secret truth. You think you're making a
joke, when in fact you're confessing a terrible fear or desire. They
don't call this business the dream factory for nothing, although

they're supposed to be the dreams of the audience, not the makers.

Maria's voice breaks into his thoughts. "Why are we watching this, Mr. Jimmy? It is too horrible."

"Then go to bed if you don't like it!"

"No. I have to see how it ends. If I don't know, I will be tossing and turning in worry."

Yes, that was all he intended here. He wanted to amuse himself by telling a story that would give simpler souls nightmares. Maria's soul is simpler than most. She seems to feel no sympathy for the Monster, no pity, only fear. She also believes in life after death, eternal punishments and rewards.

The Monster has kidnapped Frankenstein's wife—that was what upset Maria—and the doctors are in the laboratory now. The end of the picture is near.

Where was he? He had been riding a train of thought toward something interesting when Maria made him jump the track. But he cannot recover what he'd been thinking. All he can think now is that the picture will end soon and he'll have to go to bed. He worries over how he'll sleep tonight. His body is exhausted, but his mind is too agitated, too full of unfinished thoughts and images. If only his damned yardman hadn't told him he'd be on the late show, he wouldn't be trapped with this old dream in his living room.

There are no people in the movie now, only a race of rapidly cut shots, machines and sparks. They are making the Bride.

Whale crosses one bony leg over the other and discovers an erection under his robe. Not a full erection but a slight thickening of prick, warm and fat. He cannot remember the last time he got hard—certainly not since his stroke. He cannot be hard for Karloff, can he? But he had been thinking about death.

All he can see in his mind's eye is the murky sketch from yesterday afternoon, a sketch that had turned into an enormous doodle when he gave up the pretense of even pretending to draw. He blindly penciled layers of cross-hatching and squiggles over the clumsy outline while his mind concentrated on finding words that would enable him to unpack aloud the sensations that had flooded up from a commonplace jar of dripping—his very head was like a jar of dripping. And on the other side of the easel, with the skittish repose of a horse standing at rest in its traces, was his shirtless yardman, Death Before Dishonor. No, the fellow has a name. Clay Boone: a lump of Clay, a Boone of contention.

"She is hideous," exclaims Maria to the ringing of wedding bells.

"She is beautiful," Whale declares.

He is looking at Elsa in her Nefertiti hairdo, but he is thinking about Boone, stocky and motionless, a patchwork of tan and pink and white, lightly sweating like marble. What will Boone make of this movie? Will he think its maker monstrous or merely silly? Will he even be watching tonight, or did he mention the show just to butter up his employer? Why should it matter? Who was Boone anyway that he should matter to Whale except as a challenging game? Whale is suddenly angry that he had lost sight of yesterday's real purpose to natter about a past that was best forgotten. He never did get Boone out of his boots, much less his trousers. It had worried him when the shirt came off so easily. He did not want to finish his game too quickly.

"We belong dead."

Exactly. But not yet. Not until the game is played out.

Karloff pulls the lever and blows everyone to atoms.

A cheap stunt, a theatrical flourish to end this particular game. And a sly trick on the poor masses who went to the movies for love stories. He gave his monster a mate, then promptly killed them both. A *Liebestod* for monsters, with more *tod* than *lieb*. The scale model of the tower blows up nicely. The Laemmles' little white airplane circles the plasticine globe.

"Ugh," goes Maria, shivering as she stands. "I am sorry, Mr. Jimmy, but your movie is not my cup of tea. Still, I am glad there is a happy ending. The bad people are dead and the good people live." She goes to the Magnavox and hits the button with the flat of her palm, as if cuffing an unruly child. She closes the cabinet doors and becomes herself again. "Time for bed, Mr. Jimmy. The doctor will not forgive me if he hears you stay up so late."

"He won't give a damn."

"No. We want you to get better. You must have your sleep." She stands before him to offer a hand up.

He peevishly waves her hand aside and levers himself from the chair on his own. His joints ache and the eternal headache softly throbs in his crown. He readjusts his robe, but his erection faded long ago, almost as soon as he started to think about Boone.

"Let me finish here," she declares, lifting the TV tray on its stand and nodding him toward his bedroom. "Then I will come with your medicines."

Whale shifts his cold feet deeper into his slippers and shuffles down the hall. Love dead, hate living. He lives in his own guest room now, on the ground floor in the elbow of the house, facing the garage. He wants to move back upstairs to the master bedroom, despite the twin beds up there, one of them empty. But they say that is too far from Maria if he should need her in the middle of the night. Maria's quarters are over the garage, with stairs going down to the utility room at the end of the downstairs hall. He comes to his door and turns on the light: curtains covered with a modern geometric print, an Italian dresser and headboard, a white slab with one corner of the covers neatly turned down. He crosses to the bathroom, refusing to look at his bed.

He hates the end of each day, despises and fears this hour when he must turn in. Life can be a fog when he's awake, especially when he's tired, but real things, voices and objects, still come to him through that fog. The night, when he's expected to sleep, is all fog, infinite and empty. It would be different if there were true sleep, but he must choose each night between two lesser sleeps. He can lie down naturally and suffer the fragmented dreams and constant wakings of a man who only floats on sleep, a night that will last forever. Or he can take his pheno and sink like a stone into a chemical torpor, dreamless and unreal. The drug lingers the next day, so that every thought will be slow and soft, like rotting sugarplums, every sensation standing off at a distance.

He is sitting in the bathroom with his robe bunched behind him, his pajama bottoms around his ankles. He does this every night, whether or not his bowels need to move, a precaution taken from his fear of incontinence. He is not incontinent, not yet anyway, except for his memory. Sitting on the cool seat now, surrounded by chromium fixtures and tiles like pink-glazed biscuits, he remembers remembering the outdoor privy in Dudley. He did not hallucinate the smell of it yesterday, and he doesn't now, but he does remember how pleasingly familiar that smell could be, even though it was damp wood and human shit, his own family's shit. A muddy landscape of curds and snakes and his own childish worms were jumbled together below, in twisted, broken folds, like wrinkles of brain.

His head is full of shit, but his bowels are dry. He pisses, not in a virile stream but in spurts and dribbles. There's the customary stinging at the end when he wrings out his bladder. He neatly folds a silken length of tissue—it was coarse newspaper in Dudley—but there's no flicker of old pleasures in touching his own anus anymore. It's knotted up like a tightly wound rubber band.

If his mind is going to lurch backward, why won't it dwell on the pleasures of the flesh, not its embarrassments? He pulls up his pajamas and buttons them. He touches the handle and there's a clean roar of water. He is like the proverbial drowning man whose life flashes before his eyes. Or no, he is like a city during a blackout, all manner of deformed, forgotten creatures coming out to wander his pitch-black streets.

Yesterday, when it happened at the easel, he had exorcised his creatures in talk, completely squandering that first session with Boone. And yet, the talking made him feel better. He had finished their session exhausted yet relieved. Why? He doesn't know, unless it's that the talking made him aware of just how far he's come.

He is sitting up in bed, legs pinned beneath clean, sunbaked sheets, when Maria knocks. She enters with yet another tray, this one loaded with bottles and vials and a handblown venetian glass filled with water. He wonders if telling Maria about the privy in Dudley will wash out his mind; he does not want to lie in the dark with images of family turds.

"I can trust you to take them all, Mr. Jimmy?" The nurse who lived with them during his first weeks home used to stand by as he took each pill. Maria knows how he hated that.

"I'll be fine, Maria. Thank you." He looks at her heavy, woeful eyes. "You should go to bed," he tells her. "I'm sorry I kept you up so late."

"Not at all, Mr. Jimmy. I was curious what shows you make when you were working. I hope it will not give me nightmares." Her jaw trembles, but then she opens it wide in a yawn. "Sorry, it is late," she agrees. "Good night," and she goes, pulling the door behind her, not shut but with a gap of six inches.

No, he could not talk to Maria about shit. Even before the yawn, there was something about her large, impassive face that dispersed any desire to tell stories. Unlike Boone's face, which had focused that desire, made Whale want to talk, as if that meaty statue might be amused or teased or confused into life with the right, peculiar anecdote from the past.

He takes the pills, one by one, swallowing each with a mouthful of water, with no thought until he comes to the last bottle, the phenobarbital. He holds the bottle of Luminal, looking at the label, trying to decide which form of sleep he wants tonight, the sleepless sleep or the deadly sleep that will make him a zombie tomorrow. But he has nothing scheduled tomorrow, no fabulous parties, no joyrides up the coast, no visitors. He will not see Boone again until next Tuesday, which is unfortunate. He finished yesterday's session so exhausted he didn't think he could do it again anytime soon, or would need to. He opens the pheno bottle to shake out a capsule.

A dozen spill into his palm. Ugly purplish brown jellies. He holds a landscape of shit in his hand.

Luminal. Like light. Such a droll name for a pill full of shadows and darkness. It would be so simple to take two, three, four—all of them. That would end this idiotic business once and for all. But it feels too much like the death he fears, not so much a coming of death as a slow failing of life, consciousness dispersing itself in sleep and dreams and oblivion. He wants to see death coming at him.

One by one, he returns the capsules to their bottle, until a single capsule remains. He places it on his tongue, finishes the water and sets the beautiful glass on the dresser. He turns out the table lamp and lies on his back in the dark, waiting.

They used to say you never hear the one with your name on it. But Whale wants to hear and see death coming at him. He wants it to be sharp and hard, with a human face. He wants it to have a man's face, brutish and dumb, with a wide nose like Clay Boone's.

A romantic thought, a pretty thought, but the barbiturate is already taking effect, breaking circuits, turning out lights. He can see through his closed eyelids to the ceiling overhead. He can accept as perfectly plausible his hope that Clay Boone will kill him. Yes, that is what he wants. That is what he's been wanting all along. He remembers fearing violence from the fellow, but you often fear what you secretly want, or else why would you imagine it in the first place? Boone has the face of a killer. He does, although there was a moment yesterday when he smiled and looked as innocent as a box of cornflakes. But Whale can fix that. He can find the killer in the boy.

The muscles relax and the joints grow numb as mind separates from body, and here is the Monster again, not played by Karloff but by Boone. Whale is not surprised. He seems to have known all along that Boone is his monster, more authentic, more convincing than Karloff, without that actor's stuffy personality to undo the seductive fantasy of brute force. Boone takes Whale in his arms, cradles him like a child, and carries him up the hill.

And Whale does not resist but surrenders all willpower, all responsibility, becoming as weightless as a feather. The Monster shifts his tattooed arm around and eases first a finger, then the hand, then his whole arm into Whale, opening him from below to slide through his bowels until Whale can feel the fist inside his throat. The fist gently opens to stroke the brain beneath the skull, smoothing away the achy twists and convolutions that cause him so much suffering. The pain of the smoothing is intense, excruciating, but imaginable just beyond that pain, visible on the other side, is peace and clarity and rest.

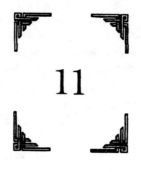

# 11

NIGHT. RAIN. THE WHISTLING OF WIND. A ZIGZAG OF LIGHTNING flashes behind a tall gabled villa. The villa stands on a hilltop over a valley full of bottlebrush pines. Its lone illuminated window comes toward us through the trees, closer, closer.

"Cut!"

The wind instantly stops. The rain flutters a moment longer, only it's not water but shredded tinsel. Something rises behind the villa, a man with a necktie and pencil-thin mustache, exposing the villa as a three-foot-high model. The pines like bottle brushes *are* bottle brushes, dipped in tar. Valley and model occupy a large table in the corner of a dark warehouse. A movie camera bigger than the villa glides back on four feet of track and a boy in a crushed fedora steps forward to brush the landscape with whisk broom.

"What do you think, Mr. Whale?" asks the man behind the table.

In the shadows beneath a blinkered key light, a trim figure goes, "Hmmmm"—a wince made audible. "No. Much too literal. Dreadful. Like a Christmas window at Harrod's."

He steps into the spill of light, an elbow in one hand, the other hand gripping his chin. He wears a suit with wide lapels and a polka-dot display handkerchief. James Whale at forty-five has full lips and a smooth complexion that enable him to pass as thirty-eight, his face scored only by the scowl lines running down from his nostrils.

It is February 13, 1935, Day 28 of Production #729 at Universal Studio, *The Bride of Frankenstein.* Elsa Lanchester has been contracted for seven days of work. They spent last week shooting the prologue where she played Mary Shelley. Today they begin the scene when the bride is unveiled. The actors are still getting into makeup, so Whale has dropped by Special Effects to see how the shot of the Shelley villa exterior is coming, important to him because it's the first shot of the movie.

Everyone prepares for another take, the men at the lights and camera, the fellow operating the blower, the partner who worked the oversized flour sifter that shook out the chopped tinsel. Whale remains calm and still in the middle of it all, the axle of a furiously spinning wheel.

Fulton, the man behind the villa, has climbed out beneath the table. "I'm not happy with the shot either," he confesses.

"It needs something. Mystery?" Whale wonders. "We begin with the cliche. The dark and stormy night. And then, when the audience thinks this is only another horror picture, we cut inside the villa, to the genteel folderol of Byron and the Shelleys. That should make them sit up and pay notice."

Fulton knows how directors love to hear themselves talk, thinking aloud in the presence of others. Actors might find it useful, but technicians only want the specifics.

"The audience knows the cliché already," Whale tells himself. "They could do this shot in their sleep. So yes. Kill a few lights. Shoot it dark. It's the lights you don't turn on that count.

Maybe a soft light on the roof. Those gables are worth seeing."
That's as close as he comes to complimenting Fulton on the
model. "The lightning bolt, however, is wretched."

"We need to work on the lightning," Fulton admits. They
flashed a light on a shiny zigzag of metal hung behind the table.

"Forget the lightning. Or no, diddle a spot on the side of
the villa. That and the sound of thunder should be sufficient.
We'll be inside before the audience realizes they didn't see any
lightning."

Fulton looks at the Fresnels and baby spots mounted around
the table. "Benny! Kill three and seven, four and eight." He
turns back to Whale. "How about some smoke coming from the
chimney? Or would that be too literal?"

"Smoke? Hmmm." His eyebrows go up.

"The telephone, Herr Whale." A fat young man with thick
glasses and sleeveless argyle sweater stands by: Heini, his personal
assistant. "Cousin Carl is on the line."

Whale ignores the boy and concentrates on picturing the
shot with smoke.

"He is wanting urgently to talk, Herr Whale." Heini points
to a desk in the corner with an unhooked telephone under a
gooseneck lamp.

Whale finishes his thought. "Yes. Smoke. Twirling in the
wind," he tells Fulton. "Can that be arranged?"

"Water off a duck's ass," Fulton replies, and heads toward
the table.

Whale strides to the desk to see what his bloody producer
wants. "Good morning, Carl."

But Junior isn't on the phone, only his secretary. "I'll connect you to Mr. Laemmle."

"Jim! What are you doing at Special Effects? You should be
at Stage C. Do I have to remind you we're four days behind
schedule on this picture?" Junior is in his baby mogul mood this
morning, acting as though the world would stop turning if he
weren't there to keep it going with phone calls.

"They're still setting up, Carl. And Jack won't be finished

with Elsa for another hour. I wanted to see how they're coming with our opening shot. Good thing too, because what they've done is no more frightening than a model train set."

"You've been spending too much time on this prologue, Jim. And nobody I've talked to thinks it's necessary."

"It's necessary, trust me."

"I trust you. You know I trust you. But I wish you'd give as much attention to your actors as you do to these toys."

"My actors can take care of themselves, thank you. It's up to me to insure that these toys, as you call them, have a bit of life."

"Jim. I didn't call to argue. Could you just get over to the lab set? Please? I'll feel a lot better."

"Certainly, Carl. If it makes you feel better. Good-bye." He regrets having to humor the boy, but Carl Junior is the ostensible head of the studio, and personally producing this picture. It's like having no boss at all and Whale's been free to do whatever he wants, so long as he lets Junior believe now and then that he's in charge. It could be much worse. David speaks in worshipful tones about his chief over at MGM, the almighty Thalberg, but Whale knows he would hate working for such a meddlesome know-it-all, a businessman who knows just enough to mistake himself for an artist.

They are finishing at the table. The unit cameraman fears it's too dark, but Fulton is confident. The boy in the fedora has rigged a thimble in the chimney and is packing it with smoke gum. Whale is sorry he can't stay and watch another take, but Fulton is a good man. He can trust Fulton to do his best.

The bright sunlight outside is made brighter by the whitewashed walls of squat offices and high hangarlike soundstages. It's early yet, and the cool air feels good after the acrid simmer of hot lights, rubber, and machine oil. Whale walks briskly, left hand in his pocket, right hand cupping a newly lit cigarette. His straight-legged gait barely breaks the crease of his slacks. Heini huffs and puffs beside him like an asthmatic little pig.

"We'll stop by Makeup and see how Jack is coming. See how

the look works on Elsa. My chief fear is it'll bury her unearthly quality. Or make her appear no worse than a trollop after a bender. Well, if it doesn't work yet, we can spend the morning shooting inserts."

"*Ja ja*, Herr Whale."

Whale doubts that Heini's English is good enough for him to understand half of what he's saying. He talks to the boy only to save himself from having to greet any acquaintances they pass while he collects his thoughts.

A director must perpetually think about a dozen different things at once while shooting a picture. Whale has already put the opening shot out of his mind and now worries about the sobriety of his chief cameraman today, the tilting of the table that wouldn't tilt yesterday, the prickliness of Thesiger, who resents being upstaged by sparking appliances in this sequence, but, most of all, the makeup for the bride that Whale sketched and Pierce has executed, but only on a female assistant. They have not yet seen how it works on Elsa.

Extras pour out of a soundstage to crowd around a canteen wagon. A small mountain of breakfast cereal stands in an alley, puffed wheat that was used to simulate a blizzard and now attracts a yellow constellation of bees.

"*Guten Morgen*, Herr Doktor Rauss," Heini calls out to a fellow in pince-nez and a jet-black suit.

"*Guten Morgen*, Heinrich," the fellow replies, gripping a packet that shows he's only an errand boy now.

There are more Germans on the lot than ever. Fearing bad times ahead in Germany, Carl Senior is bringing relatives over from his hometown of Laupheim. David says that Thalberg and other American Jews think the old man's simply sore that his hometown changed the name of Laemmlestrasse to Hitlerstrasse. Whale has no animosity toward these Germans. He gives the orders now, and if Universal occasionally reminds him of his year in a prisoner-of-war camp, his memories of that time are mostly good ones. What does annoy Whale is that Uncle Carl didn't assign him a leaner, more handsome nephew, as if fearful for his kinsmen's virtue. As if his horror king could think of monkey business when he's in the middle of a picture—even David complains during production. Still, it would've been nice to have a pretty face to look at.

Special Makeup is located across an alley from Stage C. Heini jumps forward to open the screen door for Whale. The waiting room suggests a dentist's office and, in the shop itself, Jack Pierce wears a dentist's white tunic. Elsa and Karloff sit side by side in dentist chairs, cloths around their necks, heads tilted back. Pierce is patting the hair drawn over a cage on Elsa's head. He looks up, sees Whale, and breaks into a sly, conspiratorial grin.

Pierce has outdone himself and knows it. Elsa looks marvelous, a beautiful corpse.

Her eyes are closed; she hasn't heard Whale enter. "You done yet, love? I am absolutely dying for a fag."

Whale tiptoes in for a better look. Her dead-white skin is bruised around the cheekbones. Her cylinder of hair suggests a body preserved a thousand years by Egyptian black arts.

Karloff watches from the immobilized, squared head that's now as familiar as an old shoe. He has a mouthpiece so he can breathe while the assistant adds another coat of green sizing. "Goo' 'orning, 'ames," he gurgles.

"Good morning, Boris. And a very good morning to you, my dear."

Elsa's eyes snap open.

Yes, it's darling Elsa in that ruin. Her enormous eyes. The lively pupils haunt her face like a lost soul trapped in a corroded statue. At long last, Whale has provided his friend with a role worthy of her. He looks for something wrong, something to improve, but she is uncanny, perfect.

"Uh-oh," she murmurs. "The way you look at me, James. What have you done to me this time?"

There are no mirrors on the walls; she has no idea.

"I just thank my stars I'm through with being muzzed up in bandages. Please, love. Tell me we're finished with that. No more retakes?"

"You know how much I regretted putting you through that, my dear." Whale can't help smiling. The smile wickedly deepens when he tells Pierce, "Bring a mirror. Let the Bride feast upon her visage."

Elsa pulls herself up and is confused by the weight on her head. "Boris? Do I look a fright?"

Karloff cuts his eyes at her and shrugs, not only blasé over this but irked that she's getting all the attention.

Pierce lifts a large mirror in a wooden frame. "Behold, the Bride of Frankenstein," he proclaims in nasal New Yorkese.

Elsa stares. She snaps her head left, right, up, down, startled by the sight of herself, electrocuted into frightened, spastic jerks. "Oh, James."

And Whale instantly sees the spasms as camera angles, close-ups left, right, middle, quickly cut together, the camera startled by the sight of the Bride. He wants to use that. He has to use it, even if it means reconceiving the scene. This head deserves a frantic flurry of angles.

"And you said there'd be some of me," Elsa says in a small, injured voice. "Nobody's going to know me in this getup, not even Charles."

"Nonsense, my dear. You look extraordinary." Actors are the blindest people in the world, even one with as little conventional vanity as Elsa. "Today's script," he tells Heini. "Quick. And a pencil. Give me a pencil."

"I suppose I should be grateful," she sighs. "Nobody will know this is me and I won't do my career any harm. But you said this would be jolly fun, James. I should have known you'd be the one having the lark, not me."

No longer listening, Whale scans the page of shooting script, the margin marked in pencil: CU, MS, MLS, lines running into the text so the editor will know where to cut. They had planned to cover three pages today in medium shots, up to the Monster's entrance. Whale pencils in a bracket and scribbles, "CU a, b, c, d—MOS." It will work. Whale holds the entire movie in his head and knows instantly that this will work.

"Jack, send Elsa to the set as soon as you're done. I want to get on this right away. And don't worry about finishing Boris before lunch. Sorry, Boris, we won't get to you until this afternoon."

"I 'ish you 'old 'e 'ooner," Karloff grumbles. The assistant removes his mouthpiece so he can finish in his plummy, mournful lisp. "I could have spent the morning tending to my roses."

Whale doesn't have the heart to tell him they might not need the Monster at all today, not when Karloff has already spent three hours in Pierce's chair. He hurries outside to Stage C, delighted by the new shots, eager to try them. Spur-of-the-moment discoveries like this make the chore of production exciting. He couldn't do this working for a Thalberg, who insists you stick to the script and change neither dialogue nor even camera angles without his approval. As if one could paint a picture by telegram.

The cathedral interior of Stage C is completely filled by the laboratory set. A stone wall of plaster and canvas goes clear up to the flies four stories overhead. The floor below is full of cables and lights and the shiny electrical gizmos Strickfaden concocted. A glorious set, although a week of shooting has made it less startling, more ordinary. Electricians adjust the klieg lights on the wooden tower beside the Bride's table. Stagehands hoist a two-story tarp like a sail to absorb the echoes.

Colin Clive and Ernest Thesiger are in, sitting off to the side in full makeup and costume. They have their own dressing rooms, but nobody except Karloff stays in the airless beaverboard cubicles longer than necessary. Clive mumbles earnestly over his script. Thesiger pinches his face over the needle he dips in and out of an embroidery ring.

Whale goes straight to John Mescall, the cameraman, while Heini fetches the assistant director and script girl for a quick conference. Mescall's face is already unfocused, his hair mussed, his breath like a medicine cabinet. When Whale describes the close-ups, however, he snaps out of his stupor and is full of ideas for the lighting. So long as they can get him to the studio, Mescall is often at his best when he's had a few too many. Another man operates the camera. Dolores, the script girl, duly annotates new sheets in the log. Only the assistant director is skeptical, wondering how they will cover this in the master shot.

"Oh, damn the master," Whale tells him. "Only schoolboys and producers worry about masters."

Not until everything is set in motion does Whale go over to greet his actors. They express little interest when he tells them he's seen their bride and she looks wonderful.

"So long as the dear little bitch doesn't step on my lines," Thesiger mutters as he tugs a thread.

"When she touches my arm?" Clive worriedly asks. "Should I feel disgust? Or pity?"

"Don't concern yourself with that, Colin. We'll see what works best when we shoot it."

"Excuse me, Herr Whale. Cousin Carl on the telephone."

"Again?" Whale has to walk thirty yards across the soundstage to see what Junior wants this time.

"Have you done your first take, Jim?"

"No, Carl. We're waiting for Elsa, who'll be here at ten sharp, just as I told you."

"I don't mean to pressure you. I just want to know that we're on top of things."

"We're on top of the world, Carl. Good-bye." He sees no need to tell Junior about the additional shots that will set them back half a day at least.

Whale is with the assistant director and prop man, talking about the operating table—it still won't tilt properly—when all the banging and shouting suddenly changes pitch, then stops.

Pierce has come on the set, with Elsa on his arm. He is so proud of his creation he wants to show her off. She walks regally beside him, her hands and arms wrapped in bandages, the train of her long white robe thrown over one arm. She is smirking.

There's a wolf whistle from overhead, and laughter. Mescall

begins the applause that's taken up by everyone, causing Elsa to turn, model her outfit, and curtsy to her admirers. She is beginning to understand how striking she looks.

"My God," says Thesiger, who's set his needlepoint aside to come over and look. He leans backward when he studies her. "Is the audience to presume that Colin and I have done her hair? I thought we were mad scientists. Not hairdressers."

"Only a mad scientist could do this to a woman," Elsa titters, petting her piston of hair.

"Oh no, my dear. You look absolutely amazing." He shakes his head. "There's no way I can compete with you. The scene is yours. I can only pay homage to your creator"—he nods to Pierce—"and kiss the hem of your garment." He bows down and actually takes the hem but, instead of kissing it, draws the enormous robe away from her. "Oh my. You could fit all of Charles under there, couldn't you?"

"You old bugger," Elsa laughs, and snatches the robe away. "In the sequel, James, two lady scientists should make a monster. Me and Garbo, I think. And our monster would be Gary Cooper."

"How daring of you," says Thesiger. "I would've thought Leslie Howard would be more your line."

"More your line," Elsa quips.

"Oh no, my dear. My line nowadays runs to Rin Tin Tin. Dogs are so much more interesting than men. And I've never caught Robespierre rifling my drawers for loose cash or jewelry."

Whale smiles, without hearing a word of their banter. He stands apart, watching, thinking. He needs an establishing shot before the frantic close-ups. The damn table won't pivot, but Elsa is so striking that they shouldn't need to tilt her slowly toward the camera as planned. They will begin with a simple tableaux, the Bride flanked by her creators.

"John? Here's what we're doing." He explains the shot to Mescall. The assistant director listens in so he can relay the information to the sound people and props. Then Whale returns to his actors. "Colin? Please. It's time."

"Yes, Colin," says Thesiger. "Come see what they've done to our Elsa."

Clive walks over, glumly, timidly, as if afraid he's intruding. Whale has never known an actor to take so little pleasure in theater life. The son of a British army colonel, he treats his profession as something dirty, even criminal.

"Relax, my boy. You could do this scene in your sleep," Whale tells him.

Clive grits his teeth and nods.

It often requires repeated takes to get him up to pitch, bringing out the manic quality that can look like a nervous breakdown. If worse comes to worse, Whale can get Mescall to share a few nips from his flask with Clive.

Whale positions them in front of the upended table, Clive and Thesiger holding Elsa's robe out by the hems so that the first glimpse of her will suggest a Pre-Raphaelite angel.

The shadow of the sound boom passes back and forth while they rehearse. They are surrounded by technical people, all Americans, but in front of the camera is a corner that will be forever England.

"I gather we not only did her hair but dressed her," says Thesiger drily. "What a couple of queens we are, Colin."

Elsa giggles. Whale smiles. Clive looks distraught.

And that distraught look brings some life to his stiffness. Whale decides to tune it higher.

"Yes, a couple of flaming queens," he declares, mincingly, knowing how Clive hates effeminacy. "And Pretorius *is* a little in love with Frankenstein, you know."

Clive thinks he can hide his distress, but it reads clearly now. Years ago, when Whale directed him onstage in *Journey's End*, he talked the guilty fellow into bed, once. When you know what makes a man tick, you can get from him whatever you need.

"Yes. I think it's coming together," says Whale. "Shall we have a go?" He's afraid to look at his watch and hopes they can complete this shot before they break at noon. The close-ups will have to wait until after lunch.

He sits in the canvas director's chair that Heini set a few feet to the left of the camera. He will watch each take with his legs crossed, jogging his raised foot as if conducting the scene with his shoe. People who work with him have learned that the shoe stops wagging when he's displeased.

He nods to the assistant director.

"Quiet on the set!" the fellow shouts.

The warning bell rings.

"Lights!"

The kliegs sizzle and blaze, a handful of white suns.

"Sound!"

"Okay for sound," a man around the corner calls out.

"Camera!"

A young man with a clapboard steps in front of the camera. Whale won't notice until he sees the rushes that this new man is quite beefy and handsome.

"Scene two-fifteen. Take one," the assistant calls out.

Whale uses his most masculine, military voice to declare, "Action."

And the scene is no longer his. He can do nothing now except watch and listen and hope.

It is only a horror picture, but he gives it his complete attention. James Whale would never call his current state of mind happiness, but he is very happy here, fully engaged, intensely alive. He uses more of himself directing a picture, any picture where he is allowed to work freely, than in all other spheres of his life. There is the excitement of riding a dozen horses at once, the egotistical delight of having a hundred talented people at his command, the thrill of knowing that whatever he imagines can be made to happen. He feels enlarged by a studio soundstage, his imagination magnified, his wit and love of theater turned into magical powers.

Nevertheless, when he thinks about this particular project in the evening, he tells himself that it's a lark, nothing more. Great fun, not least because, when it is finished, he will have killed off his monster for good, and will never have to think about monsters again.

# 12

LIGHT. BRIGHTNESS. THE GLARE FADES TO RED, THEN PINK. A CRE-
pey pink light stitched with blood vessels.

What time is it? He overslept. And they're expecting him at
the studio! Bloody hell. He cannot remember what day it is, what
scene they are shooting, or even the name of the picture. He
might be able to fake his way through until he can steal a glance
at the script—except that he can't see. He panics when he understands: everything is pink because he's blind. His heart races,
his breath quickens. Not even the Laemmles are so foolish as to
overlook blindness in a movie director.

The pink cracks open, then rises like a curtain on a sunlit
landscape. Knobby ridges grip a snowy slope. His own hand grips
the pillow. Of course. He hasn't lost his sight. His eyes were
closed. He's in bed. Now, if only he can remember something
about the picture in production, everything will be fine. But as
he steps inside his thoughts, searching for a title, an actor, some-

thing, the pinkness returns. He sinks back down into his own warm blood and falls back to sleep.

He wakes again five minutes later, with no memory of his panic. This time there is only sunlight, body, and bladder. His body remembers more clearly than his mind what one must do: sit up, legs to the floor, feet into slippers. He waits for Maria to walk him to the toilet. He cannot find his way without Maria. He seems to have called her, because suddenly she is here. His mind is numb, dark except for a glimmer in the back corner, like a memory of himself that unhappily watches in the bathroom as a stooped woman indifferently plucks apart three buttons of his pajama fly. He can handle his own prick, thank God, but the buttons overwhelm him. He supports himself with a hand on a round shoulder. They stand side by side, frowning away from each other. His first clear emotion each day is shame.

In bed he sits up and waits for Maria to return with the breakfast tray. It will be another hour before he regains enough mind to shower, shave, and dress, all of which he insists on doing for himself. He is not yet ready to renounce those dignities.

He stares down at the plate of toast, cut-glass dish of marmalade, the cup and saucer filled with a black hand mirror of coffee. Every thought, every sensation comes to him through the wrong end of a jeweler's eyepiece. He sees one detail at a time, his mind stopping there, unable to see through to the activity that once knitted the details together. The threads of orange rind in translucent jelly are edged with sepia; he loses himself in their tangle. A new train of thought is required for him to take a knife and spread marmalade on a stick of buttered toast.

A life made up of isolated moments, epiphanies of trivia, is exhausting. Time doesn't help. Changing the phenobarbital dosage doesn't help. It seems to take longer each morning for him to regain himself, and all he regains is enough awareness to know his mind's not right. He vaguely remembers stumbling upon a better solution last night. He made an exciting discovery last night. What was it?

Oh yes. His yardman is going to kill him.

He calmly chews a mouthful of tartly sweet toast.

Yes. Why not? It's an odd, original notion, but he has always been attracted by what others find odd.

Then his thoughts slide into the topological twist and curl of a bone-china cup as his fingers slip around the delicate question mark of its handle; he forgets about murder. He continues breakfast in a tranquilized time out of time, each minute as mentally crowded as an hour, the hour afterward seeming to have lasted less than a minute.

When Maria removes the tray and he climbs up to enter the bathroom—on his own now, thick and headachy, but pain too comes to him through the wrong end of an eyepiece—all that remains of his discovery is a weightlessness at the back of his mind, a premonition that he has something to look forward to, something wonderful like Christmas or a birthday party.

In the bathroom he showers and shaves and combs the hair of several different bodies, some seen directly, others glimpsed in the mirror or his mind's eye. Out in the bedroom, he finds clothes neatly laid out on the remade bed, nice clothes, expensive clothes. It would be so much simpler to live in bathrobe and slippers, but he refuses to give in to the temptation, not when he worked so hard to win this life and the wardrobe that goes with it. He inspects the figure in the gilt-framed mirror over the dresser, hoping the clothes will bring him back to himself. They don't. The white shirt and paisley ascot are a costume worn by someone else, an old man with loose basset-skinned face and moist, bloodshot eyes. He goes into the hall, letting the momentum of routine carry him to the dining room table and the morning paper he is not yet able to read.

Maria comes from the kitchen and greets him as if this is her first glimpse of him today. It was another man whose breakfast she served in bed, another fellow whom she assisted over the WC.

"Good morning, Maria. I trust you slept well." He shakes the newspaper open and pretends to read the headlines.

"I had a nightmare, Mr. Jimmy. My husband comes to visit, only he is not my husband anymore but the Monster. I should never have watched your movie."

"Yes? You saw one of my pictures?"

"Your old monster movie. We watch together, remember?"

"Of course." Had they gone to the movies? He can't remember going out. Has he become so senile that he forgets something so rare as a night out? He is furious with himself for forgetting, then relieved to remember this fog will not last. Isn't something going to happen that will bring him back to himself?

"I think I'll take my coffee in the living room. Yes. Save us both the hike to the studio."

The sunny, grassy slope looks too steep for him this morning. And he does not want to be alone down there. Something about the studio, its paint-spattered floor, the easel that suggests a medieval instrument of torture when there's no canvas to prove its harmlessness, worries him. Here in the living room, at least, he can hear Maria knock about.

He sits in his leather club chair and makes a show of turning the enormous pages of the newspaper. Maria sets the collapsible TV tray beside him, places the silver-plated coffee service on it, and withdraws to the utility room. The soft warmth of the leather enters his bones. The drumming of the washing machine in the distance is as soothing as the drum of engines aboard an ocean liner. Very quickly, despite the coffee, despite the elaborate effort he put into preparing himself for daylight, the newspaper drops from his hand and softly crashes. His sleep is opaque and dreamless.

When he wakes again, the tall windows are full of light, the living room full of plush shadows and polished wood. There is more of him than before, more mind, more headache. His teeth are like lead. The power of the reversed eyepiece is decreasing. Another half dozen wakings and he might recover his focal length, only then it will be time for bed.

He can hear the wheezy inhale of a vacuum cleaner upstairs. He slowly stands up into gravity, a heavy marionette. He goes to the bay window. On the other side of the glass is the grassy slope with a square blue green eye at its foot. He goes to the door and opens it. He steps into an oven of light.

A spicy aroma of hot brush stings in his nostrils. Vertical blasts of green stand suspended in the air, cypress trees like tall, silent explosions. The day is so bright that he has to look down, at the grass. It needs mowing. Each blade is tipped with a tiny white scar where the sun singed the wound of its last cutting, but it already grows long and confused. Where is his man? Where is his Boone? He wants to see Boone. But there is nobody out in the sun, no living thing, not even birds. He will have to ask Maria when the yardman's next visit is scheduled. Because there is something else he wants Boone to do. Something nice. Oh yes. He wants Boone to kill him.

He blinks. He turns, stumbling as he scans the hedges, the crowd of bedsheets glaring on the clothesline, afraid someone saw him thinking what he thought. He did think it, didn't he? Where did the idea come from? He seems to have been thinking it for a long time. He is stunned by the idea, appalled. It's insane. But even when he recognizes the idea is absurd, it doesn't go away. He wants it. He expects it. A masculine American killer. All one has to do with such a fellow is kiss him and he will break every bone in your body. Is it really that simple?

He hurries back indoors, into cool shadows that are pitch-black after the sunlight. He stands at the dining room table, grinning at himself, wanting to sneer at the absurdness of his fantasy. But his grin seems to balloon with lewd joy and hope. He, who pulled good performances out of Colin Clive and others, certainly could pull a good death out of Boone. True, this is not make-believe but real life, with more consequences than any movie. But it's his life and he should be able to make up whatever story he pleases.

Maria comes down the stairs, lugging a vacuum cleaner shaped like a small iron lung. "You have a good nap, Mr. Jimmy? You be wanting your lunch soon."

"When is the man coming to do the yard? The man who's modeling for me?"

"I know who you mean." She clacks her tongue in exasperation as she puts the machine in the closet. "He comes Mondays."

"What's today?"

"Friday."

"Only Friday? He's not coming to sit today, is he?"

"No. You say you did not want him until Tuesday."

He is disappointed; he is relieved. He hopes his senses will come back to him over the weekend. Perhaps he'll forget he even thought such a thing. Only he doesn't want to forget.

"What time is it in New York?"

"Late. Early. I don't know." She gives him a sidelong look.

She doesn't understand. Nobody could, but he has to talk about it with someone.

"I wonder how David is doing. Perhaps I should ring him up this morning."

Maria brightens. "Yes? Good." She loves and trusts David more than the dull fellow deserves. "Call him, Mr. Jimmy. He will be glad to hear from you. Tell Mr. David hello for me. I will be fixing your lunch." She goes into the kitchen.

Whale goes to the telephone table in the hall, sits, and pulls out the flat, brass-lidded address case. He slides the tab down to *L*, presses a bar, and the case springs open to a page empty except for David's address and telephone. Under it is penciled the number of MGM's New York offices.

He dials a single digit; the wheel slowly rotates back into place. The long-distance operator clicks on. He gives her the number. Circuits crackle; an undercurrent of voices whisper through the miles of wire, an electrical confusion that extends across the continent. Whale listens and waits, wondering if he is really so desperate he needs to abject himself like this, questioning what he might gain in letting David know how far over the edge he's gone.

CHRISTOPHER BRAM

"Metro-Goldwyn-Mayer," a woman answers through a Brooklyn nose.

"Mr. David Lewis, please."

"One moment, please."

His shame increases while he waits for David.

The Brooklyn voice clicks on again. "I am sorry, sir. Mr. Lewis is only taking messages here. May I take a message?"

"No. Unnecessary. Thank you very much." Click.

He returns the heavy receiver to its cradle. But instead of feeling relieved that nothing came of his impulse, he's sorry he didn't leave his name and ask David to call. He needs something real in the future, a hope of contact or intervention to counter the insane future of his imagination.

He opens the drawer and pulls out a sheaf of stationery. Yes, a letter is more dignified, less desperate. He takes the ballpoint from the marble stand. The fountain pen would be a disaster, but even the ballpoint turns his once elegant cursive into tangled snarls. He throws the sheet away and tries again, printing in crude block letters:

Dear David,

How are you? I hope the picture is well. Maria sends her best.

Could you please ring up one night at your convenience? I know you are busy, but I must talk to someone who knows me through and through. Not to alarm you, but I fear I am going mad with my illness and may do something very odd. . . .

# 13

THE WEEKEND STINKS. CLAY SPENDS SATURDAY BEHIND HIS LAWN mower. Memorial Day is coming and customers want their grass cut for parties and cookouts later in the week, but because they don't want the neighbors to see a hired man working on a Sunday, Clay has to cram in as many lawns as he can on Saturday. The sun goes down and he's still at it, in a backyard on the edge of Brentwood, cautiously plowing around twilit garden trolls. When he can no longer see the trolls or even where he's cut, he goes to the back door to get the owner to turn on a light.

"Should have been here when you said you would," gripes a fellow in Bermudas, sheepishly holding a dinky paintbrush in one hand and the plastic model of a World War I biplane in the other. "You whack off a toe, don't think about taking me to court."

"You said you needed your yard cut today. You're lucky I squeezed you in."

"Don't take that tone with me, bub. There's Japs in this

town trying to make something of themselves. They work cheaper and do flowers too.''

Clay can't afford to get angry. He has to swallow anger and pride, telling himself it's beneath him to get angry with a man who plays with toys. "Will you just turn on the porch light? Sir."

He does, and Clay finishes the yard in low white beams that fill with the shadows of moths projected as big as buzzards. He gets his money—the model maker doesn't tip him for working late—and goes home to collapse, too exhausted to go out. He has no place to go anyway. He hasn't been able to show his face at the Beachcomber since Thursday night.

He can't remember the last Saturday he went to bed sober. He wakes up the next morning as clearheaded as a baby, only to find himself with nothing to do. Between church and blue laws, Sunday is shut up tighter than a rat's ass. He sits outside his trailer and takes apart the two-cylinder engine of his mower. Dwight and his wife and their two little girls, all in their crisp Sunday best, go out to the car, Dwight giving Clay a snooty nod before they drive off. A Red Sox game from another time zone buzzes on the radio next door, the announcer talking in lazy monotones over the drone of a crowd. Clay lays out parts on a sheet of newspaper—pistons, gaskets, and gears—cleans and oils each piece, then puts the whole thing back together. He wants to feel good about that, as if he's breaking down and reassembling himself. After his blowup the other night, he really wants to be Thoreau with a lawn mower; he doesn't need Betty or anyone else in his life. But he dislikes this perfect solitude. He's got nothing to look forward to until Monday. He isn't scheduled to sit for his personal famous man again until Tuesday, but he cuts the man's grass tomorrow and should at least get a chance to say he saw his movie. Happy to remember that there's somebody out there he can talk with, or listen to anyway, Clay takes the detached screw of blades in his lap and diligently uses the whetstone to put a shiny edge on its scythelike spirals.

Monday morning is bright and hazy. Clay feels surprisingly

good as he loads his pickup and heads down the milky sunlit coast with the traffic through Malibu toward Santa Monica. He drives up into the pines of the canyon, then down into the houses and around to the back of Amalfi Drive. He parks by the gray-shingled studio and the pool speckled with leaves. The hillside is sprinkled with new poppies; the white house sits back at the crest like a friendly old man with his chin tucked in his collar. It's good to be at a job where he knows he won't be treated like shiftless white trash.

But after Clay fills the tank and yanks the cord, as he begins the easy swatches around the pool, he finds himself embarrassed to be cutting the grass here. Like he's ashamed to remember he's just the help. It's a stupid thing to feel, but he feels it. Who else did he think he was? In the week since their first session, and since seeing Whale's movie, Clay has imagined they are something like friends. Clay may have been special last Wednesday, but on Mondays he's only the yardman.

He begins his cockeyed march up and down the hill, telling himself this house means nothing to him today except that it's got a bitch of a slope. Up at the house, there's only the maid at the kitchen window doing the dishes. Clay wonders if he's come too early, then hopes he's so early that he'll finish before Whale is up and about. He likes the idea. That way, when he returns tomorrow he'll be just the guy sitting for his portrait, without also being the nigger who does the yard.

He finishes the back and goes around front without the old man so much as showing a face at a window. Clay finishes off the strips beside the forsythia and the island in the half circle of driveway, and kills the engine. He wheels its heavy silence behind the garage and around the corner.

The maid is standing by the kitchen door in her black dress and white apron, frowning.

Clay begins to smile. *"Buenos días, señora."*

She skeptically lifts her chin at his Spanish. *"Buenos días* yourself."

"Something I can do for you?"

She takes a breath through pinched nostrils. "The Master wants you for lunch."

"Yeah?"

"He wants to know if you are free for lunch. I tell him you will be having other plans, but he insists I ask."

And Clay promptly forgets his resolve—never mix, never worry—tickled that Mr. Whale wants to see him. "Got a lawn this afternoon, but I'm free until then. When's lunch?"

"Not for another hour."

"Okay." He doesn't want to appear too eager. "Gives me time to clean the pool and start the hedges." He plucks at his soggy T-shirt. "I stink like a goat right now."

"Yes. I tell him that too. But he insists he wants you."

"It's his nose," Clay laughs. "I'll be up in an hour."

Her frown remains, like something stamped in her face with a cookie cutter. "Expect nothing fancy," she declares and goes in.

Clay rolls the mower down the steep path, happily crowing to himself. He is more than just the yardman here. Not a friend, maybe, but somebody. He turns on the pump in the studio shed to filter out the pool, adds a few ladles of dry chlorine to the water, then takes the pole and skims the surface, wondering if anyone famous swam here over the weekend. He pulls up the filter when he finishes skimming. He's found strange stuff on other filter screens—wedding rings, flowered panties, and a truss—but there's nothing to scrape off this one except a gruel of spinach and drowned bugs.

Deciding the hedges can wait until after lunch, Clay peels off his T-shirt and hoses himself down. He brought a real shirt today, just in case, a short-sleeved madras shirt he left in the truck while he worked. He buttons it up with the shirttail out.

The top half of the kitchen's Dutch door is open. Clay knocks on the bottom as he lifts the latch and walks right in.

The maid is at the counter with an onion in her hand. She

looks at Clay. "The Master is dressing. I am to offer you a drink. We have no beer. There is whiskey and there is iced tea."

Boone tells her tea is fine and sits at the kitchen table.

"No. You are a guest now. You go in the living room."

"That's okay, Maria. I'm more comfortable here. It is *Maria*, isn't it?" He wants to get on her good side, feeling generous now that he's sure he's more than a servant himself. You don't invite a servant to lunch. He wants to know her better, and learn more about her boss.

She eyes him suspiciously, shrugs, and pours a glass of tea.

Clay settles back, a sweet exhaustion like sugar in his muscles. He swigs the tea and lights a cigarette, feeling quite at home. "So what's for lunch? Something English?"

"No. Mr. Jimmy—the Master. He hate English food. He is no fool. English food have no sense, no taste." She stands at the counter with her back to Clay, gutting a green pepper. "We will be having omelettes. You know omelettes?"

"Eggs, right?" Clay notices a Bible on the counter with rosary beads dribbled on top. "How long you worked for Mr. Whale?"

"Long enough."

"You were working for him when he made movies?"

"Oh, no. I begin when he was quit working. Only his friend Mr. David was working. Is working still."

He wonders who this David is but sticks to what he wants to know. "I bet you've seen a lot of famous people come and go? Movie stars?"

"No. We live simply, Mr. Jimmy and I. Good thing, because I cannot do so much alone. But even when Mr. David was here, and my dear friend Ellen was cook, we do little entertaining. People come to play bridge. And now and then, young men to swim." She cuts her eyes at him, looks away, and takes a stoop-shouldered, bulldoggy walk to the Frigidaire. "You have people, Boone?"

"People? You mean family? All in Missouri."

"Your wife?"

"I'm not married."

"Why?"

Her bluntness only makes Clay chuckle. "Oh, I don't know. Because no girl in her right mind will have me? Because I don't make enough money to keep a wife? Lots of reasons."

She stands at the open refrigerator, a clutch of eggs in her hands. "You must get married. A man who is not married has nothing. He is a man of trouble."

Clay chuckles again, at her stony face, her righteous tone. Beliefs that irritate him when he reads them in other people's minds become comical when delivered by an old woman with a funny accent. "I'm a man of troubles, I won't argue with you there, Maria. But marriage'd only double my trouble."

"No. Marriage makes one's troubles into virtues. In the eye of God. Be fruitful and multiply."

"Yeah. Well." Clay flicks his cigarette over the ashtray. "You ever been married, Maria?"

"Of course. I am married still."

"Yeah? What's your husband do?"

"Nothing. He does nothing." She is at the counter again, setting down the wobbly eggs, taking up a block of cheese. She rubs the cheese against a grater. "He is dead. He is dead now, oh, twenty years."

"Oh. Okay." Twenty years is too long ago for sympathy. "So you're as single as I am."

"No. I have children. In San Bernardino. With my brother. I have grandchildren too. I send money and visit when I can. But now that I am alone and Mr. Jimmy cannot be left very long, I cannot get away much. It is many bus rides. A whole day, morning to night. There is little I can do when I get there. They think they do not need me anymore." She stops grating. "You do not need to go poking your nose in my business."

"Just curious." He shouldn't be surprised that even a Mex maid has a life elsewhere.

"There is nothing to know. I am of no matter. But I am telling you God's truth when I say this: You need a woman."

Clay wants to get her off the subject. "You proposing what I think you're proposing, Maria? I don't know. Ain't I too young for you to want to shack up with me?"

She twists her head around with such an indignant look that Clay bursts out laughing.

And she realizes he's teasing. "Anglos. Always pulling legs." She tries to laugh herself but can't bring it off. "Everything is comedy. Nothing is serious. 'How very amusing,' " she says in an odd, new voice. " 'How marvelously droll.' "

Clay is startled by her perfectly mimicked English accent.

"All is a joke. But life is not a joke. We pay for our sins soon enough. The blessed go to heaven, but most of us go to hell. Which is why I want to make Mr. Jimmy's last days on earth as happy as possible."

She says it so cheerfully, her tone softened by her attempt at humor, that she sounds more batty than pious.

"I don't think he's going anywhere soon," says Clay, then catches himself. "Is he?"

"One cannot tell. He is better now, but he is sick too. He is old before his time. His sins make him old. But God will decide when his time is come. Not before. Not later."

"He looks okay to me."

Maria listens for something in another part of the house. "Poor Mr. Jimmy. There is much good in him, but he will suffer the fires of hell. Very sad."

"You're sure of that?"

"I am sure of nothing. This is what the priests tell me. They know better than I."

Despite himself, despite his usual response when someone gets religious, which is to nod patiently until religion goes away, Clay has to fight her belief that Mr. Whale will go to hell. "Why they so sure? Because he's not Catholic?"

"Protestants can go to heaven, but it is harder. Only the

very best get in. But even if he comes into the Church, his sins of the flesh will keep him from heaven."

"Sins of the flesh? Everybody has those." It's funny picturing the old fellow with a young girl, even when he was young too.

Maria glances toward the dining room, bending sideways. She folds her arms and faces Clay. "No. His is the worse," she whispers. "The unspeakable."

Clay leans across the table to hear her better.

Her dark brown eyes stare deep into his. "The deed no man can name without shame?"

All Clay can think of is jacking off.

She loses patience with his blank look. "*Maricón*. You know?"

He shakes his head. It sounds like Spanish for 'Merican.

"What is the good English?" she mutters to herself. "All I know is bugger. He is a bugger. Men who bugger each other."

"A homo?"

"Yes! You know?"

Clay slowly sits up.

"That is why he must go to hell. I do not think it fair. But God's law is not for us to judge."

"You're telling me—" He stumbles from the make-believe of somebody else's religion into real life. "Mr. Whale is a homo?"

Maria tightly nods, her eyes full of hurt and pity. "You did not know?"

"No, I—" He wants to dismiss the charge, like he did with Betty. What is it with women that makes them think any old man who's friendly to Clay must be a fruit? But the maid would know.

"You and he are not doing things?"

"No!"

"Good. That is what I hope. I did not think you a bugger too. I fear only that you might hurt him if he tries. If you are a bugger and buggering him, that is of no matter. Your sins are on your head. And a few extra cannot make it worse for Mr. Jimmy. Only he must not tire himself."

"He hasn't touched me!"

She nods in approval. "But if he does, you must not hurt him. Promise me that. God will hurt him soon enough. I want his last days on earth to be comfortable."

Clay's mind remains empty, blank. "I don't intend to hurt anyone!" he says angrily.

"You are a good man. I trust you. Thanks." And she begins to crack eggs into the bowl, as if they'd just done no more than agreed on a new task to be done to the lawn.

She's nuts. That's the simplest explanation. And yet Clay believes her. He is angry for not having understood this about Whale before, then angry for believing it now.

"I can't believe the man who made *Frankenstein* is a homo."

"You know many homos?"

"No, I–no."

Maria continues to crack eggs. "I came here innocent. I did not know such men exist. And by the time I knew, it was too late. I like the job and did not care. The spirit is weak. They are always nice to me. Mr. Jimmy respect me and he was happy for many years. Happy people are always easy to work for. I care now only because Mr. Jimmy's time is coming. I am too old to start new work with new people."

Off in the distance, a throat loudly trumpets itself clear.

Maria turns again. "You must go to the living room. Quickly. He will not like to think I have had you in the kitchen. Please."

Clay gets up. He wants to get away from her. He goes out into the dining room, hoping to laugh off her accusation as cracked. But he can't laugh it off. It feels like something he's known all along, only he didn't want to know he knew it—and the dining room table is neatly set for two. He hurries toward the living room through the open double doors.

As he crosses the threshold, another figure enters on the right, simultaneously, like Clay's entered a room with a mirror. The two figures see each other, and halt.

The other figure is older, with snowy hair and a burgundy blazer. Mr. Whale, of course, the very fellow Maria said will go to hell for wild, unspeakable acts. The neck in the open shirt is long and ropey, like the neck of a turtle stretching from its shell. He breaks into a timid smile. He comes forward, offering a hand at the end of a spindly wrist.

"How are you, Mr. Boone? So glad you are free for lunch."

He is smaller than Clay remembers, and older. Clay thinks it's his mental picture of the man that changed over the past week, and while talking to Maria. The handshake is bony but firmly masculine.

"All right, I guess. How're you?"

"Can't complain. Can't complain."

With his chin raised and slightly turned, he has one blue gray eye fixed upon Clay, wider than the other, as forceful as the isolated eye of a bird or fish in profile.

"I assume you worked up an appetite with your labor."

"I'm hungry, yeah. Thanks for inviting me in."

The wide eye keeps its cold, determined focus, judging Clay or simply demanding Clay pay attention. "I hope you don't mind a light lunch. Maria can make up in extra helpings for what it lacks in heft." The eye is briefly deflected by a telephone table beside them, and a stack of mail there, then completely covers Clay again.

"Got to be better than what I usually eat." Clay wants to step out of the eye, but that would seem rude or nervous.

"A marvelous cook, Maria. I don't know what I'd do without her." He glances at the telephone table again. "Afterwards, perhaps you'll want to come down to the studio and see how our portrait is coming?"

But before Clay can answer, before he remembers anything about the portrait, Whale turns away.

"One moment."

He picks the stack of mail off the table.

And Clay can think more clearly. If Whale wants to get into his pants, would he be so concerned about what came in the mail? He looks too old and distinguished for sex, normal or otherwise. Clay relaxes while Whale rifles through envelopes, most of them with windows.

"Hmmm?" He examines a squarish one with a handwritten address. If he's looking for something in particular, this letter isn't it. He keeps it in his sorting hand and goes through the other envelopes again. "Forgive my rudeness. At my age, the post is the cream of the day." He returns the stack to the table but holds on to the square envelope. He rereads the return address. He sniffs the back.

"Lady's perfume?" says Clay, hopefully.

"Perhaps." Whale smiles. "I have no idea who this might be. Do you mind?"

"Go ahead." Clay looks off while Whale opens the envelope.

"Hmmm? Princess Margaret? What's she doing over here?" He is examining a folded card.

"Sister to the Queen," he explains, rubbing a thumb over the printed lettering. "For what that's worth." He opens the card. " 'Her Majesty's Loyal Subjects in the Motion Picture Industry . . . Cordially Invited . . . reception for Her Royal Highness . . . Tuesday, May 28 . . .' " He pauses.

"That's tomorrow," Clay tells him.

But Whale isn't listening. " 'At the home of *Mr. George Cukor!*' " His lips smack open in disgust. His face screws up in disdain—the name means nothing to Clay. "That pushy little— Loyal Subject, my arse. Horning in on Princess Margaret, then offering to share her with the whole damn raj?" He flips the invitation front and back, looking for an explanation. "And why me? What makes him think I have any desire to meet that royal debutante?"

"You're British?" Clay suggests. "Maybe he wants to get everybody British there."

"Mr. George Cukor doesn't know me from Adam. And I live in this country to get away from this—rubbish!" He tosses the invitation and envelope on the table, then stares after them. "Where did he get my name? My address? Is this David's doing? Certainly David knows a gathering of fops is of no help to me."

There's that name again. "This David's a friend?"

"What? Yes. An old, useless friend." Whale looks up at Clay.

He resumes his timid smile. "Stuff and nonsense." He flicks the back of his hand at the mail. "You must excuse me. This is a world I finished with long ago. I pay them no mind and expect them to return the compliment." He takes a deep breath and recovers his repose. "Lunch should be ready. Shall we?" He holds out an open hand but does not intend that Clay take it, only that he precede him into the dining room.

Clay goes in. So what if the guy's a fruit? Clay can enjoy a free lunch with a famous old man, even one who might be queer.

The places are set catty-corner, Whale at the head of the table, Clay on his left. There's a white linen tablecloth, a basket of warm rolls, and another basket holding a wine bottle at an angle. Clay wants to be proud of disrupting this fancy spread with his dungarees and madras shirt, his smell of gasoline and grass. But he resists the impulse to sniff his armpit. When Whale opens a napkin in his lap, Clay does likewise.

"A little wine for the stomach's sake?" Whale takes the basket and pours red wine into two glass goblets. "Cheers." He takes a sip.

Clay takes a swallow. He associates wine with winos and would rather have a beer, but he's determined to play this game through.

Maria enters with two steaming plates.

"Wonderful, Maria. Yes. Smells lovely."

She has her smooth expression of indifference again. Sliding a plate in front of Mr. Whale, she seems to steal a glance at Clay, but it's hard to tell where the pupils are aimed in her dark brown eyes. She goes out and lifts the little cast-iron Sambo that props the kitchen door. The swinging door flip-flap-flaps and settles shut.

Clay waits for Whale to speak. The old man gives his full attention to his food, solemnly spreading butter on a roll. Clay cuts into the yellowy packet on his own plate; a gust of steam puffs up from a viscous mess of cheese and peppers.

"Simple yet tasty," Whale assures him.

It looks too hot to eat, so Clay takes another gulp of wine.

This is what he wanted today, better than what he expected. What exactly had he expected from seeing Whale? Clay can't remember. All his expectations and satisfaction in knowing the old man are blocked by what that damn Maria told him.

"Oh. Saw your movie the other night," he suddenly remembers. "On television. *Bride of Frankenstein?*"

Whale glances up. "Did you, now?"

"I liked it. Was strange. Stranger than I remember from seeing it as a kid."

"Yes. I suppose it was."

"Watched it with some friends in a bar."

Whale thinks a moment. "Did anyone laugh?"

"Uh, some. Yeah."

Whale considers that, nods to himself, and lowers his head to take a forkful of omelette. "Of no matter," he grumbles. "No matter at all."

Clay worries he hurt his feelings. He doesn't know what else to say about the movie. He bends down and stuffs his mouth. "Mmm. Good." He takes more bites; eating is easier than talking. He eats as he always does, with his elbows on the table, but more quickly, bolting the hot food in stringy, half-chewed knots.

He can feel Whale watching, as if he asked Clay to lunch only to study his lack of manners.

"In Korea, Mr. Boone?"

Clay looks up.

"In Korea?" Whale repeats. He tilts that scrutinizing eye at him again and gently smiles. "Did you kill anyone?"

Clay freezes. He can't remember feeding his Korea line to Whale, but he must have. "I don't like to talk about that."

The gray eye grows a little wider. "Nothing to be ashamed of. I gather that killing is an American rite of passage. One's not a real man until one's killed another man. For the sake of one's country, of course."

Clay shifts in his chair. The old man must suspect something phony. His little digs at Clay are meant to dig out the truth.

"That's horseshit," says Clay. "Any jerk with a gun can kill somebody."

"Quite true. Yes. Hand-to-hand combat is the true test. Did you ever slay anyone hand-to-hand?"

"No."

"Pity."

Clay refuses to be needled by a fruit. "I could have, though."

"Yes?" The eye blinks. "Yes, I believe you could." He takes another bite of omelette, another sip of wine, looking quite pleased, as if he just paid Clay an enormous compliment. "How free is your schedule this afternoon?"

The change of subject is a relief. "Full up. I got the hedges to do here, then another lawn out by La Cienaga."

"What if we say phooey to the hedges? This week anyway. Could you spare an hour after lunch? To sit for me?"

"Can't today," Clay says automatically.

"Just an hour. While you digest."

But sitting for Whale no longer feels like a harmless hoot, a flattering honor. Having a homo touch you, even with just his eyes, should be humiliating. And Clay already let him do it once.

"I'll pay our going rate. Plus what we'd pay if you did the hedges."

"I'm not in the mood today. To sit still."

"You're certain of that?"

"Yeah."

Whale nods, sighs, and says, "All righty. I understand. More wine?"

He drops the matter, so easily that Clay wonders if he's been unfair to the guy.

"Did you enjoy the omelette? Maria can fix you another."

"Thanks. I'm full."

"I've had quite enough myself." Whale glances at the egg left on his plate. He opens his blazer and fumbles inside. "May I offer you a cigar?"

"Uh, sure."

He draws out twin cigars like tobacco billy clubs. Clay takes one, heavy and squared, with no hole in the tip like the few he's smoked before. He assumes he has to bite the tip off, the way his father's Grange Hall buddies did.

"Oh, no, Mr. Boone. Use this." Whale passes him a little gold penknife. "Just a trim. Yes. And mine while you're at it."

Clay slices off the tip of Whale's cigar.

"Fingers are a bit stiff today," Whale explains. He uses both hands to work his lighter, holding the flame under Clay's cigar, then his own.

The first puffs are as harsh as burning manure, but the nose quickly adjusts and the aroma becomes rich and heady. The smoke gives the table a reassuring man-to-man stink. Clay relaxes a little. The mild light-headedness is enjoyable when he can hang on to something solid like the warm club in his fingers.

The kitchen door thumps open, Maria coming in to clear away the plates. Is she listening to them or did she know they finished simply because she could smell the smoke? Her frown darts at Clay through the thin blue haze as she goes out again.

What if she's wrong? The elderly gent with a little cannon angled in his hand could not look more confident and masculine. What if Maria lied? What if she's afraid Clay is getting too tight with her boss and she made up this story to scare him off? Then he'd have no reason to feel ashamed of letting Whale draw his picture. It's stupid for him to fear something that might not even be real.

"A woman is a woman, but a cigar is also a smoke," Whale observes.

Clay attempts to make a smoke ring, in an effort to look nonchalant. "You ever been married, Mr. Whale?"

Whale quietly examines Clay, like a poker player judging an opponent. "No. At least not in the legal sense."

"What other way is there?"

Whale examines the crinkly layered ash on his tip. "Oh, one can live as husband and wife without the law involved."

"So you had a wife?"

"Or a husband. Depending on which of us you asked." He smiles to himself. "My friend David. Whom I mentioned earlier."

The tightly rolled leaf crunches faintly between Clay's fingers. He's not shocked or disgusted. He is angry that Whale doesn't have the decency to lie, so that Clay can stop thinking about it.

"Does that surprise you?"

"No, I—you're a homosexual."

"Oh dear. If one must have a clinical name. Although I thought we were called pansies. Cocksuckers."

The last name makes the whole business sickeningly real. "I'm not, you know."

"Of course. I never thought you were."

Clay puffs at his cigar, needing more smoke. But the tobacco tastes muddy and the sucking disturbs him; the shape in his hand suddenly feels obscene. Clay has to set his cigar down in the ashtray. "You don't think of me that way, do you?"

"What way might that be?"

"You know. Look at me like—like I look at pretty girls."

The cigar in Whale's hand wiggles. "You're not my type. And I know a real man like yourself would break my neck if I so much as laid a hand on you."

Clay fears Whale is mocking him again. But it is true. Isn't it? Not his neck maybe, but Clay would break the arm of any man who tried something. Wouldn't he? Even the man who made *Frankenstein*?

Clay suddenly laughs, like it's all a ridiculous joke.

Whale's smile deepens. "So we understand each other?"

"What you do or did is no business of mine," Clay claims. "Live and let live, I say."

So what if the guy's a homo, as long as he keeps his hands to himself? But accepting that, knowing it and accepting it, feels just as wrong to Clay, passive and cowardly.

Whale squares his shoulders against his chair. "I hope this has nothing to do with your refusal to sit for me today?"

"No. I—"

Whale continues to smile, slyly, as the single gray eye tilts at Clay again, colder and more demanding than before.

"What are you afraid of, Mr. Boone? Certainly not me."

"I don't feel like sitting still today. That's all."

"What are you afraid of?" Whale repeats. "I'm hardly man enough to take your virtue by force. And one can seduce only those of like minds."

Is he calling Clay a homo? Or is he calling him chicken? Either way, Clay feels insulted and challenged.

"Yes? No?" Whale quietly persists. "An hour of your time. That is all I require. A simple little hour. Could you perhaps think about it over dessert and coffee?"

Clay responds with a put-upon sigh and smart-ass smirk, knowing that the man's got him and he can't walk away now without looking like he's yellow.

The studio again, dark and faintly chilly after their walk down. The blaze of noon does not spill inside but stops at the windows, so bright that the eye must choose between seeing what's indoors or what's outdoors but cannot take in both.

Clay sits sideways on the chair again. Mr. Whale stands at the easel again, attaching a fresh pad of paper to the board. He won't show Clay the work-in-progress. "It's not your concern and will only make you self-conscious." All he wants today are details he says he will later add to the picture he keeps hidden.

The space is smaller than it was a week ago, made closer by what Clay knows and can't pretend he doesn't. It feels secluded and a bit sinister without Maria in the next room but up at the house fifty yards away. There is only a catbird outside in a cypress tree, screeching like a blue jay, and the occasional dry rustles of an old man breathing through his nose.

Clay feels stupid for being here, and stupid for feeling stupid. He has nothing to fear. He has nothing to gain either. What's he want to prove by putting himself through this?

Whale seems ready to start yet doesn't. The stillness that begins as a single deep breath is held, like a radio silence that lasts so long you don't know if it's dead air in the broadcast or if a tube in your radio burned out.

Clay can't see the other side of the easel. He is unaware of the pinched, quizzical look Whale gives to the porous paper, a blank whiteness as intimidating as the Antarctic, even today when he has no intention of even attempting to draw. He might be looking into a mirror. His eyes have the skeptical excitement of a young man steeling himself to attempt a first kiss, when he's not yet experienced enough to read the signals and know if a kiss is possible or where it might lead.

"You'll have to remove your shirt," he commands.

Clay tugs at the tail. "Sorry. Not today."

Whale's face peers around the easel, blinking as it changes focus. "My interest in you is purely artistic, Mr. Boone."

"I know. I just feel more comfortable keeping it on."

"Do I make you uncomfortable?" His voice is mocking, his mouth on the edge of a smile: it's like he *wants* Clay to be uncomfortable.

"Just self-conscious. And you said you don't want me self-conscious."

Whale steps forward. His hands shyly go up in front of him; the pale skin on the backs have a faint sheen like vinyl. "But we need to match the other sketch. Perhaps if we open the shirt and pull—" The hands go in.

Clay's flesh tightens; he shrinks back.

The hands stop, palms raised. "Oh dear. I *have* made you nervous." He sounds amused.

"I'm fine. I'd just rather keep my shirt on." Clay's fear is all in his body, not in his mind. His mind knows Whale won't try anything, and that Clay can knock him on his ass if does.

Whale is smiling to himself. "Maybe if we unbutton the top and pull it down around your shoulders?" A hand goes up again but only to pat the air a few inches off, as if afraid to touch. "Like an evening gown. Would you be comfortable with that?"

Clay's body wants to strike out, push the man away, but it feels dangerous to hit him. Whale looks so brittle that the lightest blow might do real damage. The fear of injuring Whale leaves Clay powerless, helpless in his strength.

"Two buttons. Is that so much to ask? Just two little buttons." Thumb and fingers unpluck buttons in midair.

"No! Just—!" His shoulders jerk to shake off the squirminess. "Look. I'm just a hick. What you told me at lunch is still very weird for me. So if you don't mind, could you back off today? Either you sketch me like I am, or I'll say forget it and go do your hedges. *Comprende?*"

Whale takes one step backward. He does not look offended. He looks frightened, but it's a strange kind of fright, his breath quickening, his eyes locked on Clay, fascinated by this temper.

"I don't mean to be a prick," Clay mutters, "but that's how I feel."

"Yes. Of course, Mr. Boone. Whatever you say." Whale continues to step backward, eyes still fixed on Clay. "I certainly don't want to scare you off before I'm finished." He glides behind the easel. The pencils rattle in the tray.

"How did you want me to sit?" Clay won't apologize, but he wants to show he's willing to cooperate.

"Like you were. Yes. That will do fine."

He doesn't seem to care. The scratching of his pencil sounds equally careless, beginning immediately, without a pause to take aim. Scratch, scratch, scratch: circles and zigzags.

Head turned to the right, arm on the back of the chair, Clay should be used to this by now.

"Am I right in assuming, Mr. Boone, that you've had little to no experience with men of my persuasion?"

"There's no people like you in my crowd."

"Really? A manly speciman like yourself. I would think the pansies would be around you like flies."

It's like he wants to keep Clay uneasy, nervous, daring him to stay. "They know by looking at me I'm not like that."

"Perhaps. Or your size frightens them off? Although there are those who'd find that stimulating. And some men love a lost cause. I am surprised to be your first."

Scratch, scratch, scratch.

Clay wishes he'd talk about something else. This thing poisons all the pleasure he took in knowing the man. It makes anything they say to each other weird, suspect. Clay misses the stories Whale told last week, tales from long ago that had nothing to do with Clay. This has nothing to do with him either, but Whale talks as if it did.

"It must be lonely, being what you are." Clay wants to make clear that he knows nothing about this life.

"Not at all. I have more people than I know what to do with. And one needs fewer as one grows older. We are born alone and we die alone. What company we get in between is gravy."

Clay at his toughest thinks like that, but a queer's solitude has got to be different. "How long were you and your friend together?"

Whale pauses. "You don't *really* want to talk about David."

"I'm curious."

"Curiosity killed the cat." A mild sigh. "Twenty years."

Clay's not surprised. He doesn't know enough to be surprised. He's heard about the lone predatory homos—the stories in the barracks at Pendleton—but he's also noticed occasional men in couples, doughy twosomes as sexless as maiden aunts. They're as weird as the loners, but harmless. Whale and his friend must be that harmless kind of homo.

"Too long," Whale adds. "Much too long. We were like a play whose run outlasted the cast's ability to keep it fresh. We continued long after we ran out of tricks to amuse each other in our parts. Several years after I retired, I finally decided it was time we close down the show. I wanted to kick up my heels, have some fun. I was not about to spend my golden years as merely 'the friend.' The dirty little secret of a nervous little producer."

Scratch, scratch, scratch.

"So I fell in love. With somebody else. One last fling. A young fellow I met in Europe and brought back with me. Very handsome, very virile. Almost as virile as you, Mr. Boone."

"But a foreigner," says Clay, wanting to point out he couldn't have been all that virile.

"French."

"Figures."

"You think sodomy is un-American, Mr. Boone?"

"There's just more of you over there than there are here."

"Oh, no. We're quite common in this country too."

"I wouldn't know."

Whale is silent for a moment. "I wonder at your inexperience, Mr. Boone. Are you certain there haven't been fellows who were sweet on you without your knowledge?"

He keeps turning the subject back to Clay, but Clay can hold his own now. "Nope. Never."

"No teammates in football? No comrades in Korea?"

Like a dog marking out his territory, he pisses on everything, even Clay's lie. "You must think the whole world is queer. Well, it's not. War sure isn't."

"Oh, there may not be atheists in the foxholes, but there are occasionally lovers."

Clay snorts. "You're talking through your hat now."

"Not at all. I was in the foxholes myself. The trenches. A few wars back."

"You were a soldier?"

"I was an officer."

Clay doesn't believe him. His lie is even more outrageous than Clay's. "But you're a homo."

"Ah. We didn't split hairs over that in my day. Homos didn't exist, in the eyes of the law. You could be sent to prison for buggery. But dreams of buggery, an inability to dream of anything except buggery? They had no idea."

Clay has broken his pose to turn and look at the man. He remains behind the easel, only his gray slacks and white hair showing. "This was World War I?"

"No, my dear. The Crimean War. What do you think?"

The "dear" doesn't even register; Clay is too stunned to think a fruit has done things Clay feels *he* should have done.

"The Great War," Whale continues. "You had a Good War while we had a—" He clears his throat. "Of no matter. We were discussing your experience."

But Clay has no experience; he wants to get to the bottom of Whale's. "You were an entertainer? Red Cross or whatever they had instead of USO back then?"

"No. I was in the line, in the trenches. On the western front. *All Quiet* and *Sergeant York* and the other pictures, which I assume is what you know."

"I had an uncle in the AEF." Uncle Frank, with the scabby mushroom-shaped helmet up in his attic.

"Yes. Well. You Yanks were there for the denouement. We were there when it looked to go on forever. War without end. There were trenches when I arrived, and trenches when I left, two years later. Just like the movies. Only the movies never get the stench of them. The mud and rain. Always it was raining. You cannot ask an actor to work for more than a day or two in knee-deep water, caked from head to toe, although we spent whole weeks like that. The boredom of it. No movie can get the long, numbing boredom. The world reduced to mud and sand-bags and a narrow strip of rainy sky. Like living in an open grave. The bombardments that went on for days and nights, earth trembling like pudding while all the great guns, ours as well as theirs, did their best to pinch our grave shut." Whale gives a dry, humorous snort. "But we were discussing something else. Oh, yes. Love. Love in the trenches. We loved each other. Some of us."

"You mean you—you did stuff?"

"Oh, no. I was an officer. It would have been like incest. And where? Certainly not in that very public open grave. And if one climbed out, one'd catch a bullet in the blink of an eye. But at night perhaps? Now there's a thought. Underneath the old barbed wire? While the Verey lights flicker overhead like stars. How romantic."

Clay wants to think he's making this up, putting him on. He talks in that flamboyant English way of his that now sounds thoroughly fruity, but about war. Clay continues to watch the easel.

waiting for Whale to peek out. Clay wants to see his face, needs to attach a homo's face to an old man's war stories and discover who the hell this guy really is.

"But there was no carnal knowledge. Only charnel knowledge. Yes. Charnel knowledge," he repeats, enjoying the phrase. "And the human body was unlovable there. You could love a smile perhaps, or a laugh, but not a body. Not when they were so filthy. Not when we already knew each other much too intimately. There are few sights less appetizing than five or six of your men on a latrine pole, trousers around their ankles, grumbling and picking at their lice. You could love their souls but not their flesh. Our love was chaste and sentimental."

Scratch, scratch, scratch.

"And you, Mr. Boone? There wasn't some pal who broke your heart when he caught it in the chest or head?"

His cruel tone is startling, but Clay is trapped in his lie. All he can say is, "No."

"Of course. Your generation of Americans is wiser. Far less sentimental than my compatriots and I. Sentiments were like lice. We had to pick them off and crush the little buggers, if we wanted to keep our sanity."

Like last week, he's only talking to himself, but he speaks coldly, irritably, without surprise, as if arguing with something that hasn't been said.

"I arrived less sentimental than most. I had no dreams of glory, no love of king and country. When war was declared and the herds ran to enlist, I was only annoyed at the interruption. The others were bored with peace, bored with order and innocence. But I was busy raising myself by my bootstraps and saw no future in playing soldier. My reluctance was my fortune. The October draft came and they were desperate for officers. Not until they said a bright young fellow like myself looked to be officer material, working class or no, did I bite. Yes, I bit. And the war gave me a foot up in the world. It taught me to laugh at pious nonsense. It enabled me to direct the play that made my career. One might even say it made room for me, killing off men who'd have had my place if they'd lived. No, I do not regret the war."

He backs away from the easel and Clay can see him. He isn't looking at Clay but continues to stare at the paper, a sour frown pinched under his nose, the pencil flicking in his fingers. He finds a windowsill at the back of his knees, lowers himself, and sits on the edge.

"Barnett. Was that his name? Leonard Barnett."

He grips the sill on either side of him.

"A schoolboy someone declared an officer. He came to the front straight from Harrow. And he looked up to me. He was taken with me. Unlike the others, he didn't notice or care that I was a workingman impersonating his betters. How strange. To be admired so blindly. I suppose he loved me. But chastely, like a schoolboy. He spent a whole week in a jealous sulk, when I chose another man instead of him to accompany me on a night reconnaissance. Like it were nothing more than choosing sides for football. But I was protecting him. I didn't know how dangerous this particular swatch of ground might be. So yes. Maybe I loved him too."

"But—" Clay is afraid to ask. "Something happened to him?"

Whale looks up at Clay, stares at him. Then, with a pained twist of his mouth almost like a smile, he says, "Oh, he caught one. Of no matter where or how, but he caught one. After less than a month. Before he could grow as faceless and expendable as the others. If he'd been there just a little longer, I might not remember him. Not that there's anything to remember. Except —yes. A morning when the sun came out. Our little strip of sky was blue, bright blue. Odd, how even there one could have days when the weather was enough to make one happy. It took so little. He and I were standing on the fire step, above the ankle-deep muck, and I showed him the sights of no-man's-land, through the periscope. It was beautiful. There was color out there. The barbed wire was reddish gold, the water in the shell holes green with algae, the sky a clear quattrocento blue. And I stood shoulder to shoulder with a tall apple-cheeked boy who loved and trusted me. I didn't kiss him, but I may have laid an arm across his shoulder. I hope I did."

It should be pathetic, disgusting, but Clay can't help being moved. So many things that should be opposites, manliness and mush, war and perversion, barbed wire and tenderness, run together here. Clay almost envies the two men's moment of closeness.

Whale leans forward on the sill. His eyes are fixed on Clay, the white eyebrows screwed down. "Don't do this to me again, Mr. Boone."

His change of tone is so abrupt that Clay takes a moment to recognize it's anger.

"I refuse. I absolutely refuse," he hisses. "You will not set me on another walk down memory lane. Not this lane. Not today!"

"I didn't—? You—"

Whale stands up, his legs shaky before the knees indignantly lock. "Why do I tell you this? I never told David this. I never even remembered this until you got me going."

"You're the one who started in. I haven't said boo."

"No. You just sit there and let me talk." He steps toward Clay, glaring at him. "You're very clever, Boone. What a sorry old man, you're thinking. What a crazy old poof. Why are you here? What do you want from me?"

He comes closer. Has he cracked up? Clay remembers Maria said something about attacks. Only now does he realize she might have meant he'd attack Clay.

"You asked me to model. Remember?"

"Of course I remember. Do you think I'm so senile—" He stands over Clay, air rasping through his nostrils. "Take off your shirt if you're here to model."

Clay actually reaches for a button before he understands it'll accomplish nothing, that it can't be what's upset Whale. "No. We agreed I'd keep it on."

Whale hangs over him. His mouth begins to open, but the dry lips remain stuck together. He lifts a long hand, spreading the knobby fingers as if to speak with them. His pale face turns left, right, looking at Clay with one cold eye, then the other.

Clay doesn't flinch but returns his gaze, worried for Whale, frightened for him.

Whale turns away. The hand goes to his pocket and yanks out the handkerchief. "Stupid. Very stupid," he mutters as he steps toward the daybed. "What have I been thinking?"

He sits on the daybed and bends over, covering both eyes with the long hand and handkerchief.

"Just go. Please. Why don't you go?"

Clay remains sitting, still frightened for Whale but angry too. "Are you okay?"

"I'm fine," Whale snarls.

"I'm sorry about your friend."

Whale lowers his hand and looks out at Clay. "Barnett? Don't be daft. That was forty years ago. Even if he lived, he might be dead."

Clay feels free to be angry. "First you creep me out with homo shit. Then you hit me with war stories. And now you're upset because I listen? I don't get it. What do you want?"

"I want—I want—" His pained eyes focus on Clay, and soften. "I want a glass of water."

Clay turns in the direction of the pointing finger. He gets up and goes to the sink, where he finds the glasses.

"A touch of headache," Whale says loudly. "Thank you," he says when Clay hands him the water.

"You don't want aspirin or something?"

Whale shakes his head and drinks, Adam's apple bobbing up and down in his scrawny neck.

Clay steps back.

"I just need a moment." Whale sets the glass down and sits with his head lowered, his body folded like a bundle of sticks.

Clay stands with his hands on his hips, looking at Whale, wondering how he could be frightened of this man, how he could feel so many different things about him. Whale keeps changing on Clay, becoming somebody new with each story he tells. The man has more lives than a cat. Clay wishes he could pick and choose the lives he likes and throw away the rest.

"My apologies," Whale tells the floor. "I had no business snapping at you."

"That's okay. No harm done."

"It was foolishness to attempt this. Utter foolishness. The portrait, I mean. You cannot force what will not flow."

But Clay knows that's not what went wrong. He glances at the easel and thinks about going over to see what Whale got down on paper today. "Maybe it'll go better tomorrow."

Whale lifts his head. "You're willing to continue this?" He sounds surprised.

"Didn't you want to continue?"

"No, I—" Whale glances at the easel too and frowns. "It makes no sense now. My heart's not in it."

"Then you don't want me here tomorrow?" Clay is surprised that he feels disappointed.

Whale looks at Clay, sadly, like he's disappointed too. Then his gaze flickers, his eyebrows ride up. "Would you like to come with me to a party tomorrow afternoon?"

"A party?"

"Yes." A little light comes into his eyes. He smiles. "We need a break from this, a diversion. I've been invited to a gala reception for Princess Margaret. Sister to the queen, you know."

He talks like he forgot Clay was there when he opened the invitation. "I thought you weren't going."

"Did I say that? If I did, it was only sour grapes. I can't go to such things alone. I couldn't ask Maria to drive, but you could. Yes. If you don't mind driving, I'd like to take you as my guest. We can go in my car."

Thrown by Whale's wild swing of mood and subject, Clay is suspicious, and tempted. "I don't have clothes for a shindig like that."

"But it's a lawn party. It'll be casual, nothing fancy. Although there should be famous people there. Not just Princess Margaret but stars and starlets. Bushels of them."

"Like who?"

"Oh, names escape me, but anyone British. Merle Oberon, maybe. Nova Pilbeam? But they're before your time. Oh, I know. Elizabeth Taylor."

"She'll be there?"

"Possibly. She *is* English." His closed mouth goes straight, like a man who's told a fib. "Does it interest you at all? Please say yes. It'll give me something to look forward to. And allow me to make up for having behaved so badly today."

Clay takes a breath. "I'm game. Sure."

"You will?" Like he can't believe it could be so easy. "Of course you will. Lovely."

Clay hears in that last word a cause for his suspicion. "Uh, are people going to think I'm your boyfriend?"

"Will they? No. I don't think so. The worse they'll presume is that you're my male nurse. Would that be too distressing?"

"Oh, I don't care what strangers think of me."

"Good. We should never let the opinions of others stand between us and what we want."

Is this what Clay wants? It is, but he can't put his finger on why. He'd be an idiot to say no to a real Hollywood party, whether Elizabeth Taylor is there or not. But beneath his conventional desire is an unexplainable relief in knowing he'll see Whale again, despite what the man put him through today.

Whale quickly sets a time and offers suggestions on attire. He seems relaxed and content in a way he hadn't been before. He shakes hands when Clay departs, saying, "Very good, Clayton. May I call you Clayton? Or do you prefer Boone?"

Clay loads up his mower and goes, without getting to the hedges, without understanding why seeing Whale again is as important as going to this party. It's strange and unhealthy to think too much about anything, but, driving to his next job on the other side of the canyon, Clay finds himself trying to get a grip on what Whale means to him now. Clay knows more about him than is safe to know about any man. He is a fruit, and foreign, and unpredictable, and he keeps spilling secrets Clay would rather not hear. But the old fellow has done and seen more than anyone else Clay's ever met. His war was too long ago to count for much, but it does count, doesn't it? It's a privilege to listen to him, a privilege and a challenge. Maybe he has dirty thoughts about Clay, but he's too old to do anything about them, too old to even have a body somewhere beneath his clothes. Clay would never admit it, but with a younger, more physically real homosexual, he would've fled long ago.

By the time he's mowing his next yard—a flat shady lawn with a perky housewife who has bells in her crinoline petticoats—Clay's unease has shifted from sex to the confusion of knowing such a man as Whale even exists, someone who evokes such a mix of fear, admiration, envy, and pity. He screws up everything Clay's been taught to feel about the world, and yet Clay does not want to avoid him. It's like he *wants* to be confused, which makes Clay feel oddly guilty.

# 14

IT HAD BEEN BEAUTIFUL IN HIS IMAGINATION, BEAUTIFUL AND immediate, as simple as stepping into a lion's cage. The beast would seize him in his claws and tear him apart with no more thought than a hungry boy ripping open an orange.

He had his lion where he wanted him. He was keying him up to a pitch where a kiss or less—any trespass in the cage of intimate space—would be enough to make the beast pounce. And suddenly Whale understood: his beast was human. He was irritable, polite, and human. When Whale petted the air around him, his look was not that of an angry lion but a puzzled house cat. And when an awful memory from the past slipped out, the beast became concerned. He could do nothing worse than swat Whale with a paw, maybe scratch his face. Where was the pleasure in that? Even the look of the fellow's nose changed, from the broken nose of a thug to a child's nose squashed against a candy-store window. His fantasy was not exhilaratingly insane but stupid. Ludicrous, stupid, and cruel.

This is what Whale thinks afterward, as he trudges up the slope to the house. He is relieved he didn't make a fool of himself but depressed that his fantasy is so thin and impractical. What does he have to look forward to now? He goes into the living room, turns on the television, and sits in his chair. Maria quizzes him with a glance when she passes through, but he pretends to be lost in a soap opera. Within an hour, without his lion there to prove otherwise, Whale is wondering if his change of mind wasn't sanity but cowardice. Not even the beginning of a phantom headache had driven him forward, a headache that lifted as soon as he decided not to pursue his line of attack. He experienced relief when he made his decision, exactly what a coward feels when he finds an excuse to do nothing. But this relief had been deeper than mere avoidance, more eager, even friendly, an anticipation of something, as if there actually are other things one man can do for another besides kill him.

Whale remains pleased that he will see Boone tomorrow. That fragile pleasure is still intact. He regrets only that the sole opportunity to present itself was a party at George bloody Cukor's.

That night, because he needs to be fully alert the next day, Whale does not take his phenobarbital. There are the usual nightmares, instantly forgotten each time he awakes, but he wakes less frequently. He sleeps through all but his worst dreams, as if something during the day drained off his bad electricity.

Sooner than expected, he wakes to the colorful cubes and boomerangs jumbled on the sunlit curtains. There is his standard achy daze—where am I? who am I?—until he glimpses an event through his daze, something he must do today: a party with Clayton Boone. And the daze disperses, snapping apart like the skin of steam on a cup of tea. He doesn't need Maria to find his way to the toilet. He promptly begins his morning ablutions, brushing his long bony teeth, turning on the shower.

He knows Boone will not pick him up until this afternoon. He knows he has no business being cheerful, but he is. The thoughts that are usually broken and scattered have a focus this morning, not in the man thinking them but around another man, someone who acts as a magnet for thoughts. That was how it had been in the studio yesterday. Only now, in the shower, with white body hair shifting like iron filings in the springy cone of water, is Whale struck by how quick and articulate he had been for Boone. His motives were murky, but he seems to have spoken with remarkable eloquence. Am I getting better? he wonders. Or is this clarity, this confidence, only another phantom, a new knot pinching in the brain? His mind has betrayed him for so long that it cannot regain his trust; he remains aware of the churned mud of broken consciousness just beneath his mood. But he can at least enjoy his clarity while it lasts.

He takes breakfast in the dining room. Maria is surprised to see him so alert and proper at this hour. He casually announces that their yardman is driving him to a party this afternoon.

"Yes, you tell me twice yesterday," she says flatly. She slowly fills his coffee cup. "He is a good boy. He will take care of you."

"Nothing to take care of," Whale scoffs. "I feel fit as a fiddle today."

"Hmmm?" She lingers by the table, fussing with the position of the butter dish, plucking a stray toast crumb from the cloth. "Boone—he is an interesting friend."

"I'd hardly call our yardman a friend."

"No. But someone you can talk to."

Her tentative concern and curiosity touch Whale and make him curious. "Do you miss having someone to talk to, Maria?"

She looks up. "I have my family. I have Father Spinelli."

"You don't miss Ellen?" When the house had a cook as well as a housekeeper, she and Ellen had been as thick as thieves.

"No, I—" She frowns. "Ellen was all right."

They were such an odd pair, a short, muffin-faced Mexican and tall, lantern-jawed Irishwoman, looking like mismatched sisters when they left for mass each Sunday morning. "I know she could be bossy, but she was obviously fond of you, Maria. The two of you were always chattering about something."

Maria stiffens. "Things I would say to Ellen I now say to

God," she declares. "I have much work to do." She walks briskly into the kitchen.

He seems to have trespassed on her privacy. One shouldn't forget the rules that make life with a stranger possible, not even this morning when his good spirits spill over in curiosity about others. Such curiosity is a surprise after his months of self-pity. Does Maria think he accused Ellen of being a lesbian? No, she probably doesn't know such women exist. Ellen quit and returned to Ireland shortly after David moved out. She said she'd saved enough money to retire, but Whale assumes she left because she disapproved of his new life, especially the little parties around the pool. Maria has always been more tolerant, in her aloof, willfully blind fashion.

Whale busies himself after breakfast with choosing clothes for this afternoon. He and Maria go through the guest-room closet together. It's a pity it'll be too warm for his best pinstripes, which he has no occasion to wear except for visits to the doctor. Maria holds up white linens—too 1920s tropical—then a flashy yachting ensemble—too nouveau riche pansy—before Whale decides on a lightweight sky blue suit, casual yet elegant, with a fine-grained pattern of blue and white lines. It needs a hat, though, something sporty to bring out the subtle dash of its cut. He remembers a wide-brimmed cream fedora that should be perfect, but it's not here.

"It must be up in your bedroom," Maria says. "I will look."

As she goes into the hall, the telephone rings. And Whale freezes. The second ring is more shrill than the first, a buzz saw of bells. It has to be Boone, calling to cancel.

Whale steps timidly along the hallway, listening as Maria picks up and speaks. Her voice changes, loosening into a cataract of syllables: she speaks Spanish. Whale relaxes and breathes again. It's only her family.

He goes to the foot of the stairs and waits for her to finish so she can find his hat. He tries a look of mild disapproval to hurry her along, but Maria has disappeared into Spanish, acting as though speaking a language Whale doesn't understand makes her invisible. He points upstairs to let her know he will look for the hat himself.

The steps are higher than he remembers, but he hasn't climbed them in months. Knees and wood creak together. The upstairs hall is warm and close. He enters the master bedroom. His slight displacement of air is enough to set the slow float of dust motes in a sunbeam into a frantic dance. Against the wall, side by side, are two twin beds.

Their headboards and quilted satin spreads are identical, but the inside bed has an immediate, distinctive personality of its own. Whale does not picture or even remember either of the bodies that slept in it. The personality of the bed has absorbed all images of David and Luc. It is simply itself, the other bed. There is a soft vertigo of remorse and nostalgia, and then, abruptly, anger with David. The little shit hasn't answered his letter, not by phone, not even with a card. Certainly David has received the letter by now. Whale no longer needs an answer, but common courtesy declares that a request for help at least be acknowledged. Oh, blast David. Where's his hat?

The closet reeks of camphor balls in garment bags. Whale goes up on his toes and takes down a stack of hatboxes from the overhead shelf, then a second cylindrical stack, eight boxes in all. He pulls a chair over so he can sit while he looks through them. He had no idea he is a man of so many hats.

Opening the first box, he finds an ugly black bowler, like a burnt pudding. When did he have cause to wear this absurdity? It makes him think of Dudley and, of all things, the Old Birmingham Canal. He does not know why.

In another box is—good God—a cowboy hat? It may have been David's joke gift to him or his joke gift to David.

The next box holds what looks like a hat that died, a rubbery wad of heavy fabric a moldy shade of bluish gray. He has to take it out and open it before he sees two round windows like eyes. It's a mask—a gas mask.

Whose? What's it doing here? The canvas feels stiff and oily between his thumb and finger. He puts a hand inside to fill the bottom half. It looks German. The tarnished inhalator is attached directly to the mouthpiece like a beak; inhalators on British masks were separate, connected by toy elephant trunks of tubing. The thick panes of shatterproof glass are yellow with age, but the leather straps show little wear. It must be war surplus, one of the props used for *The Road Back*. Yes, it's only a souvenir from a movie, not a war. Nobody died in it.

Still, Whale doesn't dare hold it over his face. He spreads the mask in his lap and gazes at it, a noseless beaky thing with goggle eyes, so abstractly human that one can't help but think of the dead. When he sniffs at the harsh rubber smell, he pictures a live dog sniffing at a dead dog, its idle curiosity confused with only a faint suspicion of what they once had in common. But Whale understands. He understands perfectly.

When the war slipped into his consciousness yesterday, he had been able to translate only small pieces into words. He was not surprised by how much he remembered, only by how alive the memories were. Of course he remembers, he's always remembered, but he thought he exorcised the emotion of those memories long ago. He had directed a play about them and turned the play into a movie. But here they are again, all the sorrow and fear and strain of a war without end, a war whose only escapes were a loss of limb, capture by the enemy, or death. Or death. He has been here before. He has lived with death before. Except now he no longer has the company of Barnett and Evans and a hundred others whose names he forgets. He faces death alone. Which is so sad and confusing that, for a moment, he regrets that he didn't die in the trenches, since he will have to die anyway.

"Oh, Mr. Jimmy."

Maria stands in the door with a forlorn frown.

"You make a mess of it." She strides into the scatter of boxes and loose papers. "Here," she says, lifting the lid of an unopened box to show him the missing fedora. She puts it aside and starts to clear the debris, then sees the thing in his lap. "Ugh. What is that?"

"It appears to be a gas mask from the Great War." He smiles at her and strokes the mask.

"Looks hideous." She makes a face and continues stacking boxes. "That is my daughter on the telephone. She call to say she and her husband are coming to town this afternoon. They want to see me. I am sorry, Mr. Jimmy. I will keep it short and keep them to the kitchen. My son-in-law only wants to borrow more money. Some quick-rich scheme to make the fast buck. And they do not even bring the children to see their *abuela*. I promise they will not stay long."

Whale only half listens to her. "I'll be out this afternoon, remember? So your family can visit as long as they like."

"No. I keep it short and sweet. I do not cook for them. My daughter's no-good husband will not take one bite of *our* food."

When she finishes with the other boxes, she holds out the box for the gas mask, wanting Whale to put it in without touching it herself. Whale pulls the mask taut between his hands and gives it a long, final look. He drops it into the box. "You can toss this one in the trash."

"Throw it away?" Her belief that nothing should ever be discarded is stronger than her squeamishness. "There is nobody who can use it?"

Whale can't help smiling. "Not much call for it here. No mustard gas in sunny California."

"Whatever you say, Mr. Jimmy. Out it goes." She clamps the lid on the box and takes it downstairs.

No, pointless to save that memento mori. As if he needs another memento to remind him where he's going. Looking into the open closet with its garment bags and hatboxes, he wonders why he doesn't throw everything out. Clothes and hats, his furniture, his car. He despises them. Already they are his personal effects, and more ungainly than the simple handfuls of letters, photographs, dog-eared bank books, pristine Bibles, and the pocket watches of all descriptions that they boxed and shipped home from Flanders. Death was so much simpler there.

He lies down after lunch, exhausted, wanting sleep yet wary of it. Every nap is a gamble. He doesn't fear not waking up, only of waking with his mind in pieces again. Not today, he prays. Please. Not today.

He sleeps and, when Maria taps on the door, he comes out of this nap alert and refreshed, enchanted. His quiet eagerness is like enchantment. His yardman is taking him to a party. The enchantment grows as Whale slips his limbs into the neatly cut sky blue suit. He remembers an earlier sadness, but the nap puts it in the distant past. He amuses himself at the mirror with different-colored neckerchiefs—a tie is too stuffy and he told Boone not to wear one—before settling on a peacock blue paisley with golden eyes. He slips an old-fashioned pair of sunglasses into his pocket, round wafers of smoked glass. He is still deliberating over whether to bring a cane—what was dashing as a prop is pathetic if required—when the doorbells chime. The pair of oval notes overlap and merge.

No cane, he decides. He flicks a last feather of crisp hair into place and goes out to meet his man.

Maria has opened the door. At the end of the hall, silhouetted against the bright afternoon, is Boone.

He is enormous. Whale was prepared to be disappointed by the reality, but he isn't. Boone's shoulders fill the doorway. The top of his head is perfectly flat. He's had a haircut since yesterday and Whale is delighted by a new idea, a startling joke: It is his monster, in the form of an American boy, and he's taking Whale on a date.

"Good afternoon, Clayton. Ready to go amongst them?"

"I guess." Boone remains on the doormat, hands in his rear pockets, looking like today's outing is just a chore to him. His lack of emotion is exactly what one wants in a monster. He abruptly breaks character to ask, "Do I look okay?"

"You look splendid, my boy," Whale replies before he bothers to examine him. But his khaki pants are clean and pressed. His orange knit shirt fits his muscles snugly, with just enough tattoo peeking from the sleeve to show he has a tattoo. "Quite splendid. The car keys, Maria?"

She fishes them from her apron and gives them to Whale, who promptly hands them to Boone.

"All yours. I trust you can drive an automatic."

"No sweat." Clay examines the keys and hurries down the front steps to the garage. His ragamuffin truck sits in the opposite corner of the driveway.

Whale fits the soft cream hat on his head just so—there's sensuous satisfaction in clutching the plump crease and dimples of the crown. "We shan't be too late, Maria."

"They will be gone by the time you return, Mr. Jimmy," she assures him. "My family."

"Oh yes. Don't worry about them, my dear. I'm in too generous a mood to deny you time with your family. Ta-ta."

Boone has unlocked the garage door; he heaves the folding sections up with a smooth clatter. When Whale crosses and comes into the garage on the passenger side, Boone is studying the Chrysler, caressing it with his eyes.

"I suppose you'd like the top down?" says Whale.

"Oh yeah," says Boone. "If that's okay?"

"Nothing would please me more."

Whale stands by while Boone squeezes behind the wheel, shifts the seat back, and explores switches. The garage has a warm sweet smell of motor oil and vinyl. Spotless garbage cans stand along the right wall, with a hatbox perched on top of one.

The vinyl top pops up and folds backward, a loud mechanical purr opening up the car's interior.

Whale gets in. He has plenty of room for his legs today.

Boone starts the engine. He's in his element at the wheel of a car. Whale admires the grace with which his body twists around as they back out of the garage, a centaur nonchalantly looking behind to inspect a hind hoof.

Maria still stands at the front door, hands tangled in her apron. Whale tugs his hat brim at her as the car clicks forward and swings around the driveway. He does not look back to see if she waves good-bye. The immovable trees of Amalfi Drive are gliding past. The tedious houses drop away. Sunlight sputters and flares on the bared upholstery and there's the delightful surprise of wide-open sky overhead. How lovely, Whale thinks, to ride in an open convertible with a large young man.

Boone looks comfortable, his posture more content. His left arm lounges on top of the door. His right hand handles the steering wheel with a surprisingly delicate touch.

"Nice car," he declares.

"You like it?" Whale immediately wants to give him the car, if not today, then when he dies. But he does not feel so mortal this afternoon.

"Where exactly are we going?" Boone asks.

"Beverly Hills."

"What's the address?"

Whale pats his coat, finding first the bones of his sunglasses, then the folded pasteboard. He reads out the address.

"Do you know where that is?" asks Boone.

"I've been here before," says Whale. "I can tell you what to do once I see where we're going."

When they come to Sunset, Boone steps on the gas and the Chrysler takes off. The airstream above the windshield thickens into a roar. They race uphill through slashes of sun and pine, the landscape blurring, the sky overhead hardly moving, and it's like flying up to heaven. This heaven will be full of people Whale does not particularly care to see, but he remains happy. He is overjoyed to be out of the house and on the road, and to have this quiet muscular fellow as his driver. He is tickled all over again by his private joke: he's being taken to a party by his very own monster, or an amiable American substitute.

# 15

GEORGE CUKOR RESIDES ON THE UPPER SLOPES OF BEVERLY HILLS, in a hillside estate above the swank mishmash of big houses, small lots and royal palms that won't climb this high for another ten years. His large, sprawling villa was modern for 1932 when he bought it, but Cukor has left the building untouched, adding and changing only the extensive grounds around it. There are three smaller houses on the property, which he rents to friends, and an elaborate series of terraces and walkways running up and around the slope. Directly behind the villa is an enormous flagstone patio with a few Roman statues and the requisite swimming pool. A twenty-foot-high brick wall obstructs the view from the road winding up the hill. In a corner between the patio and terraced slope is a garden full of camellias and, in the center, a pitch of lawn just the right size for a game of croquet.

Wickets and stakes are set up for today's party, but only a handful of very tanned children strut around with mallets. The adults are busy talking. Assorted smiles fill the open air with words, talk that is friendly, small, and self-conscious. All the guests, English or American, are here to see and be seen today. Even the children playing croquet move with the split-second hesitance of people who know they're being photographed. And photographers are present. Four of them stroll among the guests, popping their flashes in delicate flickers of light on light.

The party is clearly audible from the road, where Clay squeezes the Chrysler into a long row of shiny new cars nuzzling the high brick wall. Cedar trees bury the road in olive drab shadow, but there's sun as well as voices on the other side of the wall. Whale puts his dark glasses on when they get out. "Stars, you know. The suns of other galaxies."

Clay says nothing as they walk up the steep road to the gate-house. He remains remote and stiff, with the cramp of consciousness like a mental charley horse that's plagued him since he picked up Whale at the house. Clay wants to see movie stars, of course, and he wants to see Mr. Whale in his Hollywood world. But he's not sure how to behave toward the old man today. He's definitely not Whale's date, but he doesn't want to be his servant either. They're not family and they're not quite buddies. Clay hasn't figured out who they are in private, but here they are in public, and what a public.

"Good old George," Whale proclaims while a lady at the gate inspects his invitation. "He loves to put on the dog. Only his dogs tend to have a bit of mutt."

The lady doesn't smile but waves them through, onto a sunny patio with hedges and statues like the back of a museum. The people are lit from behind in bright halos of hair and clothing. The luminous air seems to vibrate a few feet above their heads, not with wit and fame but an airborne cloud of gnats.

All Clay sees at first are country-club types like the people whose lawns he cuts. Several clusters congregate around the swimming pool, as if it's cooler by the water—the air is dry and the sunlight very hot in the hills. Then a middle-aged woman in slacks catches his eye, her face jumping out like that of someone who spoke to him every week through an open door. But she's not one of his customers. He's seen her in movies, playing mothers and aunts.

"What did I tell you?" Whale says. "Listen."

"I don't hear anything."

"Exactly. No music. Cukor was too cheap to hire music. There's nothing but chin-wag. The cold dreary custard of English chin-wag," he adds with a frown.

Clay sees another familiar face, a fat, jowly butler type. He doesn't know their names, but the presence of recognizable faces makes everybody else look inanimate and stuffed.

"Slim pickings," Whale judges. "Oh, there's Gladys Cooper, who lives down the street from me. But she won't interest you. Well, it's early yet. Actors with pictures in production will be just leaving the studios about now. Perhaps this is a good time to pay our respects to the guest of honor. Before a queue forms and one must take a number."

Clay follows Whale off the patio into the garden, toward a trellis alcove covered in ivy. A handful of people grin at the mismatched couple who stand in the shade: a homely old man in glasses and a pretty woman in a white dress with polka dots.

Princess Margaret is twenty-seven and between romantic entanglements this month. She produces smile after dutiful smile beneath her broad straw hat, chats with well-wishers and patiently waits to see her next real movie star. Cukor introduces guests to her, his horse face breaking into the proud grins of a fisherman posing with the biggest catch of the season. When he and Princess Margaret smile together, they generate snaps of static electricity—a photographer stands off to the right.

Whale wants to get this over with quickly. He has no love of royalty. He resents the very notion of it this afternoon, when the presence of so many countrymen makes him feel like an interloper, an impostor. But they are all impostors, aren't they? He begins to see the wonderful joke on Mother England that a son of Kiev or Krakow, wherever Cukor's people are from, is playing host to Her Royal Highness, a comic twist best appreciated by a son of Dudley. He and Cukor have much in common.

Whale forgets to remove his hat when he comes forward. But before he can give Cukor their names so that he might present them—it's been a long time and he fears George won't recognize him—Princess Margaret's polite smile bursts open in a joyful display of teeth.

"I had no idea *you'd* be here," she cries, dropping protocol to seize his hand in her little white gloves. "How are you?"

Whale is so taken aback all he can say is, "Fine. Quite fine. And Your Royal Highness?"

"Smashing. Now that I know you're still around."

Standing behind him, Clay is more impressed than surprised that Whale knows a princess. His surprise has stuck on the fact that a girl in polka dots could be royalty.

"Can we get together while I'm in town?" Margaret pleads. "I so badly want to sit for you again."

"Sit?" Whale glances at Cukor, who is staring at him, desperate to place this man Her Highness finds so important.

"Oh yes. I've changed my hair, you see. Since our last session. So much more stylish, don't you think? But those old snaps look rather dowdy now. Lovely though they are."

Whale's relief at understanding that she's mistaken him for someone else is outweighed by disappointment. He tugs his sunglasses down his nose so she can see his eyes.

"Oh dear. Have I made a blunder?"

"Ma'am, the pleasure is mine," he tells her. "James Whale."

"I am such a goose." She laughs at herself. "I mistook you for Cecil Beaton. I *thought* you were looking thin. But they told me Cecil was in Japan and I assumed you picked up some sickmaking bug over there. And the hat. You're wearing one of Cecil's hats, you know."

Whale smiles and attempts to chuckle while he fights a feeling of humiliation. "Hello, George." He shakes Cukor's hand. "James Whale," he repeats. "David Lewis's friend." He turns back to Princess Margaret. "I once made pictures myself, ma'am."

The polite response would be for Cukor to name one for her—surely Princess Margaret will know *Frankenstein*. But Cukor only frowns at *friend*, afraid his guest of honor will understand the meaning; any mixed function brings out his finely tuned, nervous guilt. He directs his frown at the young man accompanying Whale. "Yes. Of course," he mumbles, then carelessly quips to Princess Margaret, "One can't throw a rock in this town without hitting one of us old movie directors."

It's not meant as an insult, but Whale feels stung. His last thread of pride snaps; he wants to sting back. He turns to see Clay standing by and sees his chance. "Your Royal Highness," he announces. "May I present Mr. Clayton Boone?"

Clay steps forward to shake hands.

"My gardener," Whale blithely adds. "Who insisted I bring him today. He so wanted to meet royalty."

And the face of George Cukor goes blank with indignation, as if an unexpected beach ball just bounced off his head.

"Pleased to meet you," Clay tells the princess, with a confused glance at Whale.

Princess Margaret pretends she heard nothing. "Quite," she says, then completely recovers with, "I adore gardens."

But it's Cukor whom Whale wants to tweak, not Princess Margaret. He narrows his eyes and sharpens his smile at him. "He's never met a princess. Only queens."

The indignant face changes color. Cukor puffs out his chest, but the presence of royalty leaves him speechless. He quivers a bulbous lower lip at Whale.

"George, Your Royal Highness"—Whale pretends to address them both—"this has been an honor. An occasion to remember for the rest of my days. Come, my boy. Her Royal Highness and Mr. Cukor have more important fish to fry."

He leads Clay away and an American couple promptly crowd in to take their place. Striding through the garden on the balls of his feet, Whale is pleased with himself. The old dog still has teeth. He can hold his own at this gathering.

"What was that about?" Clay says irritably. He felt insults being exchanged, but like insults in a foreign language.

"Nothing of importance," Whale claims. "Just two old men slapping each other with lilies." He has a twinge of regret over using Boone to achieve his hits. "Shall we have a drink?"

They find a waiter and give him their orders—a martini and a beer. Standing off to one side of the patio while they wait for their drinks, Whale finds the Englishness of the surrounding voices less distressing than before.

Then he sees him. Across the flagstone patio. He has come through the gate with a woman on his arm.

A ripple of interest spreads through the party as people discreetly look, not at the man but at the woman, lightly veiled in a scarf and sunglasses. Whale sees only the pinched face and bald head beside her.

"Who's that?"

"David," Whale mutters. "The friend I thought was in New York."

"No, the girl."

"Girl? Oh. Elizabeth Taylor."

Clay watches as she waves to someone and pipes out a happy hello. She hurriedly unties her scarf. Yes, it really is Elizabeth Taylor, beaming and whispering five yards away. She looks less magical life-size than when she was fifty feet tall at a drive-in. Clay needs to repeat her name to himself to make her magic again. She thrusts the scarf at the old man beside her and runs off on tiptoes to embrace and kiss a woman.

"You weren't shitting me," says Clay. "She really is here."

"Apparently." Whale can't take his eyes off David, who stands with the scarf in his hands, uncertain what to do with the thing. He finally holds it up and begins to fold it, like a diligent mother picking up after a child. His face has relaxed into its natural look of pained resignation. Whale is torn between avoiding the little liar and confronting him.

"You know somebody who knows Elizabeth Taylor?" asks Clay.

"Hmm. Only the producer on her last picture."

David glances around while he slips the scarf into a coat pocket. And he sees Whale looking at him. He quickly looks left and right, as if afraid he's at the wrong party, as though he'd arranged the invitation thinking his ex wouldn't actually come. He puts on his public face—a tight little rabbit smile—and strolls across the patio.

"What are you doing here?" he demands.

"Just what I was about to ask you. I thought you were in New York City."

"I was. Until last night. Publicity asked me to fly Miss Taylor in for today's reception. You should be home in bed."

"I feel fit as a fiddle."

"That's not what you said in your letter."

"You never answered my letter."

David takes a guilty breath. "I knew I'd be back. I was going to telephone tonight and perhaps drop by tomorrow."

The waiter arrives with their drinks. Only when Clay takes his glass of beer does David see that Whale is not alone.

"David Lewis," David tells him, dropping his voice half an octave and holding out his hand.

"Clay Boone." Clay shakes his hand. "We met a few weeks ago. When you hired me to cut Mr. Whale's grass."

"Our yardman," Whale confesses with a sly smile. "Who was kind enough to serve as my escort to George's little soiree." He lifts his martini at Clay and takes a sip.

David glances worriedly between the two men. He singles out the martini as safe for comment. "Should you be drinking in your condition?"

"My condition? You talk as if I'm with child. I'm with a fully grown man." He smiles at Clay.

Clay feels like he's caught in a quarrel between a husband and wife, except it's two men. "I think I'll walk around," he tells them. He was wanting to get another look at Elizabeth Taylor anyway.

"If you would, please," David says politely. "I'd like a few minutes with Mr. Whale."

"No sweat," Clay says, and hurries off.

"Don't wander too far, Clayton," Whale calls after him. "And do try to behave yourself."

David waits until Clay's on the other side of the pool before hissing, "What are you doing with the yardman?"

"Nothing. Nothing at all. Just a little friend. Although he isn't so little, is he?" He enjoys rubbing David's face in the fact of Boone.

David leans in to whisper, "You have no business bringing trade to one of George's parties."

"Is that what upsets you? Not the possibility I'm playing snuggle-bug with the yardman but that I've introduced him to your friends? Well, too late to concern yourself there. You should have seen Georgie's face when he met Clayton."

David freezes. "You didn't."

"I did. But Princess Margaret was a doll," Whale assures him. "We're all equals in *her* eyes. As commoners, I presume."

David remains frozen. There was a time when he would've laughed at Whale's pricking of Cukor, in private anyway. But the brass nameplates and wall-to-wall carpeting have got into his soul and he is as nervous and frightened as the rest of them. Whale fell out of love not when David lost his hair but later, when he lost his nerve.

"You can't embarrass me, Jimmy. You embarrass only yourself."

"Oh dear. I'll never work in this town again?"

"You know what I mean. You have your reputation."

"But I have no reputation. I'm as free as the air."

"Well, the rest of us aren't!" David snaps. "Can't you remember that?"

"You're right. Even those of us with one foot in the grave must watch our step. So as not to embarrass the living."

David winces again, guiltily this time. "That's not what I meant. Don't talk like that. You have plenty of years ahead of you. If you'd only take care of yourself."

Whale responds with a weary sigh. It's such a stock response, and so like David. The game of making this poor rabbit uncomfortable loses its savor; it's much too easy.

"For your information," Whale tells him, "the young man in question isn't trade. A perfectly ordinary, decent American boy. An ex-Marine. I haven't laid a hand on him."

"No?" David grows more guilty, more pathetic. "I know you too well to think you haven't considered it."

"Oh, I've considered it. I've considered many things that don't happen," Whale confesses. "I've had him in for tea and lunch. He listens to me tell stories. That's the extent of our relationship. He's someone to talk to. Nothing more."

The pained look remains, but David nods, as if giving Whale permission to see Boone. "You said in your letter you thought you might be going crazy?"

"Did I? That was last week. This week I feel fine." What had he wanted from David when he wrote to him? Why had he gone to the trouble of burdening this unimaginative fellow with his fears?

"You do seem fine today," David insists, to himself as well as Whale. "Fine and difficult."

It is so easy making David guilty that Whale begins to feel sorry for him. "What a nasty old man I am today. You must thoroughly regret having an invitation sent. You never dreamed I'd come, did you?"

David stares at him. "I didn't ask George to invite you," he confesses.

"No?"

"I had no idea this affair was even taking place until Friday, when the studio said they wanted Miss Taylor here."

"Then why was I invited?"

"Maybe George invited you on his own?"

"George doesn't know I exist. Hmmm. How mysterious." He smiles over the mystery, surprised and intrigued by it.

"I shouldn't worry," says David. "Maybe George's secretary got a list of citizens from the British consulate."

"You think so? Yes. Of course." Whale is disappointed the mystery has such an obvious explanation.

They turn away from each other to look at the bodies and shadows lengthening in the lemony light.

"Shall I come by for breakfast tomorrow?" David asks.

"You have time in your busy schedule?"

"I'll make time. This isn't the place for us to talk. And there are people I need to speak to professionally. I think I have a release date for my picture."

"Congratulations, David. How wonderful for you."

"You'll be fine on your own?"

"Perfectly fine. And my young friend is somewhere about."

"All right, then." David gives him a shy, skittish look, as though he'd like to touch him but can't, not here. "Very good, then. I'll see you tomorrow."

"I know Maria will be thrilled to see you again."

David nods and goes. Whale watches him stroll over to the pool and greet a gaggle of executives, the bald little man who shared his bed for twenty years. It's as peculiar as seeing that bed appear at a party and watching it chat with strangers.

Whale is suddenly very tired. Without the pleasure of fighting David to give him energy, he feels the effects of the cold martini in the hot sun. He wants to sit, but all he sees by the patio is a headless Roman torso in the flower bed. The hard shoulders and jagged neck do not make an inviting seat.

He walks along the edge of the patio, keeping away from David and his cronies. He looks around, hoping to see either a chair or Clayton. The fellow is nowhere is sight, but there's a huddle of striped canvas deck chairs under a banyan tree at the far end of the croquet lawn. He drifts toward the chairs, past people he's never seen before, English people who don't turn to look at the old man in sunglasses and Cecil Beaton hat, as invisible here as a ghost in broad daylight.

It'll make a good story, Clay insists to himself. He has nobody to tell it to except strangers, but it should make a good story to tell somebody, someday.

He looks over a garden of jabbering heads in his search for Elizabeth Taylor. All around him are conversations that seem intelligible until he tries to listen in: English mumbles thicker or squeakier than Mr. Whale's, with a sputter of enunciated consonants. Clay finds himself standing beside half-familiar faces and has to stop from peering into them, as though they were up on a movie screen and wouldn't notice him staring.

His relief at getting away from Whale and his friend or lover or pal—whatever he is—passes. He feels lost without the old man to explain things. And wandering around looking for famous faces is strange. Clay has never given much thought to fame, accepting it as what everyone believes, worships, and resents. Famous people seem more real than other people, until you're standing beside one and whatever was a mystery evaporates; they're just more people. It's not like he's going to get to know anyone here the way he knows Mr. Whale. Clay adores Elizabeth Taylor and often daydreams about her, but it's not like he can tell her his daydreams, even if he cleans them up. He continues his hunt, though, telling himself he only wants to see if her skin is as soft and creamy as it looks on film, and her eyes really violet.

Thinking he might be able to locate her from above, he goes up the stone steps on the far side of the croquet lawn. A loose jumble of terraces climb and curve around the arid hillside. A few guests stray among the fruit trees and the yuccas that look like bouquets of green knives. At the end of the terrace that overlooks the garden where Princess Margaret continues to hold court, two men and a woman make a nasty game out of identifying celebrities, has-beens and never-wases. Viewed from above, the whole party appears grand and enjoyable, more fun from a distance, which is how most parties look to Clay. The voices blend in a buzzy, open-air drone. Whale and his friend are gone from their spot on the patio, but Clay isn't worried. He has the car keys.

He approaches the narrow steps that lead to the next level. A young woman sits on a stone bench in a niche in the rocky wall, glumly leaning on a crossed knee, her fingers fiddling with an unlit cigarette. She gazes at Clay without interest as he starts up the steps.

He nods at her. She's pasty but pretty, like porcelain painted with red lips and black hair.

"You got a light, love?"

"Sure." He comes back down, digging matches from his pocket.

She sticks the cigarette in her mouth and wearily watches his clumsy hands light it.

Talking with the opposite sex is what he needs right now. Her skirt and blouse look plain compared to what other women are wearing, but that makes her more approachable.

She exhales a luxuriant cloud and declares, "Brilliant."

"Anytime." He's not sure if she's being grateful or sarcastic. "My name's Clay."

"And my name's mud. Or will be when I get back to the hotel."

Her accent is in her nose. She sounds a little drunk.

"Beryl," she adds when Clay doesn't laugh. "My name is Beryl. Roll out the Beryl?"

Clay smiles at that. He takes his own cigarettes out and lights one.

"Hooray for Hollywood," she sighs. "This is Hollywood, right?"

"That's what they tell me." He sits beside her, careful not to sit too close. "Some party, huh?"

"Nothing but kikes and cockneys here," she says matter-of-factly. "Which are you?"

"Uh, neither."

"You an actor? If you're in cowboy movies, I wouldn't know. I never go to cowboy movies."

"No, I'm not in movies. Just the friend of somebody who is."

"Me too. Or somebody who wants to be. See that runt by the pool? The one sticking his nose up the arse of the fattest producer with the biggest cigar."

Clay looks, but there's more than one fat man with a cigar, and several runts.

"My lover boy, the angry young man. The hot new playwright. Ain't he young? Ain't he angry?" she sneers.

It means nothing to Clay that she has a boyfriend or that they've had some kind of fight. He only wants to chat with a pretty girl for a few minutes.

"All they had to do was fly us from New York, wave the dollars under his nose, and he licks boots with the best of them. Voice of the working class? Ha! Angry? Double ha! He wasn't angry. Envious, that's what he was."

"What were you doing in New York?"

"His play is there. Our play. I'm in it, so I guess it's still our play. Until they cast the movie with Yanks."

"You're an actress?"

"That's what I call myself. Others might differ."

He doesn't know enough about theater to pursue that. "So how do you like America?"

"You can have it. New York anyway. Three months and I'm sick of the place. I miss London. You know who people are in London."

"If you're homesick, you should like this party. Almost everybody here is English."

She gives him a pitying look. "They may seem English to you, love. But they're a bloody wax museum. All these la-di-da accents from nowhere. Their bowing and scraping to Princess Margaret, the biggest waxwork of them all. Back home, only shopkeepers are gaga over royalty anymore. These people live in a fairy tale. Like the war and Labour government never happened."

It's strange enough to find yourself in a foreign country without somebody telling you it's all a lie.

"You mean, like real cowboys and movie cowboys," Clay asks.

"I don't know real cowboys. You a real cowboy?"

"No." He can't tell her he mows lawns. "Was a Marine."

"You don't say? Yeah." She examines him, smirking appreciatively. "You look big and strong. Make a muscle."

Clay laughs, but he crooks his elbow and flexes.

With her eyelids lowered against the cigarette in her mouth, she wraps both hands around the squared roundness of bicep. Her red fingernails don't quite meet. "We are solid, aren't we?" She glances down toward the pool. "This bench is murder on a girl's bum. Do you mind terribly if I sit in your lap?"

Before Clay knows how to respond, whether to laugh at her or play along, she stands and plops across his legs. He holds both hands out, afraid to touch her.

"Much better." She drapes an arm across the back of his shoulders, as thoughtlessly as she might sling her arm around a chair. "Not too bony, am I?"

"Uh, no." She's as light as a bird and warm. The heat of her bottom pours into his thighs. Despite her foul mouth, it's a surprise that she isn't porcelain but humid flesh and blood. Clay sets a hand on her legs, gingerly, to hold her more snugly in place.

"Oh yeah. This is lovely. Who needs a twit when one can have a nice bit of cowboy."

She turns to look down at the party again and her hair covers his face with a smell of cigarette smoke and flowers. The blouse slides silkily against his shoulder. Clay resists the impulse to kiss her moist neck.

"What were we talking about?" she asks.

"Um, England. Cowboys."

"I'm glad you're not a cowboy. All cowboys ever kiss are their horses."

That might be an invitation, except she continues to smoke her cigarette. Clay stubs his own cigarette out on the bench and lays a hand against her back. When he feels the hard strap of bra through the watery blouse, he's glad he isn't as drunk as she is, or he'd be all over her. He's usually wary of women he's just met, but her foreignness is as good as alcohol for undoing inhibitions.

Down around the swimming pool, eyes glance up and turn away. The terrace faces the back of the house like a stage.

"Sort of a big toothbrush," she says, stroking the bristles of his flattop.

Clay rubs silk against her shoulder with his chin. Her body grows damp where it presses him. His own body grows thicker, more dreamy. "You think we should be doing this?" he mutters.

"Doing what, love? Getting friendly?"

"Out in the open like this."

"Where everyone can see us? Where Princess Margaret can see us? Now, wouldn't that be too awful?" she mocks.

"You don't want to find a corner somewhere?"

"Hmmm." She fingers his hair again. "I wouldn't trust you off by our lonesome, love."

He leans back to squint at her. "You just want to get me worked up for nothing?"

"Needed some tenderness. Something to make me feel I'm really here. Do you mind terribly?"

If she were American, he'd dump the little tease on her ass. But her Englishness changes the rules, suspends them. He's not sure what to do with Beryl, although he's tempted to bite her.

"This is cozy," she claims, leaning against his chest. She turns her head against his, cheek to cheek.

If he stood up now, he'd poke out like a busted sofa. It's humiliating when a woman gets you hard and thinks you won't do a damn thing about it. Clay holds her more tightly and considers kissing her with the corner of his mouth. If he could cup a hand over a breast, maybe he could change her mind.

Her head jerks up. "Where'd he go?" She scans the party. "Who?"

"Oh balls! The little twit can't even see us?"

And Clay finally understands. "Is that what this is about? You want to get your boyfriend jealous?"

"Sorry, love." She gives a guilty snort. "Not the kind of girl who jumps on any lug for no reason. Here, let me up."

"You cock-tease."

She wiggles in his lap, but Clay refuses to let her get off.

"Be a gent. We've taken this as far as it can go."

"Maybe you have. I haven't."

"What're you going to do? Throw me on my back? Have your way with me while Princess Margaret and the rest of them watch?"

He doesn't want that. He doesn't want anything from her, but his pride is at stake and he can't just let her walk away.

She squirms again. "Let me up, why don't you."

"Not until you kiss me."

"A kiss? Good grief. You expect me to buy my way out with a peck on the cheek?"

"A real kiss."

"Oh, Beryl, you stupid cow," she grumbles to herself. "The messes we get in when we're pissed and resentful. All right. You want a bleeding kiss. I'll give you a bleeding kiss." She grabs his head and smashes their mouths together.

Clay is startled by her quickness. Catching up with the kiss, he immediately wants to slip past lipstick into naked mouth. When his lips pry hers apart, however, it's her tongue that plunges in, a hard slick muscle that pins him between his lower teeth. It's like Frenching an electrified fence. His hands open and he reaches around to touch the armored padding of bra.

Her head jerks back and uncorks the kiss. She elbows him in the chest, hard, and leaps from his lap.

"There! Happy?" She jumps back, catching her breath, smoothing her blouse.

He grabs at her, but only in his head, his body too stunned by the break for him to move. Her weight keeps him pinned to the bench even when it's gone.

"Sorry about that, love. Didn't mean to be a cunt."

"Crazy bitch," he says breathlessly.

"Bitch, yes. Crazy, no. I'm not about to be humped at a garden party by a stranger. Not in broad daylight anyway." She laughs. "My fault, love. No hard feelings, I hope. Although it's not your feelings that're hard, are they?"

He covers his anger with a sneer as he folds his forearms over his lap. "Your loss. No skin off my nose. We could've had some fun."

She lifts her eyebrows and snorts. "If I find my lover boy screwing in the bushes, maybe I'll come looking for you. But don't count on it. Thanks for the cuddle, cowboy." She hurries down the steps into the party with an audible, "Whew!"

Who is he fooling? For a minute, his prick thought it could get something, but his brain knew all along he wouldn't be dipping into any sugar doughnuts here. His mouth still painted with an alkaline taste of lipstick, Clay remains on the bench, wanting to laugh, wanting to think this'll make a good story for somebody. He can always claim Beryl was a movie star in Britain. Or he can tell Whale about her, which means telling the truth, but the old man should get a laugh, which should help Clay laugh too. Girls aren't Whale's line, but telling him how he necked with one at this very proper party should tickle the old guy even as it makes black and white how different Clay is from him.

Suddenly, his mental cramp about Whale relaxes. It's like this is what's been eating Clay all along, not that he's like Whale but that people will think he is. It's an idea he couldn't even consider until now, when he's shown anyone who bothered to glance at the terrace that girls are his line. They are so much his line they have him by the nuts every time. Beryl made an ass of him, but their tussle frees Clay, enabling him to feel confident and friendly again toward Whale.

Waiting for his chemistry to subside so he can stand without shame, Clay surveys the party, wondering where his friend went, wanting to tell him about his crazy prick-teasing countrywoman.

The shade of the banyan tree is cool. The deck chair is comfortable, although tilted so far back that Whale wonders how he'll get up again when it's time to go. The other striped chairs are empty. A waiter brings a fresh martini. Whale regrets he didn't ask for a drink that tastes less antiseptic, less like a hospital. He relaxes and sips and patiently waits for the alcohol to refloat his earlier happiness.

Faces he hasn't seen in years drift by, looking much the same except that they've grown pale and slightly blurred, as if white stockings were drawn over their heads. Nobody notices Whale, not even people he once directed. Charles Laughton lumbers past, an enormous infant grown old, looking utterly lost in a rumpled beige suit, an untied shoelace trailing through the grass. He impassively glances Whale's way but doesn't stop, doesn't nod, doesn't even seem to see him.

It must be the sunglasses, Whale decides. He peels them off. The colors of the party glow softly now, without shadows, although it's much too early for the sun to have set. Gauzy white clouds have crowded in from the ocean, turning the light flat and painterly, almost English. The clustered trunks of the banyan tree look like fantastical white plumbing.

"Mr. Whale!"

A child's voice. Whale looks out to see a boy marching across the emerald lawn, a black-haired youth in a cardigan and white open-necked shirt.

"Wow. Saw you over here but didn't know it was you." He thrusts out a childish hand for a shake. "Great to see you again, Mr. Whale."

"Mr.—?" Whale recognizes the Roman bangs; the boy was in underpants the last time Whale saw him. "Kay?"

The boy giggles. "Bet you never thought you'd see me again. How you feeling these days? I didn't know if you'd be well enough to come to this party."

"You didn't?"

"I knew you were invited." Kay squats beside the chair, his smug little face a foot away. "I'm the one who got you on Mr. Cukor's guest list."

"You, Mr. Kay? You? How do *you* know George Cukor?"

Kay twitches his wily eyebrows up and down. "I've been a busy bee since you last saw me. I interviewed Mr. Cukor after I interviewed you. I'm his social secretary now. Well, assistant to his secretary. I'm still in school too. But I've gone up in the world."

"My word." Whale bites back his disgust. "George Cukor, Mr. Kay? I had no idea you were such an ambitious little whore."

Instead of being insulted, Kay lets off another giggle. "You can't know Cukor if you think that. He likes them butch. But he likes sympathetic people working for him and took a real shine to me. Didn't hurt when I let on I knew some jocks at school."

It should mean nothing to him, Whale tells his pride. He has no cause to feel he's been jilted or has failed. He is beyond these games of success where pretty minions are drawn like flies by one's status. "I commend you on your choice, Mr. Kay. If you're going to pursue poofs, go after those who can do favors for you. You waste everyone's time when you court dinosaurs."

"Ahhhh," Kay moans sadly. "Don't think that, Mr. Whale. I love your movies. I wasn't faking that to get in good with you. That's why I got your name on the guest list. I wanted you to come to this, so I could see you with your monsters."

"My monsters?"

"They're here."

Does the boy mean enemies? More rivals?

"I know I can't interview anyone today, but it'd be neat just to see you all together. For old time's sake."

"What are you chattering about, Mr. Kay?"

"You'll see." Kay laughs and leaps up. "Don't go away. I'll be right back."

Whale is confused, alarmed. Today's invitation was a prank, a baby poof's idea of fun? And what's this about monsters? Who here has a score to settle with Whale? Has Cukor told Kay to exact revenge for his quips in front of Princess Margaret? Whale wants to escape before Kay returns, but he finds himself caught in the chair, a turtle flipped on his back. He repeatedly throws himself forward, until the chair spills him out on one knee. He is stumbling to his feet when he sees Kay returning. With Elsa at his side.

Of course. What with Charles shuffling about, could Elsa be far off? Her tomboyish gait tosses a long tartan skirt around her white socks. She approaches with her head cocked at Whale, her eyes bright, a smile half tucked in her overbite. He hurriedly brushes the grass off his knees.

"Jimmy. How are you?"

"Elsa?"

With a look of deep concern and sympathy, she takes his hand in both of hers. "I saw Una O'Connor a few weeks ago," she explains. "At the A & P. She said you'd been under the weather."

"Oh, nothing out of the ordinary," he claims. "Getting old."

"Yes? Yes." She releases his hand, understanding he prefers not to discuss it. "We're all getting long in the tooth."

The puckish schoolgirl is half submerged in the extra chin and puffy cheeks of middle age, a thicker disguise than the makeup with which Jack Pierce buried her for the Monster's Bride. This is all Kay meant by monsters, merely actors who played monsters.

"Oh, but you have no business feeling old," Whale lies whitely. "You appear quite fresh, my dear."

She swats the compliment aside and laughs, a chuckle like a low echo of her girlish giggles at the Cave of Harmony.

Kay has been standing by, grinning proudly. "Back in a sec. You two must have scads to talk about." He races off again.

But they have nothing to say to each other. It's been so long that neither knows where to begin. Whale gazes at Elsa, through the middle-aged woman and the Monster's Bride to the comic ingenue at the Cave of Harmony.

"And what have you been up to, my dear?" he asks.

"Oh, some theater now and then. A little television. And one's hands are full just living with a genius."

Is that what we're calling him? Whale thinks, but he feels much too kindly toward Elsa to be cruel. There is a surprising sensation of calm, even relief, at seeing her here, a good fairy from a happy past. "Do you still sing your comic songs at that theater on La Cienaga?"

"The Turnabout? Now and then. But rarely."

"Do you ever do—oh, what was the one you did in London? Something like, 'I Just Danced with the Man Who Danced with the Prince of Wales?'"

She laughs. "'A Man Who Danced with *the Girl* Who Danced with the Prince of Wales,'" she gently corrects him. "Funny you remember that old thing. From our misspent youths. No, I haven't done those queer old numbers in years."

He smiles, feebly. Already his pleasure in remembering the Cave of Harmony turns sorrowful. Sweet pasts are as painful to recall as horrible ones, more painful, because here there's not even the relief of knowing he won't have to relive them.

Elsa gestures at the chair. "Please. You shouldn't stand on my account."

"Perfectly all right. But if you'd like to sit—"

"Oh, I'm fine, Jimmy. I can only stay a few minutes."

"Of course." This is merely a courtesy call on an invalid.

Elsa smiles and sighs and glances out at the party. "Oh dear. What's our pesky friend up to now?"

Whale looks with her across the lawn. Kay is returning again, accompanied this time by a stooped gray-haired man with a long rectangular face and wary, heavy-lidded eyes.

"Is that Boris? I haven't seen Boris in ages," says Elsa. "Our little chum appears to be arranging a reunion."

"Oh dear," Whale murmurs.

Karloff comes reluctantly, followed by a bashful girl in a dainty saucer-shaped hat who carries a blanket-wrapped bundle the size of a watermelon.

"Boris, darling," Elsa cries. "I didn't know you were here. These public revels are hardly up your alley."

Karloff grumbles that he came for the sake of his visiting niece. "Alice," he lisps, and waves the young woman into the circle. He introduces her to Elsa and Whale in his faintly absurd, self-important baritone. "And Miranda, my great-niece." His huge hand lifts the blanket in Alice's arms, revealing a bald infant with enormous blue eyes. And Karloff's dourness melts away. He gurgles and coos at the child like a dotty old woman.

Whale smiles politely at it, without interest. He notices Kay off to the left, eagerly waiting for them to do or say something extraordinary. It's embarrassing to have your past thrust upon you and find nothing clever to say.

"And what do you make of our royal visitant?" asks Elsa.

"Perfectly charming," Karloff declares. "A real lady."

"Of course she's a lady," Elsa scoffs. "What did you expect? A hussy in tennis shoes?"

A scrap of orange flares in the corner of Whale's eye. He looks and discovers Clayton standing a few feet behind Karloff in his bright knit shirt. The fellow watches with his hands on his hips, curiously, approvingly. His shoulders are broad and muscular, his crew cut very flat. He doesn't need shoulder pads or thick-soled shoes to look powerful. The old gentleman in the foreground has no shoulders to speak of, nothing to suggest a monster except two vaccination marks on his neck where Jack Pierce attached the bolts so tightly they left permanent scars.

Nevertheless, Whale's eyes automatically try to focus Clayton and Karloff together, going cross-eyed as if he were looking at one man. The original Monster and its shadow slide over each other, even as Whale tells himself these men overlap only in fantasy. Fantasy and memory, past and present, all short-circuit here, not in his head but out on the very real lawn. Whale strains to keep a proper face over his mental vertigo.

Clay recognized Karloff right away when he came up to the group around Whale. He isn't sure who the old woman is but hopes she's the Bride. What other girls did Whale work with? Clay assumes they're all good friends. He's surprised by how cool and distant everyone is, and how little attention they give Mr. Whale. Whale stands among them like the friend of a friend. When his eyes go funny, Clay thinks he's making a face at him to announce how silly and ridiculous this is.

"Hey, you! With the camera!" Kay shouts to a passing photographer. "We got a historical moment here. Come get a picture of it."

A man carrying a bulky Speed Graphic with a flash attachment like a steel daisy strolls over, scanning the group for a famous face.

"This is Mr. James Whale!" Kay announces. "Who made *Frankenstein* and *Bride of Frankenstein*. And this is the Monster"— he points at Karloff—"and his Bride."

"Oh, Karloff. Right," says the photographer, snapping to attention. "Everybody knows Mr. Karloff."

"I want one for myself," says Kay. "I'll pay you."

Instinctively, without thinking about it, Karloff and Elsa drift into position. "You heard the man," Elsa chirps at Whale. "What's sauce for the goose is sauce for the gander."

If his mind were clear, Whale would plead no, not today, but he is too muddled to do anything except obey. He tugs at his collar, afraid his tie is tangled around his neck until he discovers that he's wearing a neckerchief.

Kay stands by, playing director while the photographer fits a bulb into his flash. "This'll be great. Can you take a few? Can you get one with me in it?"

The flash goes off, a snap and crunch of light, just Whale and his monsters. Then a shot with Kay standing among them.

"Don't you just love being famous?" Elsa mutters through her clenched grin.

The photographer sees Karloff make a kissy-face at the baby off to the side. "Whose kid? Let me get one with Frankenstein holding the kid."

Karloff wants his niece to join them, but Alice blushes and refuses. She brings Uncle Boris her daughter, however, and hurries back behind the firing line. Karloff gently cradles the child. Whale stands on his left, Elsa on his right. For lack of anything better to do, they all gaze at the baby.

"Just a minute, folks." The photographer fusses with his lens. "If this don't get us in *Look*, nothing will."

Whale finds himself staring at the baby, *into* the baby. Her tiny upturned nose is like an absence of nose. A tongue flicks and squirms between her lips as if her heart is in her mouth. The bottle blue eyes don't stare back like human eyes but blindly roam and cross each other. She can focus nothing. Her memory holds nothing. Experience pours straight through her. Looking at such helplessness is like falling into nothingness. This is how we began, Whale thinks. This is how I will end. This helpless unreality is my future. The thing squirming in Karloff's arms grows more alarming, more terrible.

The camera flashes once, then again, as bright as lightning in the darkening shade of the banyan tree.

"Got it!" says the photographer, and Whale quickly turns from the child. He should have a headache, but he feels no pain, as if the confusion that began in seeing Clay with Karloff and grew in the mirror of this infant has cut him off from his senses. The exhaustion in his head pours into his body. He needs to sit, but he can't sit, not yet. There are still people out there. He remembers to smile at the faces exchanging good-byes.

"We'll be in touch," says Elsa.

"So good to see you again," says Karloff before he strolls off, clucking and cooing at his terrible baby.

"Catch you before you go," says Kay. "I'll make sure everybody gets sent a print." He goes off with the photographer.

"Good-bye," Whale tells everyone. "So nice to see you. Good-bye. Good-bye."

Until finally he is alone. He can stagger to the deck chair and lower himself sideways into the hammock of canvas.

"You okay?"

Whale gazes from under his hat at an orange shirt. Clayton Boone. He is strangely comforted to find Clayton looming so hugely over him.

"Tired. A bit tired. Nothing more." He takes deep breaths, hoping the oxygen will clear his head. The papery leaves of the banyan tree rattle in the breeze.

Out on the lawn a waiter looks up at the sky. Everyone else continues like a herd of kettles on the boil.

The light has darkened from a sunny English afternoon to a muddy overcast morning. The change touches Whale in every nerve, so deeply that it seems to come from his nerves, his own black mood clouding the sky. And he is struck by a smell, a familiar stink: rotting fish. He knows there's no dead fish here. It's another olfactory phantom, one he's had before, memory short-circuiting in his nose. This time, however, he identifies the odor, names its origin. The trenches outside Ypres. The morning stand-to. No-man's-land stretches before him, acres of mud and half-buried corpses, men and horses, ours and theirs, churned together in a foul stew so overripe it stinks like rotting fish. And it is still out there, forty years later, lightly covered with George Cukor's lawn and garden.

He sees Clay worriedly look out, as if he too smells bad meat. But all Clay says is, "Not going to rain, is it?"

Whale spots a red smear in the corner of Clay's mouth. "Blood?" he asks. "Is that blood?" He's frightened to think his eyes as well as his nose are hallucinating.

Clay wipes his mouth and inspects the hand. "Lipstick," he says with a snort. He had forgotten all about Beryl during the picture taking. He wants Mr. Whale to ask about it.

Whale says merely, "Ah," and lowers his head.

He looks exhausted, and Clay suddenly understands. The visit with his old stars has knocked it out of him, hitting the old man with the fact that he doesn't belong here. This world isn't his anymore. He is like me here, Clay thinks, more like me than I ever imagined. Clay is overcome by feelings of pity, curiosity, and protectiveness.

"Must have been funny for you," he says. "Seeing your monsters again."

"Monsters?" Whale sneers. "There are no monsters." His tone rises in a whine. "The only monsters"—he closes his eyes—"are here."

Across the lawn, a loud female voice proclaims, "Uh-oh."

All conversation has stopped. Men stare indignantly at the sky. A few women start toward the house. There's a ticking in the grass and, further off, a loud hiss of wind, solid and vertical. A sound of birdshot spatters the banyan leaves overhead. Birdlike shrieks come from all directions.

"Oh fuck," says Clay. "And we left the top down. You want to run for it?"

"Run for what?"

"It's raining!" Clay laughs. "Can't you see?"

From the shelter of the banyan, the rain is only a flickering of air, but everyone is going nuts. People jump and shriek as if bitten, throw coats over their heads and dash toward the house. The party scatters across the lawn. The banyan tree attracts a breathless handful. The birdshot quickens to a roar. The flickers thicken to a glassy curtain, then a milky cascade.

"Here," says Clay when rain blurts through the bough overhead. He takes Whale under the arm—a sleeve filled with skin and bone—helps him up and escorts him to the trunk of the tree where the foliage is denser, the other people crowded together. They whine and grumble, but Clay can't help laughing. It's hilarious seeing these fancy folks in a panic.

The patio fills with people jammmed against locked French doors. Only one door is open and everyone shoves and squeezes to get through. A pair of drenched waiters fit their trays together in a little roof over Elizabeth Taylor as they walk her into the mob, but people won't make way for the star. The crowd is full of pretty women soaked to the skin. Clay enjoys the spectacle of wet dresses clinging to bras and girdles. He looks for Beryl, hoping to see a drowned rat in her underwear, but the tease is nowhere in sight.

Clay expects Whale to laugh too—he should be tickled by the disaster—but Whale only stares out at it, his sole response a steady rasp of air through his nose.

He is hypnotized by the deluge. Watching the rain wash away George Cukor's party, Whale imagines it washing away the sod, the terraces, the entire hillside, uncovering the corpses from forty years ago. It is a fantasy, he tells himself, a vile image with which he hopes to purge his mind of rot. He grows angry when he can't turn the image off. The twisted, segmented trunks of the tree become a bundle of bones.

"Let's get out of this funk hole," he commands.

"You don't want to wait it out? Rain should let up soon."

"We're not sugar. We won't melt." O, that this too too solid flesh— He adjusts the brim of his hat. He steps into the downpour.

Clay has no choice except to follow. His impulse is to run, but Whale briskly walks, so Clay walks too, not wanting to abandon him. Clay cringes when the first nails of water strike his back. Once he stops fighting it, however, the rain feels good after the long, hot hours here, like a rush of carbonated water.

The minute splashes on Whale's hat form an aura, a ghost hat of spray, until the felt darkens and the hat becomes a sponge. A man and woman run by, holding hands as they race for the gate and the cars outside. Waiters with umbrellas splash out to the arbor where Cukor and Princess Margaret are unhappily packed with a dozen well-wishers. Clay sees Whale turning his head to look at the swimming pool as they pass it, the surface bristled with tiny explosions and large, brief bubbles.

Out on the road, the trees provide no cover. He and Whale stride downhill with the sheets of water sluicing over the tarred gravel. When they reach the car, Whale opens the door and gets in, not seeming to notice that the top is down, the upholstery popping with rain.

Prying the keys from a sopping pocket, Clay gets in, too, and turns the switch, and the roof slowly opens over them. When the rain is reduced to a drumming of canvas, Clay says, "There. Safe and dry." They couldn't be wetter if they were sitting in a puddle. Clay squishes each time he moves.

Whale peels off his hat. He solemnly inspects the lining. "A change of clothes," he mutters. "In the trenches, a dry change was heaven. The only heaven we could imagine."

Clay starts the engine. "I better get you home so you can get some dry clothes. Before you catch your death from pneumonia."

"Catch my death?" asks Whale. "Catch my death," he repeats, as though he didn't know the phrase.

His voice sounds broken and flat, but Clay is backing the car out. He has to wait until they're headed down the hill, behind the taillights of other fleeing guests, before he can glance over and see Whale, sitting very wet and rigid, staring straight ahead.

"You all right, Mr. Whale?"

He blinks. He slowly turns. "Jimmy. Call me Jimmy." He smiles. "I'm tired, Clayton. And wet. All I require is a change."

There's a distressed, slightly cracked look to his eyes, like a crease in the pupils. But he maintains his smile, the closed-lipped, gently mocking incision of mouth that Clay knows all too well. Clay decides to trust the smile over the eyes.

"I'll get you home quickly," Clay assures him. "I don't want it on my conscience that the man who made *Frankenstein* caught his death because of me," he adds with a laugh.

Whale hesitates. He turns away. "No. We wouldn't want that, now. Would we?"

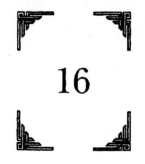

# 16

THE RAIN FOLLOWS THEM DOWN FROM THE HILLS AND ACROSS the city, not an isolated cloudburst but a seasonal freak that covers all of greater Los Angeles. The highways are a slick grayness speckled with headlights. Clay can't open a window, only the vent. The air in the Chrysler grows warm and muggy.

He tries to joke with Mr. Whale over Mother Nature's rude ending to Cukor's party, hoping to get them both laughing. Whale's only response is a thin smile. He sits stiffly behind the slap of windshield wipers, looking miserable yet aloof, like a park statue in the rain. Clay continues to feel both pity and responsibility toward him, although he can't tell if he feels sorry for the old guy because he's been made responsible for him, or the other way around.

The storm softens to a prolonged drumroll. As they come down Amalfi Drive, the sun dips below the heavy lid of clouds over the ocean to shine on an unearthly shower of bronze needles.

Clay parks by the front door of the house. Getting out of the car, he feels humiliatingly wet, like he peed in his pants. He bowleggedly follows Mr. Whale up the porch steps.

The door is unlocked. The hallway is pitch-dark.

"Maria!" Whale calls in. "Bring us some towels. We're drenched to the bone!"

But there's no response, nothing under the patter of rain except a hollow silence.

"Blast her. Come in, Clayton. Come in. If we track up her holy floor, it's her damn fault."

Whale goes squashing down the hall. Clay remains just inside the open door, prying off his tennis shoes and peeling off his socks. Not until a light snaps on around the corner does Clay close the door and follow. His bare feet slap the oak floor.

He finds Mr. Whale in the kitchen, a shriveled scarecrow in the harsh electric light. He stands over the table with his jaw open, gaping at a sheet of yellow paper.

"I don't believe this. Do you believe this? Look at this, will you?" He slides the note at Clay.

The handwriting in red pencil is very round and plump, with a pink splash where Whale dripped.

Dear Mr. Whale,

I hope this will not inconvenience you, but my husband and I have taken my mother to show her a house we are buying. We will also be taking her to dinner. We promise not to be late.

My mother requests that you ask Mr. Boon to stay with you until she returns. There are sandwiches for both of you in the icebox. She also asks me to tell you that she is sorry and this is not her idea, but I have not seen my mother for a long, long time. Thank you.

Yours truly, Mrs. Michael Ramirez

"I found it when I came in," Whale mutters while Clay reads. "I did not expect this. I didn't. It's not like Maria."

"Sounds like it's her daughter's doing," Clay offers, defending Maria, although Whale doesn't sound indignant but startled by the note, alarmed. Clay wonders what the big deal is about Maria taking the night off.

Whale fixes his gaze on the note again. His white eyebrows are pinched down, his nostrils wide, his mouth on the edge of a smile. Finally, it comes: a timid, rather sheepish smile.

"Certainly you had better things to do this evening than baby-sit an old man?"

"I didn't have anything planned," Clay admits.

"Then could you at least have dinner with me? Please. I can take care of myself afterwards. Despite Maria's impression."

"Maybe. Only—" Clay tugs at his cold, swampy armpit.

"Oh yes. We are both dampish." And, as if on cue, Whale lets go with a sneeze.

"You got to get into dry clothes right away," Clay scolds.

"And yourself," says Whale. "I think we can find you something to wear while your clothes dry out."

"I'll be fine."

"Oh no. Young men can catch their, uh, colds as easily as old men. Let me think." He presses a hand to his forehead. "Yes. There's a full bath upstairs. There are plenty of towels in the linen closet. Why don't you go up and take a nice long shower? I'll go change and see what I can find for you."

"I'm okay. Really."

"No, no, my friend. I couldn't bear the thought of dining dry while you were wet. Please. If we're going to bach it together, we should both be comfortable. That is what you say when men feed and take care of themselves? Baching it?"

Clay gives in. There's no point in prolonging his cold creep of clothes if he's staying for dinner. And he is staying, isn't he? He follows Whale out to the living room, then goes up the stairs alone. He hears shoes squeak and wheeze behind him as Whale goes off to his own room.

The upstairs bathroom is as shiny and spotless as something in a fancy hotel. Clay finds a large peach-colored towel in the closet. He turns on the shower and skins himself of his clammy knit shirt and shrunken chinos. His dead-white middle is stamped with a web of creases. Nudity is a relief and the hot water feels good. He scrubs the chilly numbness from his haunches, washes his hair, and waits for Mr. Whale to bring up some clothes. The old man seems more himself now that he's home, Clay thinks, remembering the cracked look in his eyes when they first reached the car. And before that, before the sky opened up, he had said something whose oddness now comes back to Clay, although he remembers only the oddness, not what was said.

He finishes and dries off, and Whale still hasn't come upstairs. Clay sits on the toilet and dries between his callused toes. He thinks he might kill time with a cigarette, but his pack of Luckies are a spongy mess. He grows impatient, then anxious, stuck in a strange bathroom without a stitch, nothing except a heap of soggy laundry. Has Whale forgotten him? Clay considers pulling on his khakis to go out and look. The stiff cloth has such a leadened chill, though, that he can't bear the thought of putting even his foot into them again.

He opens the bathroom door. "Mr. Whale?" he calls out.
No answer.

He wraps the towel around his waist, knots it, and shifts the knot to his hip. He steps into the hall. The only light is from the bathroom and a bit of daylight through an open bedroom door. He goes to the top of the stairs and calls out, "Where's those clothes you promised?"

Again, nothing. Rain ticks against the windows. Outside is a squeaking of birds and running water.

Now that he's out, being naked in somebody else's house is less impossible, spooky but not completely taboo. Clay goes down the stairs on tiptoe, to make his nudity less conspicuous.

"Mr. Whale? Jimmy?" But it isn't the right name for the man, even if he asked Clay to use it. "Where did you go?"

The sun has set and there's a bruised yellowy light in the living room windows. Something in the corner watches him come

down the stairs—a wing chair with shadows in its arms. On the
sofa lies a broken figure of pillows. The kitchen glows through
the dining room. There's another glow from the short hall to
the left of the dining room, between the stairs and the front
door. Clay grips the newel knob at the end of the banister.

"Mr. Whale?" His calling sounds stupid and desperate with
nobody answering.

At the end of the short hall, brightness shines in the half-
open door of what must be Whale's room. He would have to
hear Clay calling. Has he passed out? Has he suffered some kind
of attack, his heart or brain? A panic of possibilities races in Clay
as he steps slowly toward the door. He feels the whole house at
his back, following him like a shadow.

He peers in. He pushes on the door, afraid of what he might
see.

A dark bedroom. The glare of a desk lamp. The old man is
bent over the desk. His white hair is combed. He wears a clean
white shirt and, at his throat, a red splash of bow tie. He doesn't
move but sits perfectly still, one hand clamped over his mouth,
the other balancing a black gold-trimmed fountain pen.

Clay knocks.

And he jumps. He slaps a hand over his chest, twists around,
and sees Clay.

"Oh! Oh, of course. It's you." He stares like he can't quite
remember who Clay is. "Clayton. You startled me. You finished
your shower already?"

"Finished fifteen minutes ago. Been stuck up there waiting
for some clothes. Didn't you hear me calling?"

"My deepest apologies. I sat down to dash off this note—"
He looks at a sheet of paper in front of him. He turns it over.
"Lost track of time. Sorry. Terribly sorry." His eyes narrow when
he notices Clay's towel. "I promised you some clothes, you say?"

"Yeah!" Clay snaps. "You expect me to run around like this
all evening?" He is angry for getting so panicky. The empty
house did it to him, and walking around in the dark half naked.

Whale's eyes relax. The dry lips stick together in a slight

beak before they pop open in a smile. "I think we can do better than that." He stands up and goes to the closet. "You're wider than I am. And thicker. You won't want to attempt to get into my pants. Will you?"

"You said you had something that'd fit me."

"Sorry. I wasn't thinking clearly. How about this?" He takes a robe from the hook on the door, a long bathrobe of blue and maroon stripes. He averts his eyes when he offers it to Clay.

But putting his arms through the sleeves, Clay finds that the shoulders are too narrow and he can't close it over the towel. He can tell that even without the towel it'll just shut where one needs a whole foot of overlap.

"No? Alas. Oh, I know," says Whale. He opens a drawer and takes out a crewneck sweater. "Absolutely swims on me, but should take care of your upper half."

It does, the ribbed knit snug across his chest but covering his belly button. Clay pushes the sleeves above his elbows.

"Your lower half still worries me, however."

"You don't have any big trousers? Baggy Bermudas? Even some pajama bottoms."

"Sorry. My pajamas are tailored. Hmmm. Would it be too distressing to continue with the towel? No more immodest than a kilt, you know. While we do what we can to dry your pants."

"Do I have any other choice?"

"Very sporting of you, Clayton. Very well. Let's see what we can do about your things and dinner."

Going back upstairs to get his clothes, Clay feels very loose and drafty, like he's wearing a dress. This must be what girls suffer when they go without panties, except they have nothing to flop around.

He returns to the kitchen and joins Whale in the utility room. Whale wrestles open a wooden drying rack and sets it up over a drain while Clay cranks his clothes through the wringer on the washing machine. He's able to squeeze out only a few drops.

"I'm sure Maria can iron them dry," says Whale, draping

the knit shirt over a dowel. "When she gets in. In the meantime, we let them air dry. If you like, maybe we could put your drawers in the oven. See if we can dry them so you can cover up there."

Clay is tempted, but the notion of his dirty shorts displayed like a filleted flounder, with him or Whale checking on them every few minutes, is too ridiculous. "That's okay. I'm fine. When do you think Maria'll be back?"

"It depends. On whether they dine at an American hour or Spanish one."

"I don't care. I'm fine for now," Clay claims. Feeling conventional from the waist up, he feels less strange down below, especially after he sits at the kitchen table.

Whale opens the refrigerator and brings out two plates wrapped in wax paper, and a bottle of beer for Clay.

"You're not drinking anything?"

"I want to keep my wits clear. After our adventure, you know." He frowns as he fumbles with the wax paper.

Mr. Whale looks utterly out of place in a kitchen. Clay wonders what Maria would see if she walked in right now: Whale in shirtsleeves and bow tie, Clay in a terry-cloth skirt. The sandwiches are delicious, though, rare roast beef with lettuce and a touch of mustard. A mound of potato salad sits in the center of each plate. Clay gives himself over to the food.

Whale takes a bite of sandwich, and stops. He chews a moment. He sets the sandwich down, swallows, and makes a face. "How does the meat seem to you?"

"Fine," Clay says through a full mouth. "Real good."

"It hasn't gone bad?"

"Mine hasn't. Something wrong with yours?"

Whale licks at his teeth. "I guess not. My appetite must be off. But please. Go ahead. You can finish mine when you're done with yours. If you're still hungry."

He leans back in his chair and watches Clay eat. His face is calm, his eyes mildly sad.

Clay is curious again, and sympathetic, and he dislikes hearing nothing except his own chewing. "Must have been weird for you today. Being with all those people you used to work with but don't work with anymore."

"Yes," Whale admits. "But I've grown inured to the weirdness of their world. That life was over for me long ago. I had my fun. I earned my berries. I've moved on." His fingers drum the table. "I think I'll have a drink after all," he says. "Would you care for a little Scotch?"

"The beer's fine," Clay tells him.

He goes out to the living room and returns with a bulbous cut-glass decanter and a shot glass. He sits down and pours with a slightly shaky hand. "After dinner," he proposes. "If Maria isn't back? Can we try a few more sketches?"

Clay is surprised by the request after seeing his unsteadiness. "I thought you'd given up on my picture."

"The urge has returned. I'd like to try again. If you're game."

"I'm kind of bushed. Aren't you?"

"This will be casual. We won't even go down to the studio. We can work in the living room. You can watch the television."

Like Clay is a child. He wouldn't mind posing if Whale talked about his past again, but he doesn't know how to say that without sounding like a kid asking for a bedtime story.

"Oh, I don't care," Clay says. "Give us something to do while we wait for Maria."

"It will." Whale tosses back the shot, takes a deep, satisfied breath, and sets the shot glass off to the side. "I'd offer you coffee after the meal, but I don't know how to do the percolator. Can I offer you a cigar?"

"What I'd really like when I'm done is a cigarette. Mine got soaked."

"You should have told me earlier, Clayton. I can certainly scare up a pack of cigarettes."

Before Clay can explain there's no hurry, Whale is up again and out of the kitchen. Clay shakes his head over the way artists lock on their work, except Whale has been locking on this or that ever since they got back.

Clay finishes eating his sandwich, then Whale's before Whale returns with a pack of Chesterfields, a little sketch pad, and a couple of pencils. He's impatient to get started.

"You can have a smoke in the living room while I set up."

Getting up to follow, Clay is surprised again when his bare legs brush each other under the towel.

"Here," says Whale, dragging a straight-backed caned chair from the wall to the end table beside the sofa. "And here." He moves an ashtray over. While Clay lights up, Whale adjusts the table lamp and directs Clay on how to sit. His hands mold the air around Clay's head, and a cuff grazes his neck. Clay remembers how nervous he'd been in the other sessions, but he knows Whale better now, and Maria can walk in any minute. Clay is more at home in his self-consciousness.

Whale steps back. "Comfortable? Go ahead and smoke. Shall I turn on the television?"

"Naw. I don't think there's anything on tonight."

Whale stands beside the wing chair, to the left of the closed television cabinet where he's left his pad and pencils. The living room is larger than the studio, and the pattern of light and shadow cast by the table lamp makes the space larger still. Whale remains standing, examining Clay, frowning.

"Your costume makes you ridiculous, you know."

Clay looks at his sweater and towel. "Beggars can't be choosers," he says with a smirk.

But Whale is not amused. "It reduces you, Clayton. A man of your youth and physique? You should be free of encumbrance. All of a piece. Like a Greek statue."

"I'm not going to pose in my birthday suit, if that's what you're suggesting."

Whale looks startled. The sudden pinch in his eyes is followed by coldness. "Of course not. I was making an observation. Nothing more." He sits in the chair and brings the pad into his lap. He begins sketching, without looking at Clay.

Clay fears he's hurt Whale's feelings. "It's only my face you want, remember?"

"Uh-huh." Whale doesn't look up.

Clay has to take a drag of cigarette and focus on a dark window. Because, for a split second there, maybe because the sweater and towel feel as ridiculous as they look, he was tempted to take them off. If it would make the old guy happy. Clay's not sure why he wants to make him happy, except that the guy's had a miserable day and deserves some sort of pleasure, even one as unfathomable as drawing a naked man.

There's a rasp of pencil and rasp of air, Whale breathing loudly through his nose.

The only monsters are here.

*That* was the odd thing Whale said just before the sky opened up. It was the way he said it, with such bitter awe, that stuck with Clay, like something that should worry him.

"The only monsters are here," says Clay.

Whale looks up. "What monsters?"

"You tell me. It's something you said at the party. I said it must be weird seeing your monsters again, and you said, 'The only monsters are here.' "

Whale stares at him.

Aloud, the phrase doesn't sound so peculiar. "I was wondering which 'here' you meant. The party. Hollywood. Your imagination. Which?"

"I don't recall."

"You said it."

Whale resumes sketching, cutting the paper with repeated strokes. "If you say I said it, I must have said it. But I do not recall to what I was referring. Memories of the war, perhaps."

"The war?"

"I remember remembering the war," Whale mutters. "As the sky grew dark."

"When we were in the car," says Clay, suddenly recalling that, "you did talk about being wet in the trenches."

"Did I, now? There you have it. That is what I was thinking. Memories of the war."

Clay's curiosity deepens, confused with sympathy. "But that was so long ago, it can't still bother you, can it?"

"It shouldn't," Whale admits. "I don't know why I should be remembering it. Except—" He looks up, not to look at Clay but to gaze toward the closed front door. "When one is considering a journey to somewhere one has never been before, one can't help but dwell upon visits to similar places? Is that it?"

He has lost him, and Clay has no choice except to play dumb. "You're planning a trip?"

His gaze remains dreamy and preoccupied, as if he didn't hear. He looks down at the pad.

"Evans caught his between the eyes," he murmurs. "Very neat. A good morning's work for some proficient sniper. Old Cooke was less lucky. Caught in a pocket of chlorine gas without his mask. We found him flat on his back by the road, chest and mouth pumping at us like he was a landed trout. And then there was Sergeant Morgan—my God, I remember their names. Company Sergeant Major Morgan stood beside me, our backs against the trench wall. A single Boche gun out there lobbed shells in our direction, seeking its range. Morgan was tactfully correcting my attitude towards the Other Ranks. And bing! A chunk of shrapnel cut through his helmet. His skull burst open, spraying me with brains. Wet and mealy, like warm oatmeal. The very brains that enabled him to be so tactful."

Clay is thrown, not just by the sudden subject of deaths but the coldness with which Whale recalls them, a tensed, clenched telling. His earlier fragments of story had been sad and soft. These are as sharp and cutting as broken glass.

"Then there was Johnson the Younger, having a lie-down in the dugout one night. The rest of us were out shoring up a communication trench. And a shell fell just so, behind the line. Trench and dugout folded up, as neatly as a mouth clamping shut. We raced over with our picks and shovels to dig up the mud and timbers. Frantic yet delicate, terrified of digging into Johnson the Younger himself. We found his legs. We pulled and out he came. Just the legs. A beam had cut him neatly in two. We stood around with open mouths, like constables who tackle a thief and find nothing in their hands but the thief's trousers."

Why is he doing this to himself? Because Clay understands that this catalog of death is not directed at him but at something in Whale.

"And Barnett. Poor Barnett on the wire."

"Your friend?" Your sweetheart, Clay almost said, remembering that this was the boy who'd been sweet on Whale.

"He caught his one night coming back from reconnoiter. I wouldn't take him out, but McGill did. Just to give the lad a taste. They were nearly home when a Maxim gun opened fire. His body fell in wire as thick as briers. It was hanging there the next morning, a hundred yards from the line, too far out for anyone to fetch it during the day. They began a new bombardment that night, shelling us nightly, so we had to leave him on the wire. We saw him at morning stand-to and evening stand-to, just a speck in a rusty spiderweb unless one used field glasses or periscope. But one couldn't *not* look. 'Good morning, Barnett,' we'd say each day. 'How's ole Barnett looking this morning?' 'Seems a little peaky. Looks a little plumper.' His wounds faced the other way and his tin hat shielded his eyes, so it was difficult to believe he was dead. One could imagine he was napping on bedsprings and any moment might stir awake and pull free. He seemed quite close in the lens of a periscope, part of the very landscape I had shown him on a sunnier morn. I could admire his figure, without fear of impropriety.

"He hung there for a week. Until we were relieved, taken out of that section of line. We introduced him to the new unit before we marched out, speaking highly of his companionship."

Clay feels shaken open by pity, a wateriness like a head cold in his muscles. He's afraid of getting emotion all over himself. He's ashamed to think that Whale assumes he served in Korea and knows firsthand the horror he describes.

"Oh, but we were a witty lot. Laughing at our dead. Telling

ourselves it was our death too. But with each man who died, I thought, 'There but for the grace of God. Better you than me, poor sod.' Because my relief was stronger than any grief."

He begins to hum, a tune Clay has heard him hum before. Only in the second stanza does he murmur words with the tune:

> *Oh, death where is thy stinga-linga-ling?*
> *Grave where thy victory?*

"But that was years ago!" Clay says angrily. "You survived it. It can't hurt you now. It's no good to dig it up."

"Oh no, my friend. It's digging itself up. I cannot keep my mind off it. There's nothing in the here and now that's strong enough to take me out of myself. Not even you."

Clay is ferociously, inexplicably angry: at being shamed by an old man's experience, at being moved by it, at his sudden desire to comfort the man. And the only comfort he can think of offering is to snatch Whale from the past.

"Here." Clay yanks the neck of the sweater over his face. His body acts on the impulse before his mind makes sense of it. "Why don't you draw me." He tosses the sweater on the sofa. He has to stand to undo the towel.

Whale blinks, not yet understanding.

"You wanted to draw me like a Greek statue. All right, then," Clay snarls. He pulls at the knot. He doesn't want to look at Whale as the towel falls open. But he doesn't want to look at himself either. He glares at Whale.

Whale stops blinking. He sits perfectly still.

Clay has let go of the towel. His nudity feels enormous; it fills the room for a moment. His hands drift and weave, wishing for pockets. He resists the impulse to cup them over himself—a body's nakedness should be of no importance after hearing what war can do to a body. He defiantly parks the hands on his hips. "There. Not so bad," he claims.

Whale continues to look, his eyes wide and expressionless.

And Clay can't help seeing himself in those eyes, like he's

standing in front of a mirror. First he pictures his dick—the head like a little face—and fears that it looks small next to the rest of him. Then the puckered smirk of his appendectomy scar, but Whale won't know what that means. His eyes seem to take in all of Clay, a body thicker and more uneven than any Greek statue, in patches of tan and white, a stocky piebald statue.

Clay has to sit down. His bare ass waffles in the cane seat and his genitals squeeze up between his thighs. He opens his legs so they can drop down. He considers bringing his knees together and hiding himself so he's only a tuft of hair, except then he'd look like a girl.

And Whale still doesn't respond. Not so much as a smile or thank you. His gaze remains wide and blank. He opens his mouth to take a breath.

"No," he says dryly. "It won't do."

"What won't do?"

"You are much too human."

Clay tries to laugh, but he's stunned. His feelings are hurt. "What did you expect? Bronze?"

"Don't move." Whale abruptly stands up. "Stay as you are." He comes across the room.

But he walks past Clay. He goes through the dining room and out to the kitchen. The door to the garage opens.

Clay wants to cover up, which is silly now that there's nobody to see him except the ceramic dogs on the mantel. He can't believe he's doing this or that he should feel hurt that Mr. Whale isn't pleased.

The distant door closes again. The footsteps return and Whale comes through the dining room. He is smiling now, a mild apologetic smile, and carries a round cardboard box in front of him.

"I would like you to wear this."

He removes the lid as he comes around. He sets the hatbox on the sofa and steps back, afraid to come too close to Clay.

Clay takes the box and covers his lap with it. Inside is a gas mask. He immediately knows what it is, although the mask looks nothing like the ones they wore for tear gas training at Pendleton. He lifts it from the box, an old-timey antique like the face of a deflated Martian. "Why?"

"Why? Why not?" Whale becomes giddy. "For the artistic effect. The combination of your human body and that inhuman mask? Quite striking, Clayton. Very modern, very French. An attempt at surrealism, you know. Please? If it's not too much to ask."

It looks no worse than something a skin diver might wear, with a metal snout sewn into the mouth. "I don't know."

"Just for a minute, Clayton. Just long enough for me to see the effect?"

Holding the mask is like handling a pair of handcuffs: you can't help wanting to try it on. Clay doesn't buy Whale's art jabber for a minute. This has got to be a mask from the First World War. To wear it is to play some kind of game with Whale. Clay doesn't know what Whale wants from the game, but he feels obligated to play, intimidated by Whale's experience.

He holds the mask up to his face. The old rubber and oily canvas don't smell too bad. Clay fits it on the top of his head and draws the mask down. The living room turns brownish yellow in the thick glass goggles.

"There are straps in back," Whale explains.

Clay can just hear him—the rubber-lined canvas covers his ears. His fingers find a strap and little buckle.

"Let me help you." Whale is behind him.

His vision enclosed in two round windows, he can't see Whale. Other fingers work alongside Clay's, cold fingers with pointy tips, as matter-of-fact as the fingers of a father teaching a son to tie his shoes. Whale buckles the second strap without Clay's help.

"Now what?" Mouth muffled by the inhalator, Clay hears his voice from inside his head. He has no trouble breathing, although the air tastes rusty and his chin grows damp.

Whale comes around to stand in front of him. Discolored like an old snapshot, a jaundiced yellow, he grins as he steps back to examine Clay. He appears very amused and breathless out there. Everything is *out there*, as if Clay were in a fishbowl, his head anyway, completely detached from the body that's more exposed than ever when his face is trussed up. The distance between Clay and his own body makes his muscles tense, his joints queasy. He nervously taps his knees with his hands.

"All right. That's enough. Let's take it off."

"What was that?" Whale keeps his grin.

"I said I've worn it long enough!" Clay raises his voice to make himself heard. He reaches back to undo the buckles.

"You want to come out? Of course. Allow me." Whale steps in past the goggles. "We don't want to tear the straps. A family heirloom, you know."

Clay drops his hands so Whale can undo the buckles.

He can sense the weight and warmth of Whale behind him. But Whale doesn't unbuckle the straps. He does not even touch them.

Clay turns left and right. The mask cuts off his vision. He can't see Whale.

"I'm here. Oh yes. I am still here."

A shock of touch: two hands grip Clay's shoulders. All sensation rushes from his skin, then rushes back again, balled up tight beneath two bony hands.

"What steely muscles, Clayton."

The voice is toneless. Breath tickles the nape of Clay's neck. The hands squeeze.

Clay grabs the frame of the seat. He has to stop his arms from automatically swinging a fist at the man touching him. It's Mr. Whale, he tells himself. He's teasing him, spooking him. He can't be serious.

A hand slides over his shoulder. It strokes his arm, caressing the slightly stiff skin of the tattoo.

Clay jerks his shoulder to shake him off. "Just undo the mask, why don't you!"

"Relax, Clayton. I can't hear you. I can't hear a word."

The hand on the tattoo is replaced by something boneless,

breathy, and sticky. He's kissing the tattoo. Clay's skin goes tight. His muscles tense from head to toe to protect himself against touch. His body is so rigid that he can't speak, can't think.

"What a solid brute you are."

The hand caresses his chest. The flexed muscle makes touch worse, exposing his nipple to the finger that circles it. There's a sickening ticklishness beneath his skin, like a desire to puke, only it's his skin that needs to vomit.

The finger presses the nipple like a button.

"No? Maybe this, then?"

The hand slides over the bunched folds of stomach toward the numbness in Clay's lap.

And his body rebels. The tattooed arm swings backward, slamming an elbow against a skull. Clay has jumped from the chair, knocking into the end table. The light flies up as the lamp spills over. Glass pops and the room in the goggles goes dark.

Clay pulls at the mask, straining to tear it off by its chin as he steps from hands that claw at his arm and waist. His ankle is caught by a hand—no, the sofa leg—and the room flips over. Clay hits the floor, jamming the inhalator against his mouth. He quickly gets up, on his knees and elbows, pulling at the mask, hating Whale, hating himself for being such a sucker.

A body leans against his upended ass. It collapses over Clay's back and holds on, pawing and grabbing at his front.

"Death before dishonor, Clayton. Death before dishonor."

A strap breaks. His chin pulls free and Clay rips the mask off. He can breathe again. He can think again. There is light from the kitchen. For a second, the man on top of him is no worse than a kid riding him piggyback.

"Oh yes. I have you now. How much honor do you have now?"

The awful ticklishness between Clay's legs is a hand fingering and squeezing him.

"Get the fuck off!"

"I have you now. What will you do to get yourself back?"

Clay jabs with his elbow, but it's no good when he can't see his attacker. His body remembers a wrestling move. He rolls over hard, flipping Whale on his back, catching a glimpse of his own exposed front and the white hands clutching at him from behind. His body continues the move, swinging knees and legs around to straddle his opponent and pin him, face to face. Clay needs to see the face so he can hit it.

His fist has swung back. He sees an old man with white hair and wild eyes. The fist opens as it comes down; he slaps Mr. Whale across the face.

The face goes blank. Whale stares like a man slapped from a dream. "Yes? Yes?" He closes his eyes, bracing himself for another blow, tilting his face up for it.

But Clay can't slap him again. "I'm not that way. Get it through your fucking head. I don't want to mess with you."

The eyes remain shut. "Oh, but you feel good, Clayton." His hands clasp Clay's hips. "You're not such a real man after all. Are you?" A hand goes for the crotch.

Clay snatches the wrist before it can touch him. He grabs both hands by the wrists, which means he can't hit Whale again.

Whale opens his eyes at Clay. He is breathless and grinning.

"Wait until I tell my friends. I had you. Naked in my arms. Won't they be surprised."

"I haven't done a damn thing with you."

"Oh, but you have. You undressed for me. I kissed you. I even touched your prick. How will you be able to live with yourself?"

The birdcage ribs and little potbelly rise and fall between Clay's legs. Clay hates the intimacy of his breathing, but he continues to grip his wrists.

"What the hell do you want? I'm not going to let you blow me, if that's what you want."

"I want you to kill me."

His half-lit eyes are shining. It's like he's mocking Clay, insulting him. But there's a tremor in his voice, a tear stuck in the throat.

"Kill me, Clayton. Break my neck. In self-defense. No jury on earth will convict you."

His breath deepens, his grin tenses.

"Or strangle me. It would be oh so easy to wrap your hands around my neck. And choke the life out of me."

His hands come toward his throat to demonstrate, bringing in the hands that clutch his wrists.

Clay grips the wrists harder and pulls them out to the sides, to get his hands away from the throat. "I don't want to kill you."

"You have to. I've taken away your honor."

He means it. He's serious. "You're crazy."

"Utterly. And getting crazier every day. You'd be putting me out of my misery."

His wrists are two handfuls of twigs. Breaking his neck would be as simple as crushing a beetle between a thumb and finger.

"You're not man enough to kill me? Not man enough to feel dishonored by what I did to you?"

"You didn't do shit. Except make a fool of me. I thought you were a friend. Why're you filling my head with shit?"

"If you're not man enough to do it for yourself, can't you be man enough to do it for me?"

"I don't want to kill you."

"Why not?"

"Why the fuck should I?"

And he says, coldly emphasizing each word, "Because I am old and sick and I want to die."

Clay can't think clearly. Buzzing with adrenaline and anger, his mind leaps ahead of itself. "Then I'll get charged with murder. Spend the rest of my life in prison. If I don't get the chair. Thanks but no thanks."

"But I've taken care of that. I wrote a note."

"A note?"

"Explaining what would happen. That I had to have you or perish in the attempt. You'd be the innocent youth. Protecting his virtue from the dirty old pansy."

Clay is stunned to hear he has planned this, whatever it is. For how long? But just trying to figure it out while he sits on Whale makes Clay feel as if he's considering it.

He has to get off him. He holds Whale's wrists while he stands up. He releases the wrists and quickly steps back, looking around for his towel, desperately needing to cover himself. "I'm getting out of here. You're nuts. Just talking to you is making me nuts."

Whale remains on his back. "Don't leave me like this! Please. We've come this far."

Clay sees his towel, beside the overturned table and the spilled lamp. He doesn't pick the towel up. It isn't enough and his nakedness is the least of what's wrong here. He should go to the utility room, get his wet clothes, and get out of here. But he's not yet ready to leave Whale. Clay has turned away, but he continues to watch Whale across his shoulder.

Whale lets out a sigh as he sits up, a heavy moan from deep in his chest. He puts a hand to his chest as he props his back against the sofa.

"You okay? I didn't crack a rib, did I?"

Whale stares at him as if *he* were the one who was crazy. "I don't want a cracked rib. I want a broken neck."

"Look. You shit on me tonight. I trusted you, but you shit on me. But I don't feel I got to kill you for it."

"You stupid boy. This isn't about you. This is for me. Don't you understand?"

"You fucking better believe I don't understand."

"I am losing my mind," he hisses. "Every day, another piece goes. If it's not headaches, it's a daze, a fog. Either sleepless nights or wakeless days. Time has come undone. I cannot distinguish past from present from fantasy. Soon there will be nothing but fog. Fog and helplessness. It's no life for a man. It's an infant's life. A dog's life. I need you to kill me."

A new trickle of pity runs through Clay's confusion, and new anger. "If you want to die, do it yourself. I don't want any part of it."

"I can't do it alone! I don't want to die alone." He gazes up at Clay, desperately. "To be killed by you would make death bearable. Even beautiful."

Is Clay supposed to feel flattered by that? He feels horror, disgust, and pity.

"What can I give you so that you'll kill me?" Whale pleads. "You can have the car. Would you like the house? I'll sign over everything to you. I'll make out a new will tonight, if only you'll promise to kill me."

It's not real. None of this feels real. Clay waits for Whale to burst out laughing, as if it were all a joke. Then he fears Whale will think his silence means he's mulling the offer over. "No," he says. It doesn't sound forceful enough and he says it again. "No!"

Whale remains on the floor with his back against the sofa. "You disappoint me, Clayton. I should have known. You're not the cold-blooded American killer after all. You're a softhearted bloke. A bloody pussy*cat.*"

His voice tightens on the last syllable. His entire face tightens and knots.

"What was I thinking? What did I expect?" he demands in a strangled voice. "I knew all along nothing would come of this, only—have I lost my mind already?" The constriction in his throat flutters. "Oh, stupid, stupid, stupid life." He is crying. "Christ in heaven. To live through so much, and then dribble away in—? I *have* lost my mind! Only why can't I lose it completely!" He strikes at the floor with his fist. "Then I wouldn't care! I'd be indifferent to who I was. I wouldn't give a tinker's cuss to who I might hurt. I'd be free of human pettiness. And free to kill myself myself. You're right. Yes. It is *my* death. My own bloody death. So why can't I take it?"

After so much craziness, Clay is horrified to see Whale crying and snarling at himself. He doesn't know what to say except, "You'll get better. You're not that old."

"I don't get better! I only get worse. And madder. And more helpless!" His voice drowns in angry sobs. His head falls over and he grips it in both hands, his whole body shuddering and shaking.

Clay cannot leave him now. He wants to get out of here, but he can't leave Whale like this. "When's Maria coming home? She *is* coming back tonight?" Did he lie to him about her too?

"Maria?" Whale looks up.

"She is coming back, right?"

"Of course she's coming back. I just—" He rubs at his face. He clumsily smooths his hair with the hand. "I should go to bed. If I'm in bed when she comes in, she'll never know how insane I was tonight." He forces himself to his feet. His legs tremble and he has to hold on to the sofa arm. "Good God, I am tired. I really must go to bed."

"Let me give you a hand," says Clay. He needs to do something, and putting Whale to bed will bring this bizarre night to an end. He comes over and takes his arm. In the shirtsleeve is a second sleeve of skin and sinew loosely wrapped around a bone.

"Don't tell Maria," Whale whispers. "This would only upset Maria, you know."

"I got to tell somebody. You're not well."

"Poor woman. What we almost did to her. If she had come home and found you with my corpse—? How could I have forgotten what that might do to *her*?"

And me, Clay thinks. What would it have done to me? He steers Whale into the short hallway, watching him put one shoe in front of the other, not minding the cold hand that clenches his shoulder for support.

He leads him into the bedroom and sits Whale on the edge of the bed. His bow tie came undone in the scuffle and Whale tugs it from his collar. Then he sits there, as if expecting Clay to undress him. "If you can get my shoes, please."

Clay crouches at his feet. He can at least untie his shoes. One is double-knotted, and rather than pick at the knot, Clay holds the foot firmly by the ankle and pries the shoe off.

A hand lands on Clay's head and thumbs the bristles of crew cut. Touch is only a nuisance now.

"My apologies, Clayton. My deepest apologies. If I had known you were such a softhearted bloke, I wouldn't have done this to you. No matter how mad I was. Can you forgive me? Can we be friends again after tonight?"

"Forget it," says Clay, and hears how ridiculous that sounds.

"Oh, and this button." Whale lifts his chin and points to his collar. "I can never manage it when I'm tired."

Clay leans in to pinch large fingers around the button and buttonhole. His hands can't understand if they're supposed to choke or caress the sinewy throat they brush; it's odd to undo another man's button.

His face is six inches from Whale's. The blue star bursts of his irises waver as water passes over them. Clay has to blink as if the water were in his own eyes. The button comes undone. The throat swallows.

"If I had seen you like this a few months ago, Clayton?" Whale whispers. "I'd be in heaven. Alas. You're not Ganymede tonight. And you're certainly not Charon. Oh, the fantasies we tell ourselves."

He turns, breaking their shared gaze, and Clay can step back.

"I can undress myself, thank you." He hauls his legs up and stretches out on the bed. "In a minute. I need to catch my breath first."

"All right. Did you want me to close the door?"

"If you would." He is flat on his back, without a pillow, a disheveled, unraveled man in stocking feet. He turns his head to the side. "When *you* die, Clayton, be sure your brain is the last organ to fizzle. Or if you have a stroke, pray that it obliterates everything."

"You'll feel better tomorrow."

"Tomorrow and tomorrow and tomorrow," he mutters at the ceiling. "Good night, Clayton."

"Good night."

Clay pulls the door shut and it clicks. He stands there a moment, unable to remember who he is or why he's here. Then he remembers his clothes in the utility room. He pads down the hall and through the kitchen, feeling like a very large, dumb bull who's blundered indoors where he doesn't belong.

His clothes are still wet. He decides to wait for Maria to iron them dry, since he has to wait for her anyway. He needs to tell her what happened, not everything but enough to let her know that her boss is cracking up. There are bedsheets on a shelf over the washing machine. Clay shakes one open and wraps himself in it, like the survivor of a shipwreck.

The decanter of Scotch is still on the kitchen table. Clay takes it with him when he goes to the living room. He finds the pack of cigarettes on the floor and promptly lights one, then goes about setting the furniture back up, the chair and end table and table lamp. The lamp didn't break, only the bulb, and there's no other evidence of violence, except the gas mask. He picks it up from beside the sofa. How did he look in it? Half robot, half man. A monster with a dick. Is this what Whale wanted? Not Clay Boone the yardman, but Clay Boone the monster. His very own monster, like Frankenstein's only bug-eyed and naked?

Clay shoves the mask into its box. He needs some light in this room. There's a floor lamp behind the wing chair in the corner. Clay goes over and turns it on, and sees the drawing pad in the chair. He takes it up, sits in the chair, takes a swig from the decanter, and opens the pad.

There are no pictures of him. As either a monster or himself. There are nothing but scribbles and scrawls, two pages worth. An occasional eye emerges from the jagged coils. It hurts just to look at these ragged knots and snarls. He's not surprised there's nothing here but has to wonder if the pages in the studio are covered with anything better. Did any of Whale's pictures resemble Clay in the slightest? Or was it fake, every bit of it? Every minute of the hours they spent together?

He is exhausted. He drops the pad and props his feet on the hassock, adjusting the sheet around his shoulders. His mind and body are equally numb, deadened by all that's happened.

He tries to lighten his heaviness with the Scotch and cigarette.

Won't this make a tale? A once-famous man offered him his house and car if only Clay would kill him. Clay doesn't remember the offer until now, when his chance has passed and the old loony-tune is safely asleep at the other end of the house. Is he a pussy for not doing it? A chicken? Would it be so awful to have a death on your conscience if you got a Chrysler convertible out of it? Maybe if it'd been a Corvette, Clay thinks with a smirk.

But he knows that these smart-ass thoughts aren't half of what he's feeling. Underneath are emotions packed so tightly together that he can't begin to identify them. What kind of crazy pain does the old guy suffer that he'd want someone to kill him? And that Clay would be his killer? Good old Clay Boone? Yet there were moments tonight, split seconds, when Clay seemed close to becoming that. It certainly would've given him the great drama he sometimes thinks his life needs, the war story to end all war stories, but one he would have to tell to the cops. And Mr. Whale finds no satisfaction or peace in having such enormous experiences in *his* past.

Clay takes a deeper swallow of Scotch. He is amazed to discover himself full of murder, tenderness, and sorrowful awe. And a strange joy in knowing that he could have killed Whale yet didn't. It's terrible to feel so many things about one man.

The rain seems to have stopped, and Clay wants to open a window but can't bring himself to move from the chair. Now that the excitement is over, he wishes Maria would return so he could go home, put tonight behind him, and become himself again.

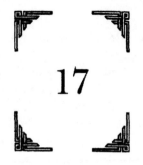

# 17

NIGHT. RAIN. A HISSING OF WIND. LIGHTNING STRIKES, SO CLOSE that the sight and sound are simultaneous, a crash of light.

James Whale bolts up in bed. He gasps for breath and stares around in panic. But he's in his own room, his own bed. He's home in California, safe from harm, although he cannot remember where he was in his dream or what frightened him there.

An electrical storm flashes and cracks in his window. He gets out of bed to watch it. Reddish sparks and white sheets of electricity jump between earth and sky. The thunder sounds exactly like a stagehand shaking a sheet of tin, more convincing in life than it ever is in theater. The hillside is illuminated in blinks and bursts. There are no trees tonight. His trees have disappeared. All that remains of his lawn is a barren slope covered with stumps. Whale can't see his swimming pool either. Has he lost his pool? He hasn't used it in months, but he's grieved to think that the storm has washed away his pool. He should go out and look for it.

He goes through a door, before he remembers that there is no door leading out from his bedroom. But it's too late, he's already outside, descending stone steps to the black grass of his lawn. Everything is black or gray, except for the crimson flashes behind the obelisks and splayed tombstones of his little cemetery. He has always disliked cemeteries, despised their sentimental morbidity. He cannot understand David's annual visits to the grave of his old boss, Thalberg, in the sunshine and flowers of Forest Lawn. At least his own cemetery is dark and Gothic and mockingly theatrical.

Walking away from it, he finds that the hill levels out where it should descend. The grass gives way to mud. He isn't dressed for mud but wears wing tips and fresh seersucker. Everything has washed away and only mud remains. Where is Boone? He must ask Boone what happened to their grass.

There he is. A flash of light catches a figure stepping past a reddish hedge of briers. Whale hurries toward him. It has to be Clayton. Who else could have such broad shoulders and such a flat head? Whale fears that he frightened the boy badly tonight and that Clayton will flee him. He walks more quickly, but it's difficult stepping over the convoluted furrows and folds of sick earth. He tries shouting to Clayton. He has no voice, but the boy should certainly hear him *think* the shout.

Whale reaches the hedge, which isn't briers but squashed coils of rusted barbed wire. Another burst of light shows Clayton farther off, following the hedge toward its end. The lightning is now tuned to Whale's mind; when he needs to see something, a new burst illuminates it like a photographer's flash. The boy turns again, away from the wire. He grows shorter in each bright flash, sinking into the earth as he walks. His head bobs along the surface, then it too is gone.

Whale rushes to the spot where the boy began to disappear. He finds the entrance to a ditch, a parting in the earth that begins level with the ground and gently slopes downward. He enters, full of old, familiar anxieties. The ditch deepens, the sides rise above his head. The sky narrows to a long gash of flickering gray. He walks on springy, half-rotted duckboards, in a ten-foot-deep corridor of timbered mud and sandbagged walls.

His chest thuds like a bass drum with the shock waves of shell bursts he cannot hear. He goes numb as he always went numb in the long approaches to the front lines. He makes no effort to understand how a ditch in his yard could lead to the endless maze of trenches in France. He disconnects all willpower and emotion, surrendering his will to whatever might happen. As he did each time they went over the top into no-man's-land. As he had one night near Zonnebeck when he and his patrol were surrounded by Germans. Like men under hypnosis, they lowered their guns and raised their hands. Surrender saved his life. Another six months in the trenches and he'd be as dead as the others. He is suddenly filled with guilt and regret, not because he surrendered but because he's alive. Are there Germans here tonight? He can't tell if this trench is German or British, abandoned behind the lines or waiting to be recaptured. There's nobody here, not a living soul. The burlap sandbags shoring up a corner suggest a mound of soft skulls. The sides of the trench are splashed with a whiteness like moonlight, the quicklime used to stop the rot of corpses buried in the walls.

He comes to what must be the forward trench. He turns right and promptly sees a man, a soldier propped outside a funk hole with his legs across the duckboard. His puttees are neatly wrapped around his calves, his tin hat pulled over his eyes, and it takes Whale a moment to understand that he's dead. He steps gingerly over the stiff legs. But there are other bodies ahead, a dozen or more men sprawled across his path. He is alone in a trench full of corpses. He feels no satisfaction in outliving them, only horror and shame and loneliness.

A little bell tingles. The bells of hell? No, the bell of a lamb. A startlingly real lamb comes trotting around the next bend in the trench, black-faced and woolly, splashed up to its belly in filth. The little bell around its neck jingles as it hops over the dead. Whale has seen her before, one morning after an artillery duel, some soldier's pet, German or English, whose dugout must have been smashed open by a near miss, freeing a lamb to wander no-man's-land. They tried to whistle and call her in—nobody dared go out and risk his life for a sheep—but she remained out there, tiptoeing in hell like a four-footed ballerina. Now she has come into the lines on her own. She prances past Whale and he reaches down to pet her. A coarse woolly warmth brushes his palm.

"Hey!"

He looks up and the lamb jingles off. Clayton stands above him, up on the parapet against the dark clouds. Whale is frightened for him, terrified that a sniper will see Clayton and pick him off. But the American shows no fear. He leans down in his crew cut and pumped-up knit shirt, gesturing to Whale to come up too, excitedly pointing out a ladder against the mud wall.

Whale hesitates, then surrenders his will again. He goes to the ladder and begins to climb. Whether or not there is gunfire up there, the surface of the earth is terrifying. The narrow sky opens, wider and wider. His heart races and his mind freezes on its last thought, like the mind of a man going under anesthesia.

Unfolding and stretching around him is the endless plain of death. The artillery flashes along the horizon illuminate the shattered bones of trees, water-filled shell holes like empty eyes, the torn nerves of concertina wire. Clayton stands out by the wire, fifty yards away, startlingly small against such desolation.

He signals Whale to follow. He has something to show him.

Whale obeys, numbly, blindly, his mind shut down against the hiss and snap in the air around him. The very air can kill you here. But Clayton shows no fear. He stands quite tall on a slight rise of ground, the rim of a crater, a blasted pock of earth the size of a swimming pool. He points down into it.

Whale comes alongside him and looks. The crater is full of men, bodies gathered around a puddle at the bottom like animals sharing a water hole.

Clayton proudly gestures at the dead, thinking Whale should be pleased by what he's found for him.

Whale wants a closer look. He somehow knows that these

men are important to him and needs to see why. He stumbles down into the crater, braking his descent with his feet turned sideways and one hand against the scored earth, ashamed of spilling dirt on their faces.

He reaches the bottom and bends over the nearest corpse in khaki. Barnett. Leonard Barnett. Bareheaded and pale, but he was always pale. Whale is thrilled to see his boyish face and silky hair again, even if the boy is dead. There are no wounds, no rips or gaping holes in his muddy tunic. His eyes are closed in breathless, dreamless sleep. Beside him lies Company Sergeant Major Morgan, without his helmet, his head shaved like a convict's but his skull roundly whole again. And over there is Evans. And Cooke. And Tozer! He forgot all about John Tozer, who was killed while Whale was in a training camp in England. Who made love with him by the Old Birmingham Canal many years before. Are all his dead here? He eagerly looks for his father, his mother, even Colin Clive, but there are only soldiers here, men who died in battle. People who died in peacetime must be in a prettier, more appropriate spot. But these dead are more than enough. They are good company if he's to die too.

He remembers that Clayton is waiting for him at the top of the crater. When he looks up, however, the fellow is gone. There is only the dark, silent sky. No matter. He does not need Clayton now. These are his people. He lies down among them, finding a spot between Barnett and Tozer. There is no putrefaction, no stink of rotting meat. There's no smell at all, only a soft warmth as if he lay among breathing pillows. No, he is the only one breathing here. The others are perfectly still, at rest, at peace. He shifts down among their peace, takes a last breath and closes his eyes.

He opens his eyes.

He is in his bedroom again. The desk lamp is on. The night outside is silent. He wears what he was wearing hours ago, when the nude figure like a soft, bulky sculpture left him here and pulled the door shut.

The emotion of his dream remains intact. He knows immediately it was only a dream but wakes from it so easily that the emotion remains intact, the peacefulness, the clarity. His head is startlingly clear, like the air after a storm.

He lies very still. He knows what he must do. He is confident he can do it. He knows how too. It seems to have been in the dream. The crater in no-man s-land was like the dark green eye of his swimming pool at night.

He sits up, into the familiar fog of gravity and headache. Good. He cannot mistake his peace for the return of health. It's only a clearing in the woods. The dark thorny thickets will close around him again. He must act quickly while his peace lasts.

He sees paper and pen beneath the desk lamp. He should write a note to let anyone who cares—Maria, of course, and David—understand that he knows what he's doing. He goes to the desk and sits down. But the sheet of stationery already has something written on the other side:

To ALL I LOVE,

   Do not grieve for me—My nerves are all shot and for the last months I have been in agony day and night—except when I sleep with sleeping pills—and any peace I have by day is when I am drugged by pills.

He already began his suicide note? He wrote one two weeks ago, let it sit in a drawer for a few days, then threw it away. This is a new one. He remembers it now. He wanted to suggest that any injury done to him by his yardman was his own fault. That he was mad and dangerous. He recalls sitting here, struggling to find a way to explain all that, when Clayton came into the room looking for clothes. He never finished the note. Lucky for the boy he didn't do what Whale wanted him to do.

Whale decides to continue this note, free to write what he wrote before.

I have had a wonderful life, but it is over and my nerves get worse and I am afraid they will have to take me away.

The words catch up with him and he stops. Has he had a wonderful life? Or is this an empty courtesy of the dead? He rereads the salutation: "To ALL I LOVE." But such phrases do not sound dishonest. At this moment, he seems to love everyone and everything, even his life. He resumes writing:

So please forgive me—all those I love—but it is best for everyone this way.

The future is just old age and pain. Good-bye all and thank you for all your love. I must have peace and this is the only way.

JAMES WHALE

There. He folds the letter and sticks it in an envelope. He looks for a stamp before realizing a stamp isn't necessary. "To Those I Love," he writes on the envelope, and props it against the gooseneck lamp.

All right, then. Now he can go. Without barbiturates or blood. He is too familiar with pills and blood for either to have any mystery. His death will be new. And it will be clean, immaculate, without a trace of filth. He has loved his swimming pool without ever learning to swim. After weeks of drowning in the past, it seems only right that he drown in the present. Everything is coming together.

He changes his shirt. Even death by water requires a clean shirt. He considers a shower and shave but knows he must act quickly while his clarity lasts. He puts on his shoes and a sand-colored blazer. He decides against a tie. Death should be informal and intimate.

He is combing his hair at the mirror when he remembers he had something else scheduled this morning. Oh yes. David is coming to breakfast. But he cannot postpone this to have one last breakfast with David. Not when the moment feels so perfect. Now or never, he thinks. The note will explain everything, although David is so overly sensitive that he'll probably assume his ex-lover chose this particular morning to strike at him.

He leaves his room and walks calmly down the hall. He pauses at the living room to give it a final look. The sky outside is pale. Gray light spills in at the windows—it's not as early as he thought. Then he sees the thing in the wing chair, something white, a corpse wrapped in a shroud. He nervously approaches, afraid that he's not awake but is still dreaming, and his act will accomplish nothing. The shrouded body loudly snores. It's Clayton. He's sunk in the chair with his legs on the hassock, cocooned in a bedsheet. He did not go home after all but spent the night.

Listening to his snores, watching his saggy, sleeping face, Whale remembers what he wanted from him. Death before dishonor. The tattooed shoulder peeks from the sheet. You can't believe everything you read. He knows he went mad last night, believing fortune and accident might enable him to fulfill a fantasy. Maria was out, Clayton was naked, and Whale surrendered to what he might make happen with a few well-chosen pokes and prods. But a nude American isn't death, even with a gas mask. The body that pressed him to the floor was a contradictory weight of hard muscle and soft flesh. It had been cruel and selfish to think he could turn a fellow's delicate stupidity into a beautiful murder.

He considers returning to his bedroom to add a postscript to his note, an apology to Clayton. But no. He should leave the boy out of this altogether. He hopes Clayton will go home this morning before they discover the body.

He tiptoes through the dining room to the kitchen. The table has been cleared, the dirty dishes stacked on the counter, which means Maria did come home last night. He regrets how this will upset her, but it can't be helped. She's a tough bird, she has her religion to protect her. And Mexicans are supposed to be at home with mortality, what with their candy skeletons and

Day of the Dead, although Maria pooh-poohs all that as the superstitions of bumpkins.

The knob of the kitchen door turns and he tugs on it, gently, so as not to make noise. He pushes on the screen door. The stretched spring twangs like a plucked string. He steps into the cool morning air.

The sky looks very immense and deep with the horizon at his feet. The canyon is full of misty shadow; the orange pastels along the crest shade upward into the rich chemical blue of a stage-light gel. The slope of the hill carries his footsteps over the wet lawn toward the greenish blue of the swimming pool. On the roof of the studio, a catbird does a dazzling string of impersonations, ending in the sweet rendition of a nightingale.

He comes to the concrete border of the pool. The water is beaten smooth by last night's rain, its only motion the sway and break of reflected sky. There's a smell of chlorine, not poison gas but summer nights with young men laughing and splashing in the dark. All around the pool stand the vertical blasts of green, not exploding earth but serene and living cypress trees.

Everything is coming together. Past and present, life and death, all dissolve together in the solution of the pool. He has enough clarity of mind to wonder if his peace is real or if he's simply lost his mind completely. What difference does it make? If one could suffer phantom pains, why not phantom peace, phantom wisdom? Yet his calm feels right, his resolve firm. He is ready to go. And he suddenly understands: It was to prepare for this moment that his past has been pouring into him these recent weeks. Against his will, everything came home to him, his fantasies, his childhood, his war, either in silence or aloud with Clayton, his life insisting on telling its true story before he declares it over. He has been breathing in the scattered pieces of himself, so that he may breathe them out again.

He strolls to the other end of the pool, the deep end. He decides to jump rather than wade into death. He stands with his hands at his sides, gazing down into the faintly milky water, waiting for one last good thought.

From the murk of the Old Birmingham Canal to an emerald swimming pool above Santa Monica Canyon. What a life he has had. What a rich, extraordinary life.

The sky grows paler, brighter. The pool is covered with a skin of light, like a crinkled sheet of quicksilver. A single crack patched with bitumen wiggles in its depths. He waits for the wiggle and crinkles to subside, so that the pool might be a mirror and he can fall through the open sky.

# 18

Something plops into Clay's sleep like a stone. He fills with circles and ripples, then closes over and is still again, without waking.

A roar of bells blasts him awake. The telephone is ringing. A hard pair of little shoes thunder out to answer it.

"Hello? Oh, Mr. David!"

Clay blinks at the sight of a softly colored, sunlit room and his pig-knuckled feet sticking rawly from a bedsheet. He recognizes Maria in black dress and white apron chattering on the phone by the far wall.

"No, no, Mr. David. He did not tell me. But no problem. We would love to see you for breakfast." She scoldingly cuts her eyes at Clay.

There's a half-empty whiskey decanter on the television cabinet. Clay doesn't feel hung over but like he's been punched in the kidneys. He fell asleep with his back wedged low in the chair.

He's got nothing on under the sheet. He quickly remembers why.

"We will see you at ten? Very good, then. Good-bye." She hangs up and faces Clay with haughty nostrils and a stern frown.

"It's not what you think," he croaks.

She holds up her palms. "I will not ask. I do not care. I have brought you your clothes." She points at the neatly folded stack beside the hassock. "All I ask is that you get dressed and go. We are having company for breakfast. It is better that you are not here."

Clay rubs at the sleepy thickness on his face, and remembers the gas mask. "I need to talk to you about Mr. Whale."

"There is nothing you can say that will surprise me."

"Maybe. But I still need to talk. Do I at least have time for a cup of coffee before I go?"

"Of course. I do not blame you for what happened."

"Nothing happened."

"Uh-huh. And that is why you need to talk?" she scoffs. She rolls her eyes and takes a breath. "I come home and find you like this? Out like a light. No, I do not blame you. I blame my daughter for keeping me out so late. And myself for enjoying her company so much. It is dangerous to have too good a time." She pauses. "I only hope you did not get him excited. It could give him a new stroke."

Before Clay can begin to explain, she turns and stomps into the kitchen.

He gets up and finds his undershorts in the stack, starched and ironed. He shyly slips them on under the sheet, which feels odd considering how naked he'd been in this room last night. The world is a different place by daylight. Last night was unreal, as impossible to describe to anybody as a bad dream.

It would be so easy just to go, Clay thinks. Without telling her what happened. Let Maria find out on her own that her cracked boss wants to be murdered. Clay doesn't have to come back to this house again, not even to mow the grass. But he can't leave now. He feels full of open windows and doors, which he thinks he can close by talking to Maria.

He's zipping up his chinos when she comes out again with a breakfast tray. "Here," she says, setting the tray on the telephone table and coming over with a rolled pair of socks. "I forget to bring you these."

"Thanks." Then, before she can go, Clay quickly asks, "Why do *you* do it?"

"What do I do?"

"Look after him the way you do. Take care of Mr. Whale like he was your flesh and blood."

She stares at Clay, amazed that an explanation is necessary. "It is my job. I do it well. I did it when he was happy and it was easy. It is only fair I do it now when he is ill." She cocks her head, wondering if that answered his question.

"So it's mostly for the money?"

"Money?" she says, and abruptly looks insulted. "Salary, yes. But not just money. Is it for money that you are with him?"

"No!" Is that how she sees him? "The only money I've gotten is what he's paid me for sitting."

"No, I did not think so, Mr. Boone. But I do not know what you want from Mr. Jimmy."

Clay doesn't either, but that's why he needs to talk. "So how come you're so loyal to him? Even now, when he's a little . . ."

He can't say it, but she can. "Crazy? *Nuts.*" She nods to herself. "Old and mad. I do not know. Maybe I feel sorry for him? Maybe I think that if I take care of him, God will provide someone to take care of me when I am old and sick?" She sounds skeptical. "That is anyway how I live my life. And I have known him a long time. He is like the family dog that one takes care of even when it is old and sick. You cannot forget it was once a good dog. Enough talk. I must take the dog his coffee."

She returns to her tray, picks it up, and breezily marches around the corner toward Whale's bedroom.

Yes, he can tell Maria what Mr. Whale wanted him to do last

night, thinks Clay. She's every bit as possessive as Whale once said she was, although not like a wife for a husband. Where Clay feels respect and fear as well as pity for the man, Maria seems to have only pity. Which can't be right, but she's not going to be too shocked when she hears what happened.

He hears her knocking on a door. "Mr. Jimmy? Mr. Jimmy? Morning, Mr. Jimmy." The door slowly opens. "Mr. Jimmy?"

Clay is pulling on his shirt when she comes back around the corner, without the tray, fists swinging at her sides. "Where is he?" she demands. "What have you done with him?"

"He's not in bed?"

"No. What did you do with him?"

"I didn't do a damn thing with him."

She goes to the foot of the stairs and shouts, "Mr. Jimmy! Mr. Jimmy!"

"I put him to bed," Clay tells her. "That's all I did. He's not there?"

Maria doesn't answer but races up the stairs.

Clay tucks himself in. He refuses to give in to her alarm. The old man has to be somewhere. It's like she thinks he did what Whale wanted him to do. For a moment, Clay wonders if he had.

Her short legs come tumbling down the stairs. "He is not up there. Look for him! We must find him!"

"Maybe he doesn't want to be found. Maybe he's playing hide-and-seek." But Maria is too upset for him to be sarcastic. "Maybe he went down to his studio?"

"Yes!" She likes that idea. "You look there. Let me look in his room again."

"You think he's hiding under his bed?"

"I do not know!" she snaps. "This is not like him. He is not well. He cannot be gone!"

"Relax. You check the bedroom. I'll look outside. Maybe he just went out for a walk."

"Yes. You are right." She angrily shakes her head. "Only out for a walk," she spits. "Wandering the streets in pajamas.

What will the neighbors say?'' She hurries toward his bedroom again.

Clay goes through the kitchen to the back door. He wants to think that she's as batty as her boss. And yet, once he's away from her, uneasiness and fear fill Clay's chest. His windows and doors are still wide open. The old man isn't well and it's easy to imagine that something terrible has happened.

"Mr. Whale!" he shouts as he starts down the hill.

He can't tell if the studio door is opened or closed. The little hut at the foot of the hill looks peaceful and toylike in the morning light.

"Are you down there?"

He went nuts last night, but he was mostly all right when Clay put him to bed. He was all right enough to apologize for going nuts. The wet grass is very cool and real on Clay's bare feet. He waits to hear Maria at his back, calling from the house that she's found him.

Still walking toward the studio, Clay senses from the corner of his eye that the swimming pool is different. The blue green smoothness is no longer solid but marred by something in the far end. He looks. An object keeps splitting apart and coming together in the jostled plates of water. Like the stick figure of a man.

Suddenly, Clay is running. His feet are pounding over the grass, his elbows springing forward. He leaps headfirst through the slap of water. When his eyes open, he is arrowing through green silence toward a tinted figure beside the drain. It is a man. It rests lightly on its back in a float of clothes, with an upward sway of straight white hair. A stroke and frog kick bring Clay close enough to grab the front of the shirt. He scissors his legs together to drive himself toward the light. The body weightlessly follows.

He breaks the surface, gulps the air, and treads water, hauling Mr. Whale toward the side. He catches a glimpse of closed eyes and paraffin face.

"Almost there," Clay tells him. "Almost there."

He gets an arm around the chest and heaves the body over the curb. He pulls them both out with one desperately strong arm. The body is instantly limp and heavy. It falls backward on the concrete, hitting its head, but Mr. Whale doesn't moan or complain. Clay drags him forward to rest the head in the grass. The legs bend at the knees and hang over the curb.

Clay grips a wrist. Nothing. He presses his hand against the chest. Again, nothing.

"Son of a bitch," he says breathlessly.

He grabs Whale's chin and jerks it back.

"You crazy son of a bitch."

His thumb and fingers pry open the locked jaw. He takes a deep breath and fits his mouth over Whale's mouth. He has to do something and the Marine Corps also taught him this. He slowly exhales into the mouth; the rib cage ballons upward. And Clay suddenly knows that the man has done this to himself, that he wanted to die and Clay is attempting to deny him his death. But nothing done to the lungs can bring back a man without a heartbeat. The mouth in his mouth is like raw liver. He is blowing air into a dead man. Nevertheless, Clay cannot pull his mouth away until he has emptied his lungs and finished his breath.

He sits up and takes a deep breath for himself. Then another. He remembers to wipe off his mouth. He is looking at Whale's face.

The skin is whiter than the eyebrows or stringy hair. It catches the sun like a block of wax. A blue shadow deep inside approaches the surface under the closed mounds of eyelids. The features of the face disappear in the whiteness. Clay suddenly sees how well he's come to know that face, now that it's gone.

I have never been so close to death, he thinks, even as he realizes he's never been so close to another life.

"Ohhh!"

Pebbles scattering in front of her, Maria comes down the path, her run slowing to a walk. The apron is balled up in her fists, one fist crushing a sheet of paper with the cloth. She stares at Clay.

And Clay sees what she must see.

"I didn't do it," he says. "This wasn't me."

"Oh, Mr. Jimmy," she moans in a scolding, disappointed tone.

"He wanted me to kill him, but I didn't." He can't give the denial the desperate voice it deserves. "He did it himself. He wanted it done and nobody else would do it."

She doesn't seem to hear him. Her round face closes like she's about to burst into tears. "You poor, foolish man. You couldn't wait for God to take you in his time? You had to take it in your own hands."

And Clay understands: she's talking to Mr. Whale. She already knows. How?

"He says here good-bye." Maria waves the folded paper. "I find it in his room. He is sorry, he says. He has had a wonderful life, he says."

Water runs over the chin, the pool water coming up as the chest empties itself of Clay's breath. There's a trickling motion beside the wax shell of his ear: an ant scurrying through the yellowish stalks of grass. The interior of his half-open mouth is as blue as a cow's tongue. This isn't Mr. Whale. Mr. Whale is gone. This is only his shape, his footprint. He wanted to go and he's gone. Clay wants to be happy for him, but all he can feel is helplessness and disbelief. A wonderful life?

He slowly stands up. He gestures heavily at the note. "Can I see that?" He needs to see Mr. Whale one more time. If he's not in the body, perhaps he's in the note.

Staring at her boss with such steadiness that her tears remain balanced in her eyes, Maria is about to let Clay take the note. She suddenly jerks it away. "No. You are wet. If you get the paper wet, the police will wonder how and why—" Her eyes widen and the tears retract. The grief in her face gives way to fear. She looks around in a panic, at the neighbor's house beyond the hedge, at the little road that runs past the studio. "You must leave," she whispers. "Quickly. Get away from here. You were not here this morning. You did not spend the night."

"But I didn't do this!"

"The police will not know that. The police will want to investigate."

"We have his note."

"But they will investigate! You will be questioned."

Clay can't understand how she can worry about him when she should be full of grief for Whale.

"Do you want to be questioned about you and Mr. Jimmy? And it will be written in the newspaper. They will write lies about Mr. Jimmy. Please, Clayton. It will be better if you are not here. If I find the body alone."

Half of Clay burns to read the note, but the rest of him is surprised at how tough and practical the old lady can be.

"Does he mention me?"

"*You?* No." She unfolds the note and glances at it. "He mentions no one. Only 'All I Love.' "

Clay is disappointed. He does not know why, but he wanted Whale to mention him. As if he needed to be a part of his death.

"All right, then. I'll go. I was never here."

He hates the sound of that. But if he's not part of Whale's death, the death is certainly part of him now. It will always be part of him, whether he wants it or not.

"But how're you going to explain this?" He points at the figure in its dark halo of wet concrete.

"What do you mean? He murdered his self."

"No. How did he get out of the pool? Did *you* fish him out?"

Maria grimaces. "You are right. Yes. We must put him back."

"I guess."

They both hesitate, looking down at Whale, finding the idea of returning him to the pool strange and cruel, like tossing back a fish they don't want.

Maria slips the suicide note into her apron pocket. She bends down to lift Whale by the shoulders. He's too heavy.

"I'll do it," says Clay.

He grabs the jacket by its shoulders and drags the body around parallel with the pool. It grinds against the concrete, leaving a fresh smear that immediately begins to evaporate. Clay is ashamed to turn the man's death into something awkward and ludicrous. Despite the bright sunlight and singing birds, the act has the midnight weirdness of a scene in one of the dead man's movies, only this time the Monster and the housekeeper clumsily work together to dispose of the doctor. One doesn't know whether to laugh or gasp.

Further thoughts and feelings about this morning will come to Clay over the next days, months, and years, whenever he attempts to understand what the past two weeks—it will never cease to amaze him that they knew each other only two weeks—means to him, how they might have changed who he was.

Maria stoops over to adjust the collar of his shirt. "Poor Mr. Jimmy. We do not mean disrespect. You will keep better in water." She nods to Clay.

He rolls the body over and it splashes on its belly. It bounces a moment in the waves of the splash, then begins to sink. As it drops along the steeply curved wall, the air in the chest slowly flips the body around. Looking up at them with closed eyes and a mouth half open for a sigh, Mr. Whale sinks backward into the softly bleared, thickening light. His legs are weighted by the shoes, but his arms trail upward and the hands lightly flutter as if waving good-bye.

# 19

THE NEWS THAT THE DIRECTOR OF *FRANKENSTEIN* AND OTHER
horror pictures was dead appeared two days later, tucked in corners of local obituary pages. "Discovered in his swimming pool
by his housekeeper, the drowning was judged an accident by the
coroner's office." David Lewis, as executor of the estate, did not
release the suicide note. He thought he was protecting his friend.
In the years ahead, the implausibility of the accident spawned
rumors of jealousy and foul play among gay circles in Hollywood.
Nobody else much cared or remembered who James Whale was.
The truth did not become public until twenty years later, when
Lewis took the note from a shoe box in his closet and gave it to
Whale's biographer.

The body was sent to Forest Lawn and cremated. A funeral
service took place that Sunday at the north wall of the Great
Mausoleum. Two dozen folding chairs were set up facing the
outdoor honeycomb of niches and plaques like a mammoth
chest of drawers. It was Memorial Day weekend and less than a

dozen people came. Lewis was there, of course, and a few former bridge partners. Carl Laemmle, Jr., couldn't come, but he sent a card saying that six trees would be planted in Whale's memory in one of the new forests in Israel. The only veteran of the movies to attend was Una O'Connor, who played the housekeeper in *Bride.*

His real housekeeper was there, seated in the last row with the yardman. An odd pair—a middle-aged Mexican woman with a black net hat and old-fashioned parasol, a husky young Anglo in a snug borrowed jacket and necktie—the former employees kept to themselves, with a secretive air of sorrow and pride, as if they believed they were the only true mourners.

There was a reading of the Twenty-third Psalm. The Elgar *Pomp and Circumstance* march that provides the tune for "Land of Hope and Glory" played through the loudspeakers, a standard selection at Forest Lawn when the deceased was English. Then it was over and the mourners drifted out to their cars, guiltily thinking about lunch or the day's races at Santa Anita or how well attended their own funerals might be. Only the yardman lingered to watch the masons cement a marble square over the little urn, then caught up with the housekeeper under the trees and awkwardly offered his arm to escort her out.

# HOMAGE TO MR. JIMMY
## An Afterword to the Paperback Edition

People of my generation first encountered his movies on the Friday night late show: *Frankenstein*, *Bride of Frankenstein*, *The Invisible Man*, and *The Old Dark House*. We were kids and it was past our bedtime, so these movies were like dreams—dark, disturbing, wonderful dreams we could share with friends. There were other horror movies too—*Dracula*, *The Wolfman*, and *The Creature from the Black Lagoon*—but even then many of us knew that the first set of titles were better, classier, somehow funnier *and* scarier. Not until we were older did we notice that they'd all been made by the same man, a director named James Whale.

I went to college in Virginia in the 1970s, which was a golden age of cinema, foreign and American. I fell in love with movies. I thought of myself as a would-be director long before I became a would-be novelist. I was a movie snob for a long time, turning up my nose at old Hollywood, avoiding the monster flicks until I was well into my thirties. I was living in New York with my boyfriend, Draper, another movie junkie (we were already making short films together; I wrote and he directed and we divvied up the other tasks), when one winter the local PBS station showed all the horror classics. That's when I truly discovered Whale.

His movies were a revelation. First there was their look. They were playfully stylish, mixing expressionist camera angles with elegant long shots and manic, silent movie editing. The emotions were oddly sophisticated. *Frankenstein*, his first horror picture, is almost classical in its feeling, yet with surprising sympathy for the monster. In the next films, however, Whale began to mix things up. *The Invisible Man* and especially *The Old Dark House* are black comedies. *The Bride of Frankenstein* is blacker still, and marvelously slippery, leaping from horror to comedy to pathos to parody. Whale was playing games of genre-fuck long before Billy Wilder and Francois Truffaut.

Whale made other movies beside the horror films. His *Show Boat* remains one of the best screen adaptations of an American stage musical. His version of *Waterloo Bridge* is a perfect little melodrama, and *By Candlelight* is a deft little comedy in the style of Ernst Lubitsch. But the monster movies were different; the monster movies were new. There was nothing quite like them when they first came along. They are where Whale made his mark on cinema history. I sincerely believe *Bride of Frankenstein* is one of the great American films, right up there with *Citizen Kane*, *Sunset Boulevard*, and *Godfather II*.

Around the time I rediscovered the horror movies, I learned that Whale was gay. A gay man myself, I couldn't help being intrigued. Vito Russo in his groundbreaking book, *The Celluloid Closet*, repeated the rumor that Whale's career ended in 1941 because he was too open about his sexuality. There was also the mystery of his death: he was found drowned in his swimming pool in 1957. I read conflicting reports of accident, suicide or murder. And then, one night over dinner, a British friend, a documentary filmmaker, told me something I hadn't heard yet: Whale had fought in the First World War; he was a working-class boy who'd served in the trenches—which gave a whole new dimension to the man. The horror movies weren't just spooky kids' stuff anymore, but war stories, pieces of autobiography. I became utterly fascinated with Whale that night. I couldn't stop thinking about him.

I didn't know what to do with my obsession. I'm a novelist, not a biographer or I would've written a biography. I began to make notes for something, maybe a screenplay, about the last weeks of Whale's life. "I don't know," said Draper. "Sounds like a novel to me."

Reading around, I found there wasn't much about Whale, and a lot of it was clearly make-believe. Then I stumbled on a small book published by Scarecrow Press in 1982, *James Whale* by James Curtis. It was a gold mine. I didn't always agree with Curtis's interpretations (I agreed even less when he expanded the book for a new edition, *James Whale: A New World of Gods and Monsters*, in 1998), but his facts always rang true. When Curtis didn't have a fact, he was silent, which might be maddening for the general reader but gave my imagination more room to work in. A few facts go a long way in fiction. You don't need or even want to know everything. There's a fine movie by the Swiss filmmaker Alain Tanner, *La Salamandre*, where two friends, a novelist and a journalist, research a murder. The journalist uses facts; the novelist uses narrative logic. At one point the novelist insists, "No more facts! They only get in my way!" The two men arrive at more or less the same solution.

The Curtis book gave me something else I needed: it solved the mystery of Whale's death. Debilitated by a stroke, aware he would never get better, he took his own life. Curtis published the suicide note that Whale's well-meaning ex-lover, David Lewis, hid for twenty-four years. This carefully chosen death seemed fitting for a man whose monster famously said, "Love dead, hate living."

My original intention was to write a hybrid of biography and fiction, one of those meta-novels where the novelist regularly pokes his head through the backdrop to tell the reader what's real and what's made up. It was my overly scrupulous way of writing fiction about a real man. Then I hit upon the character of Clay Boone, who is entirely fictional. Clay was going to be minor figure, an occasional visitor whom the general reader could identify with. But Clay took on a life of his own; the dangerous friendship between him and Whale grew and deepened and became the center of the novel. I took out the pesky authorial commentary: it had eased me into the story but now only got in the way. The story had its own momentum and I stopped worrying about historical truth. As I neared the ending, I actually began to resent history. One day I confessed to my agent that I was feeling frustrated. "No matter what I invent for Whale, he still has to end up dead at the bottom of that damned swimming pool." My agent laughed and said, "Quit grousing. Most authors don't know how their novels end, and you've been handed a great ending."

I finished a first draft and showed it to a few trusted readers. I learned what worked and what didn't, then wrote a new draft. My agent sent the novel out. There were rejections, some politer than others, until Matthew Carnicelli at Dutton took it. He loved the book, but wondered if I might put more Hollywood in, just to juice it up for the general reader. I resisted, until my friend Ed Sikov read it. Ed is a film historian, and I only wanted him to catch my errors. Ed found the history accurate, but he too wanted more Hollywood. "Not for juice," he said, "but because I want to know more about Whale's life when he was successful." Of course, I went back and wrote two new flashback scenes, including the premiere of *Camille* where Whale meets Garbo, one of my favorite chapters.

The book was published in 1995 as *Father of Frankenstein* to good reviews and decent sales. I began to hear from other people who knew and loved Whale's movies. There's a huge world of monster fans out there and some are very smart. I became good friends with one, David Skal, author of an excellent cultural history of horror, *The Monster Show*. David had arrived factually at some of the very ideas that I discovered imaginatively, in particular the role of the First World War in the horror films. Whale incorporated not only the horror of the trenches, but its gallows humor, which he mixed with the bitter gay sarcasm that is part of "camp." The monster movies opened the door on a new twentieth-century sensibility that drew upon humor, history, and sexuality.

I also heard from people who'd known my protagonist. There was a letter from the niece of David Lewis, the ex-lover: she understood I was writing fiction but was sorry I'd made her uncle bald. She told me politely but firmly that he died with a full head of hair. Yet I failed Lewis in another, more important way, which I heard about from other people, including the writer Gavin Lambert. Lewis was not closeted but fairly open about being gay. When he worked at Warner Brothers, before he and Whale broke up, Jack Warner called him into his office one day and said, "Do you have to live with Mr. Whale?" "I don't *have* to live with him," said Lewis. "I *want* to live with him." I'd misread between the lines in an account about Lewis, but my mistake wasn't just factual. For the sake of the story, I needed a gay man who was more guarded than Whale, more representative of their time. Lewis was my fall guy. You should also remember we see Lewis only from Whale's point of view, and ex-lovers aren't always objective sources. Nevertheless, David Lewis was a richer, more complex, bolder man than the figure in the novel.

But you probably want to hear about the movie, don't you? Everyone enjoys hearing about the movie, and I don't blame them, especially since it turned out so well. Novelists are supposed to hate the films made from their books, but I love mine.

I never think in terms of a future movie while writing a novel, not even this one. However, shortly after finishing the final draft, I saw the film of *Six Degrees of Separation* with Stockard Channing and Donald Sutherland. In the part of a charming friend was the great British actor, Sir Ian McKellen. Afterwards I told Draper, "McKellen would make a great Whale. He even looks a little like him." I mentioned this to my agent, who not only agreed but knew McKellen's address. We sent him an advance copy with a note: "If this were ever made into a movie. . . ." I got a nice note back. "I'm terribly busy with *Richard III* right now but look forward to reading your book one day." I figured that would be the end of it.

Over the next months, before the novel came out, a couple of major studios asked to see it. My agent and I were pleasantly surprised. This interest promptly disappeared after the new Tim Burton movie, *Ed Wood*, opened to great reviews and bad box office. They must have thought movies about weird old directors were the next new thing and wanted to be ready with one of their own. Their curiosity didn't last long enough for me to get a lunch out of it.

Finally, the book was published and I heard from my agent again. A young director wanted to option it for a possible low-budget independent feature. "His name is Bill Condon. His last film was *Candyman II*. Shall we pursue this?"

Well, beggars can't be choosers. Some wonderful directors

started out making B-pictures, although at this point, to be honest, I just wanted the option money.

Only after the contract was signed did Bill and I talk on the phone. And we liked each other instantly. He too loved movies, all kinds. He loved Whale's work and understood how the horror films were simultaneously funny and profound. And we had friends in common, including Ed Sikov. I told Bill the book was his baby now, but he was free to pick my brain. He said there were a few changes he was considering, including making the housekeeper, Maria, Central European rather than Mexican American. "Go ahead," I told him. "I realized in the middle of writing the book that she's based on my Swiss-German grandmother." He also wanted to try something different for the ending. I told him about an epilogue I couldn't make work, where Clay is married with two kids and he wakes his son one night to watch *Bride of Frankenstein* on the late show. "Hmm," said Bill. "Do you mind if I try something like that?" He asked if I had any ideas for actors to play Whale. I told him how I'd sent the bound galleys to McKellen. "Ian McKellen, huh? Hmm."

Bill wrote the screenplay that summer and showed me the first draft. He listened to my good suggestions and ignored my bad ones, but the truth is we saw things the same way ninety percent of the time. He kept me posted on what was happening with money and casting. Clive Barker came on as executive producer; his chief contribution was the use of his name and the loan of a nice house where Bill could meet Sir Ian. When Ian first read the script, he said no, it was a gay suicide story. "With my politics, I can't play such a role." "Please read it again," said Bill. "You'll see something else is there." Ian did and liked what he saw and he committed to the project. He was good friends with Lynn Redgrave; they'd always wanted to work together, so Lynn came on as the housekeeper, now renamed and renationalized.

A very talented, up-and-coming actor named Brendan Fraser was approached for the part of Clay. He liked the script but didn't like the title. He thought *Father of Frankenstein* sounded like a cheesy horror picture, which is the point, of course, but Bill couldn't bring him around. My theory is that after starring in *Airheads* and *George of the Jungle*, Brendan felt that if he were going to do a serious movie, it damn well better have a serious title. Since his involvement meant that Showtime would put up a million dollars, what Brendan wanted Brendan got. "What do you think of 'Gods and Monsters' for a title?" asked Bill apologetically. "The only other one I can think of is 'Mr. Jimmy'"—the housekeeper's name for Whale. "No, 'Gods and Monsters' is better," I agreed. (There was talk of changing the title back, but it didn't happen. Since the movie is now better known, it's easier to rename the novel, which I'm happy to do, not least because the novel's title has become *Father-of-Frankenstein-basis-for-the-movie-Gods-and-Monsters*. The new title is shorter.)

Filming began in July 1997, a little more than two years after my first talk with Bill—virtually overnight in Hollywood time. There was a twenty-one day shooting schedule and a budget of only three-and-a-half million dollars. Draper and I flew out to Los Angeles toward the end of the shoot. We arrived one afternoon at Occidental Studios, an old soundstage from the 1930s, and walked into the vast empty set for *Bride of Frankenstein*. "My God," I said. "I write one little paragraph and look at all the work somebody had to do."

"You're the novelist?" a nervous production assistant asked. "Does Bill know *the writer* is here?" We assured him that Bill had invited us.

We hung out for three days, talking to Ian, Brendan and Rosalind Ayres, who plays Elsa Lanchester, the monster's bride. (Lynn Redgrave had already finished her scenes and I didn't meet her for another five years. "You were channeling my grand-mother and didn't know it," I told her. "My family is thrilled.") Ian didn't remember getting an advance copy of the novel. "Did I write back? Oh good. I read your novel, but only after I read the script. You see, one is sent so many things that I read nothing unless there's money attached." Then he added, "But a friend read the book when it came out and he told me, 'There's a nice part for you if this ever becomes a movie.'" Brendan was terribly earnest, telling me he'd read the novel three times and asking if Clay were named Clay as an allusion to the subtitle of Mary Shelley's *Frankenstein*: "A Modern Prometheus." He said, "Prometheus makes a man out of clay. James Whale makes a man out of Clay Boone." "Uh, yeah, that works," I said. "But to be honest, I just wanted a good white trash name."

Also on the set was David Skal, who was making a behind-the-scenes documentary. The shoot felt like a party, a joyful meeting of the Friends of James Whale.

Two months later, back in New York, Draper and I sat in our living room and watched a video rough cut of the movie. It was one of the strangest experiences of my life. This was something that was mine yet not mine. I'd read the script and seen the actors, but I had never guessed how close the land-scape on the screen would be to the landscape in my head.

"That must've been weird for you," said Draper afterward. "Like hearing somebody retell the dream you had the night before."

"Oh yeah," I said. "Only I can't get over how close the telling is to my dream. Is it any good?"

Because I couldn't tell. The movie *is* true to the novel, and the artist has no distance from his work. I could see it was well done. All through it are bits of business added by the actors or director that are so good I couldn't help thinking, "Why didn't I do that?" And yet, it is my story. I couldn't tell if it worked or not. Only when I began to watch the film with other people, first the rough cut on video with friends, then the finished print in theaters full of strangers, could I see that it actually was good. Which means the book is good. Doesn't it? Believe it or not, one is never sure.

Books and movies are often discussed as if they were enemies, with the implication that visual cultural is destroying literature, and literature is superior. But bad books are as common as bad movies. It's true that a movie can drive a book out of your head, even a book you wrote yourself. Movies are so strong visually, the physical presence of actors more solid than anything that can be conjured with words alone. And yet, as Jean Renoir said, "A movie is such a little thing." Only so much can be packed into an hour or two of screen time, and it's all surface. Good as the movie of *Gods and Monsters* is, there are huge swatches of the novel that were left out, whole realms of interior life and past history that only get hinted at. A movie must concentrate experience, like a dream, while a novel is more like waking life, full of prose as well as poetry.

I love novels and I love movies. I like to think that the book and the film of *Gods and Monsters* complete each other. Most readers of a book make a movie in their own head anyway; some moviemakers are better than others, but it's the risk all novelists take. We put ourselves in your hands. I was in excellent hands with Bill Condon and his amazing cast and crew. I find I'm usually in good hands with readers, too.

*Gods and Monsters* opened in November 1998. The reviews were terrific and the distributor, Lions Gate, knew how to find an audience, starting the film in Los Angeles and New York, then slowly opening it wider. Bill took to referring to it as "the little movie that could." In February, Oscar nominations were announced. *Gods and Monsters* was nominated for three: Ian McKellen for Best Actor, Lynn Redgrave for Best Supporting

Actress, and Bill Condon for Best Screenplay Adapted from Another Source. We all assumed I'd attend the ceremony with Bill, until we found out that tickets were limited and Lions Gate had scarfed up all the extras. I was actually relieved: I didn't have to worry about renting a tux.

On Oscar night I was in Virginia, where I was writer-in-residence that semester at the College of William and Mary, my old alma mater. I invited a few friends and a couple of students over to watch the show. The "buzz" was that *Gods and Monsters* would lose in all three categories. As the evening progressed, the predictions appeared to be accurate. Lynn lost to Judi Dench in *Shakespeare in Love*. Ian lost to Roberto Benigni in *Life Is Beautiful*—the sight of Benigni leaping seats like a monkey is unhappily burned into my brain. It was getting late and my guests began to leave.

Finally, the screenwriting nominees were read out by Goldie Hawn and Steve Martin. "And the winner is," said Goldie Hawn, "Bill Condon for *Gods and Monsters*."

There was silence in my living room for three long seconds. Then we all jumped up and began to yell.

Bill raced on stage to accept the award. "First I have to thank Chris Bram who wrote *Father of Frankenstein*. This is a very faithful adaptation." Down in the audience, Ian, Lynn, and Brendan arranged themselves into a trio of beaming faces for the TV camera.

And my phone rang. It was Draper back home in New York, watching in an apartment full of noisy friends.

Bill continued to thank people until he closed by thanking Whale himself. "Sixty years ago, Hollywood sort of turned its back on him because he insisted on living the way he wanted. So, Mr. Jimmy," he said, lifting the Oscar at the camera—I later held it myself, and it's quite heavy—"This is for you."

—Christopher Bram, 2004

P.S.

Insights,
Interviews
& More...

❋

## About the author

**2** Meet Christopher Bram

## About the book

**3** Behind the Pages

**5** A Discussion with Christopher Bram

**9** Snapshots from the Filming of
*Gods and Monsters*

## Read on

**10** Novels into Movies:
The Good, the Bad,
and the Totally Reimagined

**16** The Web Detective

# Meet **Christopher Bram**

Rob Kinmonth

CHRISTOPHER BRAM grew up outside
Norfolk, Virginia, where he was a paperboy
and an Eagle Scout. After attending public
schools and the College of William and Mary,
he moved to New York City in 1978. He
worked for seven years at Scribner's
Bookstore—"My equivalent of grad
school"—while he learned to write fiction. He
published short stories and book reviews in
*Christopher Street* magazine, then movie
reviews in the *New York Native* and *Premiere*.
He published his first novel, *Surprising Myself*,
in 1987. Seven other novels followed,
including *In Memory of Angel Clare*, *Almost
History*, *Gossip*, *The Notorious Dr. August*, and
*Lives of the Circus Animals*.

He has written screenplays, including the
scripts of two short films directed by his
partner Draper Shreeve. He and Shreeve also
collaborated on several feature screenplays.
Bram's literary essays have been published in
*Booklist*, *Meanjin* and *James White Review* and
his memoir essays have appeared in such
anthologies as *Hometowns* and *Boys Like Us*.
He has taught writing at Vassar; William and
Mary; and Stonecoast, Maine. He was a 2001
Guggenheim Fellow and winner of the 2003
Bill Whitehead Award for Lifetime
Achievement. ❧

# Behind **the Pages**

THIS IS A WORK OF FICTION about a real man. I've kept to the general facts of James Whale's life but have taken liberties elsewhere. Clay, Maria, and Luc are completely imaginary. Davis Lewis is real, but my characterization of him is speculative.

There are a handful of published sources about Whale, of varying degrees of reliability, and I've used most of them. They include *James Whale: Ace Director,* by Clive Denton; *Passport to Hollywood,* edited by D. Whitmore and P. Cecchettini; and Philip Kemp's entry on Whale in *World Film Directors.* The best single work, however, is *James Whale,* by James Curtis. Along with collecting a wealth of details about the man and his career, Curtis cleared up a major mystery when he published the letter that's the basis for the note quoted in Chapter Seventeen. Also useful were *The Genius of the System,* by Thomas Schatz; *George Cukor,* by Patrick McGilligan; *Elsa Lanchester Herself,* by Elsa Lanchester; *No Leading Lady,* by R. C. Sherriff; and, on the First World War, *The Great War and Modern Memory,* by Paul Fussell; *Rites of Spring,* by Modris Eksteins; and *A War Imagined,* by Samuel Hynes.

I owe a special debt to filmmaker Brian Skeet, whose conversations about a possible documentary gave me the first sparks of this novel. I can't thank Brian enough for his artistic generosity and friendship. Eric Ashworth, Edward Hibbert, and Neil Olson provided advice and encouragement; Matthew Carnicelli, a fresh editorial eye; and Ed Sikov, Mary Gentile, Patrick Merla, ▶

*About the book*

66 Draper Shreeve is so enmeshed in this book, in ways great and small, that a dedication only begins to suggest his presence here.

3

**Behind the Pages** *(continued)*

and John Niespolo for their readerly
intelligence. Doug Clegg and Raul Silva
showed me Santa Monica Canyon, Ron
Caldwell brought me into the twentieth
century, Maureen Wilson and Meg Stewart
gave me needed space, and David Drane
shared his library card. Draper Shreeve is so
enmeshed in this book, in ways great and
small, that a dedication only begins to suggest
his presence here. ∾

# A Discussion with
# Christopher Bram

*What's it like to write fiction about real people? Are there any rules or restrictions?*

I use real people all the time, my friends and family, but in bits and pieces, never whole. Friends are used to seeing a phrase or trait of theirs tossed with other people's traits and phrases, like a salad. It's different with a historical figure, of course. There's a different responsibility. Legally speaking, an author is free to say whatever he wants about someone who's dead. You can't libel the dead. The dead are public domain.

Morally speaking, however, it's tricky. You want to be true to the person who existed, without losing yourself in facts. You want to be fair, you want to be generous. But I find that, after a while, I forget about the facts and pay attention only to the figure in my story. I don't care if he's true or not, only that he's alive and interesting—which is a kind of truth. Fiction can be as expressive as a dream, and dreams are never literal.

*Since you love movies so much, do you ever imagine particular actors playing your characters while you write them?*

No, I don't, which is odd, because I love actors. Even in a case where I began with an actor, I didn't picture him while I worked.

In my latest novel, *Lives of the Circus Animals*, one of the main characters, a British theater star named Henry Lewse, was inspired, ▶

" Fiction can be as expressive as a dream, and dreams are never literal. "

5

> I never actually picture my characters while I write. I feel things about them, quite strongly too, but I never literally see them.

I admit, by Ian McKellen. If I hadn't met Ian on the set of *Gods and Monsters*, I don't think I could've come up with Henry. However, almost as soon as I started writing, Henry stopped being Ian and became someone new, someone shorter and goofier and with a very different history. As with James Whale, he took on a life of his own.

I never actually picture my characters while I write. I feel things about them, quite strongly too, but I never literally see them. I see the landscapes plainly, but the people remain vague. They have bodies but blurry faces.

As soon as I'm done, however, and Draper and a few friends have read the manuscript, we often sit around casting an imaginary movie. It's a whole new way of thinking about characters. It's interesting to discover how elastic they are, how you can stretch a fictional character over this or that actor and discover new dimensions and qualities.

*The novel was published in 1995 at the height of the AIDS crisis in the United States. Since the novel is about death, one can't help but wonder if AIDS influenced you in any way.*

AIDS was present during the writing, both consciously and unconsciously.

Early on, when I was thinking about the project and not yet committed to it, I was uncertain why Whale even interested me. Then I went to a writer's conference where there was a keynote address by Allan Gurganus. And Gurganus compared what AIDS was doing to our generation with what the First World War did to that generation in Europe.

And I realized: here is why this story is speaking to me. Here is something my readers and I have in common with Whale: we are surrounded by death, we are trying to make sense of it in our fiction and nightmares and even our jokes. There's a private acknowledgement of that in the novel. When Whale tells Boone about men who died in the trenches, his catalogue of the dead includes the names of two close friends of mine who died.

Bill Condon and I never discussed this. But then we were both on a panel after a screening and someone asked what if any part AIDS played in the story. Bill immediately began to talk about the epidemic as something that had enabled him to understand Whale. I listened openmouthed, but I shouldn't have been surprised. For gay men of my generation, AIDS forced us to think about things we might not have thought about otherwise.

> Here is something my readers and I have in common ... we are surrounded by death, we are trying to make sense of it in our fiction and nightmares and even our jokes.

*What novelists have influenced you?*

I love to read, so I don't know where to begin. I read so much, in fact, that the influences dilute each other. There were authors I read in high school who made me want to write in the first place, Thomas Wolfe and Thomas Mann, a very weird duo. Then there were scores of writers afterwards who taught lessons about writing or offered exciting examples: E. M. Forster taught me the pure pleasure of storytelling, Marcel Proust the power of metaphor and the joy of big party scenes, Tolstoy and Henry James both showed me how everyone is the hero or heroine of his or her life and that's what makes our time on earth so dramatic and complicated. And so on. ▶

## A Discussion with Christopher Bram *(continued)*

I should also add that I learned a lot from filmmakers. As I've said elsewhere, I came of age during a golden age of film. I learned about storytelling and human behavior from people like Robert Altman, Paul Mazursky, and Martin Scorsese. And I learned from classic directors, too, in particular Preston Sturges, whose screwball comedies showed me how you can say serious things by being silly. He liberated me. He had a comic sensibility so fine no moral idea could violate it. He is the Henry James of American film.

At the other end of the spectrum, although not as far off as you might think, is Ingmar Bergman. I recently saw a retrospective of his films here in New York and was amazed by both his greatness—his best work doesn't date—and how deeply he had soaked into my bones. He was not just the grim Swede of reputation, but a man of the theater, a real showman. I learned a lot from him: the theatricality of real life, the power of long scenes, the fact that one can address almost anything through emotions: religion, despair, and complex philosophical ideas. An occasional joke doesn't hurt, either. ∾

> I learned about storytelling and human behavior from people like Robert Altman, Paul Mazursky, and Martin Scorsese.

# Snapshots from the Filming of

## *Gods and Monsters*

*Christopher Bram (left) and Sir Ian McKellen on the set of* Gods and Monsters

*Left to right: Christopher Bram, Rosalind Ayres (as Elsa Lanchester playing the Bride), and Draper Shreeve*

# Novels into **Movies**

*The Good, the Bad,
and the Totally Reimagined*

Because both forms tell stories, movies are often based on novels. Not very many feature films have been made from paintings, symphonies, or math problems. However, some adaptations work and others don't. Critics like to pretend there are clear guidelines—be faithful, don't be faithful, avoid the classics— but I disagree. (There are also critics who claim good novels don't make good movies since what's good in a novel will inevitably get lost in translation. I hope this isn't true, for obvious, selfish reasons.)

Below is a very personal list of novel-based movies that succeed and novel-based movies that fail. As you will see, there are no hard and fast rules.

—Christopher Bram

## SUCCESSES

*Election* (1999). Alexander Payne's movie of the Tom Perrotta novel is remarkable not only for what was changed but what was kept from the original. Payne and his screenwriter Jim Taylor shifted the locale from New Jersey to Nebraska and made the overachieving teenage villainess, Tracy Flick, human enough that I, for one, cannot help identifying with her—a little. However, the movie keeps the novel's multiple first-person narrators—usually a no-no in film but dazzling here—and does not shy away from the novel's more dangerous topics: teenage lesbians, student/teacher sex, and Republican moms.

> Payne ... made the overachieving teenage villainess, Tracy Flick, human enough that I, for one, cannot help identifying with her—a little.

*Frankenstein* (1931). Let's say it right off: Mary Shelley's novel is one of the world's most disappointing classics. People love the idea of it, not the book itself, which is diffused, wordy, and only intermittently dramatic. Every ten years or so, some filmmaker wants to do the *real* novel, then doesn't, since the original is about as filmable as *Paradise Lost* or *The Anatomy of Melancholy*. The movie that James Whale and screenwriter John Balderston drew from a play by Peggy Webling has a very tenuous relationship with the novel, yet it keeps Shelley's best ideas and themes. And it works! It's as if a magician had pulled a hat out of a rabbit instead of the other way around.

*Jules and Jim* (1961). The Francois Truffaut film is so different yet so similar to the Henri-Pierre Roche novel that one doesn't know where to begin. Both race along at high speed, giving more information than can be absorbed by reader or viewer. Both are cheerfully amoral, in a quick, dry, and rational manner that outmaneuvers conventional judgments. But Truffaut radically simplified the plot, eliminated characters and, best of all, used Georges Delerue for the score, one of the best soundtracks ever written. (My greatest frustration as a novelist is that books don't get to have soundtracks.)

*The Last Picture Show* (1971). Larry McMurtry wrote a mean, entertaining *Peyton Place*-style revenge novel about his hometown, then went back years later and turned it into a screenplay with Peter Bogdonavich. He was able to find the sadder, more tender tale hidden under the dirty laundry. It's not often that a novelist gets to return to old material and give it the richer, fuller treatment it deserved.

*The Leopard* (1963). Giuseppe Tomasi di Lampedusa wrote a historical novel about Sicily that is all mood and setpieces and no plot, and it's absolutely wonderful. Luchino Visconti made it into a movie that is all mood and setpieces and no plot, and it too is wonderful, especially in the longer Italian version. Here's a film that shouldn't fly, and maybe it doesn't, yet it floats and that's enough. ▶

11

> [*Lolita* is]
> surprisingly close
> to the original,
> especially when
> you consider
> when it was done.
> The only major
> change—and it
> is a doozy—
> was the casting
> of Peter Sellers
> as Quilty.

*Lolita* (1962). Stanley Kubrick commissioned Vladimir Nabokov to adapt his novel, then threw the script away and pulled his own text directly from the book with producer James Harris. It's surprisingly close to the original, especially when you consider when it was done. The only major change—and it is a doozy—was the casting of Peter Sellers as Quilty, who becomes a real antagonist for Humbert Humbert and not just a shadowy doppelganger. The second half of the movie might drag, but it doesn't evaporate the way the novel does. (Nabokov's screenplay was later published and is a fascinating study in wrongheaded brilliance.)

*Oliver Twist* (1948). David Lean's movie is fearlessly faithful, keeping not only the sentiment and violence of the Dickens novel, but the stage-villain Jewishness of Fagin and the subplot about Monk, the evil heir bent on destroying Oliver. One can understand why every other screen or stage version cut Monk, but the movie effortlessly carries him along as just one more villain in its ensemble.

*Passage to India* (1984). David Lean again, this time actually improving a great novel by adding one new scene. A likable young Englishwoman accuses a likable Indian doctor of rape. Adela Quested is a difficult heroine, but Lean invented a scene that makes her accessible and sympathetic. She visits a Hindu temple covered with erotic sculpture and live monkeys. She is both fascinated and alarmed. The monkeys turn on her and she flees. It's sexual hysteria made visual, expressing something that Forster left unexplored—he was never very good at writing directly about sex, either gay or straight. Young Judy Davis built her character around the moment, turning Adela into a great figure, someone who makes a terrible mistake and then tries to fix it.

*The Secret Garden* (1993). Francis Hodgson Burnett wrote a children's novel that transcends the genre, a tough, smart, anti-sentimental tale about the destructiveness of grief and self-pity. Agnieszka Holland's movie, with a script by Caroline Thompson, plunges fearlessly into both the cruelty and joy of the story, staying true to the emotional power of the book, never fearing that it might upset children or seem mawkish to shallow adults.

*The Unbearable Lightness of Being* (1988). Milan Kundera told a story about a man and two women by discussing a few philosophical ideas about them. Director Philip Kaufman and cowriter Jean-Claude Carriere wrote a script where the characters became flesh and blood and the ideas were dropped. The novel now reads like a joyful intellectual riff on a wonderful movie. Here is a case where a book and movie do not just complement but extend each other. (And the novelist got to have his own soundtrack. Kundera suggested they use the music of Leos Janacek, and the witty, nervy, motley Czech score is perfect.)

## FAILURES

*Beloved* (1998). A smart director and even smarter screenwriter, Jonathan Demme and Richard LaGravanese, take Toni Morisson's great nightmare/folktale novel, try to make it into a conventional narrative, and produce something overly literal and ultimately ridiculous. It's hard to say why the movie went wrong—I suspect a failure of nerve—but this is a humbling example for all filmmakers.

*Clockers* (1995). Richard Price's big, edgy novel about cops and dealers in New Jersey should've made a terrific movie, but Spike Lee turned it into a Spike-Lee talkfest where people only discuss the issues, like a Bernard Shaw play set in the projects but without any jokes. The movie is full of good intentions, but loggy and inert. The only grace note is a fine performance by Michael Imperioli, years before *The Sopranos*, as a corrupt cop tickled by his own corruption. ▸

***Cold Mountain*** (2003). Now and then a novel comes along that everybody loves, but you don't. Then a movie is made of it and the movie is close to the novel, and this time people agree with you. The Charles Frazier novel is written in gloppy, pseudo-Faulkner prose that disguises a lot of bad history and improbable psychology. Not even the trees are convincing. Anthony Minghella is a gifted director and he turned two other novels—*The English Patient* and *The Talented Mr. Ripley*—into brilliant films. I can't guess what drew him to Frazier, but the movie is as phony as the book. The worse half is a *tasteful* spaghetti western (a self-defeating contradiction in terms) while the more entertaining yet silly half is basically, as someone said, "On the farm with Lucy and Ethel."

***Endless Love*** (1981). Scott Spencer's feverish, sexy novel about adolescent obsession should have made a great movie, but the Franco Zeffirelli film is laughably bad. The story needed real actors to work, but young Brooke Shields and unknown Martin Hewitt are just pretty bodies, two mannequins. Zeffirelli is reported to have pinched Brooke's toes during sex scenes to get a reaction out of her, but he is not a director known for getting anything life-like from young performers.

***The Great Gatsby*** (1949) (1974) (2001). Scott Fitzgerald's gem-like novel would seem a natural movie: it's short, dramatic, highly visual. Nevertheless it's been filmed three times and none of the versions work. Jack Clayton came closest in 1974, with a script by

> Zeffirelli is reported to have pinched Brooke's toes during sex scenes to get a reaction out of her, but he is not a director known for getting anything life-like from young performers.

Francis Ford Coppola. There's the nice surprise of Mia Farrow's Daisy, but Robert Redford is a charmless, wooden Gatsby and the movie constantly pokes us like a school teacher with a pointer so we will notice all those damn metaphors: the green light at the end of the pier, the billboard over the ash heaps, etc.

*Madame Bovary* (1934) (1949) (1991). The novel is a great piece of narrative engineering, cool and precise. But is there a movie here? Flaubert's small-souled lives don't translate well to film. Jean Renoir stayed true to their dullness and made a quiet, intelligent piece that comes to life only in moments, such as the startling deathbed scene. Jazzed up in the Hollywood version with Jennifer Jones, the story is glossy fun without being very good. The latest version by Claude Chabrol looks great but feels clipped and glib, with Isabelle Huppert as Emma skulking through most of the film like a grumpy housecat.

*The Portrait of a Lady* (1996). If you know the Henry James novel, the Jane Campion movie is a fascinating mess. If you don't know the novel, it's an incoherent mess. Nicole Kidman isn't bad as Isabel Archer, and Barbara Hershey is a great Madame Merle. But why did Campion make so many wrong storytelling choices? By the time Isabel rejects three handsome suitors in order to marry Gilbert Osmond, played by John Malkovich as the epitome of evil, you've written her off as totally nuts. ⌒

The latest version by Claude Chabrol looks great but feels clipped and glib, with Isabelle Huppert as Emma skulking through most of the film like a grumpy housecat.

# The **Web Detective**

http://www.swem.edu/spcoll/Acc2000/
bram.htm
*for information on the* Father of Frankenstein
*manuscript collection with a display of first page
with copyeditor marks*

http://myweb.lsbu.ac.uk/~stafflag/
jamewhale.html
*for more information on the Knitting Circle at
London South Bank University with first-rate
material on the real James Whale*

http://www.mckellen.com
*for more information about Ian McKellen, visit
his website with some wonderful pictures of the*
Gods and Monsters *shoot*

http://www.kjenkins49.fsnet.co.uk/
index.htm
*for more information visit the Mising Line, an
excellent website devoted to classic horror films
from the golden age of horror cinema*

http://members.aon.at/frankenstein/
frankenstein-start.htm
*for more information about Frankenstein
Castle, a wonderful website about Frankenstein
books, plays, and movies*

http://www.filmsite.org/bride3.html
*for a list of the one hundred best movies ever
made with a very detailed discussion of* Bride of
Frankenstein

# BOOKS BY CHRISTOPHER BRAM

## THE NOTORIOUS DR. AUGUST
### His Real Life and Crimes

ISBN 0-06-093497-2 (paperback)

Spanning the years between the Civil War and the early 1920s, this is the story of Augustus Fitzwilliam Boyd, alias Dr. August, a clairvoyant pianist who communes with ghosts, and who finds meaning in his life through a strange love triangle with a righteous ex-slave and nervous white governess.

## LIVES OF THE CIRCUS ANIMALS
### A Novel
A *New York Times* Notable Book and Winner of the LAMBDA Literary Award

ISBN 0-06-054254-3 (paperback)

Leaping from one life to another, one day to the next, *Lives of the Circus Animals* throws a diverse handful of theater people together in a serious comedy about love and work and make-believe. It is a cross between a Mozart opera and a Preston Sturges movie.

## GODS AND MONSTERS
### A Novel
Basis for the Academy Award–winning film

ISBN 0-06-078087-8 (paperback)

In 1957 James Whale, the director acclaimed for such classic horror films as *Frankenstein* and *Bride of Frankenstein*, was found at his California home, dead of unnatural causes. Christopher Bram, whose social insight and wit have earned him comparisons to Henry James and Gore Vidal, explores the mystery of Whale's last days in this evocative and suspenseful novel.

CPSIA information can be obtained
at www.ICGtesting.com
Printed in the USA
LVOW07s2041290517
536164LV00017B/122/P